THE ESSENTIAL GUIDE TO WORLD COMICS

TIM PILCHER • BRAD BROOKS

First published in 2005 by Collins & Brown
The Chrysalis Building, Bramley Road,
London, W10 6SP
United Kingdom
An imprint of **Chrysalis** Books Group plc

Distributed in the United States and Canada by
Sterling Publishing Co, 387 Park Avenue South,
New York, NY 10016, USA

10 9 8 7 6 5 4 3 2 1

British Library Cataloguing-in-Publication Data:
A catalogue record for this title is available from
the British Library

Editor: Chris McNab

Commissioning Editor: Chris Stone

Proofreader: Andy Nicolson

Designed by Brad Brooks of Sequential Design

Cover image by Roger Langridge

Repro by Classicscan, Singapore

Printed in China by SNP Leefung

Dedication:

Tim: Megan (the biggest Bone fan I know) and Oskar –
the next generation.

Brad: For Sophie, with all my love.

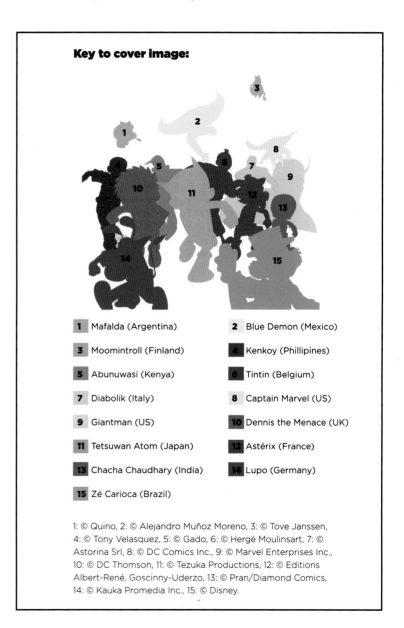

Key to cover image:

1 Mafalda (Argentina)
2 Blue Demon (Mexico)
3 Moomintroll (Finland)
4 Kenkoy (Phillipines)
5 Abunuwasi (Kenya)
6 Tintin (Belgium)
7 Diabolik (Italy)
8 Captain Marvel (US)
9 Giantman (US)
10 Dennis the Menace (UK)
11 Tetsuwan Atom (Japan)
12 Astérix (France)
13 Chacha Chaudhary (India)
14 Lupo (Germany)
15 Zé Carioca (Brazil)

1: © Quino, 2: © Alejandro Muñoz Moreno, 3: © Tove Janssen,
4: © Tony Velasquez, 5: © Gado, 6: © Hergé Moulinsart, 7: ©
Astorina Srl, 8: © DC Comics Inc., 9: © Marvel Enterprises Inc.,
10: © DC Thomson, 11: © Tezuka Productions, 12: © Editions
Albert-René, Goscinny-Uderzo, 13: © Pran/Diamond Comics,
14: © Kauka Promedia Inc., 15: © Disney.

CONTENTS

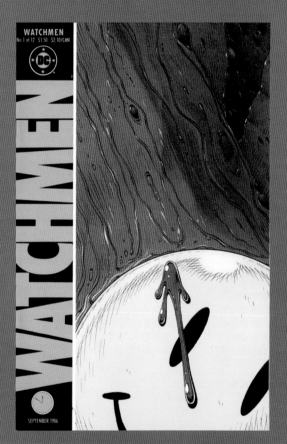

The iconic cover to the first issue of the *Watchmen* 12-issue series created
by Alan Moore (Story) and Dave Gibbons (Art).
© *DC Comics Inc.*

FOREWORD
DAVE GIBBONS

The first page of the first issue of *Watchmen*, directly following on from the cover, as seen on page six. Artwork by Dave Gibbons.
© DC Comics Inc.

As the world seems to shrink, the variety it holds seems to expand in equal measure.

In mediaeval times, Western maps would depict the few known areas in reasonable detail, becoming vague and amorphous at the fringes until, at the very edges, only the legend, "Here be dragons" was felt to be an accurate description of what lay beyond.

In Victorian society, the reading of guide books and travellers' tales engrossed millions with overblown yarns of mysterious Arabia and far Cathay. The dragons had become smaller, perhaps less fantastic, but more varied, real and interesting.

Today, orbiting cameras can show us objects anywhere on the planet in real time, down to the size and mundanity of a trash can. We might mourn the dragons, if they had ever existed, but we are no less fascinated by the novelty of the everyday as it manifests itself across cultures.

With the possible exception of recorded music, I would argue that there is no artefact simultaneously more mundane and fantastic as the comic book, seemingly universal in its simplicity and accessibility as a medium whilst, at its best, fiercely local in its content and appeal.

Like music, pictorial storytelling has a cross-cultural appeal which can transcend language and location to appeal to an audience. Just as a good song can be enjoyed without an understanding of the words, a good comic is a joy, whatever the language in the word balloons. Indeed, it seems to me that the experience of exploring popular music has many parallels with the exploration of comics. When I was younger, I became aware that most of my favourite records were, if not of American origin, at least influenced by that country's performers. Later, it transpired that American soul and R'n'B were largely imported from Africa, with native European music grafted on to create the hybrid Rock and Roll. Once that had spread, it was re-exported to North America by the British, who were, meanwhile, having music from the Caribbean brought to their shores.

At the same time, in Britain, I was discovering American comics, both in their original form, and as adapted and reprinted for the British and Australian markets. It later transpired that many of my favourite British comics were, in fact, drawn by artists from Spain, Italy and far-off South America. Other cultural anomalies occasionally surfaced, too. Admittedly, Belgium has always been a mystery to me, in popular music terms, but I knew it produced a wonderful comic in *Tintin*.

In the 1980s, Britain even exported several of its comics and creators to America, an invasion not comparable in scale with the music invasion of the Sixties, but as significant in its field. By then, international-al comic conventions and festivals had become commonplace. Angoulême and Lucca gathered many European creators together, with a scattering of attendees from North and South America.

I had a personal 'Road to Damascus' experience at the Festival in Lucca where I stumbled, dazzled, from table to table barely able to believe the wealth of good stuff there was 'out there' in the action and adventure genre, from *Blueberry* to *Kraken* to *Les Naufrages* to *Sgt Kirk* to *Un Homme Une Adventure*. I learned that there was a world full of wonderful artists of whose existence I had previously been totally unaware. So far, so local. The cultures of the Americas, Australia and Europe were, even then, pretty close in most ways and easily traversed. Not so that of Japan. Formally dressed to mimic the West, the intrinsic nature and concerns of Japanese culture are really very different. The same applies to Japanese comics. The size of telephone directories, printed on the cheapest paper, the kinetic energy and graphic attack of 'manga' is a bracing shock to Western eyes. Delighted as I was to find the term translated to "irresponsible pictures", it took me much longer to become comfortable with reading them, as it were, backwards. But, in time, even the sensibility of manga has been successfully adapted to the West, in the form of America's best selling comics

magazine, *Shonen Jump*, as well as being influential to a generation of that country's superhero artists.

All of which now brings me to what is, for someone like me who likes to think of himself as a modern citizen of the world, an embarrassing admission:

"Here be dragons."

Here was where my knowledge of world comics ran out. Maybe yours does too. Thankfully, like some modern day comics equivalent of the Victorian *Baedeker's* guide, this present volume will thrill you, as it has me, with a bold and exciting overview of what is really out there. Tales of Arabia and Cathay you will certainly find, inviting and intriguing, but all thoroughly researched and documented.

From their vantage point, the authors will also show you, far more attractive than orbital pictures of trash cans, vivid snapshots of major creators across the globe, creative giants to rival any we know in Europe or America. Maybe someday in the future, comics aficionados will have the equivalent of the technology that brings music from around the world to my computer desktop. Then, as much as now, this guidebook will be invaluable. There may not be dragons on modern maps, but there is still plenty of buried treasure out there. This book will show you where to dig.

Dave Gibbons, October 2005

The first page, drawn by Dave Gibbons, of a satirical strip from the 500th issue of the British weekly anthology comic, *2000 AD,* poking fun at the comic, its characters, editorial team and creators themselves. In-jokes abound.
© *Dave Gibbons, Pat Mills, Rebellion A/S*

A fantastic three-colour page by the American cartoonist David Mazzucchelli from his story *Discovering America*, which appeared in his self-published anthology *Rubber Blanket*.
© David Mazzucchelli

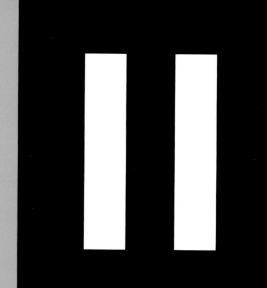

INTRODUCTION

Fareed Choudhury's first book, the hilarious *Malice Family*.
© *Fareed Choudhury*

Mårdøn Smet showing off one of his many styles.
© *Mårdøn Smet*

Comics? From all over the world? What's all that about then?

In other countries and cultures they're called manga, manhua, manhwa, bande dessinee or BD, komiks, bilderstreifen or bilder-geschichter, historietas, benzi desenate, quadrinhos or HQ, torietas, tebeos, fotonovela or fumetti. **In the USA and UK they're known as comic books and they are the most prevalent, important yet misunderstood art form in the world.**

Depending where you come from, most people's concept of comic books is either that of superheroes like *Spider-Man* and *Batman*, 'juvenile' strips like *The Beano*, *Tintin* and *Astérix* or, more recently, the all-encompassing term 'manga'. All of which is unsurprising, considering the majority of the general public's experiences of comic books extends from their own childhood or Hollywood's recent glut of superheroic movie adaptations.

But all this belies an art form that is not unique to the UK, USA and Japan. In fact, practically every country in the world has its own comics industry. In some countries, like Britain and Singapore, comics are regarded as a juvenile form of entertainment. In others such as France, they are a highly regarded form of expression – The Ninth Art – while in Japan, comics are so integral to its culture and society that it would be impossible to imagine the country without them. But whatever their social status, the cultural impact of comics cannot be underestimated.

There are many misconceptions about comics, but possibly the most frustrating is ill-educated press and fine art critics labelling them a genre. Comics are no more a genre than film, prose or music. Comics are an artform as diverse in their subject matter as any novel or film, and can relate romance, western, horror, non-fiction, autobiographical and of course, superhero stories.

SO WHY THIS BOOK?

Some further clarification is in order. This book is called *The Essential Guide to World Comics*. What does that mean? Well, if we break it down word by word, it's "Essential", as there is no other book that covers such a breadth of topics or breaks down the territories so clearly. This is the one book that any novice can pick up and instantly become more informed about global comics. There are however, plenty of surprises and hidden gems for those who think they've seen and heard it all. After a collective experience of over 30 years in comics, both of us were flabbergasted at the sheer scope across the planet – and we have been lucky enough to attend conventions in France, Spain, America and the UK, and to experience first hand, comics in Brazil, Sweden, Korea, Dubai, Egypt and Germany, to name but a few.

Obviously the book is a "Guide" and not a definitive encyclopaedia of every title, every publisher and everyone who has ever worked in comics. We'd need a minimum of five volumes (of 1,000 pages each) to do that! It is intended as a global snapshot of the history and current status of comics, not the ultimate listing. The world's comics industries are in too much

constant flux for anyone to write that book.

"World" is self-explanatory; we've tried to cover most countries here (and certainly every continent), but obviously space constraints prevent us from talking about the Bhutan, Chilean or Greek comic scenes.

"Comics" is a little harder to define. It covers a wide range of media, from traditional US-style comic books, through newspaper strips and webcomics, to pretty much any form of pictures in deliberate sequence. It must be pointed out however, that defining what comics actually are, is a little like trying to nail jelly to a wall. Most comics theoreticians can agree on the basics (panels, sequence of pictures and so on), but after that the arguments start. The noble attempt by Scott McCloud to create a definition that would satisfy everybody in his book *Understanding Comics*[1] created more controversy than even McCloud himself thought it would. To this day, nothing will cause an argument between cartoonists and comics theorists quicker than asking a bunch of them, "So what is a comic, then?" The term 'comic book', used here, refers to a publication that is solely filled with sequential comic stories. Like the actual definition of a comic, the term 'comic book' also causes discussions between fans and pros alike. It was coined by writer/editor/publisher Stan Lee, who postulated that they were neither comics

A page from the wonderful *Los Profesionales* by Carlos Giménez, parodying the comics agencies in Spain.
© *Carlos Giménez*

The interior of the best comic shop in the UK, *Gosh Comics* in London. Someday, all comic shops will be this way.
Photo: B. Brooks

A panel from the Spanish cartoonist Germán García's series *Tess Tinieblas.*
© *Germán García*

(stand-up comedians) nor books, but uniquely, *comic books*. We however, have chosen to call them 'comic books' throughout, probably annoying someone!

Unfortunately, we've also been unable to cover webcomics or minicomics in a large amount of detail. This is a shame as there are many, many creators (like Kevin Huizenga, Drew Weing, Daniel Merlin Goodbrey, Scott Kurtz, the Fort Thunder collective, Tom Gauld, Paul Hornschemeier, Derek Kirk Kim, Jason Shiga, Ben Catmull, Lark Pien, Jesse Hamm and… We could go on and on for pages) around the world

working in these forms, making fantastic comics that we haven't been able to cover. The bibliography will however, point you in the right direction to find out a little more about the comics we've been able to cover and those we haven't.

THE POWER OF COMICS

Comics are an exceptional form of story-telling completely separate from film, prose, animation or any of the other media they've been pointlessly compared to. Because we think visually, sequential art speaks directly to us without the need for translation, and most people can get the gist of a comic story no matter what its language[2]. Because of this unique power, the US Army solicited creators to develop a propaganda comic book series for the Middle East, in May 2005[3]. In a vain and cynical attempt to win the hearts and minds of young Arabs, the US Army stated, "In order to achieve long-term peace and stability in the Middle East, the youth need to be reached. A series of comic books provides the opportunity for youth to learn lessons, develop role models and improve their education." The project was thought up by US Special Operations Command at Fort Bragg in North Carolina, home to the army's 4th Psychological Operations Group, better known as 'psy-op warriors', but competition already existed in the shape of new Egyptian publishers AK Comics (formed in 2002), whose goal is, "to fill the cultural gap created over the years by providing essentially Arab role models, in our case, Arab superheroes." This example of using comics to spread information, propaganda and a particular worldview is not a new one, and it won't be the last time that comics will be co-opted to suit a political or philosophical doctrine.

SO WHERE ARE YOU FROM, THEN?

When one of us worked in a comic shop, he could tell where a customer came from, not by their accents, but by what comics they requested. Italians always wanted *Dylan Dog* or *Nathan Never*, Swedes requested *Donald Duck*, and Australians always looked for *The Phantom*. It was soon apparent to both of us that there was a whole world outside our own local comic shop. As far back as 1989, we'd often visit specialist shops in London that imported the latest manga from Japan and Bandes Dessinées from France, and even travel abroad to comics festivals like the famous Angoulême Salon de la Bande Dessinée. As the world gets ever smaller and cultures collide and merge, this cross-pollination of comics becomes more and more obvious. For more than 60 years, American comics in the shape of news-paper strips, Disney comics and certain

superheroes dominated the global comic book market. They influenced thousands of diverse creators in hundreds of countries. More recently, the cultural tide has turned and a new empire has risen; the manga, which has turned the tables on US comics, flooding the market with more economical and speedy versions of their American cousins. Just like the car industry.

The gargantuan *Comix 2000*, an anthology of wordless comics by cartoonists from all over the world.
© l'Association

New Zealander Karl Wills does what he does best in his series of school story parodies.
© *Karl Wills*

A quite simply wonderful panel from Drew Weing's exquisite webcomic, *Pup.*
© Drew Weing

A page from Paul Peart-Smith's wonderfully evocative strip *One + One.*
© Paul Peart-Smith

TRENDS IN WORLD COMICS

As we researched this book, certain trends across the countries began to stand out. We started noticing how many comic creators had started studying medicine before finding their true vocation (Osamu Tezuka, Jim Lee, Peter Madsen et al), how many countries began their comics industries in almost exactly the same way (with first, the importation of American newspaper strips and later, comic books, and how that importation of material eventually gave way to homegrown comics being created), and how many countries have clutched that most unlikely of popular characters, *The Phantom*, to their collective bosom.

TWO OPINIONS, ONE BOOK

This book is made up of two completely opposing views. One of us believes that comics should be elevated to a fine art status with the respect and attention the medium justly deserves. The other is more prosaic and believes that comics can be just big, dumb fun that allows you to escape reality for a little while. Both views are valid and the truth probably lies inbetween. Consequently, the book manages to straddle the complexities and intricacies of French comic experimentalism, with the brash rollicking adventures of Marvel and DC's most garish superheroes, with equal love for both.

And apologies to everyone who didn't make it into this book! For every country we've mentioned, there were another three we had no space for. Consequently, there was no room to talk about Israel's constantly struggling, but excellent comics scene. Similarly, Turkey missed out and we couldn't cover in depth the history of its satirical comic newspaper, *Girgir*, and the vibrant comics scenes of Chile and Uruguay likewise. Nothing personal, maybe in the sequel!

In spite of this, we are proud of what we have managed to cram in here. From the gangland comics of Hong Kong, to the political tracts for children from Egypt, via the immense creativity-under-sanctions of Argentina, what we have here is a potted history of world comics, a travelogue to send you on a journey of your own discovery. It will send you to the far-flung corners of the world and will reveal unique treasures from far-off lands. It will open up new and exciting areas of comics to be explored and savoured. And who knows, the trip might be as fun as the destination.

Bon voyage!

Tim Pilcher & Brad Brooks, October 2005, somewhere on the M23 motorway.

The first page to a 'sequel' strip (about Japanese comics) to *Understanding Comics* by Scott McCloud. This strip first appeared in the comics magazine *Wizard*.
© *Scott McCloud*

ENDNOTES:

[1]Scott McCloud's attempt was the unwieldy "**com.ics** (kom'iks) **n.** plural in form, used with a singular verb. **1.** Juxtaposed pictorial and other images in deliberate sequence, intended to convey information and/or to produce an aesthetic response in the viewer."

[2]Art Spiegelman was the first theorist to point this out in his lecture *Comix 101*.

[3]http://news.bbc.co.uk/2/hi/middle_east/4396351.stm

Patriotism or jingoism? Whichever, *Captain America* has become the embodiment of the United States, especially post 9/11. Art by Frank Miller and Roger Stern.
© *Marvel Comics*

1

UNITED SUPERHEROES OF AMERICA

No other country saw a single genre dominate the comics medium like superheroes did in America. From the moment that Superman emerged on the scene, superheroes began to be almost synonymous with comics in the USA.

There were other genres in the early days that were as diverse as anything from the Philippines, France or Japan, but superheroes managed to eventually ride roughshod over them until 90% of the market related tales of men and women in spandex. Those early days however, saw romance, monster, horror and western comics all vying for rack space in the local soda shop.

Comics had evolved – as they'd done in the UK and many other countries – out of the early newspaper strips produced at the turn of the 19th Century. Creations like Winsor McCay's *Little Nemo in Slumberland* (1905), George Herriman's *Krazy Kat* (1910) and *Polly and Her Pals* (1912, originally called *Positive Polly*) by Cliff Sterrett broke new ground in narrative storytelling by experimenting with page layouts, language structure and incorporating abstract art that played with panel and story construction. These strips were so powerful, that even after almost 100 years since their creation, artists today still reference them in their own work, and look to them for inspiration. Ever since newspaper strips like

EC Segar's *Thimble Theatre* (featuring *Popeye*) and *Tarzan* by Hal Foster debuted in 1929, their popularity kept rising.

THE FIRST COMIC BOOKS

In 1933, Eastern Color Press was trying to think of how to better use its printing equipment that was often idle between jobs, and Maxwell Gaines suggested comics to his boss. Gaines had the idea of printing an eight-page comic section that could be folded down from the larger broadsheet to form the first modern comic book, *Funnies on Parade*. It contained reprints of newspaper comic strips, and the experimental comic-book was given away. It soon proved that a market existed for repackaged strips. The following year, Eastern published *Famous Funnies* and risked selling the comic for an extortionate 10 cents in retail shops. The gamble paid off big-time, Eastern began producing numerous titles on a monthly basis and other publishers soon jumped on the bandwagon.

One of these 'Johnny come latelys', National Periodicals, launched *New Fun Comics* in February 1935. It was the first of

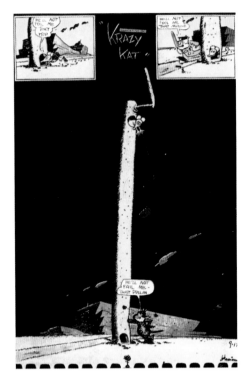

George Herriman's *Krazy Kat* featured a bizarre love triangle between *Ignatz* the mouse, *Krazy* and *Officer Pup*. Its language inspired Walt Kelly's newspaper strip, *Pogo*, and its backgrounds influenced UK cartoonist Hunt Emerson.
© *Estate of George Herriman*

its kind with entirely new material, with no reprints and original characters that continued from one issue to the next. A new type of comic book was born, and the wheels of the industry began to turn.

Meanwhile, 1934 was the year of the adventure newspaper strip, when many important and influential stories debuted, including *Jungle Jim*, *Flash Gordon* and *Secret Agent X-9* (written by crime novelist, Dashiell Hammett) by Alex Raymond. Milton Caniff's *Terry & The Pirates* also made its first appearance along with Lee Falk and Phil Davis' *Mandrake the Magician*. While this latter creation was popular, it was nothing compared to Falk's follow-up (with Ray Moore) in 1936, *The Phantom*. While popular in the USA, its staggering success was achieved abroad when the strip was syndicated around the world by King Features, and it helped spark comics industries in India, Sweden and Australia.

DISNEY EXPANDS INTO COMICS

The following year saw the launch of *Mickey Mouse Magazine* in the USA, despite having appeared as a newspaper strip since 1930, drawn by Disney animator Ub Iwerks and later by Floyd Gottfredson. It wasn't until 1938 that *Donald Duck*'s first comic was published, and it took another four years after that before writer/artist Carl Barks' first *Donald Duck* story appeared in Dell

Publishing's *Four Color Comic #9*. Barks' duck stories had a profound affect on Scandinavian creators, and even today, American cartoonists like Jeff Smith, creator of *Bone*, admits to being heavily inspired by them. Disney's influence on world comics would equal, if not surpass, that of *The Phantom*, managing to get versions of its comics produced locally almost everywhere from Italy to Egypt, and they still dominate the children's market today.

ALSO SPRACH ZARATHUSTRA

In 1933, a couple of teenagers from Cleveland, Ohio, had read Philip Wylie's novel *Gladiator*, about a man with super strength and enhanced powers. Inspired by this and *Flash Gordon*, the two young men, Jerry Siegel and Joe Shuster, created a story called *The Superman of Metropolis*. They published it in their own fanzine, *Science Fiction*, and received a positive response. The duo then wrote and drew an entire episode of daily strips, which they submitted to many newspaper syndicates.

Meanwhile, Max Gaines had moved from Eastern Color Press to become publisher of All American Comics, a part of National Periodicals. When Siegel and Shuster approached Gaines, in 1938, he looked at the pages Siegel and Shuster had created and felt he couldn't use them, but editor Sheldon Mayer and publisher Harry

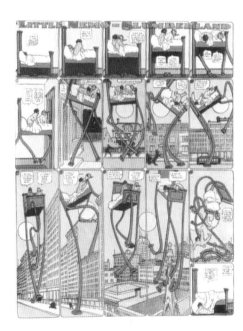

Little Nemo in Slumberland by Winsor McCay. In 1990, the newspaper strip was turned into a Nintendo computer game: *Little Nemo: The Dream Master,* and an animated film, *Little Nemo: Adventures in Slumberland,* in 1992.
© *Estate of Winsor McCay*

Donenfeld – over at DC – thought differently. Mayer looked at the pages and immediately gave the two teens a cheque for $130, with all rights included. This would come back to haunt all concerned, as Siegel entered into a long-running court battle over the rights to *Superman*, eventually winning himself and Shuster a lifetime annuity from DC Comics in 1977.

Superman first appeared in print on the cover of *Action Comics* #1 in June 1938 and was an instant hit. The following year, he got his own title. *Superman's* original abilities were more prosaic, as he could, "leap 1/8 of a mile, hurdle a twenty-storey building, raise tremendous weights and run faster than an express train." As the years went by, his powers grew to add X-ray vision, cold breath and heat vision, all of which made him too invulnerable to be of interest, and so DC Comics created Kryptonite as his main weakness. The publisher also made him more 'human', both physically and emotionally with John Byrne's 1986 revamp of the whole mythos.

DC Comics' other icon appeared shortly after 'the flying boy scout'. A yang to *Superman's* ying, *Batman* first appeared in *Detective Comics* #27 in 1939. The Dark Knight was created by Bob Kane and Bill Finger, and 11 issues later, *Robin* "The Boy Wonder" joined his mentor. Both of them then faced their deadliest enemy, the Jerry Robinson-created villain, *The Joker*, in *Batman*

#1 (1940). *Batman* has became almost as iconic as *Superman* over the years, and in many ways, is more popular than his predecessor, at least with comics fans.

MARVEL'S TIMELY EMERGENCE

In October 1939, pulp publisher Martin Goodman launched a title that would profoundly affect the American comic book industry forever. *Marvel Comics* #1 included three strips; The *Human Torch* by Carl Burgos, The *Sub-Mariner* by Bill Everett and *Ka-Zar* by Ben Thompson. The first issue was a smash, selling out and being reprinted the following month. Even Goodman's bizarre changing of the name to *Marvel Mystery Comics* couldn't stem the runaway success of the title. The entire Marvel Comics empire – that would dominate the US comic book business for over six decades – had laid its foundation stone. The comic originally cost 10 cents; becoming the embodiment of what is referred to as the 'Golden Age' of US comics, an original copy sold for an impressive $350,000 in 2001.

In 1939, Martin Goodman hired his 17 year old nephew, Stanley Lieber, as an assistant editor. In 1942, Stan Lee, as he became known, was promoted to editor and would eventually become the most potent force in the company for over 40 years.

Above: Since his first appearance *Superman* has faced many adversaries, Lex Luthor, Brainiac and but none more unusual than former heavyweight boxing champ Muhammad Ali. This 1978 special was drawn by Neal Adams and the cover featured numerous celebrities, including *Batman* and then-President, Jimmy Carter.
© *DC Comics*

Giant Man strides across the Manhattan skyline in Kurk Busiek and Alex Ross' *Marvels*. It was their homage to Marvel Comics' Golden and Silver Age superheroes.
© *Marvel Comics*

Marvel Comics #1, the comic that helped launch The Golden Age of American comics.
© *Marvel Comics*

For more than 65 years since his first appearance, *Batman* has been drawn by hundreds of artists. This is Brian Bolland's rendition.
© *DC Comics*

Justice League of America

The *Justice League of America* weren't DC Comics' first superhero team – that was the Golden Age Justice Society – but they were the most successful. After All Star Comics folded, DC Editor Julius Schwartz took the Justice Society,

© DC Comics

renamed them the JLA and launched the team in *The Brave and the Bold* #28 in 1960.

The original line-up included *Flash*, *Martian Manhunter*, *Wonder Woman*, *Aquaman* and *Green Lantern*. After just three issues, The JLA got their own title, which ran for 261 issues until its cancellation in 1987.

Since then, there have been several variations including *Justice League* (1987), *Justice League International*, *Justice League Europe* (1989) and *Formerly Known as the Justice League* (2003). Almost every superhero in the DC Universe has served with the organization.

CAPTAIN AMERICA TO THE RESCUE

Writer Joe Simon, at this point, was working with a new artist, Jacob Kurtzberg – aka Jack Kirby. They met while working at Fox Comics, and when Simon left to resume freelancing, he asked Kirby to come with him. The two partners were asked by Martin Goodman at Timely Comics to come up with new heroes. Simon and Kirby had worked for Goodman and Timely before, doing *Red Raven* #1, so Goodman had reason to trust both. The character Simon and Kirby eventually created helped to change the history of superhero comics.

World War II was raging in Europe in late 1940 and the Germans had levelled Coventry, England, in November – an attack that had shocked the world. The staff at Timely, being mostly Jewish (Goodman, Simon and Kirby among them), were very aware of what Hitler and the Nazis were doing and what their intentions were. Much of this was examined in Michael Chabon's Pulitzer Prize winning novel, *The Amazing Adventures of Kavalier & Clay*, a semi-fictional look at the work of New York Jewish comic creators such as Jerry Siegel and Joe Shuster, the creators of *Superman*. Timely was distinctly anti-Hitler. As early as December 1939, the *Sub-Mariner* had taken on a Nazi submarine in *Marvel Mystery Comics* #4. So Simon and Kirby created a new

character who embodied the patriotism of the Timely staff, *Captain America*.

Goodman liked the idea of a patriotic hero and had Simon & Kirby create enough stories for *Cap* to have his own book – an unusual move, as nearly all new characters debuted in anthology books before being given their own title. *Captain America Comics* #1 went on sale on 20 December 1940, and was an immediate bestseller. The creative duo had actually been touting *Captain America* around Timely's rivals, and managed to get Goodman over a barrel, so the publisher gave Simon 15% of the profits from the sales of *Captain America Comics*, and Kirby 10%. This was an unprecedented deal in comics.

Captain America was not the first patriotic superhero in US comics however, as Irv Novick's character *The Shield* appeared in MLJ's *Pep Comics* #1 in November 1939. Many others quickly followed *The Shield*, but they lacked the flair and pizzazz of Simon and Kirby's creation. Kirby's energetic, exaggerated, fluid and powerful art style, combined with strong storytelling skills, leapt off the page, making *Captain America* compelling reading.

Naturally, publishers MLJ, miffed at the similarities between *The Shield* and *Captain America*, threatened Timely with a lawsuit. Goodman knew he didn't have a leg to stand on and agreed to change the character's shield from a triangular shape to a

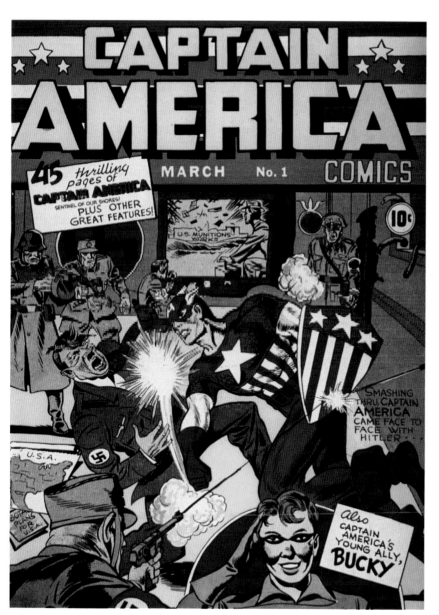

Captain America gives Hitler a black eye in the superhero's first issue by Joe Simon and Jack Kirby.
© *Marvel Comics*

Not only did psychologist William Moulton Marston (aka Charles Moulton) help invent the polygraph 'lie detector', but he also created *Wonder Woman*. His stories were thinly veiled S&M power fantasies – drawn here by the strip's first artist, Harry G. Peter in *Wonder Woman* #28 (1948). This issue was published posthumously, as Moulton died of cancer in 1947.
© *DC Comics*

A gal comes between a man and his horse in Marvel's *Western Life Romances*.
© *Marvel Comics*

Kid Colt was launched in 1948 and was only cancelled after 31 years in print.
© *Marvel Comics*

The grisly cover to EC Comics' *Crime Suspenstories #22* by Johnny Craig.
© *EC Comics*

circular one, a major sticking point with MLJ's publisher John Goldwater. At the end of the meeting, Goldwater even had the cheek to try to lure Simon & Kirby away from Timely – something that did not go down well with Martin Goodman at all.

MAKE WAR NO MORE

With the end of WWII in 1945, there was no need for these new 'super' heroes, and by the end of the 1940s the public had largely turned their backs on them. In a desperate attempt to chase the money, Marvel (the newly renamed Timely) scoured the market for what was the next big thing. It came in the form of western comics. Spurred on by the Republic cowboy serials and films, Marvel quickly cashed in with titles like *The Two-Gun Kid*, *Tex Morgan* and *Kid Colt, Outlaw*.

Simultaneously, another brief genre took off, the romance comic. Marvel went ballistic in this area, desperately wringing out every cent before the craze died, with no less than 14 titles with 'Love' in the name. But even *Best Love*, *Love Tales*, *Lovers*, *Love Romances*, *Love Adventures* and *Loveland* et al, couldn't keep their audience forever. Marvel, never a company to leave a customer's cash unspent, merged the two genres to create a bizarre hybrid – the romance western – with *Cowgirl Romances*, *Love Trails*, *Cowboy Romances*, *Romances West* and *Rangeland Love*.

However, the fire that burns twice as brightly burns only half as long, and the time in the sun for westerns and romances was barely three years, with a few exceptions, before readers moved on.

EXCESSIVE COMICS

In 1950, comics publisher William Gaines (son of Max Gaines) was panicking that his comicbooks weren't selling like they used to. Gaines needed a new formula, and pretty soon he and editor/artist Al Feldstein had figured it out. In the penultimate issue of their *Crime Patrol* title, they introduced a story with the blurb, "From the Crypt of Terror" on the cover. The issue was their best-ever seller. The next issue's cover had an obvious horror slant. It sold even better than the previous issue. The secret of success had been unlocked.

By mid 1950, EC (the initials ironically stood for Educational Comics, and later Entertaining Comics) had three horror titles on the stands: *Crypt of Terror* (later *Tales from the Crypt*), *Haunt of Fear* and *Vault of Horror*. The anthologies' stories had strange, twist endings that catapulted horror comics to the fore. Top names like Wally Wood and the often overlooked Johnny Craig drew the grisly tales. Other publishers scurried to get horror titles on the stands. Some were good, most were not, but that didn't matter. The public couldn't get enough.

Paranoid that these comics were corrupting children, when in fact the target audience was always intended to be adults, it was scenes like this that brought the wrath of parents, teachers and the moral majority down on EC Comics.
© *EC Comics*

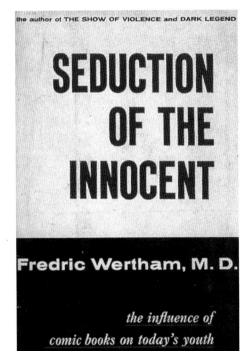

The book that almost destroyed an art form. *Seduction of the Innocent* by Dr. Fredric Wertham.
© *Estate of Dr. Fredric Wertham*

The Flash comes to terms with his, "strange, but good, feelings" about his new sidekick in *Flash* #110 by John Broome, Carmine Infantino and Joe Giella.
© *DC Comics*

Then the sky fell in. Several magazines, including *Readers Digest*, published a scathing article by a German psychologist, Fredric Wertham, who claimed that comic books and other media were responsible for the degradation of American youth. It was comics that made teenage boys rob, rape and use drugs. Comic books turned children into thieves, bullies and cold-blooded killers.

THE COMICS SCOURGE

American parents were thrown into a panic when Wertham published his book *Seduction of the Innocent* (1954) that contained supposed examples of sex and violence in comics. The book fanned anti-comics sentiment across America, and the resulting hysteria caused schools and PTA groups to hold Nazi-esque public comic book burnings. Comics were banned in many cities, and store owners refused to sell anything but *Bugs Bunny*, *Archie* and Disney comics. Even *Superman* couldn't get shelf space in some places. By this time, the public outcry was almost a roar. The Senate Subcommittee on Juvenile Delinquency had released a widely circulated report which was very critical of comics, leading to the subcommittee calling comics editors and publishers to appear before them. William Gaines, the publisher most accused of corrupting the young, appeared in front of the Senate hearings and tragically, inadvertently, did more harm to his cause than good.

In an effort to appease the public, the comics industry set up the highly restrictive, self-regulating Comics Code Authority, in one of the largest acts of creative self-censorship ever seen. The CCA imposed strict rules that prevented even the slightest suggestion of sex or hint of conflict. Words like weird, horror and terror could not appear on the covers (practically all of EC's titles had these words in them). Comics also had to have, "respect for parents, the moral code, and honorable behaviour shall be fostered. A sympathetic understanding of the problems of love is not a license for moral distortion."

POTRZEBIE

The backlash sent comics into a pit of despair from which few would crawl out. By 1955, all comics publishers had slashed their output. Many simply dumped comics and moved into other publishing areas, if they hadn't gone bankrupt. Dozens of small publishers went out of business, unable to overcome the problems the regulations inflicted. EC discovered that publishing *MAD* magazine could make more money than they ever had with comic books, and promptly shut down the rest of their output. *MAD* was created in 1954 by cartoonist/editor Harvey Kurtzman, and it went on to become one of the most influential and popular humour magazines ever, spawning local versions in other parts of the world.

DC's approach to comics helped them to avoid the disasters other publishers like EC suffered, since not one DC title needed to be changed to conform to the code, and they adopted the seal willingly. Dell Comics also didn't need to make any changes as they mostly published 'family oriented' products. Unlike DC, they didn't even subscribe to the Comics Code, as they always enforced their own code. For years, Dell was the only company not to carry the code's seal on their covers. Comics – while not dead – were certainly in intensive care, and it was unclear if they were going to make it through the night.

Ironically, the man responsible for comics near-death experience, Dr Wertham, actually recanted his position in the 1970s, and became an advocate of comics, "I had nothing whatever to do directly with the comics code. Nor have I ever endorsed it. Nor do I believe in it… I was the first American psychiatrist admitted in a Federal Court in a book censorship case – and I testified against censorship." But the damage had been done.

With the reduction of available themes due to the witch-hunt, publishers had to find new ideas. DC editor Julius Schwartz had a brainwave when, rather than looking forward, he looked back into DC Comics' past. Schwartz joined DC in 1944, editing *All Star Comics*, *Green Lantern*, *Flash* and *Sensation Comics*. He later took over editing *Strange Adventures*, *Mystery in Space* and *Showcase Comics*. The last of these titles premiered in January 1956, but its sales were dismal and by the third issue Schwartz decided to take a chance. He dug up the old Golden Age superhero *The Flash* and put him on the cover of #4. It was written by Robert Kanigher and illustrated by Carmine Infantino, and this creative team made sales figures jump. For many, this heralded the 'Silver Age' of American comics.

In 1960, another Schwartz-edited title, *The Brave and the Bold*, took another leap backward to achieve something new with issue 28. By teaming up DC Comics' leading superheroes – as it had done in 1941 with *All Star Comics* – the publishing house launched the *Justice League of America* team. Members included the *Flash*, *Green Lantern*, *Wonder Woman*, *Martian Manhunter* and *Aquaman*, occasionally joined by *Batman* and *Superman*. The JLA's popularity was so great that DC gave the group their own title a mere six months after they first appeared.

One day in 1961, Jack Kirby arrived at the Marvel offices to discover writer/editor Stan Lee distraught, as movers took the furniture out of Marvel's offices. The company that Stan's uncle, Martin Goodman,

A classic Silver Age comic, *The Atom* #10 (1964), with art by Murphy Anderson and Gil Kane.
© *DC Comics*

The first issue of *The Amazing Spider-Man* saw the Marvel Universe's first crossover with a guest appearance of *The Fantastic Four*. Art by Steve Ditko.
© *Marvel Comics*

The first appearance of *Iron Man* in *Tales of Suspense* in 1962. Cover art by Jack Kirby and Don Heck.
© *Marvel Comics*

founded in 1939 was going out of business. Kirby convinced Lee to try something new for Marvel. The two got to work on a series of titles that would not only save Marvel but also revolutionize comics forever. In September 1961, *Fantastic Four* #1 went stratospheric and was followed by the *Incredible Hulk* #1 (cover dated May 1962) and possibly the second or third most famous comic book superhero of all time, *Spider-Man*, in *Amazing Fantasy* #15 (cover dated August 1962).

A NEW REALISM

What made Marvel's comics different from the rest was their 'realism'. While many of DC's superheroes had fantastical adventures in far-off dimensions or in outer space, Marvel's were nerdish teenagers with real troubles, like girlfriends, keeping a job, school pressures and being bitten by a radioactive spider. Most importantly, Marvel's heroes were reluctant ones, forced into fantastical situations by fate rather than by choice.

Over the next two years, Jack Kirby and Stan Lee introduced scores of heroes from *Giant Man* and the *Mighty Thor*, to reviving the *Sub-Mariner* and *Captain America*.

Lee was a PR genius of unparalleled skill and an unabashed self-publicist. Over the years, if you'd just listened to Stan 'The Man' – as he labelled himself – you could be forgiven for believing that he created the entire Marvel universe single-handedly without any help from Jack 'King' Kirby, Steve Ditko or any of the other countless artists who drew *Doctor Strange*, *Daredevil* and *Iron Man*.

In 1972, Lee became publisher and editorial director of the group. When he finally left Marvel he was named chairman in emeritus. Stan Lee and Marvel clashed in 2002, when he claimed the company had locked him out of bonus payments when the *Spider-Man* film was released. In 2005, a court ruled that Lee was entitled to 10% of Marvel's profits generated since November 1998 by Marvel TV and movie productions involving the company's characters. The final figure could reach upwards of $90 million (£50 million).

GOING UNDERGROUND

Inspired by groundbreaking work Harvey Kurtzman did on *MAD*, *Help!* and *Humbug*, many of the underground cartoonists of the 1960s started writing and drawing their own strips, and some, like Robert Crumb, even ended up working for Kurtzman. The burgeoning underground scene was focused around the hippy haven of Haight Ashbury in San Francisco. Whacked out on drugs, and influenced by everything from Jimi Hendrix to Disney comics, a group of artists started

Steve Ditko

Alongside Stan Lee and Jack Kirby, Steve Ditko is also credited for ushering in Marvel's Silver Age.

The artist was first published in 1953. Three years later, he was drawing horror and supernatural strips for Atlas (later Marvel). In 1962, Ditko and Lee created *Spider-Man*. Ditko also drew the mystical *Doctor Strange*. After various disagreements, Ditko left Marvel and from 1966 through 1968 worked for Charlton, where he revived two old superheroes, *Blue Beetle* and *Captain Atom*, and created *The Question*.

© DC Comics

Ditko's more personal, self-published works, such as *Mr. A* (a more extreme *Question*) and *Avenging World*, expressed his political and philosophical sentiments . However, their moral certitudes didn't go down well with readers, and sales failed to match his superhero work. Famously reclusive, Steve Ditko remains, like his characters, enigmatic.

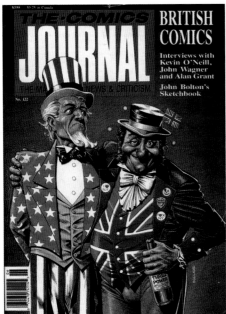

Fantagraphics' *The Comics Journal* has been providing news, critique and commentary on the industry for over 30 years. Cover by Brian Bolton.
© *Fantagraphics Books Inc*

experimenting with comic books. Creators included Gilbert Shelton (with his cult hit, *The Fabulous Furry Freak Brothers*), the political Spain, the disturbed S. Clay Wilson and many others who worked on the legendary *Zap Comics*. For a brief time, the San Francisco scene was where it was at, with music legends like Janis Joplin hanging out with cartoonists, and Crumb's characters being turned into films, namely *Fritz the Cat*, which he hated. But it couldn't last.

FROM UNDERGROUND TO ALTERNATIVE

By the late 1970s, the underground comics scene was dying out. Many cartoonists found it difficult to support themselves on a meagre income and turned to other means. Publishers found it hard going and many faded away. There were however, a few die-hards who kept the spirit of the underground alive. Publishers and editors like Art Spiegelman and Gary Groth genuinely believed that the underground movement could herald a new era of comic books for adults, and engender the intellectual acceptance that the medium deserved.

There was also a new generation of alternative comics creators growing up, who were inspired and motivated by the 1960s' originals, but had slightly different aims for their work – sex, drugs and rock and roll were still on the agenda, but so

was a more personal, even autobiographical approach.

In 1976, Gary Groth and fellow fanzine friend, Mike Catron, formed Fantagraphics Books while publishing *The Comics Journal*, a critical art magazine focusing on the comics industry. *The Comics Journal*, and Groth in particular, soon gained a reputation for being elitist and hypercritical of the industry. Groth revelled in his agent provocateur role, and the magazine continues to slaughter the occasional sacred cow, much to the disdain of certain elements in the comics industry. He has loudly scorned lowbrow superhero comics and frequently written manifestos calling for higher artistic standards. Over the years, Fantagraphics has been sued (and cleared) three times for libel and defamation of character, with one infamous case dragging on for seven years, which Fantagraphics ultimately won.

Kim Thompson became the new co-owner of Fantagraphics when Catron left to head up the short-lived Apple Comics. Under the new partnership of Groth and Thompson, Fantagraphics published its first continuing comic in 1982, *Love & Rockets*. The anthology was written and drawn by Los Angeles-based brothers Gilbert (AKA Beto), Jaime and Mario Hernandez (who left shortly after). The Latino brothers wrote and drew character-driven, semi-fantastical tales firmly rooted in their personal experiences of late 1970s' punk rock and

Gilbert Shelton's cult classic, *The Fabulous Furry Freak Brothers*. Despite there only ever being 13 issues, the comics have been almost continually in print for over 30 years.
© *Gilbert Shelton*

Sixties survivor and America's best known underground cartoonist, Robert Crumb, has fun at the 1994 Oscars when Terry Zwigoff's excellent bio-pic, Crumb, was entered in the competition. The Academy ignored it.
© *Robert Crumb*

...AND THERE I WAS, WALKING ON THE RED CARPET WITH THE MOVIE STARS... I FELT ILL AT EASE IN THE EXTREME AND VERY EMBARRASSED FOR ALL OF HUMANITY.

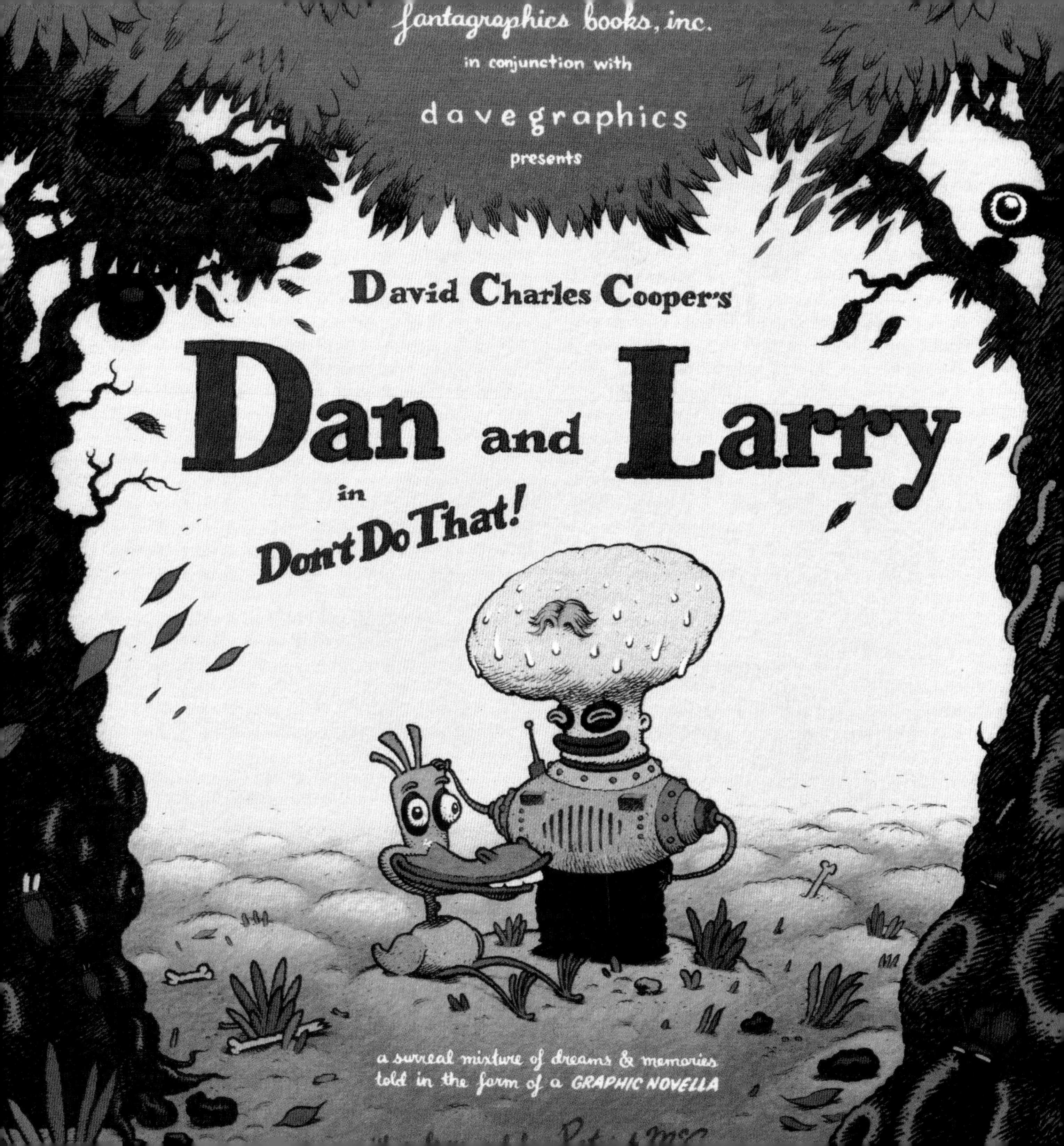

fantagraphics books, inc.

in conjunction with

davegraphics

presents

David Charles Cooper's

Dan and Larry

in

Don't Do That!

a surreal mixture of dreams & memories
told in the form of a GRAPHIC NOVELLA

life as Mexican-Americans. Jaime filled his half of the comic with tale of two friends, *Maggie* and *Hopey*, and followed their life in the barrio from teens to adulthood. Gilbert's stories of 'magic realism' examined the small fictional Mexican town of Palomar and its large, strange community. Inspired by *Love & Rockets*, other artists made tracks for Fantagraphics, and in the next few years the company published dozens of young talents who became lynchpins of the 'new wave'.

By the late 1980s, Fantagraphics was riding high on the explosion of independent comics as readers sought out more diverse material. The company moved to Seattle, where the grunge music movement was starting and a growing base of cartoonists was located, including Peter Bagge. Bagge's early professional work appeared in *Weirdo* magazine (1981), published by underground survivor Last Gasp. Originally edited by the ubiquitous Robert Crumb, the anthology was taken over by Bagge with issue 10. *Weirdo* saw new talents like J.D. King and Mary Fleener explode on to the scene. Issue 14 saw the debut of Bagge's *The Bradleys*, a strip he would develop over several years, and whose characters would provide Bagge with lots of material. By issue 18, Bagge went off to produce his own title, *Neat Stuff* (1985) for Fantagraphics, leaving the editorship of *Weirdo* in the more than capable hands of

Crumb's wife (and fellow cartoonist) Aline Kominsky-Crumb.

Neat Stuff was a collection of hilarious stories about losers and freaks including *Girly Girl*, *Studs Kirby*, *Junior* and *Chuckie Boy*, and it was here that the gruesome *Bradley* family shone. The *Bradleys* were the antitheses of every wholesome American ideal, the perfect post-nuclear family. *Neat Stuff* threw Bagge into the limelight, and in 1990, Fantagraphics published his acerbically titled *Hate*, which focused on the *Bradley's* oldest son, *Buddy*, and his attempts at living the 'slacker' lifestyle in Seattle. The tragically funny series ran for eight years, developing from black and white to a full-colour comic as the readership grew through word of mouth.

PORN SAVED THE COMPANY

Fantagraphics' boom then turned to bust. Despite the quality of material Fantagraphics had published over the years, the company had been continually plagued with financial problems, mostly thanks to both Groth and Thompson gleefully admitting that they had no business sense. Looking for a quick cash-flow fix, Fantagraphics turned to sex comics, and in 1990, it created a new subsidiary, Eros Comix, in order to cash in on the trend towards pornography. "Porn came to us in a vision," joked Thompson. Many saw this

Opposite page, left: Dave Cooper's 2001 graphic novel *Dan and Larry in Don't Do That!* is equally cute and queasy. But mostly queasy.
© Dave Cooper

A page from Peter Bagge's hard-to-find *Testosterone City!* minicomic. Published in 1989, it was reprinted by Seattle-based Starhead Comix in 1994.
© Peter Bagge

Dan Clowes' homage to the sexiest entertainment career, the cartoonist, in his series *Eightball*.
© *Daniel Clowes*

as a highly hypocritical move by Groth and Thompson, as *The Comics Journal's* mandate was about raising comics to an artform and not as an excuse to peddle smut. Despite others' misgivings, Eros saved Fantagraphics from bankruptcy within a year and now thrives as an independent revenue raiser for less commercial projects by Fantagraphics. Foreign creators from Europe and South America produced many of these titles and, in fact, Fantagraphics have specialized in scouring the planet to find new cartoonists to unleash on US readers. The most recent examples include UK-based Kiwi, Roger Langridge, Frenchman Lewis Trondheim and the Norwegian, Jason.

One of Fantagraphics' esoteric titles was *Lloyd Llewellyn* (1986) by Dan Clowes. *Llewellyn* was a beatnik PI resplendent in retro, 1950s' cool. Despite this, the comic didn't take off and was cancelled after six issues and a one-shot. Clowes' next series for Fantagraphics, *Eightball* (1989), was a completely different story. *Eightball* had a surreal, dream-like quality, reminiscent of the work of director David Lynch, and was populated by deeply-flawed, grotesque protagonists. It was a collection of short stories and longer serialized pieces, most notably *Like a Velvet Glove Cast in Iron*, *David Boring* and *Ghost World*. Clowes described *Eightball* as, "an orgy of spite, vengeance, hopelessness, despair and sexual perversion," but this

ignores the fact that it is also savage and darkly funny.

CRITICAL SUCCESS

Another Fantagraphics success was Chris Ware's acclaimed *Acme Novelty Library* (1993). Ware cut his teeth, like so many others, on Monte Beauchamp's *Blab!* (1986) and Art Spiegelman's *RAW* before launching his own title. His artwork was crisp, clean and made up of dozens of intricate panels that were a masterstroke of design. The content however, was grimly humorous stories of loneliness and alienation. The first collection of strips, *Jimmy Corrigan, the Smartest Kid on Earth*, told the tragically funny story of how history repeated itself in three generations of men named Jimmy Corrigan. In the UK, it went on to win the *Guardian* newspaper's award for Best First Book in 2001, the first graphic novel to do so.

While Ware focused on the tedium and drudgery of an empty fictional existence, Joe Sacco's work looked at the terrifying and tragic consequences of real-life war and conflict. Maltese-born Sacco studied journalism at the University of Oregon before becoming a full time cartoonist, contributing to a wide range of anthologies including *Drawn & Quarterly*, *Prime Cuts*, *Real Stuff* and *Weirdo*. In late 1991, the former Fantagraphics employee spent two months in Israel and the occupied

A page from the infamous 10-page strip *Letitia Lerner, Superman's Babysitter*. Liz Glass and Kyle Baker's story originally appeared in Elseworlds 80-page *Giant #1* in June, 1999. When DC Comics' publisher, Paul Levitz, saw the strip, he freaked and demanded that all copies be pulled and pulped, concerned that the madcap antics of putting (even Super) babies into microwave ovens would cause outrage or copycat cases. Two years later, DC relented and republished the strip in the *Bizarro* anthology, and it won a coveted Eisner Award.
© *DC Comics*

Cartoonist Joe Sacco was commissioned by the UK's *Guardian* newspaper to do an exclusive comic strip report from the frontline in Iraq in January 2005.
© *Joe Sacco*

Dark Horse

Set up in 1986 by successful, but frustrated, comicbook retailer, Mike Richardson, Dark Horse Comics (DHC) has become a powerful force in American comics and is now the fourth biggest publisher in the business.

It's first publication was *Dark Horse Presents*, that ran 157 issues until 2000 - the longest-running US anthology ever. DHC has always managed to attract top talent which has contributed to it's success and titles like Paul Chadwick's *Concrete* and Frank Miller and Dave Gibbons' *Martha Washington* series, which started in 1990.

© Mike Mignola

In 1992 Richardson set up a film division of Dark Horse and scored a massive hit with *The Mask*, starring Jim Carrey. Since then DHC has successful turned many of it's comics into films, including Mike Mignola's *Hellboy* and Frank Miller's *Sin City*, both of which were part of DHC's brief Legends imprint, along with the less successful *The Next Men*.

territories. When he returned to the USA, he combined the techniques of eyewitness reportage and comics to create *Palestine* (1993), an eight-issue mini-series for Fantagraphics. The series was collected and gained widespread praise, setting new standards for the use of the comic book as a documentary medium. In 1996, Sacco won the prestigious American Book Award for *Palestine*.

In 2000, Sacco finished *Safe Area Gorazde: The War In Eastern Bosnia 1992 – 1995*, an exploration of a small Muslim enclave in Serbia. Based upon Sacco's travels to the war-torn region, it gained major coverage from *Time* magazine, *The New York Times* and *The Los Angeles Times Book Review*, and eventually led to Sacco being commissioned to do a strip for *Time*. In 2005, the UK's *Guardian* newspaper commissioned Sacco to report from US-occupied Iraq, and he supplied a 10-page strip.

Critical acclaim doesn't pay the bills however, and again Fantagraphics found themselves going cap in hand when they lost $70,000 (£37,000) as a result of their distributor going bankrupt and, over-excited by their recent success with Ware, Clowes and Sacco, Groth and Thompson made all too frequent publishing errors, overprinting books and leaving themselves severely short of cashflow. In 2003, they were forced to put out a desperate plea on the Internet for readers to

purchase $80,000 (£42,000) worth of books in order for Fantagraphics to pay off their immediate debt. It's a sign of the loyalty and high regard which Fantagraphics has in the comic industry that they managed to raise the money in just eight days.

"It points out the inherent financial instability of publishing alternative comics," said Groth. Profit margins in the alternative comics industry are very tight and the fan base is compact. It has always been hard to reach customers, since many comics stores shun alternative comics in favour of the bread and butter superhero stuff. Mainstream bookstores are slightly more open to graphic novels, but still don't really understand how to sell and promote them. This, according to Groth, explains why, "every other remotely independent comics publisher has gone out of business over the last 16 years." Certainly there were many 'indy' companies that rose and died in the 1980s and 1990s including Comico, Pacific Comics, Eclipse, First Comics and Kitchen Sink, to mention but a few.

IDEAS IN MOTION

In the early and mid-1980s, America began to see a creative invasion unlike anything since The Beatles and The Rolling Stones in the 1960s; only this time, the British invaders weren't musicians, they were comics creators. Having cut their teeth on

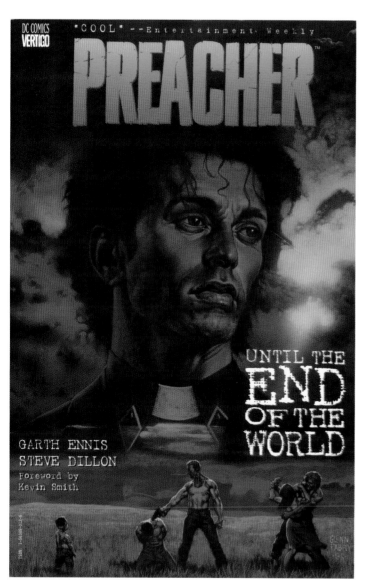

Preacher was the complete antithesis to everything previously published by Vertigo. The UK team of Garth Ennis, Steve Dillon and cover artist Glenn Fabry deliberately threw in bestiality, extreme violence and heartfelt characters to shake up what they perceived was the pretentiousness of the Vertigo imprint.
© Garth Ennis & Steve Dillon

The Sandman, written by Neil Gaiman, became Vertigo's biggest selling title, and spawned endless spin-off titles like The Dreaming series and several graphic novels. These panels are by Danish artist Teddy Kristiansen.
© DC Comics

Bernie Wrightson's cover for a reprint special of *The House of Mystery*, one of the titles that inspired the creation of DC Comics' Vertigo imprint.
© *DC Comics*

Alan Moore, Steve Bissette and John Totleben's revamp of *Swamp Thing* paved the way for serious adult themes in mainstream American comics.
© *DC Comics*

classic British comics like 2000 *AD* and *Warrior*, writers and artists led by Brian Bolland, Dave Gibbons and Alan Moore crossed the Atlantic in search of wider creative freedoms and bigger paychecks. They found them mostly in the welcoming arms of DC Comics. Bolland drew *Camelot 3000*, a series written by Mike W. Barr, while Gibbons worked on the Len Wein-written *Green Lantern*. Moore took over the ailing 'horror' series, *Swamp Thing*, threw out all the continuity and started again. His brash style and intelligent writing revolutionized American comics and paved the way for fellow Brit writers like Jamie Delano, Neil Gaiman, Grant Morrison and Peter Milligan. Many of the titles they worked on weren't the traditional superheroes, but slightly off-kilter, quirkier titles like *Shade The Changing Man* (a 1960s' Steve Ditko creation), *The Sandman* and *Animal Man*. Many titles, like *Hellblazer* by Delano, had a horror slant hangover from DC's old titles like *House of Secrets*, *House of Mystery* and *Weird Westerns*.

DON'T LOOK DOWN

The defining link with most of these projects was that Karen Berger edited them. As she saw a growing interest for more adult sensibilities in comics, she set up a new DC imprint, Vertigo Comics, in 1994. The imprint collected the disparate titles together, dropped the impotent Comics Code seal on the cover and clearly labelled themselves 'For Mature Readers' only. It quickly became a home away from home for British creators who were generally more experimental than their American counterparts. Artists like Dave McKean, Brendan McCarthy and Duncan Fregredo all found a place to stay. *The Sandman* by Neil Gaiman was the imprint's biggest selling series, reaching the *New York Times*' Bestseller list and garnering the 1991 World Fantasy Award for the best short story – the first comic ever to win a literary award – and cemented the writer's reputation leading to a string of successful novels. Other important titles included *Preacher* by Garth Ennis and Steve Dillon and *The Invisibles* by Grant Morrison and various artists including Steve Yeowell and American Phil Jimenez. Vertigo has had more than of its fair share of misses as well as hits, but it valiantly strides on and is an important voice that has encouraged more experimentation in American comics outside of the superhero mainstream. Having celebrated 10 years, it looks as if the imprint has settled into a routine of being semi-unconventional. It constantly tries new subjects, with crime being the current genre du jour, through titles like *100 Bullets* by Brian Azzerello and the Argentinean artist Eduardo Risso and *The Losers* by ex-editor of 2000 AD, Andy Diggle, and fellow Brit, Jock.

The Brazilian edition of Peter Milligan and Ted McKeever's four-issue Vertigo mini-series, *The Extremist*.
© DC Comics

Archie Goodwin

Archie Goodwin began his career as a comic book writer and occasional art assistant to Leonard Starr on *Mary Perkins on Stage*. In 1962, he joined Harvey Comics, but moved to Warren, where he wrote for artists like Al Williamson, Joe Orlando,and Neal Adams in *Eerie* and *Creepy*. He went on to edit these and *Blazing Combat* for Warren. Goodwin also wrote *Vampirella*, the newspaper strip *Secret Agent X-9*, as well as *Fantastic Four*, *Iron Man* and many others for Marvel.

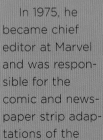

© Walt Simonson

In 1975, he became chief editor at Marvel and was responsible for the comic and newspaper strip adaptations of the *Star Wars* trilology. He launched *Epic Illustrated* magazine and headed-up Marvel's Epic imprint. He also worked at DC Comics where he revived *Manhunter* with artist and friend Walt Simonson.

Goodwin sadly died in 1998 after a long battle with cancer. Regardless of the above, there's one achievement that stands out; Archie Goodwin was the best-loved comic book editor, ever. No mean feat.

THE EARTH PIG COMETH

North of the border in Canada, there are comics creators producing interesting work, the 'big daddy' of which is, without doubt, Dave Sim. In December 1977, he started self-publishing his black and white *Conan the Barbarian* parody, *Cerebus*, under the imprint Aardvark Vanaheim. Not only did Sim write, pencil, ink and letter the series, but he also declared that it would run for a staggering 300 issues. "If you read 300 issues of *Superman* or *Spider-Man*," said Sim, "they don't make sense as a story or a life. When I started *Cerebus*, uppermost in my mind was the thought that I wanted to produce 300 issues of a comic book series the way I thought it should be done – as one continuous story documenting the ups and downs of a character's life." And that's exactly what he did. *Cerebus* began as a 'funny animal' series about an aardvark, but after 25 issues Sim realized that there were bigger issues and expanded his scope to cover the entire realm of human existence. He wove in references to current social and political events, from electoral politics to abortion, and many familiar icons like Oscar Wilde, Groucho Marx, The Rolling Stones and many parodies of classic (and not so classic) comics characters.

When Sim realized the daunting task he'd set himself, he brought in collaborator Gerhard to pencil and ink the backgrounds and colour the covers. *Cerebus* was the longest-running self-published comic of all time. It survived a very public and bitter divorce between Sim and Deni Loubert (*Cerebus*' then publisher, and Sim's wife) and numerous attacks on Sim's apparent misogyny. Both praised for his stand on creator rights and his defence of independent publishers, and vilified for his uncompromising views in the same breath, Sim is undoubtedly one of the most important influences in modern comics, bridging the old school to the new wave. The epic 6,000-page story eventually stretched over 26 years and ended in March 2004 with the death of *Cerebus*. Sim is currently taking, "A long nap."

DRAWN AND QUARTERED

The rise of the black and white comics in the late 1980s and the inspiration of Dave Sim saw a string of Canadian cartoonists emerge onto the scene. Many started out simply by self-publishing minicomics, but were soon grouped together and published by Montreal's Drawn & Quarterly. Formed by Chris Oliveros in 1990 and Drawn & Quarterly was Canada's answer to Fantagraphics. "I realized that a comic could be about anything – any viewpoint, any kind of graphic approach. In other words, it could be a kind of literature," enthused Oliveros. "Cartoonists became

James Sturm's *The Golem's Mighty Swing* tells the emotional story of a touring Jewish baseball team in the 1930s. It is indicative of the quality of the work that Drawn & Quarterly publish.
© *James Sturm*

Dave Sim's iconic character *Cerebus the Aardvark*, here seen in a plate from the *Animated Cerebus* portfolio.
© *Dave Sim*

more ambitious. Instead of 24-page comic books with one story, they began serializing longer stories that could be collected into book form." It took Oliveros almost two years to put together the first issue of the eponymous *Drawn & Quarterly* anthology.

Soon after, Oliveros began to publish important titles such as *Yummy Fur* (1986) by Chester Brown (originally released by another Canadian publisher, Vortex), *Palookaville* (1991) by Seth and *Dirty Plotte* (1990) by Julie Doucet, 'a female Robert Crumb'. Doucet was also based in Montreal, and had just been turned down by Fantagraphics when Oliveros agreed to publish her series. Another Montreal-based cartoonist, Joe Matt, appeared in *Drawn & Quarterly* #1, and shortly after spun-off his painfully honest, Crumb-like autobiographical stories into the series *Peepshow* (1992).

Drawn & Quarterly magazine evolved into an annual coffee-table anthology featuring new artists, old favourites, translations and reprints, and shortly after the company published its first graphic novel, *The Playboy* by Chester Brown, in 1992. Brown's autobiographical strip originally appeared in *Yummy Fur* and told of his guilt and angst at gaining a copy of *Playboy* in his pubescent youth. Drawn & Quarterly continues to be an important publisher of alternative comics, producing great works such as *Atlas* (2001) by New Zealand cartoonist Dylan

Horrocks, and the series *Jar of Fools* and *Berlin* (1996) by Jason Lutes.

READING YOURSELF RAW

Much of Fantagraphics and Drawn & Quarterly's inspiration was drawn from the groundbreaking work done by Art Spiegelman on *RAW* magazine. Spiegelman was a long-time contributor to underground comix throughout the 1960s and 1970s, and was co-editor of *Arcade* with fellow underground cartoonist Bill Griffith, an immensely influential comics anthology. *Arcade* however, was, "a tremendous headache and a lot of work and when it ended I swore I'd never be involved with a magazine again," Spiegelman said ruefully.

In 1980, Spiegelman moved from San Francisco to New York and met his future wife, Françoise Mouly. Spiegelman worked on several publications including *Playboy*, the *New York Times* and the *Village Voice* when Mouly finally persuaded Spiegelman to get back into magazine publishing, and after buying a printing press, they co-edited and published the first issue of *RAW*. Planning it as a one-shot, the first issue (which carried the subtitle "The Graphix Magazine of Postponed Suicides") soon sold out its 4,500 print run and gained legions of admirers. RAW's unique over-sized format had a fine-art slant, with early issues deliberately torn or containing individual inserts

Opposite page, left: Jeff Smith's *Bone*, the best all-ages comic to come out in the last 15 years. The series ran from 1991 to 2003 and won a record-breaking nine Eisner and nine Harvey Awards.
© *Jeff Smith*

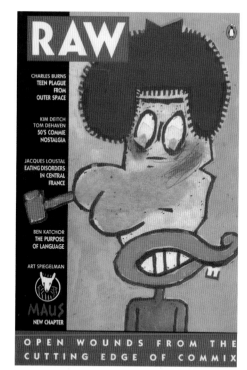

The first of the Penguin Books' editions of *RAW*, "The Graphix Magazine for Damned Intellectuals." Cover by Gary Panter.
© *Raw Books & Graphics and Gary Panter*

on coloured paper, including Spiegelman's epic, *Maus*.

With only eight issues published between 1980 and 1986, what *RAW* lacked in quantity it made up for in quality. It launched the careers of dozens of cartoonists and artists from Charles Burns and Gary Panter to Drew Friedman and Chris Ware. Spiegelman and Mouly weren't simply satisfied with homegrown US creators, however. They actively sought out European artists and writers such as Jacques Tardi, Joost Swarte and Lorenzo Mattotti, intending to give them wider exposure to an American audience. The co-editors also reprinted lesser-known classic strips from Basil Wolverton and George Herriman's *Krazy Kat*.

DAMNED INTELLECTUALS

The strip that really captured the public's attention was *Maus*. First serialized in *RAW* from issue 2 (1980), it gave a compelling and deeply moving account of Vladek – Spiegelman's father – and his experiences as a survivor of the Nazi concentration camp at Auschwitz.

Spiegelman delivered the masterstroke of drawing the Jews as mice and the Nazis as cats, using age-old cartoon stereotypes and Nazi propaganda (which portrayed the Jews as a plague of rodents). Vladek's struggle through pre-war Poland, up to the

horrors of the ironically named Mauschwitz, is interspersed with conversations between father and son. The first volume of *Maus*, *My Father Bleeds History*, was collected and published by Pantheon (USA)/Penguin (UK) in 1986. It took another five years before the second and final chapter, *And Here My Troubles Began*, would be collected and published in 1991.

The following year, *Maus* won a specially created Pulitzer Prize for fiction, the first and only comic to do so. By the time Spiegelman had finished *Maus*, it had taken up 295 pages and 13 years of the creator's life. It stands today as one of the greatest achievements in sequential art and manages to transcend its humble underground comics beginnings to become a work of literary fiction that is used in schools around the world.

During the success of *Maus*, Penguin Books began publishing *RAW* in 1989. The format changed from a large over-sized magazine to a 200-page mangaesque paperback format, but the same mix of classic comics and new experimental works remained.

Mouly and Spiegelman always stated that each issue would be the last, and after three issues of the Penguin edition, *RAW* finally closed its doors in 1991, the regret of comics amateurs everywhere. It remains one of the most important and influential comics anthologies and was instrumental

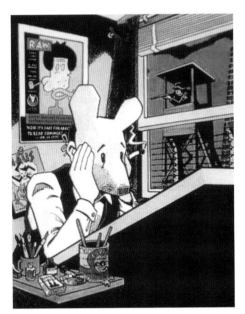

Pulitzer prize-winning cartoonist Art Spiegelman's self-portrait, surrounded by his most famous creations, *RAW* and *Maus*.
©*Art Spiegelman*

in gaining comics credibility amongst the intelligentsia.

NOVEL GRAPHICS

Around the same time as *Maus* was being serialized in *RAW*, two other, more mainstream, 'graphic novels' – a term soon coined – were released that would shake American comics to the core and launch a thousand tired newspaper headlines like "Biff, Baff, Pow! Comics aren't for kids anymore!" Both books actually started as series before being collected. The first was Frank Miller's prestige format (the first of its kind) four-part *The Dark Knight Returns* in 1986. This near future 'what if' *Batman* story rewrote what was possible in a superhero comic. Until then, superhero titles were generally escapist, light fantasies, but Miller infused a dark broodiness that spawned a mass of 'grim and gritty' comics that threatened to encompass the entire genre and very quickly became tired. Then the following year came *Watchmen* by the British duo Alan Moore (story) and Dave Gibbons (artwork). This 12-part series was originally intended as a revamp of old Charlton Comics characters, but developed into so much more. It turned superhero comics on their heads with its complex scripting, intricate art and interwoven storylines. It told the story of a world were superheroes really existed but

had been outlawed. It examined, like *Dark Knight*, the psychology of men in tights, and attempted to address why someone would dress up as an owl to fight crime. All three graphic novels, *Maus*, *The Dark Knight Returns* and *Watchmen*, became the darlings of the media and fêted as the future of comics. Sadly, the rest of the industry failed to live up to these expectations.

IT'S ALL ABOUT IMAGE

Almost as a reaction to the intelligent approach to comics that DC pursued, Marvel went in the opposite direction with big, exciting, lowbrow superheroics. Korean-born Jim Lee had worked for the self-styled 'House of Ideas' for several years before he landed the job of revamping Marvel's flagship title, *X-Men*. The title became a massive hit, selling millions and catapulting Lee to the top of the 'hot artists' lists.

At the same time, Todd McFarlane started out by submitting artwork to various editors of comic books. After receiving over 700 rejection letters, McFarlane's tenacity paid off when – just a few weeks before graduation, in March 1984 – Marvel/Epic Comics offered him a pencilling job on a back-up story in *Coyote*. Gradually clawing his way to the top, he eventually convinced Marvel to give a title that he could not only pencil and ink, but

In 2001, Frank Miller produced the sequel to his seminal *The Dark Knight Returns*, 15 years after it came out. But *The Dark Knight Strikes Again* (AKA *DK2*) received a mixed response and failed to garner the same success as its predecessor.
© *DC Comics*

After drawing *Spider-Man*, Todd McFarlane self-published his *Spawn* comic at his co-owned company, Image. The title sold remarkably well, all things considered.
© *Todd McFarlane Productions Inc*

write as well. His *Spider-Man* #1 launched in September 1990 at the height of the speculator market boom when customers often bought five copies of an issue as an 'investment'. Because of this, and the massive hype, the title became one of the best-selling comic books of all time, selling more than 2.5 million copies of the first issue. With an inflated wallet and ego, McFarlane decided to leave both *Spider-Man* and Marvel in August 1991 to form his own publishing company. Meanwhile, Rob Liefeld was hired by Marvel in 1985, and worked on *The New Mutants*, which evolved into X-Force. Like Lee's *X-Men* #1 and McFarlane's *Spider-Man* #1, *X-Force* #1 sold an obscene number of copies and also made Liefeld very rich.

Then, in 1992, Liefeld joined Lee, McFarlane and a whole group of artists to set up their own company, Image Comics. The other early founders included Jim Valentino (the 'old man' of the group who created *Shadow Hawk*), Marc Silvestri, the Filipino artist Whilce Portacio and Erik Larsen (creator of *Savage Dragon*). Liefeld's title, *Youngblood*, broke the record for the all-time best-selling independent comic, a record broken by McFarlane's *Spawn* #1, and then again by Lee's *WildC.A.T.S.* #1. But the young Turks were also hot-headed, and Liefeld resigned from Image Comics and struck out alone. McFarlane's *Spawn* spun-off a movie in 1997 and an animated

series, and after Image's very public creator spats, he focused on his highly profitable action-figure company. Lee took his Image imprint, WildStorm Productions, over to DC Comics where it had huge successes with the postmodern superhero series *The Authority* and *Planetary*, created by UK writer Warren Ellis.

INDEPENDENT'S DAY

Over the years, Image has inspired or given birth to many smaller, independent super-hero-publishing companies such as IDW and Top Cow. Since the mid 1990s, more and more smaller alternative publishers have appeared, telling non-superheroic tales as audiences tastes have grown and come into line with Europe and Japan. Companies of note in recent years have included Slave Labour Graphics, Caliber, AiT/Planetlar, Oni Press and Top Shelf.

Brett Warnock and Chris Staros' Top Shelf Productions was formed in 1997, created to promote the careers of rising talents such as Craig Thompson (*Good-Bye Chunky Rice*), Scott Morse (*The Barefoot Serpent*), James Kochalka (*Monkey Vs. Robot*), Ed Brubaker (*Lowlife*) and Peter Kuper (*Speechless*). Warnock and Staros launched Top Shelf Productions at the first Small-Press Expo (SPX) in Maryland, USA. SPX was designed as a convention to help publishers consolidate their work and gain a stronger voice. The show has gone from strength to strength and has its own prestigious and coveted prizes, the Ignatz Awards.

Two years earlier in 1995, SPX's West Coast cousin, the Alternative Press Expo (APE), was launched in San Francisco. APE was a colourful mingling of Bay Area punks and activists, underground comics creators and established stars of the independent scene. The indy comics market is expanding and in 2003, APE's attendance had grown to 3,400 with an increase in the number of exhibitors.

Comics publishing was, is, and probably always will be a monetarily hazardous business, and many of today's independent publishers perpetually hover on the brink of financial disaster. In 2002, both Top Shelf and Drawn & Quarterly nearly folded when their distributor went out of business. They survived by appealing to their fans to buy their books, just like Fantagraphics. However, while there have been casualties along the way, such as Black Eye, the US comics industry has undoubtedly grown in breadth and depth.

THE SPIRIT OF COMICS

Throughout all of this history, there was one man who remained at the forefront of the comics industry: Will Eisner. His career spanned nearly seven decades, beginning as a teenager in 1936 with his first major work, the buccaneer saga *Hawks of the Seas*. Eisner then set up a comic book content packaging company with his friend Jerry Iger. From 1936 to 1939, the legendary Eisner & Iger Studio was at the forefront of the comicbook industry. Their staff included a huge roster of future stars, from Jack Kirby and Lou Fine to Bob Kane and Mort Meskin. Meanwhile, Iger and Eisner created classic strips like *Sheena, Queen of the Jungle*, *Dollman* and *Blackhawk*.

In 1940, Eisner sold his share of the packaging company to Iger and created his most famous character, *The Spirit*, a masked crime fighter. *The Spirit* was the lead feature in a new format: the 16-page colour comic book that was inserted in Sunday newspapers. *The Spirit* insert appeared in 20 major newspapers, reaching five million readers each week.

From 1942 to 1945 he served as a warrant officer in the Pentagon, and pioneered the use of cartoons for instruction manuals with the Army Motors. After the war, Eisner continued *The Spirit* until 1952 when he 'retired'. It has been continually reprinted ever since. Eisner coined several terms that helped define what comics were, including the very first 'graphic novel', a term used to describe his seminal 1978 work, *A Contract with God*. Eisner produced almost 20 additional graphic novels over the years, including *A Life Force*, *Dropsie Avenue*,

Harvey Kurtzman

Alongside Will Eisner and Jack Kirby, Harvey Kurtzman was one of the most influential figures in American comics. His first published work appeared in 1939 in *Tip Top Comics*, and between 1946 and 1949 he worked for Stan Lee at Marvel, doing a one-page humour strip, *Hey Look!*

Kurtzman then joined EC Comics and worked on horror and sci-fi stories before editing *Two Fisted Tales* and *Frontline Combat* - realistic and moralistic war comics. In 1954, he started the revolutionary satire comic book *MAD*, which became a huge success. Kurtzman not only edited it, but also drew, wrote scripts and designed page layouts. However, after falling out over *MAD*'s direction with EC's publisher, Bill Gaines, Kurtzman left in 1956 to start *Trump* (with Hugh Hefner), *Humbug*, and *Help!* He then teamed up with Will Elder on *Little Annie Fanny* for *Playboy* between 1962 and 1988. He died in 1993.

© DC Comics

The Spanish edition of Will Eisner's *A Contract with God*, generally regarded as the forerunner of the modern graphic novel. The powerful story of a Jew who makes a deal with God, but then loses his faith in the seemingly absent deity.
© *Estate of Will Eisner*

The Spirit is one of the longest running and most influential newspaper and comic book strips in the USA.
© *Estate of Will Eisner*

The Heart of the Storm, Family Matter and *The Name of the Game*. He also taught comics art classes for years at the School of Visual Arts in New York City, and authored two definitive instructional books on the medium, *Comics and Sequential Art* and *Graphic Storytelling*, both perennial sellers with over 20 reprints. These books became the bibles for all aspiring, and working, professionals, and helped explain the 'magic' of comics. The books also inspired fellow artist Scott McCloud to take Eisner's ideas one stage further in his comics studies, *Understanding Comics* (1993) and *Reinventing Comics* (2000), both essential reading.

In 1988, Eisner received the accolade of having one of the comics industry's most prestigious awards named after him. Eisner himself presented the Eisner Awards, held annually at America's biggest comics convention in San Diego, until his death. Eisner also won several other prestigious industry awards named after his close friend, the late Harvey Kurtzman. In 2001, Eisner won two Harvey Awards for works created 60 years apart: the 1940 *Spirit Archives* won Best Reprint, while his book *Last Day in Vietnam* (2000) won Best Graphic Novel. On 3 June 2002, he received a Lifetime Achievement Award from the National Federation for Jewish Culture, only the second such honour in the organization's history. Tragically, Will Eisner died on 3 January 2005, following complications from open-heart surgery. His last completed work, THE PLOT: *The Secret Story of The Protocols of the Elders of Zion*, was published posthumously in May 2005. Eisner's legacy lives on as DC Comics reprints all 645 stories in *The Spirit Archives* colour hardcovers, and has produced new *Spirit* stories by contemporary writers and artists.

While Eisner was constantly pushing the boundaries of the medium, both DC and Marvel seemed locked in traditional superhero fare. Recently, almost out of necessity, the mainstream publishers have been forced to become more experimental to try to change the superhero genre, allowing the edgier, 'alternative' creators loose on their core characters. Previous stars of the independent comics scene such as Paul Pope, Evan Dorkin, Ed Brubaker and New Zealander Dylan Horrocks all found themselves thrust into the spotlight, giving their unique spin on what was becoming a tired and jaded genre, in titles like *The Tangled Web* of *Spider-Man* and DC Comics' *Bizarro Comics* one-shot anthology. Despite several attempts at reviving titles by luring the Vertigo writers Grant Morrison and Peter Milligan to work on their biggest titles, *X-Men* and *X-Factor/X-Statix*, both Marvel and DC's sales have dropped drastically. From the late 1980s, the high-point of the speculator market when titles regularly topped sales of one million copies,

comics sales have declined considerably. Today's bestsellers are lucky to top 250,000 per issue, with the overwhelming majority of titles selling many thousands of copies less.

THE FUTURE?

Although sales have declined in the superhero market, there is growth in other areas. The 'alternative' titles are becoming the new mainstream as the market matures and diversifies, aided and abetted by the popular rise of manga in America. Readers now demand complete stories in one book, and the graphic novel, or trade paperback collection, has certainly eaten into the monthly comics' sales. The American comic book industry seems to be evolving into the European or Japanese model. So, despite everything, and after 100 years of publishing, the future of American comics looks – if not bright – then at least glowing.

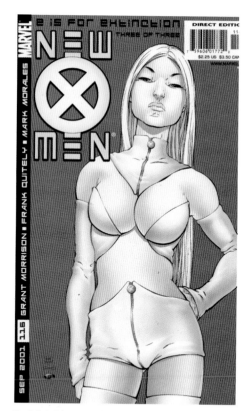

Frank Quietly's cover to *New X-Men* #116, featuring a sexually ambiguous Emma Frost.
© *Marvel Comics*

JACK KIRBY

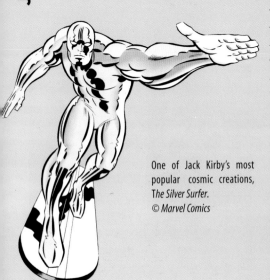

One of Jack Kirby's most popular cosmic creations, *The Silver Surfer*.
© Marvel Comics

Jack Kirby's self-portrait with the endless characters he'd created and drawn over his long career.
© Estate of Jack Kirby

Jacob Kurtzberg, better known as Jack Kirby, was born in New York on 28 August 1917. Like so many early comic book pioneers (Will Eisner, Jerry Siegel, Joe Shuster, et al), he was a second generation son of Jewish immigrants. Growing up in the tough Bowery tenements, he learned to draw early on and started his career in 1935 as an 'in-betweener' for Max Fleischer's animation studio. He moved to the Lincoln Newspaper Syndicate just over a year later, where he pro-duced short-lived newspaper strips like *Black Buccaneer* and *Socko the Seadog*. In 1939, he briefly joined the famous Eisner-Iger comic studio.

While working at Fox Comics, Kirby met writer/artist Joe Simon and the two formed the first of two important collaborations for Kirby. The pair worked together for nearly 20 years, for several publishers including, Novelty, Timely, National and Harvey.

In 1941, Kirby developed his artistic style when he co-created *Captain America*, with Joe Simon. The title brought them fame and a steady wage. The character quickly became a national icon, boosting the country's morale. But the creative duo only

stuck around for a year before being lured to rival publishers National Periodicals (who became DC Comics) with the promise of better pay and bigger credits on the covers. Both soon became fan-favourites, creating strips like *Sandman* and *Boy Commandos*. When the real war called in 1943, both men were drafted into the army, and Kirby took part in the Normandy landings. In later life, he was reticent in talking about his war years, but his military service pro-foundly affected his creative imagination, as had his ghetto upbringing.

When they returned from the war in 1945, Simon and Kirby started packaging books for several publishers, beginning with Harvey Comics, for whom they created *Boys Explorers* and *Stuntman*. In 1947, they developed *Young Romance Comics* – historically, the very first romance comic title – along with *Black Magic*, one of the more highly regarded horror titles of the 1950s – both for Crestwood.

In 1954, Simon and Kirby launched their own publishing company, Mainline Comics, with titles like *Bullseye*, *In Love* and *Foxhole*. In response to Timely's revival of their creation, *Captain America*, the duo also launched *The Fighting American*, which was a brief hit before disappearing after just seven issues.

When Dr Wertham's witch-hunt decimated the comics industry, Kirby returned to his old publishers, Crestwood (now called Prize) and again drew *Young Romance* and *Young Love*, which was edited by Joe Simon. But when Prize folded in late 1956, Simon and Kirby's artistic collaboration ended.

With nowhere to go, Kirby began working with DC again, illustrating the *Green Arrow* in *Adventure Comics*, and doing sci-fi and mystery stories. In 1957, he created the *Challengers of the Unknown*, who were generally regarded as the blueprint for his later creation, the *Fantastic Four*. Around the same time, he created and successfully syndicated the science-fiction newspaper strip, *Skymasters*, written and pencilled by Kirby and inked by Wally Wood.

Kirby's second great collaboration came in 1961, when he teamed up with writer/editor Stan Lee and created the *Fantastic Four* for the Marvel Comics Group. Kirby, Lee and Marvel rose to the top of the industry, and many claim they completely revamped the comic book world. Together they created or co-created nearly every character Marvel has published since. *Spider-Man*, *Thor*, the *Hulk*, *Ant-Man/Giant-Man*, *Nick Fury*, *Iron Man*, *The X-Men*, *Silver Surfer*, the *Avengers* and *Captain America* (revived again) all became huge hits. Exactly who created what, and how, has long since

been a huge bone of contention in the comics world. Whatever the truth, it was here that Jack Kirby was crowned 'King' by Lee. After a disagreement with Lee - over creative recognition and financial recompense - Kirby left Marvel in 1970 to return to DC Comics as a writer/editor/artist, where he created nearly a dozen titles, including his 'fourth world' titles; *The New Gods*, *Forever People* and *Mister Miracle*. He also created titles and characters such as *Kamandi*, *OMAC*, and *The Demon*.

After another brief stint at Marvel, Kirby went back to animation, but he soon leapt at the chance when Pacific Comics asked him to create new titles that they would publish, but to which he would own the rights. In 1981, he drew *Captain Victory* and *Silver Star* for Pacific and returned to DC briefly to work on *Super Powers*.

Kirby developed a unique, highly exaggerated style that added extreme dynamism to the page. Characters didn't just swing punches, they threw their entire bodies into them. This and his innovative layouts (sometimes using experimental techniques such as collage) influenced generations of artists.

In his 50-year career, Kirby drew over 24,000 pages of comic book art, making him the most prolific comic artist ever. His importance to US comics cannot be overstated, and there isn't a single serious creator who doesn't know his work, yet he remained relatively modest.

On 6 February 1994, aged 76, Jack Kirby died. The King was dead, and the comic book industry mourned.

Jack 'King' Kirby by fellow comics artist, Rick Geary.
© Rick Geary

Above: Amazing Adventures #1 (June 1961). Cover by Kirby.
© Marvel Comics

Above: On the cover of Marvel UK's *Captain Britain* #23 (1977) Jim Callaghan, then British Prime Minister, faces certain death alongside Captain America and Captain Britain. The rather poor likeness is due to the cover being drawn by American artists, Herb Trimpe and Fred Kida.

© *Marvel Characters, Inc.*

2

BRIT LIT

Tracing the ancestry of British comics is as complicated as tracing a family tree, and it is easy to become lost in the distant past. Like all genealogy, every aspect of comics has more than one parent, some influences come from abroad, styles become divorced and lost, and there is the occasional bastard child.

THE CLAIMANT.

The "Daily News" says, "On his regaining his liberty, the Claimant will appeal to the public for support." SLOPER says, "Why don't they let the poor man out at once, so that he may have the benefit of the Seaside season?"

Above: Britain's first regular comic character, *Ally Sloper*, drawn by W. G. Baxter in 1884.
© *Estates of W. G. Baxter/Charles Ross*

British comics real lineage began in the 18th Century with the arrival of satirical illustrations in the broadsheets, which gave birth to today's political cartoons. In the early 18th Century, William Hogarth, 'Father of English caricature', began illustrating his grim experiences of poverty. Hogarth's most famous works were told through sets of satirical illustrations including, *A Harlot's Progress* (1731–32) and *The Rake's Progress* (1735).

From the caricatures and prints of Hogarth, George Townshend, Thomas Rowlandson, James Gilray and George Cruickshank (also, from Europe, Rodolphe Töpffer, whose works were widely pirated in America and Britain) emerged the popular humour magazines led by *Punch* in July 1841. *Punch* honed the joke cartoon concept and developed the talents of John Leech, John Tenniel and Phil May. Leech's 'Mr Briggs' cartoons featured the domestic difficulties of a typical middle class family (*Punch*'s target audience). Rival humour magazines like *The Man in the Moon* also ran early cartoon strips, including *Mr Crindle's Rapid Career Upon the Town* by H.G. Hine and Albert Smith, serialized from April 1847.

An important element of these proto-comics and cartoons was the use of text within the illustrations; captions and dialogue balloons were already recognized tools of the caricaturist's trade. However, the great majority of cartoons were captioned below with a barbed comment or stinging libretto. This became standard format for the majority of British comic strips right up until the 1940s. New photogravure printing techniques developed in the 1880s were especially useful for artists like Phil May, whose simplified style was highly influential.

THE GRANDADDY, ALLY SLOPER

Often credited as the first regular British comic character, *Ally Sloper* debuted in the pages of *Judy, or the London Serio-Comic*, on 14 August 1867. Sloper, with his bulbous

Right: The very first issue of *The Beano* from 1938. A copy sold in 2004 for a record £12,100. Ewan Kerr, who became editor in 1984, rightly said, "*The Beano* is now as much a part of the British way of life as fish and chips and the Union Jack."
© DC Thomson & Co. Ltd

Below: *Comic Cuts*, the great grandfather of all British comics, was launched in 1890.
© Respective creators

Above: *Mickey Mouse Weekly*, the first European Disney comic, launched in 1936.
© *Disney*

Right: *The Innocents*, AKA *Weary Willy* and *Tired Tim* by Tom Browne.
© *Estate of Tom Browne*

nose and huge feet, was created by Charles Ross and named after the slang for somebody who would slope off down an alley to avoid the rent collector. In 1884, Sloper graduated to his own title, *Ally Sloper's Half-Holiday*, where W. G. Baxter became the definitive Sloper artist until his early death from consumption in 1888.

Funny Folks, launched in 1874, was a direct link between the humour magazines and the earliest comics, although it contained no ongoing strips at first. The eight tabloid pages, mostly reprinted jokes from France and Germany, were half illustration and half text. Alfred Harmsworth used an identical format when he launched *Comic Cuts* and *Illustrated Chips* in 1890, modelled on *Funny Folks* and *Scraps* published

by James Henderson, but at half the price (1/2d.).

Comic Cuts soon began running original comic strips and illustrations by Roland Hill, Oliver Veal and Vandyke Browne. The latter was the pen-name of Tom Browne, who started work on *Scraps* at the tender age of 16 and revolutionized British comic strips. Browne applied Phil May's clear line style to comic strips and in 1895 created *Squashington Flats* for *Comic Cuts*, followed by *Weary Willie* and *Tired Tim* for *Illustrated Chips* a year later. The quixotic adventures of this famous pair of tramps took pride of place on the front cover of *Chips* for 60 years.

PUBLISHING PUGILISTS

Publisher James Henderson fought these pretenders to the comics throne with his *Snap-Shots* (1890) and *Comic Pictorial Nuggets* (1892), but it was a losing battle with Harmsworth, and eventually all of Henderson's titles were absorbed into the Amalgamated Press (AP) in 1920. Newcomers Trapps-Holmes launched a slew of titles, including *Funny Cuts*, *The World's Comic*, *Side-Splitters* and, in 1898, *The Coloured Comic* (a tad misleading as full colour was limited to the front page and dropped after 18 months). Harmsworth had previously published colour specials, but it wasn't until *Puck's* 1904 launch that the four-colour cover became the norm.

Willie and *Tim* helped boost sales of *Chips* to a respectable 600,000 a week and established the popularity of comics with children. Having grown out of satirical magazines, comics were considered adult reading and even at the low cost of a halfpenny, were too expensive for children to buy. There was however, a nod to the kiddies as many comics often included a strip aimed at youngsters. *The Ball's Pond Banditti* by G. Gordon Fraser predated the famous *Bash Street Kids* by 60 years, first appearing in *Ally Sloper's Half-Holiday* in 1893. Tom Browne's *Little Willy and Tiny Tim* (the sons of his famous tramps) were the cover stars of *The Wonder* from 1898, and strips plagiarizing Rudolph Dirks' *The Katzenjammer Kids* began appearing in 1900 (*Those Twinkleton Twins* in *The Big Budget*). The use of speech balloons in *The Katzenjammer Kids* also transferred and was reflected in new strips aimed at a more juvenile audience.

FUNNY ANIMALS

The first comic specifically aimed at a juvenile audience from launch was *The Rainbow* in 1914, with its famous cover strip featuring *The Bruin Boys*, a funny animal strip inspired by Arthur White's 1898 strip *Jungle Jinks*. Julius Stafford Baker emulated White's success in Alfred Harmsworth's *Daily Mirror* in 1904, when it ran *Mrs Hippo's Kinder-Garten*. Whilst Baker was extremely good,

the adventures of *Tiger Tim* and his chums at Mrs Hippo's Boarding School really took off when Herbert Foxwell took over the artwork. Foxwell drew the strip when *Tim* graduated to his own title, *Tiger Tim's Tales* (re-titled *Tiger Tim's Own*) in 1919, which ran until 1940. Tim then ran in various other comics until finally coming to an end in 1985 after a run of 81 years.

FILM FUN

The best-selling British comic of the early 20th Century, regularly shifting 1,750,000 copies a week, was Film Fun, launched on 17 January 1920 and based around the concept of turning cinema stars into comic strips. It was not a new idea, as Charlie Chaplin had been appearing on the front page of *Funny Wonder* since 1915, drawn by Bertie Brown. George Wakefield had been a cartoonist and illustrator since 1906 and had impressed Film Fun editor, Fred Cordwell. Wakefield illustrated the serialized text adventures of *Fatty Arbuckle's Schooldays* and was assigned many of the major strips as agreements were reached with stars like Joe E. Brown, Max Miller and George Formby. Wakefield also designed characters for other strips and drew *Fatty Arbuckle* in Film Fun's cash-in companion, *The Kinema Comic*. His clear, bold style was exemplified by his work on *Laurel and Hardy*, who first appeared in Film Fun in

Above: *Laurel and Hardy* learn British football on the cover of *Film Fun* in 1938. Art by George Wakefield.
© *Estate of George and Terry Wakefield*

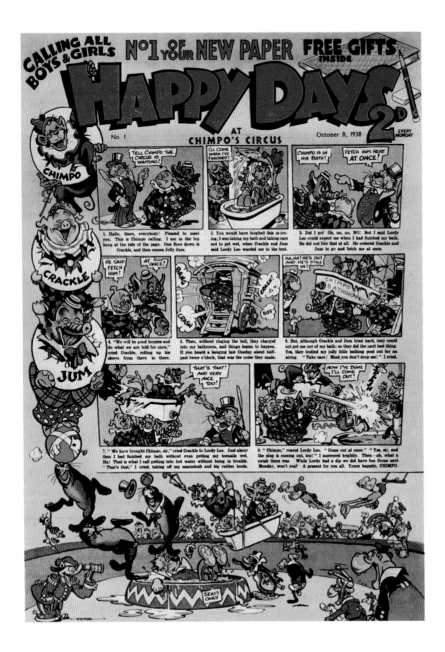

1930 and were the cover stars from 1934 to 1957 (drawn by Wakefield's son, Terry, after 1942).

HAPPY DAYS ARE HERE AGAIN...

Another major influence on humour comics was Roy Wilson, whose comic strips were usually to be found on the covers of Amalgamated Press' penny comics such as *Funny Wonder's Pitch & Toss* and *Jester's Basil & Bert*, although his best work was *Chimpo's Circus* on the cover of *Happy Days*.

Happy Days was AP's answer to *Mickey Mouse Weekly*, which was launched in 1936 by Willbank Publications. It was the first weekly comic to benefit from the popularity of Walt Disney's cartoons, which made it an instant success. Apart from its strips based on cartoons, *Mickey Mouse Weekly* also contained some influential comic strips by newcomers like Reg Perrott, Tony Weare and also Frank Bellamy, who would go on to be one of Britain's most renowned artists.

Serial adventure stories had been appearing in British comics since the arrival of *Rob the Rover* in *Puck* in 1920. Artist Walter Booth set the tone for adventure strips for the next 20 years, as editors demanded that characters were visible in every frame. Reg Perrott, a regular film-goer, revolutionized the adventure strip when he introduced a cinematic approach, varying the shape of his frames and the reader's viewpoint to produce some of the most dramatic artwork seen in British comics to that point.

A SCOTTISH GIANT AWAKES

Meanwhile, in Dundee, Scotland, the firm of DC Thomson had grown from the shipping business when William Thomson had offered financial assistance to an ailing newspaper. William's son, David Couper Thomson, helped turn the paper around and discovered his true vocation. DC Thomson & Co. Ltd was established in 1905 and became the most successful newspaper company in Scotland.

In December 1937, Thomson launched *The Dandy*, with 24 pages for 2d. Comic strips were not a new area for the company, as they were already included in a number of the publisher's story papers, and their famous *Sunday Post* newspaper had, since 1936, incorporated an eight-page supplement called the *Sunday Post Fun Section*, which made stars of *Oor Wullie* and *The Broons*. Their artist was Dudley D. Watkins, who provided *The Dandy* with its first mega-star, the cow-pie-eating cowboy *Desperate Dan*.

The Beano followed *The Dandy* onto the newsstands seven months later with another of Watkins' creations, *Lord Snooty and His Pals*. Editors Albert Barnes (*Dandy*) and George Moonie (*Beano*) managed to achieve just the right balance of humour, adventure and text stories in the two papers. The format made them seem value for money and, not surprisingly, they were an immediate success.

The Amalgamated Press tried to counter this incursion by launching *Radio Fun* in a similar format, but the developing rivalry between the AP and DCT was brought to an abrupt ceasefire with the declaration of World War II in September 1939. Paper supplies from Africa, Europe and Scandinavia were cut off and the AP hoped to continue with imports from its mills in Newfoundland, only to see its cargo ships sunk by U-boats in the mid Atlantic. In May 1940, the AP axed over a dozen titles to focus its paper supply on the most successful titles; DC Thomson was forced to turn its weeklies into fortnightlies. Both companies were forced to tread water for almost a decade and the effects of the war were still being felt as late as 1958.

America's comic book development in the 1930s had begun impacting on the British industry. *Superman* Sunday strips were reprinted in *Triumph* and imports of *Superman* and *Batman* comics were available, mainly near major ports such as London and Liverpool. The war curtailed these imports, but American comic strips were still available, albeit in depleted numbers. The US

Above: A rare British superhero, *The Falcon*, on the cover of *Radio Fun*. In 2003, stand-up comedian and former cartoonist Bob Monkhouse adapted the strip in a three-part radio series. © *The Amalgamated Press, Ltd.*

Left, opposite page: The cover to *Happy Days* #1, 1938, by Roy Wilson. © *The Amalgamated Press, Ltd.*

government produced colour comics for their servicemen overseas that proved popular with youngsters in areas where GIs were stationed in Britain. British reprint editions of US titles also began to appear: T.V. Boardman – who had been the British importer/publisher of *Wags* in 1938, publishing strips produced by the Eisner-Iger workshop – began reprinting cut-down versions of various Quality Comics' titles as early as 1940, although they would become famous for their later, post-war titles, the highly collectable *Buffalo Bill Annual*, *Roy Carson* and *Swift Morgan* comics, drawn by Denis McLoughlin.

WORLD WAR II INDY EXPLOSION

A number of small companies began to spring up to take advantage of the gaps in the market left by the demise of so many titles, printing issues whenever they could find the paper. Gerald G. Swan was the boldest of these independent publishers, producing a range of titles often drawn by artists who found themselves suddenly unemployed due to the collapse of AP and DCT's titles. E.H. Banger and Wally Robinson were Swan's most prolific suppliers of 'funnies', while brothers John and Bill McCail supplied plenty of adventure strips. Cheaply produced and poorly paid – and with virtually no editorial interference – some of Swan's comics were mostly

Above: L. Miller and Son's British reprint of Fawcett's *Whiz Comics* #65, starring Captain Marvel.
© DC Comics

notable for their violent, bizarre, down-right surreal content, especially the work of former animator William Ward. Paget Publications and Martin & Reid became the main markets for a number of artists, amongst them Mick Anglo, who had trained before the war as a fashion artist but honed his cartooning skills in army newspapers. Newcomers to comics like Ron Embleton, Ron Turner, Terry Patrick, Jim Holdaway, Paddy Brennan, Bob Monkhouse and Denis Gifford all made early sales to various independent comic publishers.

The post-war paper shortage had created a unique publishing opportunity for the entrepreneurial 'pirate' publishers, who began buying in what today would be called grey imports. American imports were almost impossible during Britain's repayment of the War Loan, a situation that lasted until the late 1950s. Both Sidney Pemberton (Pembertons of Manchester, World Distributors) and Arnold Graham (Streamline Publications) discovered that imports from Canada were exempt from this ruling and began importing comic books from a number of briefly thriving Canadian publishers. Newspapers were also exempt and attempts were made to import newspapers with Sunday supplements. The papers were thrown away and the supplements sold separately. These loopholes were soon closed and publishers like Pemberton, Graham and Len Miller travelled to America to sign deals. Miller's deal with Fawcett Publications was the most rewarding. He had begun reprinting *Captain Marvel* and *Whiz Comics* in 1944. From around 1950, Mick Anglo began supplying a steady stream of covers and features for Miller's reprints, along with new titles cashing in on the early 1950s' boom in science-fiction comics. These included *Space Comics*, *Space Commander Kerry* and *Space Commando Comics* in 1953 and 1954, mostly drawn by Mick Anglo's Gower Street studio regulars, Roy Parker and Colin Page.

HORROR COMICS HARASSED IN THE HOUSE OF COMMONS

Simultaneously, Miller's son's company, the Arnold Book Co., had been reprinting US crime and horror titles like *Black Magic* and EC Comics' *Haunt of Fear*. These titles were under scrutiny in America where Dr Frederick Wertham was condemning them as the cause of rising juvenile crime. Similar scare stories began circulating in magazines and newspapers in the UK in the late 1940s, and came to a head in 1954 when the government began discussing the *Children and Young Persons (Harmful Publications) Bill*, which became an Act in 1955. Six months later, the publishing of 'horror' comics had come to an end due to many newsagents refusing to carry them. Len Miller also had problems elsewhere. Owing

to the legal action taken by National Periodicals against Fawcett Publications over the similarities between *Captain Marvel* and *Superman*, Fawcett had given up publication of their various *Captain Marvel* titles. Miller, unwilling to give up on a good thing, asked Anglo to convert *Captain Marvel Adventures* into an all-new title. Anglo changed *Captain Marvel* into *Marvelman* while retaining much of the original content. The newly branded *Marvelman*, *Young Marvelman* and *Marvelman Family* titles would continue to run until 1963.

Most of the independent publishers folded their comics lines as the major publishers began to re-establish themselves after the war. The Amalgamated Press bought *Comet* and *Sun*, two photogravure titles, from Manchester-based publisher J.B. Allen in May 1949, and DC Thomson were able to return *The Beano* and *The Dandy* to weekly publication in July 1949.

The major launch at this time however, was *Eagle*. The ambitious amateur publisher Reverend Marcus Morris, vicar of St James' Church in Southport, had already turned his local parish newsletter into a monthly (albeit loss-making) magazine entitled *The Anvil* when he teamed up with Morris and Chad Varah, vicar of Holy Trinity in Blackburn. Varah founded the Samaritans and also the Society for Christian Publicity, whose aims included researching the idea of a weekly comic as a way of attracting

Marvel or Miracle?

It's doubtful that there's a single British comic character that has created more copyright controversy and confusion than *Marvelman*.

When Alan Moore revived the superhero in *Warrior* in 1982, the editor, Dez Skinn, secured the rights from the receivers who'd seized the assets when L Miller & Sons went bust in 1963. The rights to the new *Marvelman* stories were split among Moore, Skinn and artists Alan Davis and Garry Leach.

When *Warrior* ended, *Marvelman* continued to be published in the US by Eclipse, who changed the name to *Miracleman* after legal threats from Marvel Comics. Moore handed over the writing chores and gave his rights to fellow scribe, Neil Gaiman. He then ended up in court over copyright ownership of the character with artist/writer Todd McFarlane. The latter insisted that Gaiman had swapped the rights with him for another character's. Gaiman won, but with at least five people claiming ownership to the character, the saga's unlikely to end there...

© *Respective creators, who knows?!*

BIG FISH HUNTING UNDER THE SEA WITH HANS HASS! P. 4

Above: *Rocket* was a short-lived sci-fi title edited by famous ex-fighter pilot, Douglas Bader. Cover by Frank Black.
© News Group Newspapers Ltd

Left: The *Eagle* is probably Britain's best known adventure comic, and survived several incarnations, as did its lead character, *Dan Dare*. Artwork by the legendary Frank Hampson.
© The Dan Dare Corporation Ltd

readers. Morris already had a capable illustrator amongst his contributors, Frank Hampson, who had attended Southport School of Art. Between them, they prepared a dummy for a new comic, which Morris hawked around numerous London publishers before arriving at Hulton Press' doors.

PILOT OF THE FUTURE

Like most publishers, Hulton Press was looking for ways to expand its output after a decade of paper rationing and unlike AP – who were not interested in buying in titles from out-of-house packagers – were interested in taking on Morris and his team. Thus *Eagle* was launched on 14 April 1950 with pride of place on the cover going to *Dan Dare*, an interplanetary pilot of the future (although initially conceived as a chaplain in a futuristic interplanetary space force). *Eagle* was rushed into production and the quality of the early issues was patchy; the printing presses used were still 'bedding down' and the artists had still to discover that the photogravure process did not reproduce certain mixtures of colour well. However, these problems were soon overcome and *Eagle* looked magnificent. As well as its front-cover star and biography of St Paul on the back cover, Morris had secured two popular radio shows, the police drama *The Adventures of PC 49* and the western *Riders of the Range*, along with their

talented scriptwriters Alan Stranks and Charles Chilton.

Thanks to heavy publicity, over 900,000 copies of the first issue of the *Eagle* were sold and, despite its high price (4d.), the paper settled down to a regular weekly circulation of 800,000 copies. Surprisingly, the *Eagle* was not the most successful launch of 1950. That position was held by *School Friend*, a new comic for girls, which appeared in May and sold over a million copies of its first issue and opened up a whole new market for comics.

AMALGAMATED PRESS

British comics had changed dramatically since their 'golden age' and much of that change was the responsibility of two editors. Firstly, Edward Holmes, who had joined the Amalgamated Press in the 1930s and was the launch editor of a new weekly entitled *The Knockout Comic*.

This was the Amalgamated Press' second attempt to counter the arrival of D.C. Thomson's *Beano* and *Dandy*, but Holmes was able to draw on two very popular AP characters, *Sexton Blake* and *Billy Bunter*, to give the title the boost it needed. Unfortunately, Holmes soon departed to serve with the Royal Air Force, leaving the fledgling paper in the hands of Percy Clarke, a veteran editor at AP. Holmes had, when the new title was being planned, appointed a newcomer

Below: *Fraser of Africa* by Frank Bellamy appeared in the pages of *Eagle*. Bellamy eventually took over art chores on *Dan Dare* in 1960.
© *Estate of Frank Bellamy*

to comics as his assistant. Leonard Matthews had previously worked at a department store where he showed a natural talent for caricature that led to him joining the staff magazine. Matthews submitted samples of his work to Thomson and AP and they had caught Holmes' eye. Unlike Holmes, Matthews served his time during the war in London and was an invaluable assistant to Clarke. Holmes returned in 1946 and would become the editor of *Comet* in 1949, as well as working on an all-new project. His natural successor was Matthews, who was put in charge of *Knockout* and *Sun*.

Normally, it would be decades before a sub-editor rose to full editorship at AP; in 1949, their newest titles were in the hands of relatively young men in their mid-30s who had not grown up 'through the system'. Both wanted to bring in new artists to create modern comics for the modern youngster.

Holmes took characters from AP's vast stable, knowing that they had a built-in audience, and reinvented them as comic strip characters. Holmes and Matthews encouraged illustrators like Michael Hubbard, D.C. Eyles, Sep E. Scott, Reginald Heade, T. Heath Robinson and H.M. Brock to turn their talents to strip work, as well as trying to attract new artists. An advert placed in newspapers caught the attentions of Geoff Campion and Reg Bunn who were first employed on a new project created by Holmes.

POCKET FUN

An attempt to launch American-style comic books in Australia led to another AP innovation. The artwork produced for these (primarily western) titles was not a standard size that could be used in domestic comics. When Holmes approached his bosses about reprinting the strips, the only presses available were those that had been used to print pocket-book format text series with 64 pages and a colour cover. Holmes had the artwork from his Australian titles cut up into the new format and began producing *Cowboy Comics Library* in April 1950. These small-format titles, priced at 7d., were hugely successful and inspired the publication of *Thriller Comics* in 1951 and *Super Detective Library* in 1953. Dozens of romance and war titles followed from the mid-1950s to the mid-1980s, some series running to over 2,000 issues. *Commando Library*, launched by rivals DC Thomson in 1960, is the sole survivor of the pocket library boom and, at the time of writing, has just published its 3,800th issue. The success of these pocket libraries inspired a number of smaller publishers to produce rival titles, some of which also had long runs, notably Micron's *Combat Picture Library* and *Romantic Adventure Library*, both of which achieved runs of over 1,000 issues. The rapid expansion at Amalgamated Press in the 1950s, and the success of *The Eagle* and its companion titles – *Girl*, *Robin* and *Swift* launched in 1951, 1953 and 1954 respectively – attracted other publishers to comics. *TV Comic* was launched by *The News of the World* in 1951, with strips based around children's TV characters (it would become best known for its long-running *Dr Who* strip). *The News of the World* also launched *The Rocket* in 1956, a short-lived science-fiction comic.

Two other newspaper publishers tried their hand with children's newspapers – the short-lived *Junior Mirror* in 1954 and the more successful *Junior Express* which converted to a comic after 38 issues. The latter (successively re-titled *Junior Express Weekly*, *Express Weekly* and *TV Express*) featured popular science-fiction strips starring *Jeff Hawke* (from the *Daily Express* strip), *Jet Morgan* (from the *Journey Into Space* radio series) and the long-running *Wulf the Briton* by Jenny Butterworth and Ron Embleton.

GIRLS' COMICS

Back at the Amalgamated Press, their successful launching of a comic for girls, *School Friend*, in 1950, opened up a new market, quickly exploited with new titles like *Girls' Crystal*, and a slew of romance comics – *Marilyn*, *Mirabelle*, *The New Glamour*, *Valentine*,

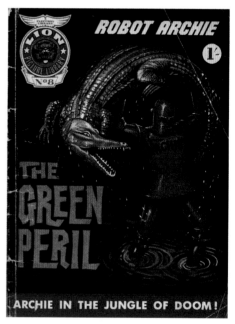

Above: At the height of the pocket sized comic boom, in 1964, Fleetway released the *Lion Picture Library*, a series of self contained stories from the *Lion* weekly anthology. The strips were re-sized and reformatted reprints. This one featured the title's most popular character, *Robot Archie*. The 'Jungle Robot' strip was created by Ted Kearon in 1952.
©AOL Time Warner

Left, opposite page: *The Express Weekly* featured *Wulf the Briton* by Ron Embleton, which he started in 1957.
© Express Newspapers

Romeo, Bunty, Roxy and Boyfriend were all launched before the decade was out. At the same time, Playhour, Jack and Jill and Harold Hare's Own Paper replaced old-fashioned nursery titles like The Playbox, Tiny Tots and Chick's Own.

THE LATIN INVASION

This exponential increase in output during the 1950s required a vast army of new artists. In the early 1950s, Belgian agency A.L.I. began representing Spanish artists working for British comics. Giorgio Bellavitis and Jesus Blasco led the way in 1954 and, before long, a steady stream of artwork from some of the top European talent was crossing the Channel. The strength of the pound abroad meant that, even working through agencies, artists could earn up to four times the amount they could working on their native comics and, over the next two decades, over 300 of the best artists from Europe and South America would work for British publications. This wealth of talent included Dino Battaglia, Ferdinando Tacconi, Gino D'Antonio, Victor de la Fuente, Esteban Maroto, Jose Gonzalez, Hugo Pratt, Alberto Breccia, cover artists Biffignandi and Penalva and dozens of others. Rinaldo D'Ami and Alberto Giolitti in Italy and Francisco Solano Lopez in Argentina set up studios to cope with the demand, which

saw Solano Lopez and his assistants producing over 100 pages a month.

British talent was not ignored. In 1949, the G-B Animation studio closed down, depositing 150 trained artists and technicians on the market, many of whom found their way into comics. Ron Clark, Eric Bradbury and Mike Western found work on Knockout, Harry Hargreaves and Bert Felstead worked in nursery comics, Bill Holroyd and Ron Smith became prolific adventure artists for DC Thomson and Roy Davis became one of AP's most prolific scriptwriters. At the same time, Ron Embleton, Ron Turner, Joe Colquhoun, Don Lawrence and others were emerging from the training grounds of the post-war independents.

To many, the 1950s were the 'silver age' of British comics, riding the wave of the post-war baby boom with new and, for the most part, superbly written and illustrated comics. The launches made throughout the decade found a ready market. Lion, launched in opposition to Eagle by Amalgamated Press in 1952, featured its own SF hero, Captain Condor, in colour on the cover, although the paper would be better remembered as the home of Robot Archie, Karl the Viking, war ace Paddy Payn and spot-the-clue American cop Zip Nolan. Tiger, which followed in 1954, gave Britain one of its most famous sons – Roy of the Rovers, the football strip, became the longest-running soap-opera in comics

Above: *The Steel Claw* by Jesus Blasco. The Spanish artist inspired hundreds of British comic creators. The character was revived in America by comic writer Alan Moore's daughter, Leah, in 2005. It was published by WildStorm, an imprint of DC Comics.
© Time Warner

Above: *The Sun* #1 from 1947 with *The Swiss Family Robinson* by Bob Wilkin on the cover. The comic also featured creators like R Beaumont, R Plummer, Serge Drigin and JB Allen. It was one of the most popular post war British comics, until its cancellation in 1959.
© *Respective creators*

Right: Ken Reid's *Queen of the Seas* from the pages of *Smash!* The series was the natural successor to Reid's earlier strip, *Jonah*, about a cursed sailor who sunk every boat he boarded.
© *Estate of Ken Reid*

Above: David Law's *Dennis the Menace* from *The Beano*. Law drew the strip until his death in 1971 and *Dennis* became the title's most popular character, even making it into an animated TV series. Today, *Dennis'* dad would probably be prosecuted for abusing his son!
© DC Thomson & Co. Ltd

as, over the years, Roy married, had children, served as player-manager of England, survived a terrorist bomb but eventually, after transferring to his own paper in 1976, had to retire from the pitch when he lost his famous left foot in a helicopter crash in 1993. Roy continued to entertain fans through newspaper and magazine strips for almost another decade.

THE BEANO AND THE DANDY

The second revolutionary front was in the humour strip. In March 1951, DC Thomson's *Beano* had introduced the anarchic *Dennis the Menace* by David Law, whose increasing popularity led him to the colour back cover in 1954 to 1958 and 1962 to 1974 and then to the cover, replacing *Biffo the Bear*. Like his American counterpart (coincidentally first published in the same week), *Dennis* spent his waking hours trying to stave off boredom, avoid schoolwork or mimic his favourite books or movies. Everything he tried caused chaos and the strip often ended with him receiving just retribution or the slipper from his father.

1953 saw the arrival of Ken Reid's *Roger the Dodger*, featuring a scheming trickster forever looking for a way to dodge work and school. Reid's masterpiece however, arrived in 1958 – *Jonah*, about a seaman whose antics sent hundreds of ships to Davy Jones' Locker, took over the back page

for four years. Reid would turn the 12-frame script into anything up to 36 frames of glorious hilarity. That same year, Leo Baxendale – inspired by David Law – created *Little Plum*, *Minnie the Minx* and *When the Bell Rings*, the latter introducing *The Bash Street Kids* and mirroring the chaos of the average school playground.

The Beano and *The Dandy* also debuted popular adventure strips like *General Jumbo* and *Black Bob* during the decade and launched two more papers, *Topper* (with female menace *Beryl the Peril* by David Law) and *Beezer* in 1953 and 1956. On the other hand, sales of their story papers were slipping and the all-text *Hotspur* was relaunched as a comic under the title *The New Hotspur* in 1958, followed by *Victor* in 1961, transferring some of the best-loved characters – athletes *The Tough of the Tracks* and *The Wonder Man*, air ace *Matt Braddock* – from text stories to comic strips.

At the end of the 1950s, a number of changes had taken place at Thomson's great rivals. The Amalgamated Press was taken over in 1959 by Daily Mirror Newspapers, who renamed the company Fleetway Publications; in 1961, they also purchased Odhams Press, bringing the *Eagle* into their fold. Fleetway and Odhams became part of the larger International Publishing Corporation (IPC) in 1963. During this period of transitions, Fleetway had been mounting a retaliation to DC Thomson's

Above: *The Dandy* celebrated its 50th anniversary in 1987 and featured *Korky the Cat* and *Desperate Dan* on the cover.
© DC Thomson & Co. Ltd

Above: In 1966, *Smash!* reprinted the American *Batman* Sunday strips by Bob Kane. In keeping with the popularity of the Sixties' TV series, the strip was camp rather than edgy.
© *DC Comics/Odhams Press Ltd*

success by creating the humour title *Buster* (originally in an old-style tabloid format similar to *The Topper* and *Beezer*) and *Valiant*. The latter was initially a disappointment, despite some strong adventure strips including *Captain Hurricane* and *The Steel Claw*, drawn by Spaniard Jesus Blasco. A merger with *Knockout*, a change of editor and a popular promotion – a bar of toffee – quickly saw the title back on track to become one of the most popular of the 1960s. The death of *Knockout*, followed by the demise of *Sun* and *Comet* in 1959, after being swallowed up by *Lion* and *Tiger* respectively, and the absorption of *Radio Fun* and *Film Fun* into *Buster*, marked the end of an era for the company.

WHAM! POW! SMASH! TERRIFIC!

Fleetway found themselves in charge of *Eagle* and made changes that lost the title its uniqueness. Alf Wallace, in charge of the Odhams' juvenile titles, began to launch new titles, starting with *Boy's World* in 1963 and *Wham!* the following year. Ken Reid was attracted to Odhams by the offer of better pay, and he produced two all-time classics, *Frankie Stein* and *Queen of the Seas*. *Smash!* followed in 1966, introducing a number of American reprints including Marvel's *The Incredible Hulk* and DC Comics' *Batman* Sunday strips. This was followed by *Pow!*, *Fantastic* and *Terrific* in 1967, which

were virtually all reprints. American comics had been distributed in the UK since 1960, although the distribution was patchy, and Alan Class, whose father-in-law had published American comics as Streamline, picked up the rights to many of the horror, weird and science-fiction stories for publication in new anthology titles like *Astounding Stories*, *Creepy Worlds* and others. Many of the reprints included classic early monster strips by Jack Kirby and Steve Ditko, and many of US publisher Dell/Gold Key's titles were reprinted in annuals by World Distributors.

RISE OF THE FANBOY

The mainstay of American comics, the superhero, had never really taken off in the UK, although masked heroes like *The Amazing Mr X* had appeared as early as 1944. Now, in the 1960s, a fandom began to grow up around American comics that led, in 1967, to the first British Comic Art Convention – actually little more than a glorified dealers' mart. With fans scattered around the country, dealers issued mail-order catalogues out of which developed the first comics fanzines, such as Frank Dobson's *Fantasy Advertiser*, Tony Roach's *Heroes Unlimited* and Alan Austin's *An Adzine*. Fanzines became the focus for new talent, especially in the 1970s, when newcomers like Paul Neary, Steve Parkhouse, Dave Gibbons and

Brian Bolland began to break into the mainstream. Specialist shops carrying American science-fiction and comics followed soon after when mail-order dealer Derek 'Bram' Stokes founded Dark They Were, and Golden-Eyed.

A fandom for traditional British comics grew up alongside the fans dedicated to American comics. *Dan Dare* achieved a unique honour of having a club and fanzine dedicated to him – Andrew Skilleter and Eric MacKenzie's *Astral*, first published in 1964. Fandom of British comics saw an upsurge in the late 1970s with the first convention dedicated to British (rather than American) comics, Comics 101 in 1976, and the establishment of the Association of Comics Enthusiasts by Denis Gifford. Fanzines *Illustrated Comics Journal*, *Golden Fun* and *British Comic World* flourished briefly, although *Eagle Times*, with its stricter focus, has survived for 18 years. *Class of '79* and *Eagle Flies Again* have kept the flag flying for British comics in recent years.

The popularity of *Batman* on 1960s' television inspired a number of strips in British comics such as *The Spider*, *It's the Rubberman* and *Johnny Future*. As the decade progressed, television began to take over as the primary form of home entertainment for children, sales steadily declined and the most successful launches were based around TV shows. *TV Century 21* was a spin-off from various Gerry Anderson puppet shows, *Fireball XL5*, *Stingray* and *Thunderbirds*. The latter strip was painted by Frank Bellamy, whose career had flourished through the pages of *Swift* and *Eagle* since his debut in *Mickey Mouse Weekly*. Bellamy's *Thunderbirds* strip is often cited as one of the best from this period. Other TV-inspired titles included *TV Tornado*, *Countdown* (later re-titled *TV Action*) and *Look-In*, the latter drawing on many of the best TV shows of the 1970s, and featuring inspired artwork by John Bolton, Martin Asbury, Arthur Ranson and many others.

IPC KO DC THOMSON

By the late 1960s, IPC's longest-running boys' titles – *Lion*, *Tiger*, *Valiant* – were struggling against rising costs, inflation and union activity that caused titles to disappear from the newsstands. A radical rethink was needed to shake up the traditional IPC weeklies, and the only source of writers and editors to breath new life into them was rival publisher DC Thomson. John Purdie, Iain McDonald, Les Daly, Gerry Finley-Day, John Wagner, Gaythorne Silvester and Malcolm Shaw were all lured down to London to take up positions on various girls' titles including *Princess*, *Tammy* and others. A new sensibility was brought to the girls' papers. The traditional 'Silent Three' style girls-as-amateur-detectives and girls-in-girly-jobs (air hostess, ballet

Below: *Zero X* from *TV Century 21* (1967). The title was based on various Gerry Anderson television series and included artwork from Frank Bellamy.
© *Gerry Anderson*

Above: *Charley's War* by Pat Mills and Joe Colquhoun.
© Egmont Magazines Ltd

Below: The brutal *Darkie's Mob* by John Wagner and Mike Western in 1976's *Battle Picture Weekly*.
© Egmont Magazines Ltd

dancer) storylines were dropped and the writers brought in cruel stepfathers and battles against afflictions as a way to give the stories a strong, if faux, emotional content. Blind tennis players and kidnapped schoolgirls in forced labour camps sat uncomfortably alongside aspirational yarns of Cinderellas struggling to earn their place in life.

As the girls' titles began to claw back the readership that they had lost to Thomson's *Bunty*, *Judy* and others in the 1960s, IPC turned to another ex-Thomson employee, Pat Mills, to produce a comic for boys that would take on DC Thomson's recently launched *Warlord*. Mills, a one-time sub-editor on romance comic *Romeo*, turned to his ex-writing partner John Wagner, and the two developed *Battle Picture Weekly*. They introduced working-class hero strips like *The Bootneck Boy* and took inspiration from TV and movies, turning *The Dirty Dozen* into *The Rat Pack*. Once *Battle* was off the ground, Mills was asked to create a second new title whilst Wagner tried to revive the fortunes of *Valiant*. Mills, working with former *Lion* editor Geoff Kemp, spent the next few months developing *Action*, which more than lived up to its title. Mills' attempts to turn traditional genre strips on their head resulted in a violent, aggressive group of stories that immediately attracted huge controversy. One of the more controversial was *Hook Jaw*, a series based on the popular

film *Jaws*, about a great white shark with a harpoon hook stuck in its jaw, which it used to rip up its victims. The tipping point came when juvenile delinquents were shown beating up a policeman in *Kids Rule U.K.* The comic received overwhelming bad press from newspapers and television and was pulled from the shelves, despite growing sales at a time when many titles were starting to free-fall.

THE GALAXY'S GREATEST COMIC

Mills had left some months earlier to create yet another title. Kelvin Gosnell had suggested a science-fiction title to IPC management, and Mills and Gosnell were now in the process of creating *2000 AD*. In an attempt to draw attention to the new title, the paper revived *Dan Dare* – actually the grandson of the original Dare – in new adventures. Reaction to *2000 AD*'s launch was positive, much of the success down to *Judge Dredd*, a "judge, jury and executioner" of a future metropolis on America's east coast called Mega-City One, where most of the 100 million population are unemployed. Created by John Wagner and artist Carlos Ezquerra (although Mike McMahon was *Dredd*'s main early artist), the stories were violent but filled with black humour, a potent mixture that has kept *Dredd* as the star of *2000 AD* and his own spin-off, *The Megazine*, for over 25 years. *2000 AD* was a

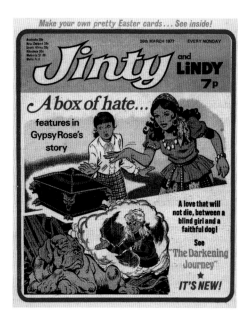

Above: *Jinty* (1977) had typical stories featuring girls overcoming handicaps or adversities, such as the slightly surreal *The Darkening Journey* — when a guide dog is separated from his blind mistress.
© *IPC Media Ltd*

Right: The comic they tried to ban. This issue of *Action* caused a furore with its apparent disregard for authority. Cover by Spanish artist, Carlos Ezquerra.
© *Egmont Magazines Ltd*

Dez Skinn

If Britain has an equivalent to the ubiquitous and bombastic Marvel publisher Stan Lee, then Dez Skinn is it. In fact, Lee was even Skinn's mentor when the straight-talking Yorkshireman helped set up and run Marvel UK's offices in the Seventies. Skinn has been involved with practically every aspect of British comics publishing. He began as an assistant editor working at IPC on titles like *Buster*.

He then edited the UK edition of *MAD* magazine before revamping Marvel UK. Next, he started his own anthology, Warrior (1982). In 1990, he launched the UK tradepaper *Comics International*, which he still publishes.

There are very few people in British comics who haven't worked for Skinn at some point, and he hired a young Steve Dillon to draw *Dr Who Weekly*. Skinn even employed Tundra UK and Atomeka Press publisher Dave Elliot and WildStorm group editor Scott Dunbier early in their careers. Equally reviled and revered, there's no doubt that Skinn's influence on British comics has been significant and controversial.

training ground for new writers and artists, who were able to build up a following thanks to the introduction of story and art credits in 1978. Dave Gibbons and Brian Bolland soon began to attract the attention of DC Comics in America, with Bolland leading the pack in 1982 with *Camelot 3000*.

WARRIOR

At the same time, former IPC and Marvel UK editor Dez Skinn had launched *Warrior*, an independent monthly drawing on talent Skinn had previously used on Marvel titles *Hulk Weekly* and *Dr Who Weekly* and his earlier horror monthly, *House of Hammer*. *Warrior* was home to Alan Moore's reinterpretation of 1950s' British superhero *Marvelman* (art by Garry Leach and Alan Davis), the dark, fascist state of *V For Vendetta* (art by David Lloyd), Steve Moore's action-packed *Laser Eraser and Pressbutton* (art by Steve Dillon), *Spiral Path* by Steve Parkhouse and *Father Shandor* by Steve Parkhouse and John Bolton. Strong as this line-up was, *Warrior* ran for only 26 issues before problems of finance, distribution, in-fighting and threatened lawsuits from Marvel US bought it to an end. However, *Warrior*'s influence on global comics was incredibly potent, and *V for Vendetta* was made into a Hollywood blockbuster by *The Matrix*'s Wachowski Brothers 24 years after it first appeared. In the mid-1980s, DC Comics began to poach the best

talent from *Warrior*, *2000 AD*, and Marvel UK (where writers Alan Moore and Jamie Delano and artist Alan Davis were reimagining *Captain Britain*, a character originally produced for the UK by American writers and artists). Marvel UK's media tie-in titles (*Transformers*, *Zoids*, *Thundercats*, *Action Force*) gave an outlet for newcomers like Steve Yeowell, Bryan Hitch and Gary Frank. Over the next few years, Moore, Delano, Pete Milligan, John Wagner, Garth Ennis, Grant Morrison and others would find a wider audience in the USA, and a new generation of British artists like Glenn Fabry and Simon Bisley would also find *2000 AD* a stepping stone to US work.

GOING UNDERGROUND

Yet more talent emerged from the home-grown underground movement which had been in full swing since the early 1970s, gaining some notoriety when *Nasty Tales* was prosecuted for obscenity. Duplicated fanzine-style comics had begun appearing in the late 1960s, and the first printed comics arrived in 1969 with *Too Much Far-Out Rock & Roll* and *Black Dog*, the latter by Mal Dean who was to work for underground newspapers *Frendz* and *International Times*. A year later, *Cyclops* styled itself "the first English adult comic paper" and showcased reprints by Gilbert Shelton, Vaughan Bode as well as British artists like Dean,

Raymond Lowry and Edward Barker. *Nasty Tales*, debuting in 1971, had full-colour covers, an underground hero in Chris Welch's *Ogoth* and the backing of distributor Moore-Harness. Its publisher, Bloom Publications, was raided by police and copies of the title seized, but it was found not guilty of obscenity when the case came to court in 1973. Despite this vindication, *Nasty Tales* only lasted seven issues. *Cozmic Comics* picked up the baton, lasting six issues between 1972 and 1974, remembered today only for a one-page strip by newcomer Brian Bolland.

Apart from homegrown comics, Tony Bennett's Hassle Free Press published British editions of Gilbert Shelton and Robert Crumb titles under the imprint Knockabout Comics in the 1970s, and developed a popular line of original comics (including the *Fanny* line of comics by women) and books featuring the work of Hunt Emerson, such as *The Big Book of Everything* (1983), *Lady Chatterley's Lover* (1986) and *Casanova's Last Stand* (1993).

Early attempts at adult monthlies – such as *Near Myths* in 1978 and *Pssst!* in 1981 – had been stifled by a lack of distribution, but gave opportunities to creators like Bryan Talbot, whose *Adventures of Luther Arkwright* series appeared in both titles. Talbot had already gained some success as the writer/artist of *BrainStorm Comix*, a trilogy of tales featuring the dope-fuelled fantasies of Chester P. Hackenbush published from 1975 to 1977. *Near Myths* was probably the first British comic to show the inspiration of European creators, in this case Philippe Druillet, whose influence can certainly be seen in Graham Manley's *Tales from the Edge*, if not in Talbot's *Arkwright*. The closure of *Near Myths* after five issues put *Arkwright* on hold until 1981, when it was serialized in the 10 issues of *Pssst!* before being reissued in book form in 1982.

GRAVETT, MAN AT THE CROSSROADS

Where the duplicator had helped spread comics in the 1960s, cheap photocopying in the 1970s meant that anyone with a pen and the inclination could produce their own comic book. The best of these were showcased by Paul Gravett and Peter Stanbury in *Escape Magazine*, founded in 1983 out of Gravett's small-press distribution service, Fast Fiction. An anthology also named *Fast Fiction* was edited by Phil Elliott and, later, by Ed Pinsent, themselves two of the leading lights of the 'Fast Fiction crowd' that would soon encompass diverse talents like Glenn Dakin, Myra Hancock, Paul Grist and Eddie Campbell. Campbell's autobiographical series *Alec* and *In the Days of the Rock and Roll Club* were outstanding examples of the achievements of the small press and its leading lights have gone on to find critical and commercial success in

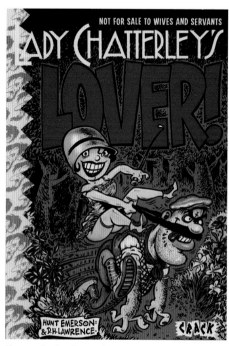

Above: Hunt Emerson's adaptation of the classic novel, *Lady Chatterley's Lover*.
© Hunt Emerson

V for Vendetta by Alan Moore and David Lloyd.
© Alan Moore, David Lloyd and Quality Communications

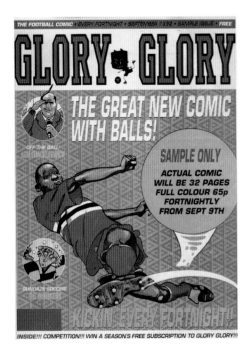

Above: One of Tundra UK's many unrealized dreams. *Glory Glory* was set to revolutionise the British football comic, but sadly never got past this 1992 preview sampler. It was to be co-edited by Stuart Green and Frank Plowright, and would've featured work by Si Spencer, Nabiel Kanan, Garry Pleece and David Leach. © *Tokoloshe Comics*

America via independent publishers such as Image and Top Shelf Productions.

COMICS GO HIP, LEGIT, AND SKINT IN THREE EASY STEPS

The boom in comics in the late 1980s, inspired by Frank Miller's *Dark Knight Returns*, Alan Moore and Dave Gibbons' *Watchmen* and Art Spiegelman's *Maus*, also helped establish the comic shop in the UK, and the concept of an older audience for comics. The audience however, was stubborn, and experiments like Fleetway's *Crisis*, launched in 1987 to good reaction and, initially, good sales, and *Revolver* (1990), failed to match expectations. It was a similar story for mainstream publishers' attempts to launch graphic novels: apart from occasional reprints of newspaper strips and one-off surprises like Raymond Briggs' *When The Wind Blows* (1982), comics were not seen as a viable market. With comics gaining much newspaper coverage, Gollancz, Pan, Penguin, Random House and HarperCollins all announced new lines in the early 1990s. Despite some interesting titles such as Alan Moore and Oscar Zartoe's *A Small Killing* (1991), and Neil Gaiman and Dave McKean's *Signal to Noise* (1992) and *Mr Punch* (1994), no imprint lasted more than a few books. Unsure of this new market, most publishers outside the industry treated it, at

best, with mild curiosity and, at worst, with derision.

The magazine-format *Deadline*, founded by publisher Tom Astor and artists Brett Ewins and Steve Dillon, was aimed at the hip new audience who were being lured back to reading comics, or had outgrown their weekly dose of mainstream titles. A mixture of music, interviews and strips, *Deadline* gave the world *Tank Girl* by Alan Martin and Jamie Hewlett, *Wired World* by Philip Bond, *Hugo Tate* by Nick Abadzis and *Several Colours Later* by the Pleece Brothers. Unfortunately, the mag was underfunded and couldn't retain the creators it had helped gain notoriety, so it folded in 1995.

BRITISH BLACK & WHITE BUST

Ambitious attempts at creating new lines of original comics in the American comic book style by independents – Harrier, Escape and Acme – had fallen by the way-side by 1992 as the comics market in the USA went into recession. Dave Elliott and Garry Leach's Atomeka launched *A1* with perhaps the best line-up of talent since *Warrior*, but it failed to gain a foothold. Backed by Kevin Eastman (of *Turtles* fame and fortune), Elliott tried again as Tundra UK, publishing *Lazarus Churchyard* by new-comer Warren Ellis and a handful of other titles before massive overspending ensured

Right: The short-lived experimental *Revolver* featured important strips including *Rogan Gosh* by Brendan McCarthy and Peter Milligan. Cover by Rian Hughes.
© *Respective creators*

Below: The socially aware and politically correct *Crisis* was Pat Mills' pet project. The comic initially started with just two strips, *Third World War* by Mills and Carlos Ezquerra, and *The New Statesmen*, by John Smith and Jim Baikie.
© *Pat Mills, Carlos Ezquerra, John Smith and Jim Baikie*

Above: *Viz* was founded by Geordie brothers Simon and Chris Donald and has spawned numerous animated TV shows and films. But it all came from humble starting point, "The aim when we began was to keep ourselves amused," said Simon. "There was nothing more to it than that."
© Dennis Publishing Ltd

the plug was eventually pulled, leaving many creators unpaid and embittered.

FNARR, FNARR...

One title that was an astonishing success was *Viz*, an adult humour comic known mostly for its gratuitous profanity and characters like *The Fat Slags*. Launched as a low-circulation fanzine distributed around pubs in the north east in 1979, *Viz* caught the eye and imagination of London publisher John Brown, who distributed it nationally; the bi-monthly paper hit a sales peak of over 1.3 million copies per issue. Other titles followed – *Poot!*, *Smut*, *Brain Damage*, *The Bog Paper* (an attempt at a weekly), *Zit*, *Acne*, *Spit! Comic*, plus Scottish contenders *Electric Soup* and *PMT* – but most failed after a few months, as they lacked the satirical edge (*Viz* was steeped in the traditional comic style of *The Beano*) and had to rely solely on toilet humour.

Viz also inspired a breed of edgier children's comics like *Oink!*, *UT* and *Triffik*, but the humour market was in steady decline. Long-running Fleetway titles like *Buster* and *Whizzer & Chips* began to fold, and even the steady stalwarts *The Beano* and *The Dandy* lost sales during the 1990s.

By 2000, the boys' adventure comic had all but disappeared. *Battle* had begun strongly thanks to long-running series *Johnny Red* and Pat Mills and Joe Colquhoun's First World War masterpiece *Charley's War*, but by 1983 it was dominated by toy tie-in *Action Force*. The paper folded into Fleetway's revival of the *Eagle*, launched in 1982 as a mixture of photo stories and strips in a style made popular in teenage girls' magazines in the 1970s. The photos soon disappeared and, despite the popular revival of *Dan Dare* drawn by Gerry Embleton, Oliver Frey, Ian Kennedy and others, the *Eagle* folded in 1994, having absorbed other short-lived titles like *Scream*, *MASK* and *Wildcat*. *Tiger* was another title absorbed into the *Eagle*, having lost its central character, *Roy of the Rovers*, to his own paper in 1976.

CAP'N BOB'S COMIC ADVENTURE

The juvenile division of IPC had been purchased by Robert Maxwell in 1987 and was renamed Fleetway Publications. The most successful launch over the next few years was *Teenage Mutant Ninja Turtles*, thanks to sales generated by the hugely successful TV cartoon. Maxwell, shortly before his death in 1991, had also negotiated a new deal with Disney and this attracted the attentions of Gutenberghus, the giant Danish publisher who controlled most of the Disney comics licenses throughout Europe. A deal was made with Maxwell to buy a 50% share in Fleetway; after his death

Above: *Tank Girl* leapt from the pages of *Deadline* to become the style icon of the Nineties, until her flop of a film killed her cool. Artist Jamie Hewlett then created the band *Gorillaz* with Blur's Damon Albarn.
© *Jamie Hewlett and Alan Martin*

Right: Brian Bolland's cover to the 2000th issue of *2000 AD* featuring (left to right): *Nemesis The Warlock*, *Nikolai Dante*, *Johnny Alpha – Strontium Dog*, *Judge Dredd* and *Rogue Trooper*. Note the pile of cancelled British comics including: *Eagle*, *Action*, *Hotspur*, *Valiant*, *Look & Learn*, *Escape*, *A1*, *Hammer House of Horror* and *Lion*.
© *Rebellion A/S*

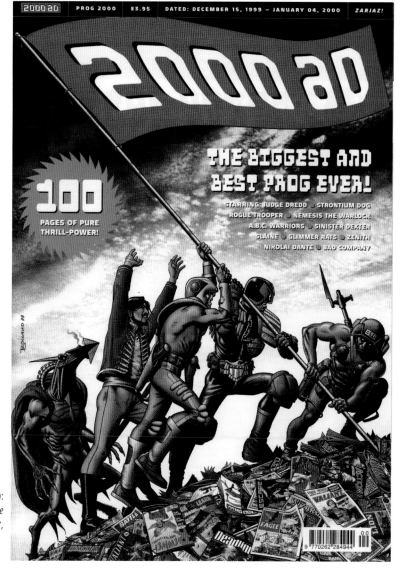

Left: Although short lived, the Scottish title *Near Myths*, featured future British comic legends' early work, including Bryan Talbot's *Luther Arkwright* and Grant Morrison's *Gideon Stargrave*. The latter was re-worked into *The Invisibles* by the writer for American publisher DC Comics.© *Respective creators*

Left*: Judge Dredd*'s arch-nemesis, *Judge Death*, makes his debut drawn by Brian Bolland in *2000 AD* #149, 1980.
© *Rebellion A/S*

Right: *Bullet* was launched in 1976, but by 1978 it had merged with its more successful companion title *Warlord*.
© *DC Thomson & Co, Ltd.*

Gutenberghus bought Fleetway outright and merged it with London Editions – who reprinted DC Comics titles – to form Fleetway Editions, later renamed Egmont Fleetway.

Gutenberghus had little knowledge of British adventure titles and declining sales offered no incentive to revive them, when nursery titles like *Tots TV* and *Budgie the Helicopter* were so successful. Sales of even the flagship *2000 AD* were in freefall, dropping from 100,000 in 1990 to 70,000 in 1993, a trend which continued over the decade despite a hoped-for boost from *Judge Dredd: The Movie* (1995). The movie bombed and didn't improve the comic's fortunes. *2000 AD* and *Judge Dredd Megazine* were subsequently sold to computer games developer Rebellion, appropriately in August 2000. Rebellion has maintained the profile of the title and its star characters through the publication of computer games, books, collections, audio adventures and the promise of more movies.

One recent attempt at an old-style boys' football title is *Striker*, based around Peter Nash's hugely successful newspaper strip. Using computer-generated artwork, the comic had a rocky launch and survived only through issuing shares to its fans who raised over £200,000 ($380,000) to keep the title going.

Despite this loss in one area, comics for younger readers remains a thriving business in the UK, although most successful titles are now concentrated in the primary school age group, and are usually based around a popular TV series (*Teletubbies, Tweenies, Fimbles, Balamory* and so on). Panini UK (who took over Marvel UK in 1999) maintain a stable of around 20 titles, mostly reprints from Marvel and DC but also including UK-originated material in their junior titles which range from *Cartoon Network* to *Postman Pat*. In all, there are still some 60 newsstand titles appearing in the UK.

DEATH OF THE NEWSSTAND COMIC?

DC Thomson's adventure and girls' comics (*Warlord, Buddy, Crunch, Judy, Bunty* et al) have also died out over the past 15 years, leaving their output limited to *Commando* and their ailing humour titles, *Beano* and *Dandy*. The *Beano* had maintained reasonable sales, thanks mainly to the popularity of *Dennis the Menace*, but sales of *The Dandy* had slumped to below 50,000 a week, forcing a revamp and hefty price hike in October 2004. Strangely, nostalgia for the title has never been stronger and both *The Dandy* and *The Beano* have begun attracting the kind of prices previously only seen for Golden Age American comic books. A copy of *The Dandy*'s first issue (complete with its metal whistle free gift) was sold for over £20,000 at auction in 2004, while other early issues also command high prices.

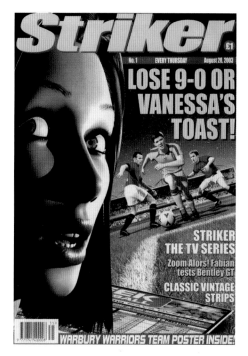

Above: The worthy successor to *Roy of the Rovers, Striker* has had a long, if not trouble free history, first appearing in *The Sun* newspaper in 1985. It got its own title in 2003, but tragically, poor distribution saw the comic cancelled in 2005.
© *Striker 3D Ltd.*

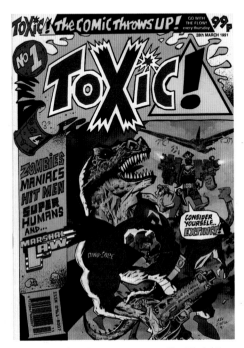

Above: Pat Mills' solo attempt at a weekly title in direct competition with *2000 AD*, saw many of the latter's creators defect, including Alan Grant and Kev O'Neill. But the bold move didn't last out the year (1991) and *Toxic!* folded.
© *Respective creators*

Right: Captain Britain's re-vamp look by Alan Davis rescued him from the Seventies' cheesy outfit (see page 54).
© *Marvel Characters, Inc.*

DCT still maintain a department to produce comic strips for licensing abroad that are never seen in the UK. Licensing strips has been a vital part of the British industry for over 75 years. To take just one example, *The Rise and Fall of the Trigan Empire* was syndicated around Europe and, 20 years after its demise in the UK, is still being reprinted abroad. Whilst major strips from *Dennis the Menace* to *Roy of the Rovers* are essentially British in their character and comedy, the purchase of IPC by AOL Time Warner in 2001 has created the opportunity for American publisher DC Comics to draw on old IPC-owned characters.

TINY ACORNS...

The small press continues to bring new talent to the fore and continues to attract a hardcore following who are looking for something out of the ordinary. *Six Degrees* by Martin Shipp and Marc Laming took the Jamie Bulger murder as its starting point; *Strangehaven* by Gary Spencer Millidge sees a man trapped in a *Twin Peaks*-esque English village; *The Astonishing Adventures of Julius Chancer* by Garen Ewing is a Tintin-styled adventure set in the 1920s.

The whole landscape is very different to that of years gone by, but British comics still have much to offer and a vast pool of creative talent drawing its inspiration from Europe, America, Japan and elsewhere, as well as from Britain's own history and culture. Diversity has always been one of the strengths of the British small press, and nowadays it is the strength of the country's top creators, whether they work for the small press in the UK or for the mainstream in America.

Right, opposite page: Simon Bisley made his name with his spectacular painted artwork on *Slaine* in *2000 AD*, but had worked on *ABC Warriors* two years earlier in 1988.
© *Rebellion A/S*

LEO BAXENDALE

Leo Baxendale

Left: Leo Baxendale's creations have spawned countless merchandise, including this *Little Plum* statue by Robert Harrop Designs.
© *DC Thomson & Co, Ltd*

Right: Baxendale's *Sweeny Toddler* first appeared in *Shiver and Shake* #1 on 10 March 1973 in the 'Shiver' section. The two year old "toddler from hell" caused havoc with his dog, Henry.
© *IPC Media Ltd*

Born in 1930 in Lancashire, Leo Baxendale's first job was designing paint labels for the Leyland paint manufacturer, before being called up for his national service in the RAF. After being discharged, Baxendale started to look around for work as a cartoonist, and began to draw cartoons for the *Lancashire Evening Post*, where he also contributed a series of illustrated articles.

In 1952, he decided to draw up some 'sets' (as cartoonists in the UK called comic pages at the time) to send to the publishers of the *Beano* and *Dandy* comics, DC Thomson. Baxendale had been very influenced by the *Beano* as a boy, and this had inspired him to try to work for the Dundee-based publisher and their comic papers. The work he sent impressed the editor of the *Beano*, George Moonie, and he set Baxendale to work on new series for the comic. The following year, 1953, saw the first of Baxendale's original characters appear in the pages of the *Beano*: *Little Plum*. This was quickly followed by *Minnie the Minx*, and in early 1954 by *When the Bell Rings*, a large splash panel full of havoc and destruction set

in a school. This last series later became a two-page colour spread and changed its name to *The Bash Street Kids*. This strip was to take on iconic status, and was to provide a high-water mark in humour comics. In many ways, *The Bash Street Kids* shows us what made Baxendale such a master cartoonist. Every panel was alive with his action-filled and evocative drawing, while his scripts were often ridiculous, silly and downright hilarious. Baxendale specialised in filling his panels with minute detail and small signs that paid dividends for anyone who took the time and the effort to look for and read them all, as well as the often grotesque physiognomy of his characters.

In 1956, Baxendale contributed to the launch of a new comic from DC Thomson called the *Beezer*, for whom he contributed a new strip called *The Banana Bunch* about a team of juvenile delinquents similar to the *Bash Street Kids*. Feeling that he was somewhat pigeonholing himself, Baxendale later created the strip *The Three Bears* in 1959. Developed from the bears that appeared in his earlier strip *Little Plum*, *The Three Bears* was yet another trademark Baxendale creation, featuring incredible situations, slapstick action, hilarious dialogue and bears. By his own admission, Baxendale drew around 2,500 pages for DC Thomson during the Fifties and early Sixties.

Feeling the need for a new challenge (and perhaps tired of the Scottish firms' legendary miserly behaviour – it has often been said, maybe apocryphally, that they would seat left- and right-handed artists together to share the same inkwell to save on ink costs), Baxendale accepted an offer to create a new comic for DC Thomson's rival in London, Odhams. In 1964, the first issue of *Wham!* was launched. Baxendale created most of the characters, and drew and coloured many of the strips including *Eagle Eye Junior Spy*, *The Tiddlers*, and *General Nitt and his Barmy Army*. *Wham!* was followed two years later with *Smash!*, a companion comic, for which Baxendale contributed other new strips including *Grimly Fiendish* and *Bad Penny*. Odhams were bought out by the giant publishing conglomerate IPC and *Wham!* and *Smash!* didn't last very long after the takeover, being absorbed into other IPC titles in the great British tradition.

Nevertheless, Baxendale continued working for IPC, producing more and more strips (around 3,000 pages), until in 1975 he left the UK comics industry completely. From then on, Baxendale devoted his time to

creating comics more for himself, and his other great passion – political and sociological essays. He created the series *Willy the Kid* for the book publisher Duckworth, who also brought out his autobiography *A Very Funny Business* in 1978. The following year, Baxendale started working for the Dutch comic *Eppo,* contributing his *Willy the Kid* and *Baby Basil* strips to the magazine.

By 1980, Baxendale had filed suit against his former employers DC Thomson for the rights to his *Beano* characters. This lawsuit lasted for seven years, and was finally settled just before the case went to trial in May 1987. Neither party would comment on the settlement, only to say that it was, "mutually acceptable". Baxendale used the time that he was suing Thomson to start writing *On Comedy: The Beano and Ideology*, and by 1989, had set up his own publishing imprint, Reaper Books.

The Guardian newspaper asked him in 1990 to create a daily strip, and he responded with *We Love You Baby Basil*, a madcap but intellectually superior series. He also started working on plans to create the UK centre for comics in much the same vein as the CNBDI in France, plans which have only culminated in a series of exhibitions thus far. Baxendale continues working on limited edition books and prints sold through his imprint, and is still one of the finest cartoonists working today.

Above: *When the Bell Rings!* eventually became *The Bash St. Kids*, a strip so popular that it still runs in *The Beano* – over 50 years after Baxendale created it.
© *DC Thomson & Co Ltd*

Above: Baxendale's super villian, *Grimly Fiendish*, was the inspiration for the eponymous 1985 single by UK punk band, *The Damned*.
© *Leo Baxendale*

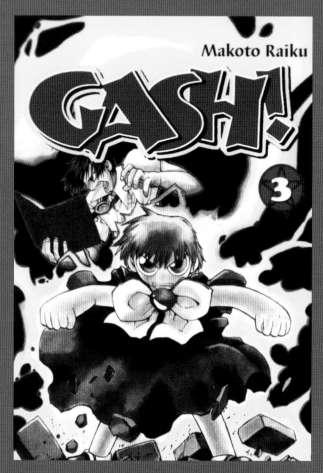

Above: Intense demonic drama in Makoto Raiku's *GASH!* It has been described as "Highlander with humor."
© *Makoto Raiku*

3

MANGA MANIA AND ANIME ANGST

If you'd mentioned the word 'manga' to anyone in the West in 1985, you would have been greeted with blank or quizzical stares. Yet in just under 20 years, the Japanese term is so ubiquitous that it's becoming the homogenized norm for comics.

Comic Amour is the top selling redikomi, or erotic manga for ladies, and sells around 430,000 copies a month.
© San Shuppan

No other 'style' has so successfully dominated global sequential art as manga. From Korea to France via Sweden and America, the Japanese have managed to influence every aspect of the art form. So how did this cultural locust manage to sweep so successfully across the world and change comics forever?

Japan is the biggest comic book producing country in the world with the highest amount of readers. Roughly two billion comic books and magazines are sold in Japan every year, and nearly 40% of all publications released in Japan each year are manga titles. By contrast, the US comic industry's output is approximately 3% of all American publishing.

With sales approaching the equivalent of $7 billion (£3.8 billion) a year, it's impossible to fully explore every aspect of the manga scene in one book, let alone one chapter. Manga caters for every age and social stratum, from children, teens and young adults to housewives and middle-aged men. It's a tired old cliché – that the West often wheels out when describing manga's popularity – that businessmen are often seen reading them on commuter trains with none of the embarrassment that may have occurred in the UK 20 years ago. Things have moved on in all respects.

IRRESPONSIBLE PICTURES

Manga gets its name from two words, 'man' meaning involuntary or irresponsible, and 'ga' meaning pictures. Today, certain aficionados, upset by the negative connotations prefer the term gekiga (dramatic pictures). The Japanese have always loved comics from the earliest forms. The fact that the language originally developed out of various pictograms that actually represented an icon of the word it described, has much to do with their affinity for comics. For example, a small image of a tree eventually evolved into the word for tree. This meant that the Japanese have always been more of a visually based society, rather than a word-based one as in the West.

Modern-day Japanese comics first exploded onto an eager public after World War II. Almost single-handedly, Osamu Tezuka (see creator profile on page 118) dragged Japanese narrative art kicking and

Right: The insatiable baby dinosaur that is *Gon*. Masahi Tanaka's strip mixes cartoon styles with finely detailed animals as they battle the prehistoric throwback which attempts to eat them and everything in his path. Silent, surreal, silly and sensational.
© *Masahi Tanaka*

Above: *Weekly Morning* magazine from 1992.
© *Kodansha*

screaming into the 20th Century. A huge fan of Disney films, the 'God of manga' helped develop the pace of Japanese comic storytelling by extending the page count from an average of 30 pages to several hundred, and by adding many silent panels that had the effect of a camera zooming in or out. This frenetic and kinetic style means that the average 320-page manga is read in 20 minutes, at a speed of 3.75 seconds a page. This is the closest to 'film on a page' as comic books get, and is the real magic of comics that American comic artist Scott McCloud pointed out in his seminal book, *Understanding Comics*. The brain fills in the blanks between the panels, creating a cinematic, moving picture effect in the mind.

THE JAPANESE COMICS MARKET

Over the years, Japanese comics gradually drifted into defined markets and now generally fall into five main categories; shonen (boys), shojo (girls), redisu or redikomi (ladies), seijin (adult erotica), seinen (young men – which actually refers to 14 to 40 year olds). There are countless subgenres and categories however, such as shonen ai (boy love) heta-uma (bad-good, relating to the art style) and rorikon (Lolita complex). While there are only 21 shonen anthologies, they actually make up the largest percentage of sales (38.4% in 2002). Men's titles are second with 54

dedicated publications claiming 37.7%, and shojo trailing at 43 manga titles (8.8%). Finally, there's a paltry 6.7% share for women's comics, even though there is a huge choice of 59 publications. Despite the vast variety of weekly, monthly and quarterly manga, these anthologies are ephemera, read quickly and thrown away. The Japanese readers tend to keep the collected works of their favourite strips from the weeklies. These bunkobon (300-page collections) and tankobon (200 pages) are small and easier to store than their brick-sized parents.

The cornucopia of choice first started in 1959 when one of Japan's biggest publishers, Kodansha, launched *Shukan Shonen Magazine* (Weekly Boys' Magazine). It was the first all-manga 300-page anthology and ran up impressive sales of over one million. Many of the bigger publishers released titles, but this never stopped smaller players muscling in. One of these was Seirindo run by Katsuichi Nagai. In 1964, he launched the experimental *Garo*, primarily as an outlet for creator Sanpei Shirato and others to try out new stories and styles. The artist delivered *The Legend of Kamui*, an Edo-era Japan saga dealing with ninjas rather than the more traditional samurai. While the monthly anthology never set the world on fire in terms of sales (7,000 – 20,000), it remains a highly influential and important part of manga publishing. Rival publishers

Shueisha, then went on the offensive in 1968 with *Shukan Shōnen Jump* (Weekly Boys' Jump) and it has become the biggest selling manga comic in Japan. The title helped launch serialized strips like the basketball drama *Slam Dunk* and space saga *Dragon Ball Z* to international stardom. It's common to see both schoolboys and 'salarymen' (who have grown up reading manga) picking up copies on the way to school and work. Published every Tuesday, the telephone directory sized comic (428 pages) at one point sold an unbelievable five to six million copies a week, making it the biggest selling magazine in the world (*TIME* magazine only sells four million). However, after Japan's recession hit in the 1990s – which saw manga sales universally dip – *Jump's* sales dropped to a 'mere' three million. *Morning* (1982) has always been aimed at men, but its 'manga energy' has never been directed into the area of porn, but instead, rather intense dramas. It sells around a million copies every week. Other anthology titles include *Big Comic Spirits* (1980), *Big Comic Superior* (1987) and *Big Gold* (1992).

AN UNPARALLELED RANGE OF CONTENT

The most breathtaking aspect of Japanese comics is the sheer breadth and depth of subject matters. Everything is covered, from cooking (Tochi Ueyama's *Kukkingu Papa* –

Cooking Papa) to parenting for young hip mums (*Yan Mama Comic*, 1993). There are even manga magazines specifically based around the Japanese pastimes/obsessions of mahjong (*Kindai Mahjong Original*, launched in 1977) and Pachinko – a form of Oriental pinball (*Manga Pachinker*, 1991). Other titles include *Business Jump* (business comics for boys), *Reggie* (the story of a black American baseball player in Japan) as well as countless others on martial arts, computer games, basketball and ping pong.

CENSORSHIP, JAPANESE STYLE

As in the West, manga has always had its fair share of detractors to deal with and associated issues with censorship, however lax they may appear to Western standards. Article 175 of the vaguely worded Japanese Penal Code prevented the depiction of explicit sexual intercourse and adult genitalia in comics. Unfortunately, as publishers tried to circumnavigate the laws using loopholes, they created another apocryphal tale of schoolgirls earning pocket money in the holidays working for publishers, whiting out offending penises, vaginas and pubic hair. Yet another Japanese dichotomy, leading to the question of who's protecting whom from what? The loopholes around adult genitalia also led to the unfortunate rise of rorikon (Lolita complex) comics. These titles portrayed pre-pubescent girls

Above: The experimental and cutting-edge anthology, *Garo*. © *Seirindo*

Left: A panel from Mitsuhiko Yoshida's *Paper Theatre*, published in 1990. The short story, *The First Visitor* is the tale of a girl's first period, a subject that would have been unthinkable in Western comics until recently.

© Mitsuhiko Yoshida

Right: The erotic comedy, *Mouse*.

© Hiroshi Itaba and Saturo Akahori

Below: Modern manga is rife with naked flesh, such as this series from *Monthly Champion*, set in a bath house.

© Respective creators

Below: Mangaka superstar, Masamune Shirow gets hot and heavy with one of his many sexy posters.

© Masamune Shirow

with excessively sized breasts in sexual situations, in what would be regarded as paedophilia in the West. The whole uneasy image of sexy schoolgirls has a firm grip on Japan's manhood.

OTAKU TAKEN TO TASK

In 1989, there came a major crackdown after the infamous – and horrific – kidnapping, murder and mutilation of three pre-school girls by Tsutomu Miyazaki, an Otaku (an obsessive fan-boy), who was a huge devotee of rorikon manga. This caused a furore in parents' and teachers' groups concerned over the sexual and violent content of certain manga. However, the Miyazaki murders are the exception rather than the rule, and the island state has far fewer incidents of rape and murder than America. Alongside numerous other reasons – including a high sense of social responsibility in Japanese society – many have argued that because the Japanese so openly explore their deepest, darkest fantasies in manga, animation and live-action film, very few individuals ever feel the need to act them out. Titles like the infamous *Rapeman* (a manga series that some said condoned the use of violence against women; its premise was of a 'rapist for hire' employed to get back at women who had spurned their boyfriends) act as a cathartic release for readers. Simply put, most Japanese can tell

the difference between fantasy and reality. The other anomaly with these sexually violent comics is that the vast majority are created by women themselves and, if examined closely, actually put the woman in a position of power rather than that of the victim, further confusing the issue.

THE INDUSTRY REGULATES ITSELF

To counter the general public's outrage over the schoolgirls' murders, the manga industry set up the self-regulatory group, the Association to Protect Freedom of Expression in Comics. Headed by several high-profile mangaka (comic professionals), they went on a counter-offensive, fighting for creative freedom and attacking censorship. It eventually worked, and by 1994, the manga witch-hunt was off, as Japan's moral minority trooped off to right wrongs elsewhere. As one pundit put it, "There was a big fuss about it for a while, but now everything seems pretty much the way it's always been." However, in 2004, the whole censorship issue kicked off again when on 13 January, Suwa Yuuji's pornographic *Misshitsu* (Honey Room) was deemed "obscene" by a Japanese court and the artist was sentenced to one to three years in jail. To avoid this, he and his publisher Monotori Kishi, reluctantly accepted the guilty verdict. The first major obscenity trial in Japan for 20 years sent shockwaves

Hino Horror

Hideshi Hino is Japan's horror manga master. If there is such a thing as a Japanese underground comics artist, Hino is it.

Born in China in 1946, Hino moved to Tokyo with his mother, where the post-war devastation stayed with him and reoccurs throughout his work. After seeing Masaki Kobayashi's film *Seppuku*, he decided to become a director, but at high school his drawings captured the imagination of classmates and he changed tack to a career in manga. Hino initially created self-published comics, or doujinshi, until a publisher friend asked for a few filler pages for a magazine, and his career took off. His first graphic novel was published in 1978.

© Hideshi Hino

Horror and suspense, Hino suggested, are "deeply hidden emotions that surface when we are confronted by a disturbance of our everyday lives." Hino's huge body of work has managed to fill over 400 books, influencing a new generation of manga artists, like Kanako Inuki.

Above: Takao Saito's Series about an amoral assassin, Gogol 13, was launched in 1969.
©Takao Saito

around the manga world, with many artists and publishers self-censoring, as before, and shops scrapping their adult-only manga sections.

WORKING CONDITIONS

There are over 3,000 mangaka working in Japan today. Many scrape a living, but for the top 10%, the rewards are astronomical, and almost unattainable for Western creators. *Dragon Ball's* creator Akira Toriyama has managed to sell 120 million copies of his manga since 1984. Artists' royalties are as good as the sales of the books, with Yoshihiro Togashi, creator of *Yu-Yu Hakusho* (The Yu-Yu Report on Apparitions), making approximately $7 million (£3.7 million) in 1994 alone, while *Ranma 1/2* creator Rumiko Takahashi made so much money, she was listed as one of the 10 richest people in Japan.

Two of the most successful mangaka ever, Kazuo Koike and Goseki Kojima, got together in 1970 and created an epic story that would set a new benchmark in manga in terms of storytelling, scale and viscera. *Lone Wolf and Cub* first appeared in *Manga Action* (launched in 1967), published by Fuso-Sha. The impressive saga told of a Ronin (a masterless samurai) called *Itto Ogami* and his infant son, *Daigoro*, as they follow the assassin's path down the road to Hell, seeking revenge for their clan's massacre. Despite

his ferocity and cunning as a killer, *Itto Ogami* is among the most noble of men in Japan.

This tale of staggering proportions took six years and over 8,000 pages to tell, and is one of the most remarkable works ever created in the medium of comics. "It takes you to another time, and to a frightening, alien land, windswept and grey, dying in quiet obedience to insane decrees of insane leaders," said American comics legend Frank Miller, a huge fan. "Its authors took the time and space to tell their tale in its every moment, often devoting many pages to scenes that wouldn't last three panels in a monthly American superhero comic book."

Miller's early work, *Ronin*, for DC Comics, was heavily influenced by Koike and Kojima's series. *Lone Wolf and Cub* was turned into six highly successful live-action films between 1972 and 1974, which Koike also helped to adapt. It has been made into three popular television series and 2005 also saw the planning of a remake by cult American director Darren Aronofsky. Not bad for a comic created over 35 years ago!

One of Japan's foremost manga writers, Koike was born in Akita Prefecture on 8 May 1936. Soon after graduation from college, he became a pupil of the historical novelist, Kiichiro Yamate. In 1968, he joined the production team of the classic

Right: A classic silent sequence from *Lone Wolf and Cub*.
© *Kazuo Koike, Goseki Kojima and Dark Horse Comics*

Below: The US reprint of *Lone Wolf and Cub* with cover by Frank Miller. This was the second company to reprint the series in the US. When the original publishers, First Comics folded, Dark Horse picked up the rights.
© *Kazuo Koike, Goseki Kojima and Dark Horse Comics*

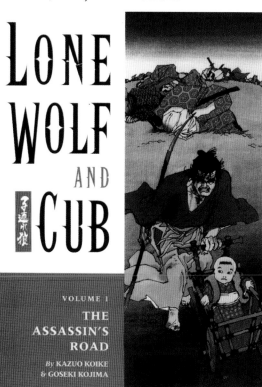

Left: *Inu Yasha*'s creator, Rumiko Takahashi, is known as The Princess of Manga. Her light humorous tone and passionate characters mean she's had many popular series including *Urusei Yatsura* and *Ranama 1/2*.
© *Rumiko Takahashi*

Below: The manual for the *Fist of the North Star* Playstation game. Tetsuo Hara's futuristic Kung-Fu epic was also adapted into a cult anime.
©*Tetsuo Hara*

assassin strip *Golgo 13*, working for the creator, Takao Saito. Two years later, he'd launched *Lone Wolf and Cub* and his career was assured. In 1977, the writer set up the Koike Kazuo Gekigason-juku (Kazuo Koike's Character Principle), a manga course in the vein of Joe Kubert's school in New York. The Japanese course launched the careers of several remarkable young manga creators, including Rumiko Takahashi, creator of *Ranma 1/2*, and *Fist of the North Star* writer/artist Tetsuo Hara.

With the money he made from the various successful manga titles, Koike set up his own publishing company, the Koikeshoin Corporation. At a bizarre tangent from manga, Koike indulged in his other passion when he launched 1987's *Alba-Tross-View*, a golf magazine. In 2000, Koike was made a professor of Osaka University of Arts' Literary Arts Department and he maintained his fascination with historical action when he launched *JIN*, an all-samurai manga magazine in 2004, reprinting classic material and new stories. The following year, Koike became professor and dean of the newly created Character Figurative Arts Department in Osaka University of Arts.

Koike and Kojima went on to collaborate on several other, equally successful, Bushido series including *Kawaite Sourou* and *Samurai Executioner*. Koike's other epic, *Crying Freeman*, drawn by Ryoichi Ikegami, was also made into a series of animated films. The manga told of a hitman forced to work for the sinister organization, the 108 Dragons. Unable to stop himself, he sheds a tear with every assassination until he meets a female artist who is the key to his freedom. The creator duo also worked on the series *Offered* and *Kizuoi-Bito*.

ANIME AND MANGA

Just as Osamu Tezuka couldn't separate his manga from his anime work, he also motivated many creators to work in both media and in Japan the two are intrinsically linked. Two of these director/artists, Hayao Miyazaki and Katsuhiro Otomo, became equally legendary as their inspirational forefather.

It's safe to say that Hayao Miyazaki is truly Tezuka's successor as Japan's premier storyteller. Miyazaki started his career, unlike many mangaka, in reverse. The traditional route of mangaka was to establish themselves in manga before moving into animation. However, Miyazaki's first major job was in 1963 as an animator at the famous Toei studios, after graduating from Gakushuin University with a political science and economics degree. He was 22 and was involved in many early classics of Japanese animation. From the beginning, he commanded attention with his incredible drawing skills and seemingly endless stream of ideas for film proposals. In 1971,

Above: *June* was the first of the Shonen ai, or 'boy love' manga.
© *San Shuppan*

Above: Miyazaki's *Princess Mononoke,* as interpreted by Ryoichi Ikegami, the artist of *Mai The Psychic Girl* and *Crying Freeman.*
© Hayo Miyazaki and Ryoichi Ikegami

he moved to A Pro studios with Isao Takahata, then to Nippon Animation in 1973, where he was heavily involved in the TV animation series *World Masterpiece Theatre.* He directed his first TV series, *Mirai Shonen Conan* (Future Boy Conan) in 1978, and then moved to Tokyo Movie Shinsha to direct his first movie, *Lupin III: The Castle of Cagliostro* (based on the manga series by Monkey Punch), the following year.

In 1982, Miyazaki began his epic manga, *Nausicaä of the Valley of Wind,* an eco-logical warning of the future – a recurrent theme in his work – and he worked inter-mittently on the series for the next 12 years. In 1984, the film adaptation was released to critical and commercial acclaim. Another manga, *Hikoutei Jidai,* later evolved into his 1992 film *Kurenai no Buta* (Porco Rosso), about a fighter pilot pig based in the Adriatic Sea during World War I.

The success of *Nausicaä* led to a new ani-mation studio being set up, Studio Ghibli, for which Miyazaki directed five films and produced another three between 1986 and 1997. These included *Tenkû no Shiro Rapyuta* (Laputa: Castle in the Sky) in 1986, *Majo Tonari no Totoro* (My Neighbour Totoro) in 1988, and 1989's *No Takkyûbin* (Kiki's Delivery Service). Miyazaki had the golden touch, and all the films enjoyed box office and critical success.

Miyazaki takes his work very seriously – not only did he write, direct and edit

Princess Mononoke – but he personally correct-ed or re-drew more than 80,000 of the film's 144,000 animation cels. The hard work paid off, and in 1998, *Princess Mononoke* won the Japanese Academy Award for Best Film, and was the highest-grossing domes-tic film in history, making about $150 mil-lion (£83 million).

Ironically, the man often called the 'Walt Disney of Japan' – a title Miyazaki hates – has recently had all his films distributed in the US by Disney/Miramax. The American company asked to cut some of the footage from *Princess Mononoke,* but were refused as it was contractually obliged not to edit the film for the American release. The US ver-sion's dialogue was written by British-born, US-based comic writer Neil Gaiman.

Princess Mononoke's success however, mere-ly paved the way for even greater triumphs, when Miyazaki's 2001 film *Sen to Chihiro no Kamikakushi* (Spirited Away) won not only the Japanese Academy Award for Best Picture, but also an Oscar for Best Animated Film and a BAFTA for Best Foreign Language Film. Miyazaki's latest film, *Hauru no Ugoku Shiro* (Howl's Moving Castle), is based on the novel by Diana Wynne Jones. The Japanese director, artist and creator stated that this would be his last film, but he's said that before, so hopefully we will see a few more cinematic treats before he retires.

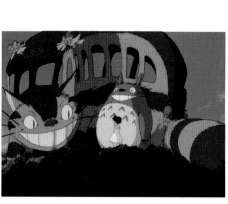

Above: A scene from Hayo Miyazaki's film, *Majo Tonari no Totoro* (*My Neighbour Totoro*).
© *Hayo Miyazaki.*

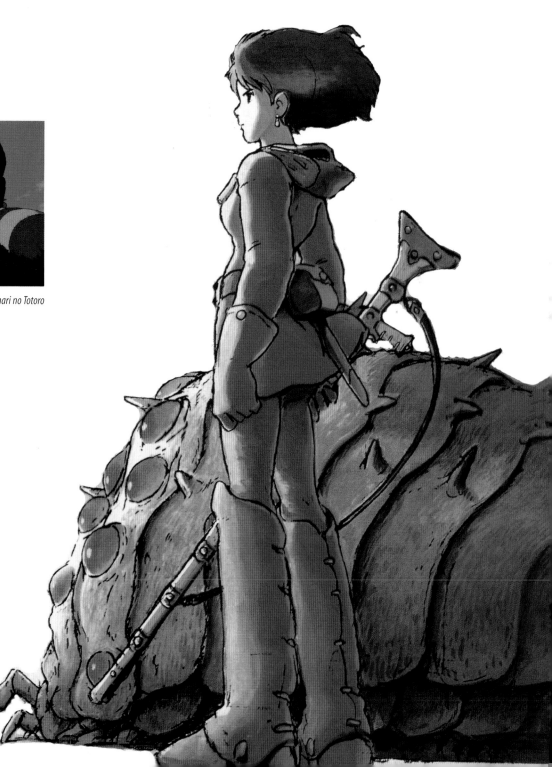

Right: *Nausicaa of the Valley of Wind* was Miyazaki's ecological fable set in a future where mankind threatens to destroy the natural world.
© *Hayo Miyazaki.*

AK-III-RRRRAAAAAA!

Katsuhiro Otomo was born in Miyagi, 13 years after Hayao Miyazaki. As a young man, Otomo's great passion was watching American movies, just like his predecessor, Osamu Tezuka. He often travelled three hours just to get to the nearest cinema. Otomo moved to Tokyo in 1973 and made his debut in comics that year, with *Jyu-Sei* (*A Gun Report*), an adaptation of *Mateo Falcone*, the classic French writer Prosper Mérimée's novella. Otomo then went to work regularly on *Manga Action*, the seinen anthology that was launched in 1967.

In 1979, Otomo's first major series, *Fireball*, broke all the rules with its unique art style, and changed traditional manga forever. It also marked the beginning of Otomo's interest in science-fiction themes. The following year, his story *Domu* – about the battle between two psychics, a little girl and an old man in a tenement building – was a bestseller and won Japan's Science Fiction Grand Prix Award.

Then in 1982, Otomo launched the ambitious series that would make him and his creation, *Akira*, international household names. The story was first published in *Young* magazine and was an immediate success that grew into a massive blockbuster. It took Otomo 2,000 plus pages, 10 years and six volumes to complete his saga of biker gangs, psychics and political machinations

in a post-apocalyptic neo-Tokyo. In 1987, *Akira* was one of the first manga to be translated in its entirety, and was published in the USA by Marvel's appropriately titled Epic imprint. It was a global hit, as was the animated adaptation Otomo directed. For many, it was the first experience of the new generation of anime, and it launched the West's demand for Japanese manga and animation that remains unabated over 15 years later.

GIRL POWER

Another successful 'artist' is CLAMP, the four-woman manga studio that has created some of the planet's most popular recent manga. The group consists of Ageha Ohkawa, the team leader and writer; Satsuki Igarashi, art assistant; Tsubaki Nekoi, art assistant and lead artist on several titles; and Mokona, lead artist.

For the past 15 years, they have worked non-stop, creating everything from the cute shojo hit *Cardcaptor Sakura*, to the dark and brooding *Tokyo Babylon* and the sci-fi romantic comedy *Chobits*. Amazingly, these workaholics are simultaneously producing four series: *Legal Drug*, *X*, *Tsubasa: Reservoir Chronicle* and *xxxholic*. The group has a close relationship with anime studio Madhouse, which has adapted most of CLAMP's manga into successful anime.

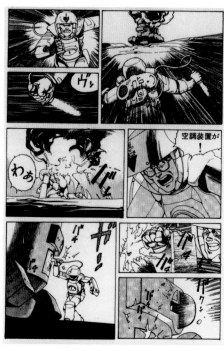

Above: Katshiro Otomo's earlier work, the anti-war story, *A Farewell to Arms*.
© *Katshiro Otomo*

Left, opposite page: Otomo's epic masterwork *Akira*. This is the cover to the third Japanese volume.
© *Katshiro Otomo and Kodansha*

Above: Cel from Akira Toriyama's international phenomena, *Dragonball*.
© *Akira Toriyama*

THAT DARN ROBO-CAT

One of the most popular children's characters that also made the successful leap to anime, is the robotic cat from the future, *Doraemon*. Created in 1970 by Fujiko F Fujio (real names Hiroshi Fujimoto and Abiko Motoo), the eponymous strip originally appeared annually in publisher Shogakukan's school specials. His popularity grew, as did the frequency of his appearance, until the strip was published in the kid's monthly *CoroCoro* (founded in 1977). *Doraemon* has the same iconic status as fellow cat *Garfield* has in the USA, with the same enormous merchandizing empire, and has created vast profits amounting to ¥15.3 billion ($153 million/£81.6 million) in just 15 years. Since 1980, a new *Doraemon* animated movie is released every year, and his funny, yet gentle adventures with schoolboy *Nobita Nobi*, meant it was the first manga to achieve international success in Europe, South America and both the Middle and Far East.

CYBERMANGA

Another manga creator who has received critical and commercial success abroad is the cyber-punk cartoonist, Masamune Shirow. He was born and raised in Kobe, the second largest port city after Yokohama. At college he was introduced to manga by a friend, and in 1983 he self-published the series *Black Magic* in the fanzine *Atlas*. Shirow was 22 when *Black Magic* was noticed by Harumichi Aoki, president of Seishinsha, an Osaka-based publisher. After Shirow graduated in 1985, he drew *Appleseed* for Seishinsha, making his commercial debut. At the same time as *Appleseed*'s launch,

Right, opposite page: *Subasa,* one of the many series by the creative team CLAMP
© *CLAMP*

Left: The robotic cat from the future, *Doraemon,* and his schoolboy pal, Nobita, build a flying saucer.
© *Fujiko F Fujio/Shōgakukan*

RESERVoir CHRoNiCLE

3

Below: *Deunan* and her cyborg partner, *Briareos* from Masamune Shirow's most famous series, *Appleseed*. The strip won the Galaxy Award for Best Science Fiction Comic in 1986, and it has been adapted for the big screen twice in 1988 and 2004. In the series, Shirow correctly predicted the rise of international fundamentalist terrorism 15 years before 9/11.
© *Masamune Shirow*

Above: A cover to Shirow's other big hit, *Ghost in the Shell*, a cyber-punk epic, featuring *Motoko Kusanagi*, a sexy cyborg specializing in counter-terrorist activities. Like many of his stories, Shirow succeeds in creating a bleak, yet hopeful future, as seen in films like Blade Runner.
© *Masamune Shirow*

Shirow became a high school teacher, but after teaching for five years, he left, disillusioned with the educational system. He then started work on *Ghost in the Shell* and *Orion* (1988) for Seishinsha. The latter was first published in the monthly anthology, *Comic Gaia*.

Shirow's primary influences were animation shows such as Yoshiyuki Tomino's *Gundam* and *The Macross Sagas*. Both dealt with the manga and anime sub-genre of large cybernetic robot suits controlled by a human user inside. The whole giant robot manga scene was started partly by Tezuka's *Astro Boy* and other earlier giant robot stories, but it mostly took off with Go Nagai's 1972 *Mazinger Z* series. Shirow's influences however, came from many sources, "When I was working on the animated version of *Black Magic M-66*, I concentrated very intently on the techniques of Hayao Miyazaki. Looking back at *Appleseed*, I seem to find nuances strongly reminiscent of Katsuhiro Otomo, Terry Gilliam and many others."

Shirow's works – *Dominion Tank Police, Ghost in the Shell* and others – reflect his extensive and varied interests. Medicine, general science, the supernatural, philosophy, military strategies, mythology, biology, nanotechnology and sword fights are all key elements in his work. In his spare time, Shirow looks after and photographs his pet spiders, and the influence of arachnids, insects and crustaceans is apparent in the design and atmospheric nature of his comics.

Shirow is the 'Thomas Pynchon' of manga. He guards his privacy intensely, to the point that he never (knowingly) appears at conventions, and any interviews are done either by phone or email. Even his name, Masamune Shirow, is actually a pseudonym. When the 1995 earthquake destroyed his Kobe home and studio, he moved to another part of the Hyogo Prefecture. Living and working in virtual isolation, his primary contacts are Harumichi Aoki and long-time friend and editor, Shigehiko Ogasawara. Shirow did have an assistant, Hagane Kotetsu, for a while but, "I really couldn't keep him busy," Shirow regretted. "Since there aren't too many artists here, the poor fellow would practically starve."

JAPANESE FANDOM

Comic conventions aren't big in Japan. They're vast! Tokyo's two-day Super Comic City is held in April in five giant halls. In America, the majority of San Diego Comic Con's 87,000 attendees are male. Conversely, 90% of the 200,000 people at Super Comic City are girls in their late teens or early 20s. There are over 18,000 booths selling every genre and format. Yet this isn't a professional convention – despite being twice the size of the USA's

The Mother of Manga

Riyoko Ikeda studied philosophy while she was first published in the *Kashihonya* magazine. In 1967, she made her debut with *Bara-Yashiki no Shoujo* (*The Girl of the Rose*) and in 1972, she began her most famous series, *Versailles no Bara* (*The Rose of Versailles*). The title ran for over 1,700 pages and was set in the court of King louis XVI. It began the trend for historical manga, and was turned into a stage play and live action and animated films.

Riyoko Ikeda mysteriously disappeared from the manga scene around the mid-1980s, but in 1998, she returned with a new series, *Orpheus no Mado* (*Orpheus' Window*). Her other work included titles such as: *Jotei Ecatherina* (*Empress Chaterina*).

She was the first female manga artist to achieve great success and respect and is consequently called the 'Mother of Manga.'

Above: Cover to CLAMP's *xxxholic*, demonstrating the team's diverse range of art styles.
© *CLAMP*

biggest pro show – this is entirely for dojinshi, or self-published fanzines. There are 50,000 manga societies in Japan who pool their resources so that they can publish their own manga with impressive print runs of 100 to 6,000 (as big as some independent US publishers). These societies, or mini-publishing houses, are similar to how L'Association started in France; the artists are doing it for themselves. Copyright laws are much more relaxed in Japan, allowing for fans to create homages, pastiches and parodies of their favourite manga. Whereas in the US, publishers would have sued the fanzines out of business, Japanese publishers tolerate the part-time artisans, as they don't want to alienate their fan base. Another reason why publishers allow the dojinshi market to thrive, is that it's an excellent source of tomorrow's mangaka. Masamune Shirow and CLAMP were both

discovered at these shows. Thousands of amateur auteurs assemble, selling their wares on everything from small humorous pamphlets to hardcover, hardcore pornographic graphic novels. In fact, some of the more salacious material saw the show shut down by police in 1994. There still remains a slight stigma for fans, as many girls don't want their parents or teachers to know that they've attended.

Even the immense scale of Super Comic City is still a blip compared to Comiket or Komiketto (Comic Market), also in the capital. Held twice a year – in December and August – it is a non-profit fair run for, and by, fans. Started in December 1975 by Yoshiro Yonezawa and others, the three-day convention was originally intended as a way to get manga out to a wider audience, and for fans to connect up and trade books, as it was much harder to find manga in the

Right: Eikichi Onizuka, aka *Great Teacher Onizuka* (*GTO*), prepares to teach his students a lesson they won't forget.
© *Tohru Fujisawa*

Right, opposite page: *Rin* and her bodyguard *Manji* from Hiroaki Samura's epic samurai tale, *Blade of the Immortal*.
© *Hiroaki Samura*

Right: The global hit comedy, *Love HINA* by Ken Akamatsu.
©*Ken Akamatsu*

Above: The incredibly macho-looking international art thief, *Eroica*, from the 1976 strip *From Eroica with Love* by Akita Shoten.
© *Akita Shoten*

mid-Seventies than today. The first show had 600 attendees, a figure that has steadily increased to a mind-blowing 400,000 plus, who spend over ¥3 billon ($30 million/£16 million) in one weekend, an average of $75 (£40) per person. By comparison, Europe's largest convention, Angoulême in France, only achieves around 210,000 visitors. A regular sight at the Japanese conventions is the thousands of fans who dress up as their favourite manga characters. Known as 'cosplay', this fad has grown year on year, with huge numbers of young ladies dressed as *Sailor Moon* or any one of numerous girly manga characters.

MANGA AND LITERACY

Recently, publishers have been creating illustrated novels based on popular manga titles, but overall the trend for traditional books has been downwards. Based on the fact that sales of novels are declining and that manga is the primary form of communication, it appears that Japan has finally produced what British writer Alan Moore called the, "post-literate generation" – not a criticism, but simply a comment on the future of mankind's cultural development

As Japan's comics become increasingly popular in the United States and Europe, proponents predict the Land of the Rising Sun's anime and manga styles will challenge the West, to form the backbone of

21st Century world pop culture. It's already started.

THE JAPANESE ARE COMING!

The first major manga translation tsunami to crash onto American shores was in fact brought over, not by the 'big two' – Marvel and DC Comics – but by many of the smaller independent US publishers such as First and Eclipse at the end of the 1980s. The man surfing the crest of the wave was American, Toren Smith, who was already scouting and translating Japanese manga with the intent of finding publishers in the USA. "I think it was summer of '87," recalled Smith. "I quit my job in America, sold my car and all my worldly goods and went over to Japan to try and somehow survive over there and get involved with comics and animation." Smith would find and purchase the North American publication rights for promising manga, then, with the help of freelancers, translate and reformat the material for the American market. In those early days, manga was quite alien to most Americans, and Smith felt his job was to introduce the best manga, while rendering it more palatable to Western tastes. That meant not only changing the vertical lines of Japanese text to horizontal English, but also reversing the sequence of panels. Smith undertook the vast, and tedious, job of reformatting the

Above: This regular issue of *Monthly Champion* makes most Western comics look like mere pamphlets. Many mangaka are under intense pressure to produce a lot of artwork to fill these pages and often hire several assistants to draw backgrounds, fill in shadows, etc. This cover features *Worst*, the story of high school gangs, by Hiroshi Takahashi, who also wrote the screenplay for the cult horror film *Ringu* (*The Ring*).
© *Monthly Champion*/Hiroshi Takahashi

Junko Mizuno

Junko Mizuno made her comic debut in the rock magazine *H.*, combining cute girls with wide eyes and beaming smiles, with grisly skulls and corpses. Her early work included *The Life of Momongo,* and in 1996 she achived recognition with her self-published book, *MINA animal DX.* Like her characters,

Mizuno is petite and cute. She is an avid collector of toys and figures and many of her own designs have been turned into figurines. In recent years, she has received great acclaim in manga circles, not only for her unique way of juxtaposing the cute and the grotesque, but for her savvy sensibility and beautiful colour work.

Mizuno has adapted several classic fairy tales, all with her black humorous twist, including *Cinderella, Hansel and Gretel* and *Princess Mermaid.* In the latter, three seductive mermaid sisters, Tara, Julie, and Ai, lure unsuspecting sailors into their underwater pleasure palace, only to eat them.

material to fit the average American comic-book, reversing the order of the pages and flipping each individual page so that the action could be read from left to right.

One of the earliest manga translations was one of the best, *Lone Wolf and Cub.* It was first introduced to English readers by First Comics in 1987, and immediately captured the attention and fascination of readers with its intelligent, action-packed stories and stunning artwork. Unfortunately, First went bust before they could complete the series, but in August 2000, Dark Horse reissued the series in a new 28-volume format.

One of the most important forerunners of the 'Asian Invasion' was Viz Communications (not to be confused with the British humour comic *Viz*). Two Japanese businessmen, Seiji Horibuchi and Satoru Fujii, founded the San Francisco-based publisher in 1986. They formed partnerships with two of Japan's biggest manga publishers, Shogakukan and Shueisha, and began translating the material for American audiences. Toren Smith advised Horibuchi on the launch of Viz, and expected to do re-write and translation work on the company's first titles. However, Smith found Viz frustratingly slow to acquire rights to manga and anime properties not already owned by Shogakukan or Shueisha. Despite this, he was able to make enough contacts with Japanese creators and companies to form his own packaging

operation, Studio Proteus, in 1988. The studio's first client was Eclipse Comics, for which Smith adapted Shirow's *Appleseed.* Smith also packaged Johji Manabe's *Outlanders* for Dark Horse.

After reading Smith's article in the Japanese edition of *Starlog* magazine, which tore apart the poorly edited and translated American release of Hayao Miyazaki's anime film *Nausicaä* (as *Warriors of the Wind*), the manga writer/artist picked Studio Proteus to adapt his *Nausicaä* manga for Viz.

Titles like *Pineapple Army* by Naoki Urasawa, and *Grey* by Yoshihisa Tagami (both translated in 1988), and *Ranma 1/2* by Rumiko Takahashi, and magazines about manga like *Animerica* and *Mangajin* all helped keep the insatiable American manga fans happy. It still it wasn't enough. Shirato's ninja epic, *The Legend of Kamui*, was published by Eclipse in 1987 and the same year Eclipse also released *Mai the Psychic Girl*. This was the more popular of the two and Kazuya Kudo and artist Ryoichi Ikegami's moving tale of a young schoolgirl who develops telepathic abilities, was collected into four graphic novels.

Since those early days of translated material, manga has exploded around the globe and continues to gain fans at a staggering rate. The current English-language market is estimated at $60 - $100 million (£33 - £55 million) for the USA alone. All these early manga imports inspired young

Right: Gô Nagai's lengendary creations, *Goldorak* and *Mazinger Z* (later renamed *Great Mazinger* and *God Mazinger*) helped launch the craze for giant robots that transform, which continues unabated in manga and anime to this day.
© *Gô Nagai*

Above: Gô Nagai's vision was fully realised in the Eighties' epic, *Robotech*. It spawned several anmie TV and comic series and was a huge hit both in Japan and America. Art by Adam Warren.
© *Harmony Gold USA, Inc*

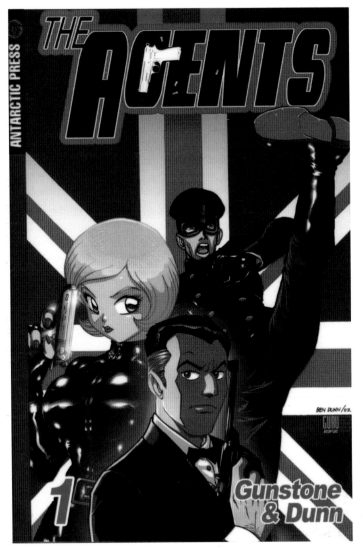

Above: Toren Smith and Adam Warren's *Dirty Pair* helped kick-off Western manga.
© *Toren Smith and Adam Warren*

Left: Kevin/Ka Gunstone and Ben Dunn's *The Agents*, a manga homage to super Sixties' spies, *James Bond, Joe 90* and TV shows like *The Green Hornet* and *The Thunderbirds*.
© *Kevin/Ka Gunstone*

Below: *Missive Device #23: Globulelicious*, by the UK's Infinite Livez, owes a nod to manga.
© *Infinite Livez*

American creators to launch their own manga titles. At the forefront of this was Ben Dunn and his company Antarctic Press which released the popular semi-parody, *Ninja High-School*. Toren Smith even began to write his own successful US manga, *Dirty Pair*, drawn by fellow American Adam Warren in the early 1990s. In 1991, The First International Conference on Japanese Animation took place in San Jose, California. Better known as AnimeCon '91, it was the tipping point for manga and anime fans in the USA, and ultimately led to a wider audience discovering Japan's creative output. Many artists from Japan attended as guests, and were overwhelmed by the positive fan response in America.

When Stuart Levy founded Tokyopop in 1996 with $12 million (£7 million) financial backing from Japan, Korea and America, it's doubtful that even he envisaged it would become the single most successful non-Japanese manga publisher in the world. In 2001, Tokyopop made a major breakthrough into a previously unconquered land for graphic novels, the bookshops. The US manga market expanded exponentially and profits went through the roof, roughly doubling in 2003, with the vast majority of growth in bookshops who dedicated whole sections to manga.

Tokyopop now ships more than 400 titles a year and sells more graphic novels through the book market than either of America's previous kings of comics, Marvel or DC. Tokyopop now has beachheads in Los Angeles, Tokyo, London and, most recently, Hamburg. Every year it organizes the Rising Stars of Manga, a competition to find the next generation of American manga creators, highlighting how deeply the Japanese influence has gone into Ameri-teens' psyches. Every winner gets to have his or her work published, and 2004's winner, M. Alice LeGrow, launched her gothic Alice in Wonderland-esque graphic novel, *Bizenghast*, at the end of 2005.

In 2002, the Japanese anthologies were launched in the USA. The American version of *Shonen Jump* reported a circulation of 300,000, whereas *Rajin* became the first English-language weekly manga in America.

Realizing that they had to compete with this new publishing phenomenon, DC and Marvel released manga versions of their numerous comics. Marvel launched its *Mangaverse*, headed up by Ben Dunn, with fellow US-based artists Jeff Matsuda, Kaare Andrews and Lea Hernandez. Suddenly, *Spider-Man* and *The Hulk* had bigger, cuter, rounder faces and eyes, and lots of speed lines behind them. However, the experiment was short-lived and the heroes reverted back to their original look. DC took the alternative route and actually hired Japanese creators such as Yoshitaka Amano (*Vampire Hunter D* and *Final Fantasy*) who collaborated

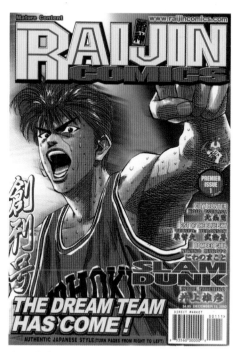

Above: The first issue of the American manga reprint title *Raijin Comics*, featuring the basketball drama, *Slam Dunk*.
© Shueisha Inc / Viz Communications

Above: A Spanish edition of an American comic featuring Japanese versions of the *Fantastic Four*, *Captain Marvel* and *The Watcher*. A truly international comic! Cover art by Benn Dunn.
© *Marvel Comics*

Right, opposite page: Bounty hunting Rashomon Emi, aka *Bomber Girl*, by Niwano Makoto, has the final word as usual.
© *Niwano Makoto*

Right: UK artist Andi Watson's early work, like *Samurai Jam*, *Skeleton Key* and *Geisha* were heavily inspired by manga creators like Rumiko Takahashi.
© *Andi Watson*

with Neil Gaiman on the graphic novel, *The Sandman: The Dream Hunters*.

Having seen the huge success of manga in bookshops, many traditional publishers are also belatedly attempting to cash in on the manga craze, with Random House being the most recent. In a joint venture between Random House's Del Rey imprint and Kodansha, the publisher launched a manga graphic novel line in the spring of 2004, including two of CLAMP's series, *Tsubasa* and *xxxholic*.

It appears as if the Japanese invasion is permanent, like Sony televisions or Nintendo GameBoys. Manga has irrevocably changed comics, not only in the States, but right across the globe. In South Africa, Spain, Germany or India, no matter what happens now, for better or worse, manga is here to stay.

WORLD-CLASS CREATORS:

Above: Tezuka's medical drama, *Black Jack*.
© *Tezuka Productions*

From a very young age, Osamu Tezuka was obsessed with film. His father used to screen 8mm American films such as *Charlie Chaplin* or Fleischer cartoons, and this formative experience had a profound effect on Tezuka's storytelling skills when he started drawing comics. In particular, he had a love of Disney animation. Heavily influenced by Disney cartoons' stylized big eyes, Tezuka took up a wide-eyed 'cutesy' style that became synonymous with his work. Tezuka, in turn, influenced countless numbers of Japanese cartoonists, and the large eyes and big gaping mouths of extreme exaggeration became the West's primary preconception of manga, which mistakenly continues today.

Tezuka started drawing manga young. As World War Two raged around him, he drew over 3,000 pages of strips in private, a lifetime's work for some creators, but Tezuka was just warming up. He started his career as a comic artist in 1946 with *Machan no Nikkicho* (Machan's Diary) for the children's magazine *Mainichi Shogakusei Shinbun* while he was a student at Osaka University. Tezuka's

parents were determined for him to have another career to fall back on in case the comics vocation didn't work out, and so, like many other cartoonists around the world, he went to medical school and graduated as a fully-fledged doctor. He put his medical knowledge to good use when he created *Black Jack* (1973). His longest series, it was the story of a mysterious 'rogue' surgeon who performed freelance operations other doctors dared not do.

His first big hit, *Shin Takarajima* (New Treasure Island) appeared in 1947 and sold 400,000 copies. He was just 19 years old. Three years later, he launched the ecological saga *Jungle Taitei* (Jungle Emperor) in *Manga Shonen*. It ran until 1954 and was turned into Japan's first full-colour animated TV show in the 1960s. The series was shown in America as *Kimba the White Lion* and in turn, inspired Disney's 1994 film *The Lion King*, closing the circle of influence.

What made Tezuka so important was that he pushed the manga medium forward, as he worked in practically every genre feasible, from science-fiction, historical fiction and horror, to fantasy and funny animals. He even created diverse manga adaptations of *Faust* (1949), *Pinocchio* (1952) and *Crime and Punishment* (1953).

In 1951, he created *Atom Taishi*, later renamed *Tetsuwan-Atom* (Astro Boy). It was the heart-rending tale of a rich business inventor whose son is killed in an accident. In an effort to bring him back, the philanthropist creates a robot version but realises his folly and abandons his creation. *Tetsuwan-Atom* then teamed up with *Professor Ochanomizu* and together they helped foster peace between humans and robots, while seeking a way to turn Astro into a real boy, in this futuristic Pinocchio tale. The character became an international icon and new animation shows are still broadcast on television all over the world, over 55 years since his creation.

Other Tezuka creations included the girls' strip *Ribon no Kishi* (Princess Knight), the western *Lemon Kid*, the science-fiction stories *Majin Garon* and *Captain Ken*, the horror tale *Vampire*, *Hinotori*, and the historical strip *Dororo*. In 1972, Tezuka started work on *Buddha*, a manga adaptation of Siddhartha's life, and he also created the equally ambitious *Adolf ni Tsugu* (Tell Adolf), an epic tale of more than 1,000 pages, about World War II and beyond.

Tezuka often stated that manga was his wife, and animation was his mistress, and he straddled these two media with equal vigour and verve. Tezuka's skill on the screen was just as successful as it was on the page. He created the first animated show in Japan (*Astroboy*, 1963), and he turned many of his other manga creations into successful anime. It was Tezuka's success in both fields that led to many mangaka/directors experimenting in the two media, and Katsuhiro Otomo and Hayo Miyazaki in particular owe a huge debt to the trail blazed by Tezuka.

Tezuka died in 1989. His final creation was *Hidamari no Ki* (A Tree in the Sun), but his work has been continually in print ever since, earning him the undisputed title of 'God of Japanese Comics'. Like Jack Kirby in America, Tezuka was prolific, producing 160,000 pages of comic art in his life. In 1994, his home city of Takarazuka inaugurated the *Osamu Tezuka Museum of Comic Art*. The impact he has had on Japanese comics is almost impossible to exaggerate. Without Tezuka, manga certainly wouldn't have become the dominant force in global comics that it is today. That's not speculation, it's a fact.

Above: A cover from perhaps Tezuka's most celebrated creation, *Tetsuwan-Atom*.
© *Tezuka Productions*

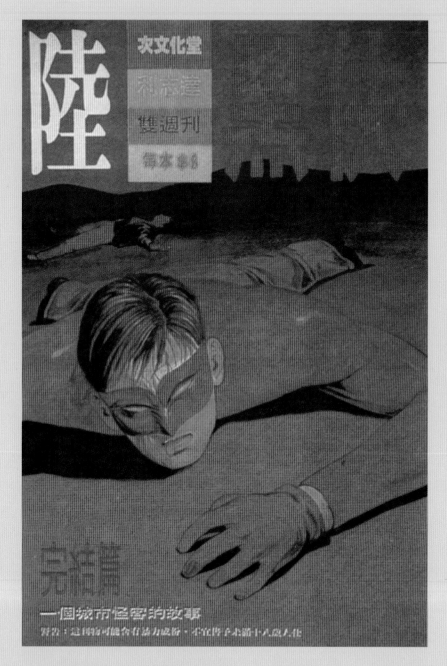

Above: *Black Mask* by Hong Kong's Pang Chi-ming and Li Chi-tat. This martial arts vigilante was turned into a popular film starring Jet Li in 1996.
© *Pang Chi-ming and Li Chi-tat*

4

CROUCHING ARTISTS, HIDDEN COMICS

Japan dominates the West's view of Far Eastern comics, but that is only half the story. The fine line and brush strokes of the other islands and continental Southeast Asia differ from those of Japan, both artistically and thematically.

Above: Chinese communism was heavily criticized in the excellent 1955 manhua *Cry for the Death of a Crazy Man*. Written and drawn by Lui Yu-tin it explored the internal power struggles of the Communist Party. Most of Lui's propaganda was published by Asia Press Ltd, a US-backed company.
© *Lui Yu-tin*

Japanese manga are read all over Asia, but until recently many of the copies sold in other countries were pirated versions. However, Asian economies are increasingly developing systems for licensing translated editions from the Japanese publishers. The percentage of pirated manga has fallen to about 10% in Taiwan and Hong Kong, but in some countries, such as Indonesia, pirate editions still account for 80% of all manga publications.

Many opportunists quickly print pirate editions before the official licensed version is published, while others have found a new market in publishing comics that are aimed at 'mature readers'. Most of the pirated manga in Thailand are adult and gay comics, and because of their salacious content, they have provoked controversy and public concern, tarnishing all Thai comics with the same brush and unfairly giving them a poor reputation.

PULP PIRATE PROBLEM

This has concerned the general manager of Tomorrow Comix, Rop Ponchamni, who worries that the government, "will become too serious and exercise more control over all kinds of comics. Therefore, [pirates] can cause a lot of damage to the market both directly and indirectly."

The earliest traditional Thai comic book publishers included Nation, Siam Inter Comics and Bongkoch, who published a variety of titles including popular humour comics like *Kai Hua Raw* (*Selling Laughter*), *Seu Hua Raw* (*Buying Laughter*) and *Mahasanuk* (*Super Fun*). They often featured the comedy of marital tension, similar to the UK's classic *Andy Capp* newspaper strip with wives angrily wielding their sark (a large pestle) just as Capp's wife, Flo, brandishes her rolling pin when he comes back from the pub drunk.

Yet it was the explosion in Japanese manga that helped boost the Thai comic industry. Manga comics had always been on Thai newsstands, but they really took off in huge numbers in the early 1990s. Competition is fierce amongst Thai comics, retailing for 5 baht (12¢/6p), while the more dominant, and lucrative, imported Japanese manga – aimed at rich middle class children – sell for around 35 baht

Right: A Pirate version of *Batman*, from 1962's *Flying Black Batman* by Ho Yat-Kwan. Many American superheroes were used in this way, without permission, including *Superman* and *Spider-Man*.
© *Ho Yat-Kwan*

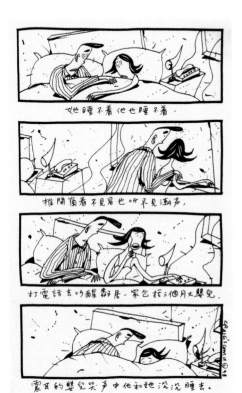

她睡不着他也睡不着

推開窗看不見屋也听不見潮声

打電話去吵醒鄰居一家包括三個月大嬰兒

震耳的嬰兒哭声中他和她沈沈睡去

Above: Hong Kong cartoonist Craig Au Yeung also works as a DJ, radio producer and image director for local pop artists. He has also published nine books and edits the impressive comics quarterly, *Cockroach*, which features the work of comics artists from Hong Kong, Taiwan and mainland China.
© *Craig Au Yeung*

(89¢/48p). Generally, Thai trends follow those of Japan, with popular titles including, *Detective Conan*, *GTO*, *Love HINA* and *BERSERK*.

In 2000, two new comic publishers, Burapat Comics and Tomorrow Comix, entered the market. Burapat Comics successfully imported titles from Hong Kong, Korea and Japan, while Tomorrow Comix started printing homegrown Thai comics, before licensing manga as well. This new wave of recent Thai comics has, unsurprisingly, a strong manga influence and they are seen as fashion accessories, with around 35 - 50 titles on sale per week. The majority of comic readers still want to read as many as they can, so they rent them first and only buy only the best. Despite the libraries, the comic industry in Thailand now generates more than 3 billion baht ($79,000/£42,000) per year, a high amount by Thai standards.

BOY LOVE IN BANGKOK

However, not everything is a bed of roses. A 1997 survey discovered that 47% of parents thought comic book material inappropriate for children, and several Thai children's organizations have even embarked on public crusades against Japanese comics, missing the point that the majority of the titles are aimed at adults. Citing images of violence and premarital sex, some Thais declared many comics unsuitable for youth and argued that they could lead to unacceptable and dangerous behaviour (just like Dr Frederick Wertham did in America in the 1950s). Articles and letters condemning Japanese comics appeared in the national newspapers. Then, in 2001, a big scare exploded over Japanese 'boy-love' comics, (known as shonen ai in their homeland). These homoerotic love stories focussed on the everyday lives of gay men as they sought romance while being discriminated against by society.

Like much of Japanese manga, the boy-love genre contained explicit kissing, oral sex and intercourse. In Thailand, more than 80% of boy-love readers are teenage girls and women in their early 20s, while the rest are homosexual. Girls in their teens are particularly interested because they are keen to see love scenes in cartoon books, but are too embarrassed to purchase comics about boys and girls, so they buy unthreatening boy-love comics instead.

Television reports claimed the comics were a, "bad Japanese influence", while one newspaper reported, "Most of the boy-love cartoons are not copyrighted, as publishers fear being arrested over their sensitive content, according to one publisher who requested anonymity." In reality, this is probably because the majority are illegally pirated from Japan. Business is good however, with comic shops selling between 30 and 50 boy-love comics a day. Like most scares, it eventually died down and Thai comics carried on regardless.

It's hard to imagine boy-love comics taking off in neighbouring Islamic Indonesia, but other manga is popular there. Jakarta-based *Animonster* magazine covered comics and animation and reprinted information and strips from Japan via the Internet. This was pirating out of necessity, rather than malice, as the editors would have loved to contact the Japanese publishers to license strips, but simply didn't know how.

Ignoring imported manga, many indigenous Indonesian comic book heroes often suffer some kind of physical handicap, with characters such as a blind swordsman (similar to Marvel's *Daredevil*), a young man who is mute when awake but tough in his sleep, and a hideous boy with a good heart learning martial arts. Similar to Japan's rental comics, many titles had erotic and/or surprisingly violent scenes, including some verging on rape, aimed at adult readers.

INDONESIAN COMIC LIBRARIES

Indonesian comic books were mostly loaned out from rental libraries called Taman Bacaans, which stocked 50-page serials. Many of the earliest Indonesian rental comics first appeared in the 1950s,

as in the Philippines, but suffered competition from American comic imports on the newsstands, and so the libraries had all but disappeared by the 1980s.

Following the resignation of Indonesia's President Suharto in May 1998, there was a more liberal attitude towards the country's press and publishing companies. As a result, one trend that emerged was that comic books with political themes began to sell very well and so publishers began releasing satirical and historical titles based on famous politicians, the first being Amien Rais.

MALAYSIAN MASTER CARTOONIST

Another political cartoon driving force, from nearby Malaysia, was Lat. Mohamed Nor Khalid, better known as Lat — short for bulat, or 'round' — one of the most-read and prolific cartoonists in Southeast Asia. Coming from very humble beginnings, growing up in a typical Malay village, Lat's life was simple and friendly. As a child he adapted Raja Hamzah's *Pahlawan* (*Warrior*) novels and sold the comic books to his classmates for 20 cents each.

Lat got his big break while he was still at school, aged 13, when publishers The Sinaran Brothers paid 25 Ringgit ($6.60/£3.50) for his comic strip *Tiga Sekawan* and published it in June 1964. By 1968, Lat was earning 100 ringgit

Above: Malaysian cartoonist Lat contributes his newspaper strip, *Scenes of Malaysian Life* to *New Straits Times* three times a week.
© *Lat*

Above: Sargent *Uncle Choi* and his howler monkey commandos! Even Korean simians do their bit in the war against Japan. Art by Hui Guan-man.
© *Hui Guan-man*

Below: The battlin' *Boy Scout* (aka *Siu-ming*) was launched in 1960 and succeeded in getting on the Scouting Association's nerves as the comic had Scouts fighting the Japanese. Notice the *Eagle* logo from the UK comic in the top right corner.
© *Ng Gei-ping*

($26.25/£13.85) a month from his comic strips *Pemimpin* and *Dewan Pelajar* in the *Berita Minggu* newspaper. His strip *Keluarga Si Mamat* (*Mamat's Family*) ran in *Berita Minggu* for 26 years. Lat moved to Kuala Lumpur and worked as a crime reporter for the *New Straits Times* for a while, but eventually returned to full-time cartooning in 1974. His upbringing inspired his most famous creation, *The Kampung Boy* (aka *Village Kid*), and he has played a pivotal part in championing positive family values. Lat's character went on to spawn a movie, a musical, an animation series, adverts, merchandise and even a McDonald's Kampung-burger.

In 1993, Lat created the character *Mina* for a UNESCO literacy campaign animation video, and the following year he was awarded Malaysia's honourific title, the Darjah Paduka Mahkota Perak (AKA Datuk), the equivalent of a knighthood. The influential and celebrated cartoonist still contributes three new cartoons a week in the *New Straits Times* on Mondays, Tuesdays and Saturdays, and his designs have even graced Malaysia Airways' planes.

FROM LIANHUANTUS TO MANHUA

Moving north to China, it's easy to see that Asia's most populous country has a rich comic history. For the first half of the 20th Century, Shanghai's lianhuantus were Hong Kong's main source of sequential art. These earlier comic prototypes consisted of an horizontal book with a single large panel on each page. The text usually appeared either as a caption along the top or as a speech bubble, similar to a political cartoon. This eventually evolved into a single page with four squares, depicting sequential events. Each of these pages had a title, usually consisting of four words (the standard number for a phrase in Chinese) explaining the situation. The most popular genre was wu-shu, or martial arts. After Mao's communists took over the Chinese mainland in 1949, communications between the two British colonies grew thin and Hong Kong began to develop its own titles. Initially, these looked like Singapore's lianhuantus, being horizontal in format and recounting Chinese myths and legends.

HONG KONG COMICS FOR ALL

As Hong Kong's manhuas, or comics, industry developed in the 1950s, however, the subject matters became more diverse. The economy was struggling to get back on its feet and the manhuas from the early days reflected the harsh reality of everyday life. There were comics for everybody – the re-telling of myths for the boys, comics on clothes and dressing-up for the girls and social/political comics for the adults. They all aimed to get an instantaneous message across, or to preach a moral to the

Above: Funky fashions in the girls' comic *13-Dot Cartoon* by Lee Wai-Chun. Launched in 1966, it was the first comic created by, and specifically for, a female readership. The heroine, *Miss Thirteen Dot*, was a female version of *Richie Rich*, as she was a millionnaire's daughter.
© Lee Wai-Chun

Left: Master Yidung gives *Chou Lee* the finger in the Hong Kong manhua, *The Legendary Couple* by Tony Wong.
© *JD Global IP Rights Ltd*

Below: Martial arts madness with the massively popular humour comic, *Old Master Q*. The manhua has been turned into numerous live-action and animated films since its creation in 1964.
© *Wong Chak*

readership, and so were often very short and simplistic.

In 1958, Hui Guan-man created one of HK's favourite action manhua, *Uncle Choi*. Originally played for laughs, *Choi* grew more serious when became a war hero fighting the Japanese, a Chinese *Sgt Rock* or *Captain Hurricane*. The title became a huge success and was the best-selling comic book for years. It broke the mould in terms of format and the way it dealt with real-world issues. As the spy genre took off in the 1960s, *Choi* followed, swapping his machine guns for hi-tech gadgets. Yet, while the change worked for *Sgt Nick Fury* in America's Marvel Comics, it wasn't a popular one for *Choi* and sales began to wane. The title was finally cancelled in the mid-1970s, but only after an impressive run of almost 17 years.

Another war comic that followed *Uncle Choi*'s lead was *Boy Scout* (1960) by Ng Gei-Ping. The series saw *Siu-ming* and *Siu Sam-ji*, boy scouts with attitude, kicking Japanese butt as they fought to drive them from China. Unfortunately, it didn't go down well with Baden-Powell's scouting organization, and they eventually succeeded in forcing the writer to change the comic's title to *Siu-Ming*.

Humour was equally as important to the manhuas as fighting, and in 1964, creator Wong Chak unleashed *Old Master Q* onto the world. The goofy adventures of this wise man and his two side kicks, *Big Potato* and *Mr Chun*, instantly captured Chinese readers' hearts and spawned endless animated and live-action films. Wong Chak was inspired by Ye Qian-yu's character, *Mr Wang*, who appeared in the *Shanghai Sketch* anthology in 1928. Wong obviously hit the right tone, as *Old Master Q* remains in print over 40 years later.

While Wong Chak was the most popular humour comic creator, the undisputed king of 1970s' action manhua was another Wong, Wong Yuk-long. He burst onto the scene in 1968 with *Little Vagabond*, the adventures of a drunken Chinese god. Then, in 1970, he released what would become one of HK's most controversial comic series, *Siu Lau-man* (the misleadingly titled *Little Rascals*). Drawn in a cutesy sub-manga style, it was actually a savage and brutal examination of street life and gang culture in Hong Kong's tenements. It told the tale of two brothers who fought the gangs to bring justice to the weak. Growing up in the harsh housing projects himself, these were the kind of comics that inspired film director John Woo, who grew up reading them. The comic had a huge following, but its graphic violence caused the authorities concern, and in 1975, they passed the Indecent Publication Law. Wong switched the name to *Lung Fu Mun* (*Oriental Heroes*), toned down the violence and adapted his art into a more realistic style in

Above: Wong Yuk-long's *Little Rascals* get up to the sort of hi-jinx that saw them almost banned in Hong Kong in 1975. Wong toned down the graphic violence.
© *Wong Yuk-long*

the mid-1980s, following fellow artist Ma Wing-shing's lead. This seemed to appease the powers that be.

A contemporary of Wong's was creator/publisher Seung-gun Siubo, who worked on *Lee Siu-lung* (Bruce Lee's Chinese name), *Hei Bo* and *Ching Bo*. In the 1980s, Seung-gun and Wong joined forces in the latter's company, Jademan Comics, which saw staggering success in the decade's big comic boom. Wong continued publishing *Oriental Heroes* along with *The Chinese Hero* (1983), *Drunken Master* (1982) and *King Manhua Weekly* (1982). Just as the 1980s boomed for comic books however, the 1990s brought a bust, in Hong Kong as in America. In 1991, Wong's Jademan comic empire was failing and he desperately tried to keep the company afloat, but was eventually convicted of fraud and sent to jail for a hefty two years. Undaunted, he launched a new company, Jade Dynasty, in 1993 and continued writing and drawing.

MARTIAL ARTS MANHUA

In recent years, Hong Kong comics have been revitalized thanks to the resurgence of historical kung fu comic books such as Tony Wong's *The Legendary Couple*, and the best-selling *Storm Riders* by Ma Wing-shing. The latter's adaptation of the blockbuster kung fu novel, *Heaven Sword & Dragon Sabre* — written by Louis Cha — tells the story of

WuJi Chang's bid to reunite China against the invading Mongol hordes, using the eponymous swords. Much of modern Chinese manhuas contain beautifully detailed, finely feathered artwork, which looks as if it's been painted with a single-bristle brush. This style, which differentiates them from most manga, harkens back to more traditional Chinese classical painting and was pioneered by Ma Wing-shing as early as 1978.

HK CINEMA AND COMICS COMBINE

Many of these comics also owe much to Chinese cinema, and the two have had a healthy symbiotic relationship for decades, with manhua being influenced by classic kung fu films such as *Chinese Ghost Story*, *The Golden Harvest* and Shaw Bros studios' output. Nowhere is this more obvious than in writer Du Lu Wang and artist Andy Seto's epic *Wu Ho Cang Long*, better known as *Crouching Tiger, Hidden Dragon*. Originally published as part of the *Crane/Iron* pentalogy, the saga was written by noted kung fu novelist Du Lu Wang, who died in 1977. Despite the success of the comic book adaptations of the first three novels, Seto's version of the fourth novel was slated, so he re-watched the film, gaining inspiration on how to depict the fight scenes. Telling the tangled love story of two kung fu warriors, Shu Lien and Li Mu Bai, *Crouching Tiger...*

Above: More cheeky shenanighans with those *Little Rascals* (*Siu Lau-man*). The main character, *Wong Siu-fu*, dispenses some ghetto justice with a chain.
© *Wong Yuk-long*

was a massive hit in Hong Kong, and in 2000, it broke through to international audiences when it was adapted by director Ang Lee into a multi-Oscar winning film.

Another movie adaptation Andy Seto drew was of Stephen Chow's 2001 cult classic film, *Shaolin Soccer*. In this humorous homage to martial arts movies, a young kung fu adept realizes that the sport may be the way to spread the Shaolin temple teachings. A young Andy Seto got his start in manhua when he joined Freeman Publications in 1989 and created *Sword Kill* followed by *Gambling Saint*. During 1993, he drew his first big hit series, *Cyber Weapons Z*, with writer Chris Lau. It was adapted into an animation series and launched him as a star of Hong Kong comics. In 1997, he adapted the novel, *Story of the Tao*, and set up his Neo Company. Seto and Neo Company acquired the copyrights to illustrate *The King of Fighters Z* and *Saint Legend*, both of which were well received.

Seto was originally inspired by Japanese manga, in particular the creator of *Venus War*, "Yasuhiko Yoshikazu is my favourite and most respected teacher. He taught me the basics of comic making, so he has the most influence on me in all aspects," explained the Chinese artist. "When I first started working as a comic artist, I had never thought about foreign fans. When French and American audiences accepted *King of Fighters Z* and *Crouching Tiger & Hidden Dragon*, it

was a great encouragement, and at the same time I felt blessed that my works were being published in other languages," said the modest Seto.

Elsewhere in the Chinese-speaking world, comic books haven't been quite as successful. Singapore is a relative newcomer to the world of panels as most Singaporeans had previously generally disparaged the medium. Then in 1990, Chuang Yi Publishing launched a mission to expose the local populace to comics, with flagship titles including translated manga like *Dragonball*, *Slam Dunk* and *Tian Long Ba Bu*. Another publisher, Asiapac Books, took the more traditional route and released a range of titles mostly based on classic stories set in China's past, including *Return of the Condor Heroes*, *Romance of the Three Kingdoms* and *The Water Margin*. Constantly seeking to gain the biggest audience share, and with an eye on the foreign markets, both companies publish simultaneously in Mandarin and English.

NOT COMICS OR COMIX BUT KOMIKS

The Philippines is unique in Asia regarding its comics' influences. Whereas the rest of region succumbed to the mighty manga in some form or other, the archipelago state was in the thrall of Spanish and American influences, thanks to years of colonialism and occupation. Before Filipino komiks

Above: Actors Chow Yun Fat and Andy Lau on the cover of the manhua adaptation of the 1989 Hong Kong action flick, *God of Gamblers*. The film kicked off a sub-genre of movies and comics including, *Youth God of Gamblers* and *The Unbeatable Con Man*.
© Sze-to Glim-kiu, Wing Yan, Lau Ding-gin and Man Dik

Left: *Nobela Klasiks* specializes in comic adaptations of popular novels and prose books. Romantic themes are particularly popular in The Phillipines.
© *GASI Publications*

Below: *Pogi,* ran *Marissa,* a typical 'tart with a heart' strip in 1984.
© *Ace Publications Inc*

really took off, the only comic strip of note was Tony Velasquez's 1932 *Kenkoy* (see the creator feature). Regarded as the founding father of Filipino sequential art, Velasquez set up numerous companies and helped launch the careers of many creators. In the post-World War II years, komiks began appearing, modelled after American comic books discarded by the GIs. In 1946, the first big anthology, *Halakhak Komiks*, was launched featuring many creators who'd later become cartooning legends, including Francisco Reyes, Larry Alcala, Francisco Coching and many others. While the comic only lasted 10 issues, it was the snowball that started an avalanche. The following year, publisher Don Ramon Roces and Tony Velasquez launched their komik publishing company, Ace Publications. The first titles included *Pilipino Komiks* – which sold 10,000 copies fortnightly – followed by *Tagalog Klassiks*, reprints of the US *Classics Illustrated* (1949), *Hiwaga Komiks* (1950) and *Espesyal Komiks* (1952).

Velasquez left Ace in 1962 and set up Graphic Arts Service with his brother Damy. Together they launched what would become household names like *Aliwan Komiks*, *Pinoy Komiks*, *Holiday Komiks*, *Teens Weekly* and *Pinoy Klasiks*. Early artists who made a name for themselves included Mars Ravelo, Virgilio Redondo and Nestor Redondo. Mars Ravelo helped 'Filipinize' *Tagalog Klassiks* with his story *Roberta*, the first locally

created tale to be published in the title. It was made into a box-office smash, as were many of the creator's komiks, and his adventure and fantasy stories set the benchmark for the industry. He went on to launch his own company RAR Publishing House, in 1970. RAR's originality lay not only in the quality of its titles (such as *Ravelo Komiks*, *Kampeon Komiks* and *18 Magazine*), but also in their format, which Ravelo changed from standard US comic size to the *TIME* magazine shape more associated with British comics. RAR continued to be a key player until economic depression and Ravelo's illness forced the business to fold in 1983. As compensation, the following year Ravelo received a lifetime achievement award, not only from the comic industry, but also from the film industry, highlighting the breadth of the creator's influence.

The industry flourished and by the 1970s, almost half of all Filipino movies were based on komiks, which had become the most-read medium in the country. The sheer diversity of genres in the Filipino industry have included everything from fantasy, adventure, humour, science-fiction and jungle adventures (in the vein of *Tarzan*).

ROMANTIC READERS

As the highest proportion of readers are aged 20 to 29, and because female readers

Above: Generally considered the first 'proper' Filipino comic book, *Halakhak* (Laughter) *Komiks*. The title ran a mix of humorous and adventure strips, like *Bernardo Carpio*.
© *Halakhak Komiks*

exceeded male readers by 7%, it should be no surprise that romance komiks are incredibly popular. Titles like *Sweetheart*, *Aliwan* and *Love Story Illustrated* all recount tragic tales of romantic triangles, damsels in distress and unrequited love, with familiar Western figures such as Cinderella and slightly less kid-friendly 'tarts with hearts'.

KOMIK CREATORS GAGGED

Kitchen sink dramas and political satire were also introduced in comics until 21 September 1972, when President Marcos declared martial law (for the next nine years). All mass media was banned, but komiks were allowed to continue after the industry had set up a self-regulating code that promised no criticism of the government or military, no explicit sex scenes and little or no crime stories. Social issues like poverty and social unrest disappeared overnight and were replaced with antiseptic, government-approved, soulless tales of 'family values'. Despite this repression of creative freedom, komiks eventually got back on track after Marcos was deposed in 1986.

By 1999, there were 89 different komik titles on the newsstands, but as with the rest of the world, Filipino sequential art has had to compete with film and computer games, and today there remain about 50 titles with readers spending an average of

two million pesos ($35,541/£19,754) a week on komiks. A full 40% of Filipinos (17.6 million) read a comic every day, while only 500,000 (about 1%) read a daily newspaper. Adults read comics with no sense of embarrassment, as being seen to be literate is a mark of distinction, and while the best-selling US titles sell around three million copies a year in America, the number one comic in the Philippines sells 1.5 million copies each month.

Comics are so ubiquitous that the Philtranco bus company even produced an on-board publication, the *Biyaheng Pinoy Komiks-Magasin* in 1999. This 52-page colour monthly was distributed free to over 300,000 passengers. The University of the Philippines/ Philippine General Hospital also created its own comic book, *The Rayuma Komiks*, to help explain medical procedures and terms to patients.

ARTIST EXODUS

In the 1970s, Filipino komiks suffered a 'brain drain' as many well-established artists looked to America to expand their creative horizons, their financial incomes and as a way of escaping the repressive Marcos regime. Established names like Tony Zuñiga, Nestor Redondo, Alex Niño and Alfred Alcala became household names in the USA as they all either emigrated or started working for the big publishers, like

Below: *Tagalog Klasiks Illustrated* #2 (1949). This title was the third comic series to be published in The Philippines.
© Ace Publications Inc

Marvel, DC and Warren, and creating a school of Filipino comics art within the US comics community.

The Filipino/American comic book connection continues today, "I've found myself sort of the bridge between that initial wave of Filipino artists," said US-based artist Rafael Kayanan, "and the next wave which came onto the scene during the late Eighties and Nineties, artists like Whilce Portacio (who set up Image comics with Korean Jim Lee), Gerry Alanguilan, Lenil Yu and others established a separate look to the earlier wave. They had dynamic layouts and the ink work had more of an angular look to it. They have quite a huge following to their work from east and west." Kayanan has worked on many leading titles such as *Spider-Man* and *Conan* for Dark Horse.

KOREA: LAND OF THE MANHWA

While Filipino komiks were influenced by American titles, modern Korean manhwa are closer to Japanese manga than any other Asian country's output. Japan's close proximity to Korea and its annexation of the country from 1910 to 1945 have left an indelible influence on Seoul's comic-book publishers. However, unlike manga, manhwa are actually read in the Western way, from left to right. The titles tend to be more story-led, like the Chinese manhua, than the Japanese character-led manga.

Despite the heavy cultural influence of Japan, the importation of all Nipponese movies, music and comics had actually been technically illegal until 1998 because of Korean animosity over the occupation.

Born in 1912, Kim Yong-hwan was one of the best Korean comics artists of the 1940s and 1950s. He made his debut in Japan under the name Gita Koji, but returned to Korea after the liberation in 1945. He started out working for the *Seoul Times*, an English-language newspaper, and created *Kojubu Samgukji*, who became the first popular Korean comic character. Kim Yong-hwan went on to found *Manhwa Haengjin*, the first real Korean comic book, in 1948. During the Korean War, the writer/artist produced the hard-hitting *The Soldier Todori*, which told the story of South Korean soldiers fighting the communist North. Kim finally passed away in 1998. One of Kim's contemporaries, Im Chang, was also born in Korea and left to study art in Japan. He also returned to Korea after the liberation, where he became a teacher at several schools. He moved to Seoul in 1955, where he began illustrating and drawing comics for *Sintaeyang* magazine. He started the daily strip about a robot, *Machistae*, in 1964 for the children's newspaper *Sonyeon Hanguk Ilbo*, and devoted himself to creating juvenile comics meant for distribution through libraries. His most famous creation was *Taengi*, and he produced several

Above: Mars Ravelo and Nestor Redondo's popular superheroine *Dana*.
©Mars Ravelo and Nestor Redondo

Below: *Espesyal Komiks* #1 (1952).
© Ace Publications Inc

collections from the late 1960s. Im Chang died unexpectedly in 1982 at the age of 59.

Ko Woo-young made his manhwa debut in 1954, and went on to create titles such as *Im Keokjeong*, *Suhoji*, *Iljimae* and *Samkukji*. His witty style and classic historical themes ensured that he grew to become one of Korea's leading comic artists, alongside newspaper cartoonist Park Bong-seong. Park was born in Korea in 1949 and broke into comics 10 years after Ko. Park's creation, *A Man Called God*, appeared in the *Daily Sports* newspaper, and follow-up titles like *Son of God* and *Samgukji of Park Bong-seong* were equally successful.

A FEMININE TOUCH

Korea has an almost unsurpassed amount of women working in comics. Almost half of the manhwa creators working today are female, bringing a unparalleled perspective to what is generally regarded as a male-dominated medium in the rest of the world. An important figure in the development of female manhwa was Hwang Mi-na, who started her career aged 19 in 1980 with *The Blue Star of Ionie* (published in the anthology *Sonyeo Sidae*). She helped push the boundaries for female creators and contributed to the expansion of women's and girls' comics in Korea with several romance titles. Five years later, she founded *Nine* magazine, a literary comics magazine.

Unlike many other female artists, Hwang Mi-na often used Korea itself as the setting of her stories.

Kim Jin was another female comic artist who achieved huge success, proving that female Korean comic artists can easily hold their own against their male counterparts. She made her debut in *Yeogo Shidae* magazine in 1983, and created several feminine series including *The Gods and the Twilight* and *Certain Birds Fly Towards the South Before the Winter Comes*. She won 1997's Great Prize for Korea Cartoon Publishing for *The Name of the Forest*. Her historical fantasy-epic *Barameui Nara* (*The Land of the Wind*) began in 1991 and has reached an impressive 17+ volumes. Mixing myth with Korean history, Kim created a massive hit which was adapted into a popular online game, *Genesis Jin*. Kim was also a professor in the Social Education School of Myoungji University.

Similar to Japan and Thailand, private reading libraries, known as Manhwabangs, are now popping up all over South Korea. These libraries are open 24 hours, and charge customers by the hour to come in and read comics. And there are many to read. In 2002, over 9,000 different comic titles were published, 40% of them Korean.

MANHWA GOES GLOBAL

South Korea is maturing along the lines of Chinese manhua and is fast on the heels of Japanese manga. With a $2.3 million (£1.3 million) publishing deal brokered at the 2004 San Diego Comic Con, Korean comics are set to explode onto the US market. Indeed, the biggest manga publisher outside of Japan, the American Tokyopop, has already published many Korean artists' work, possibly without Western fans even realizing the strips don't come from Japan. Series like *King Hell* by Kim Jae-Hwan and Ra In-Soo, and the gothic vampire tale *Model* by Lee So-Young are both Korean, but could easily be mistaken for manga.

KOREAN ARTIST MAKES GOOD

Like the Filipinos, Koreans are making a name for themselves by working for the big American publishers. One of the most famous is Jim Lee. Born in South Korea in 1964, Lee went to America to study. He graduated from Princeton University with a degree in medicine, but realized his true calling was comics (just like Osamu Tezku, and many other comic creators – medicine's loss is comic books' gain). Lee began working on Marvel's *Alpha Flight* in 1986, and achieved international stardom with his artwork on their flagship title *X-Men*. He left Marvel in 1992 to co-found the independent Image Comics with fellow creators Todd McFarlane and Rob Liefeld. Lee's imprint at Image, WildStorm Productions, launched several successful titles including

Left, opposite page: Despite the image and the heading "Hindi Porn", *King* was described on the cover by the publishers, Atlas, as "Wholesome Family Reading Material."
© *Atlas Publishing Corporation*

Below: *Hiwaga Komiks* specialized in mystery and horror stories, such as the classic *Darna* and *Roberta* by Mars Ravelo. The comic anthology was published twice a week. This is the first issue from 1950.
© *Ace Publications Inc*

Right, opposite page: The brutal martial arts epic, *Dangu* by Joong Ki Park, obviously inspired by the manga artist Goseki Kojima. © *Joong Ki Park*

Above and Right: A propaganda comic published by NKChosen in North Korea. In it, two communist boys foil a couple of capitalistic thieves. © *NK Chosen*

Wild C.A.T.S., *Stormwatch*, *Deathblow* and *GEN13*. He then successfully transferred the whole imprint over to Marvel's competitors DC, where he remains as editorial director. Ironically, Lee is now probably more famous for his comics work in his adopted country than back in Korea.

Of course this doesn't even account for the material produced behind the Iron Screen in North Korea. Most of the comics produced there are typically weighed down with communist propaganda, more ideology than entertainment.

All around South East Asia, comics are thriving in one form or another and even in those isolated states such as North Korea and the slightly more open Vietnam, there is a market for sequential art.

VIETNAM VETERANS

While there are many Vietnamese cartoonists working today, there are few actually living in the country, as many fled during or after the bitter war that lasted between 1957 and 1975. Many went to France, which was the original colonial ruler before America became involved. One of those artists was Pham Minh Son, whose nom de plume is Son or Sonk. He founded a comics magazine in his native Vietnam before becoming an industrial designer. When he moved to France in 1973, he found work in advertising illustration. He

met writer Didier Convard in 1981, and together they produced *Songe et les Forges de la Guerre* (1985) and *A L'Ombre des Dieux* (1986). Son also drew *Croc Blanc* with scripts by Jean Ollivier for French publishers, Hachette. Other albums Son has drawn include *Margot*, *L'Enfant Bleue* and *Phénix et la Dragon*, both of which were created in the early 1990s.

In 1990, Son began the series *Maître Chang* with Robert Genin on script duty. The story was serialized in *Hello Bédé* magazine. Another Vietnamese creator is Kohoa Vinh, AKA Vink. Born in 1950, he originally worked as a journalist in Saigon, but moved to Belgium in 1969, where he took classes in medicine (like Peter Madsen, Jim Lee and Osamu Tezuka). In 1975, he changed course once more and studied fine art in Liège.

Vink made his professional comics debut in *Tintin* in 1979 with *Contes et Légendes du Vietnam*. The short stories were collected in the 1983 album *Derrière la Haie de Bambous*. Vink also created *Pays de Liège*, *Vie d'un Église* with writer Michel Dusart as well as the humorous *Deux Hommes dans la Neige* in *Vers l'Avenir*. For the relaunched *Charlie Mensuel* magazine, Vink wrote and drew a series set in ancient China, *Le Moine Fou*. In 2000, he took on art chores on *Les Voyages d'He Pao*, and in 2003, he created the excellent *Le Passager*.

A Vietnamese refugee cartoonist who didn't flee to France was Tak-Thach Bui. Instead he headed for Canada.

Understandably, as Bui describes that he grew up, "in an environment of political chaos, guerrilla terrorism and countless military coups."

He found escape in drawing cartoons and collecting manga from Japan and bande dessinée from France. In 1967, he went to the United States on a high-school student scholarship and spent a year with an American family. The following year, he moved to Canada. Bui studied at the New School of Art in Toronto and began his professional cartoon career in 1973. He founded the Artattack Studio in Toronto, and produces the strip *PC and Pixel*. The strip features *PC Odata*, who works as a freelance consultant from home, with his Net-surfing cat, *Pixel*.

COMICS FROM THE KILLING FIELDS

Tragically, Cambodia is one of the rare exceptions where comics never had a chance to evolve, as the Khmer Rouge succedded in practically wiping out all forms of artistic expression during their reign of terror. One artist who managed to escape was Phoussera Ing (also known as Séra). Born in Phnom Penh, he fled the bloody communist revolution to France, with his mother in 1975. He continued to study art, and his first short story was published in *Circus* in 1979. He wrote and drew the strip *La Vespasienne* in 1993, for the manga

Below: *Model* by Lee So-Young is just one of the many manhwa being translated for eager Western readers. The gothic horror-romance owes much to the Japanese shonen ai (boy-love) romantic manga art style.
© *Lee So-Young*

Below: This beautiful drawing from Korea illustrates one of the very subtle differences between Japanese manga and Korean manhwa. While the face and eyes are exaggerated in a cartoon style, the figure is more realistic and in proportion. In truth, it is very hard to distinguish between the countries' art styles as there has been so much cultural cross-pollination over the decades.
© *Korea Culture & Content Agency (KOCCA)*

anthology *Morning*. In 1995, he drew *Retour de Soleil* and created *Impasse et Rouge*, about a child-soldier during the Cambodian war.

That same year saw Séra return to his homeland for the first time in 20 years. Afterwards, he created two strips for *P.L.G.* and contributed to the anthology album *Alfred Hitchcock*. He then began his series *HKO* in *À Suivre* magazine in 1997.

As comics continue to grow in credibility and popularity, more and more Asian artists are sure to make their presence felt on the international stage.

Left: A page from Park So Hee's Korean historical drama, *The Palace.*
© Park, So Hee

TONY VELASQUEZ

TONY VELASQUEZ

Above: A portrait of Tony Velasquez as a young man.
© Estate of Tony Velasquez

Right, opposite page: A classic Kenkoy strip, which went colour after a year in print. © Estate of Tony Velasquez

Left: Pocket-sized *Kenkoy Komiks* #9 (1959). © Estate of Tony Velasquez

Just like his peers Anant Pai in India and Osamu Tezuka in Japan, it's hard to imagine Filipino Komiks without Antonio S Velasquez.

Born in Pace, Manila on 29 October 1910, Velasquez got into publishing while still at high school, working part-time at Ramon Roces Publications. The 'Father of Tagalog Komiks' got his big break by default, after working as a photo-engraver and then as an assistant artist on *Liwayway* magazine. In the ad department, Romualdo Ramos wanted to create a comics supplement, but head artist Procopio Borromeo was too busy so the job fell into Velasquez's lap.

With Ramos supplying scripts and Velasquez on art chores, the duo got to work on the new strip in 1928. Their efforts were rewarded on January 11 1929, when the strip *Mga Kabalbalan ni Kenkoy* was launched in *Liwayway* magazine. The strip was so popular it had songs and poems written about it and its success inspired the creators to quickly launch another, the wonder-fully phonetically titled *Ponyang Halobaybay*. *Kenkoy* was a flashy 'wide-boy' who constantly got into scrapes while poking fun at the

modernization of The Philippines. *Ponyang* was a beautiful woman con-stantly pursued by the loveable and goofy millionaire *Nanong Pandak* (who later got his own strip). Ponyang was so stylish that outfits Velasquez created for her started fashion trends. But the winning writer/artist team came to an abrupt end when Ramos unexpectedly died in 1932 and Velasquez continued on his own. Three years after Ramos' death, Velasquez was promoted to chief advertising artist for *Liwayway*, *Graphic*, *Bannawag*, *Bisaya*, *Hiligaynon* and *Bikolnon*, and he pioneered car-toon advertising, creating character icons for numerous companies – the equivalent of one man creating Ronald McDonald, The Jolly Green Giant and countless others.

But Kenkoy remained the artist's true love, and as time passed he expanded the dude's family and sup-porting characters. Then World War II broke out and the Japanese invaded. Almost all publications were shut down except *Liwayway*, which the Japanese used to spout propaganda, including Kenkoy, who became a spokes-cartoon for their health drive.

Velasquez was even ordered to create a new strip, the *Kalibapi Family*, that depicted life in the Philippines under a 'benevolent' Japanese occupation.

After the Americans liberated the country in 1945, Tony and his brother Damy, set up the Velasquez Advertising Agency. The following year, Jamie Lucas launched the anthology *Halakhak Komiks*, generally considered the first real Filipino comic book. However, Velasquez had previously published *Album Ng Kabalbalan ni Kenkoy*, a collection of *Kenkoy* strips, in 1934.

In 1947, Velasquez's old boss, Don Ramon Roces, made the artist an offer he couldn't refuse and helped set up the Komik company, Ace Publications. Their first title, *Philipino Komiks*, launched in June 1947, was an instant hit. Velasquez went onto launch a sister company, Graphic Arts Service, which created household names like *Aliwan Komiks* and *Pinoy Klasiks*. After 44 years in comics, Velasquez finally retired as general manager of Graphic Arts in 1972. Sadly, Tony Velasquez died in 1997, but the creator/editor/publisher's legacy lives on. When Filipino komiks historian Dennis Villegas discovered a rare, pristine copy of *Album Ng Kabalbalan ni Kenkoy*, he had 1,200 facsimiles reprinted in 2004, with the approval of Velasquez's widow.

Above: A gorgeous panel from the first book, *Triple Jeu*, in the series *Vénézia* written by Lewis Trondheim with beautiful artwork by Fabrice Palme. Trondheim and Palme also created the series *Le Roi Catastrophe* for Delcourt.
© *Lewis Trondheim, Fabrice Palme, Dargaud*

5

THE NINTH ART

Above: *La Mouche*, the charming wordless strip created by modern master, Lewis Trondheim.
© *Seuil, Lewis Trondheim*

Right, opposite page: A detail of a panel from *Le Jeune Albert* by the late Yves Chaland. Chaland was a master of the style of artwork called La Ligne Claire, and *Jeune Albert* was something of a masterpiece, detailing the misadventures of a young Belgian boy growing up in post-war Brussels.
© *Les Humanoïdes Associés, Yves Chaland*

Comics respected as a highly regarded and viable art form contributing to a country's culture and heritage? Sounds like a myth to the English speaking world, but in France comic books have achieved the exalted status of 'The Ninth Art.'

French comics are more commonly known as bandé dessinée or BD (pronounced bay-day), which literally translates as 'drawn strip'. In terms of credibility, sophistication and diversity, France's BD are second only to Japan's manga.

Culturally, France has, in many ways, been progressively light-years ahead of America and Britain, and so it's no surprise that alongside architecture, music, painting, sculpture, poetry, dance, cinema and television, comics have become the 'Ninth Art'. They received their eloquent moniker from Claude Beylie, the leading French film critic and Sorbonne professor, who stated in 1964 that television and comics should be added to the Italian critic Ricciotto Canudo's original 1923 *Manifesto of the Seven Arts*. The French media picked up the phrase, making it stick in the public's mind, and so comics' standing in France was assured.

FRANCOPHONE FUNNIES

To be fair, the label 'French comics' is a bit misleading, as a huge portion of the greatest Francophone creators in fact came from Belgium. Yet a substantial proportion of these creators made a name for themselves working for publishers in their larger southern neighbour. The two countries' comics history is so inextricable, the term 'Franco-Belgian' is far more accurate. Even today, the comics output of both countries is completely mixed, with cross-pollination of talent happening on a scale that is seen nowhere else in the world.

The current comics scene in the Francophone countries can best be described as 'vibrant', and has been so for many years. Ever since the student riots in the 1960s, the cultural life of France particularly, has been one of fresh ideas and experimentation, and this is as true for comics as for any of the other eight art forms.

Across the board, from comics aimed at children to the most avant garde postmodern experiments, there's a spirit of exuberance and confidence in French comics that is possibly unequalled anywhere else. Cartoonists often take their time when creating, and many will take a year or more to complete a 56-page 'album', a rate that

Above: *Spirou*, the *Marsupilami* and *Spip*, *Spirou's* pet squirrel, here seen in a panel from one of André Franquin's many albums featuring the characters.
© *Dupuis, André Franquin*

makes their counterparts in the USA and Japan green with envy. This leisurely pace, combined with the sense of freedom that many creators feel even when working for mainstream publishing houses, ensures that the climate for fresh and new BD is alive and well.

A SENSE OF HISTORY

Such creative license has its roots in the way that the Francophone comics industry evolved. Unlike many countries, where mainstream comics publishing has been the often bastard child of larger, 'more serious' publishers, the comics industry in France and Belgium was, for the most part, pioneered by people who had a fondness for, and understanding of, the medium. Also, the creators rarely made assumptions about their target audience. The result was comics for children that weren't patronising and that could be read by adolescents and adults, as the material worked on many levels.

The watershed for French and Belgian comics was the 1950s. This was the time of *Pilote* in France and *Tintin* & *Spirou* in Belgium. These magazines introduced the comics-reading public to iconic characters, cartoonists as artists, editors as near-demigods and self-referential strips that bordered on metafiction. The cartoonists who launched their careers in this heady

time then went on to be international stars, and two major schools of comics style were created.

THE MARCINELLE SCHOOL

Marcinelle is a suburb of Charleroi, a large town in the southern, French-speaking half of Belgium. It's a bustling, picturesque Wallonian town. It's also the place where Jean Dupuis decided to set up his printing business. The business did well, but in 1936, Dupuis decided to boost profits by publishing a magazine for children. Nineteen year old Charles Dupuis was put in charge of the project, quite an undertaking for a young man still in his teens. However, Charles took to the project like a duck to water and started to assemble a roster of strips and creators that would produce a comic magazine of rare and sustained quality. The magazine's name was *Spirou*, and its eponymous lead strip featured the adventures of a young bellhop.

Illustrated at first by the pedestrian French cartoonist Robert Veltier (AKA Rob-Vel), the character would eventually become one of European comics' most enduring heroes. As sales started to increase, Dupuis Junior started to add more talented artists to the magazine's staff. Foremost was a cartoonist named Joseph Gillain, or Jijé. Gillain was an incredibly gifted artist and one who could command the comics form effortlessly. He could also turn his hand to realistic and cartoony strips with equal skill. After helping to create such series as *Blondin et Cirage*, he was given the job of taking over the creative reins of *Spirou*. His effect was instant and enormous: he turned the series from a simple gag-strip to a rollicking comedy adventure series. Buoyed by this, Jijé became the hot ticket at the magazine and his work piled up. In order to cope with his ever-increasing commitments, and to enable him to complete a personal project he had started (*Emmanuel*, a biography of Jesus Christ in comics form), Jijé started to look around for assistants. The men he found to help him would become some of the most famous and well-respected cartoonists ever to work in comics, and formed the basis of the so-called Marcinelle school.

Hence, cartoonists such as André Franquin, Peyo (Pierre Culliford), Eddy Paape, Will, Morris (Maurice de Bevere), Maurice Tillieux and Victor Hubinon were introduced to an unsuspecting public. *Spirou* was also blessed to have a visionary editor-in-chief in the person of Yves Delporte. His willingness to allow artists the freedom to run with ideas that many other editors would dismiss out of hand – allied with his ideas of what made great comic strips – allowed *Spirou* to flourish and become a hotbed of invention and superlative story

telling. He pioneered such innovations as 'micro-comics', small comics printed in the middle of the magazine that could be removed and folded up into mini-books, and *Le Trombone Illustré*, a supplement of *Spirou* that featured more mature stories.

Of all the cartoonists to follow on from Jijé, the most popular were Franquin, Peyo (*Les Schtrompfs* or the Smurfs) and Morris (*Lucky Luke*). Franquin, in particular, became the true heir to Jijé's throne, taking over *Spirou* from Gillain and introducing several new characters to both that strip and others he created. Possibly his most famed creations were the fantastical creature, the *Marsupilami* – later bought by Disney for some truly awful cartoons that completely missed the point of the character – and the idiot copy-boy, *Gaston Lagaffe*, who, in a brilliant metafictive twist, works for the *Spirou* comic itself where he daydreams, creates fabulous, useless inventions and thwarts the ambitions of the editor on a daily basis.

It is hard to estimate the true and lasting impact that Jijé and Franquin had on Franco-Belgian (and indeed, world) comics. Not only were their stories and characters loved by generations of children and adults, but they influenced countless cartoonists to this day. In fact, the only real rival to the Marcinelle school, in terms of its inspiration on the minds and brushes of Franco-Belgian cartoonists, was the group of artists and writers who were based in

Above: Franquin's fantastical creature, the *Marsupilami*, here seen from a 3D exhibit at the Angoulême comics festival. Photo: B. Brooks © *Marsu Productions*

Below: A panel from one of André Franquin's original pages of *Gaston Lagaffe*. This panel is reproduced at the same size as the original artwork.
© *André Franquin, Dupuis*

PFFOUH! C'EST DUR À PERCER...

Flemish Comics

Although the main comics-produc-ing part of Belgium is French speak-ing, there is a significant number of cartoonists from the Flemish, or Dutch-speaking, part of the country. Fiercely proud of their language and culture, the Flemish cartoonists have a long and accomplished place in comics history.

Some famous Flemish cartoonists include Willy Vandersteen, Marc Sleen, Bob De Moor, Kamagurka (Luc Zeebroeck), Ever Meulen and Johan De Moor (the cartoonist son of Bob De Moor).

While the Flemish cartoonists may have not had the impact that the French-speaking Belgians had, their influence on Francophone and Dutch comics is undeniable.

Right: The wonderful *La Vache* by Stephen Desberg and the Flemish cartoonist (and son of *Tintin* collaborator, Bob De Moor), Johan De Moor. © *Stephen Desberg, Johan De Moor, Casterman*

the Belgian capital, Brussels, and who worked for the main rival to *Spirou: Tintin* magazine.

THE BRUXELLES SCHOOL AND 'LA LIGNE CLAIRE'

The most famous member of the Bruxelles school was also its founder, and in fact probably the most famous Belgian ever: Hergé. By the time that Hergé met Raymond Leblanc, a Belgian publisher, in 1946 to discuss the formation of a new publishing venture, he had been working on his famous creation *Tintin* for a number of years. The proposition that Leblanc put to the cartoonist was an exciting one: the creation of a new magazine that would not only feature the serialized adventures of the boy reporter and his entourage, but would also take his name as its title. Thus Leblanc's publishing house, Lombard – and its magazine *Tintin* – was born.

Tintin was the place for realistic series in Belgium until its final demise in the early 1990s. It boasted a roster of cartoonists who were at the top of their game, includ-ing the likes of Edgar P. Jacobs, Paul Cuvelier, Jacques Martin, Dino Attanasio, Willy Vandersteen, Bob de Moor, Jacques Laudy, Tibet and Raymond Macherot.

The art direction of the magazine was overseen by Hergé and his studio, leading to the prevalence of cartoonists who drew

somewhat like Hergé himself. This style, later termed 'La Ligne Claire' (the Clear Line), became one of the mainstays of European comics with many followers. La Ligne Claire is a deceptively simple style that in reality is quite complex. If the art of cartooning is the art of reducing images to as few lines as possible, then the Clear Line is the logical extension. Cartoonists who have a Clear Line style endeavour to draw using just the right lines. This approach involves a huge amount of preparatory drawings; the irony is that it makes an intensive task (the creation of comics art-work) even more intensive in order to appear seemingly simple and effortless. Today, La Ligne Claire has many adherents and is still seen in the styles of many car-toonists. The best have been authors like Serge Clerc, the Spaniard Daniel Torres, and the late Yves Chaland who mixed a Clear Line style with a love of the work of André Franquin.

Tintin magazine was a success from the start. Its mix of realistic stories and clear, concise artwork were an immediate hit with the public to the point that in 1948, Leblanc made a deal with French publisher Georges Dargaud to create a French ver-sion. Of course, the main attraction of the magazine was the serialized adventures of the eponymous title character. The impact of *Tintin* on the Francophone public (and ultimately, the world) cannot be underestimated. It was, quite simply, enormous. Not only did Hergé's character set the bar for adventure comics in France and Belgium, its mix of humour and high drama defined what a good strip should be, for more than a generation. The fact that *Tintin* was serialized in the pages of a magazine before being collected in books ensured that it was a raging success and that Leblanc's efforts were amply rewarded.

Traditionally, comics in France and Belgium have been treated better, format-wise, than their counterparts in the rest of the world. After serialization – or, more often, after being commissioned – strips are collected into 40- or 64-page colour hardcover books.

A curious side issue was created when *Tintin* the magazine became successful. Obviously, pages needed to be filled every week, and cartoonists were needed to fill them for both *Spirou* and *Tintin*. It soon became apparent however, that there was no cross-pollination of talent between the two magazines. Indeed, it became a unwritten rule that if you worked for one of the magazines, you didn't work for the other. There are exceptions to every rule however, and only one cartoonist ever went from *Spirou* to *Tintin* and back again, and indeed worked for the two magazines at the same time: André Franquin. After a dispute with Dupuis, the publisher of *Spirou*, Franquin approached Leblanc and signed a five-year contract with *Tintin* magazine to create a series called *Modesté et Ponpon*, a charming yet relatively pedestrian (for Franquin, anyway) gag strip about a young family. Soon after signing this contract, Franquin's dispute with Dupuis was resolved, and he went back to working on the *Spirou et Fantasio* series whilst still creating *Modesté et Ponpon*. He was relieved to leave *Tintin* once his contract was fulfilled, but *Modesté et Ponpon* continued in the pages of *Tintin* under the hands of other cartoonists like Dino Attanasio and Griffo.

Unlike *Spirou*, *Tintin* magazine isn't around today. Its sales started to decline in the 1980s, and although many initiatives tried to turn the title around – including changes of name – the rot had set in, and by 1993, the plug was pulled on what was once one of the most vibrant comics magazines in the world.

Above: The cover to an issue of *Tintin* from 1959, created by Jacques Martin.
© Jacques Martin, Le Lombard

Left: One of the more beloved characters in *Tintin* magazine, *Cubitus*, created by the late Belgian cartoonist Dupa (Luc Dupanloup).
© Dupa, Le Lombard

Above: The cover of the first issue of *Pilote*, featuring the line-up of characters inside.
© *Dargaud*

Below: A half-page from Greg's humour strip *Achille Talon*. This sequence shows one of Greg's famed forays into postmodernism.
© *Greg, Dargaud*

PILOTE GETS ITS WINGS

The success of *Spirou* and *Tintin* magazines led to a whole range of rivals being launched onto an eager public. While some of these went on to moderate success, only one really hit the big time, becoming even more influential than its Belgian rivals: *Pilote*.

The brainchild of two writers, René Goscinny and Jean-Michel Charlier, an artist, Albert Uderzo, a publisher, Jean Hébrard, and two journalists, François Clauteaux and Raymond Joly, *Pilote* was a true turning point in Francophone comics. For the first time, the editorial thrust of a comics magazine was to be decided by working cartoonists rather than former journalists or interested parties.

The genesis of *Pilote* had its roots in the agencies that Goscinny, Charlier, Hébrard and Uderzo set up, Édipresse and Édifrance. Under the Édipresse banner, the men created *Le Supplément Illustré*, a special supplement for newspapers, and worked for Radio Luxembourg's magazine *Radio-Télé*. Soon, the team started toying with the idea of creating a new magazine for children that would have backing from Radio Luxembourg in terms of promotion and publicity. The idea quickly gelled, and on the 29 October 1959, the first issue of this new magazine, called *Pilote*, went on sale. All 300,000 copies sold out in one day,

aided by the promotion of the radio station.

In the early days, the bulk of the magazine's writing was taken on by Charlier and Goscinny. Between them they created several popular series, right from the first issue. Charlier created *Barbe-Rouge* with Victor Hubinon and *Tanguy et Laverdure* with Uderzo (the artwork of both these series was later taken over by Jijé), while Goscinny created *Le Petit Nicolas* with Jean-Jacques Sempé and more famously, *Astérix* with Uderzo (see sidebar). Other cartoonists like Maurice Tillieux, Christian Godard and Raymond Poïvet also weighed in with series, ensuring that the magazine had a balanced cast of creators.

Although the magazine was successful, a financial crisis caused *Pilote*'s backers to pull out in 1960, throwing the magazine's future into jeopardy. Fortunately, a saviour appeared in the nick of time. Georges Dargaud – already versed in publishing comics with the French edition of *Tintin* magazine – stepped in and took over the reins of publishing *Pilote*. Under his wise counsel, *Pilote* went from strength to strength, both in sales and in creative talent. Many new and popular series were introduced, and the magazine became the home to many influential cartoonists, notably Jean Giraud (who co-created the iconic western Lt. *Blueberry*), Morris (who transferred his very popular, humorous western *Lucky Luke* to *Pilote* from *Spirou*) and Greg (*Achille Talon*, a series notable for making Goscinny and Charlier characters in the strip, as well as playing with the comics form itself).

Resources opened up to *Pilote's* editors through their association with Dargaud, including the acquisition of rights for foreign properties, such as series from the British *Eagle* comic created by Frank Bellamy and Frank Humphris. This, along with the influx of creators doing fresh and innovative work, meant that *Pilote's* readership were treated to a creative wellspring that went far beyond the norm.

The late 1960s marked another high-point in *Pilote*, as many new, young cartoonists got their chance to appear in the magazine's pages. One of Goscinny's strengths as an editor was spotting and nursing new talent, and artists like Marcel Gotlib (whose series *Rubrique à Brac* was a genuine revelation), Claire Bretécher, Nikita Mandryka, Jean-Marc Reiser, Jacques Lob, Pierre Christin, Alexis and Mézières were regularly featured. During this time, the content of the magazine became more adult, dealing with politics and social themes. Artists like Philippe Druillet and F'Murr began to aim their strips at older readers and satire began to replace slapstick. Goscinny went along with these changes, but by the time the 1970s arrived he began to feel more and more uneasy

with the direction that the magazine was taking. He began to clash with many cartoonists, over the material they were turning in for publication and, feeling frustrated with what they saw to be editorial interference and even censorship, several jumped ship to other publications. Others, including Gotlib, Bretécher and Mandryka created their own magazine, *L'Écho des Savanes*.

These defections hurt Goscinny badly, especially when cartoonists he had nurtured, like Jean Giraud, started to submit work to the other, newer magazines. Goscinny stepped down from the editor's position in 1973 (staying on as director until the following year) to be replaced by Guy Vidal. Vidal turned *Pilote* into a monthly, rather than a weekly title, and brought in the types of comics that Goscinny felt were wrong for the magazine. The name of the magazine was also changed to *Pilote et Charlie* in 1986, after merging with another Dargaud comics magazine, *Charlie Mensuel*, while later still, it dropped the *Pilote* name completely and became *Spot BD*. While these initiatives worked for a time, by the early 1980s the sales began to decline again and by the end of the decade, *Pilote* was gone, and an era was over.

Astérix

The only real rival to the worldwide success story that was Hergé's *Tintin*, was René Goscinny & Albert Uderzo's series *Astérix*. Created for the magazine *Pilote*, it had its roots in the series that Goscinny and Uderzo had worked on for *Tintin* magazine, *Oumpah-Pah*, but instead of a wild west setting with a Native American as its hero, the strip featured a small, fiesty Gaul and his large, slightly slow, but mighty comrade and their battles against Roman invaders in the time of Julius Caesar.

The strip quickly caught the public's imagination, appealing as it did to a particularly Gallic mindset, and became a phenomenon. Thirty one (a 32nd is in progress at the time of writing) albums in over 100 languages later, the series has survived the death of one of its authors (Goscinny died in 1977 while undergoing a medical check-up), charges of racism and a battle for the publishing rights between the original publisher and the surviving author.

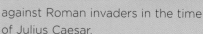

© Éditions Albert René/Goscinny & Uderzo

THE SOUND OF THE PLAINS

The 1960s were a time of massive upheaval in France (as well as the rest of the world) in terms of social, political and cultural life. Inevitably, these changes spilled over into the world of comics. Cartoonists working in the mainstream became dissatisfied with the status quo, and wanted to reflect the climate of the times in their work. The need to get more 'adult' in their work wasn't exactly met with open arms, and in order to move with the times the artists needed to move away from the mainstream.

When Marcel Gotlib, Claire Bretécher and Nikita Mandryka broke away from *Pilote* to form their own magazine, they summed up the zeitgeist of the age. Free to do the work that they felt was impossible in the mainstream, they created comics that were more personal and reflected their artistic ambitions. *L'Écho des Savanes*, as they called the new magazine, was the vanguard of a new type of comics magazine publishing this new, more personal material. Soon, they attracted other like-minded artists such as Jean Giraud, Philippe Druillet and Ted Benoît and the pages were filled with satiric and often scatological comics. The magazine also reprinted and commissioned new work by foreign cartoonists, particularly Harvey Kurtzman – the creator of *MAD*, and the father of Underground Comix – and those responsible for the US underground scene like Robert Crumb.

L'Écho des Savanes also created and courted its fair share of controversy over the years, not least when, in the late 1970s, a young cartoonist named Philippe Vullemin joined its ranks. His comics reached a new high in upsetting people, frequently featuring extreme scatology, weird sexual content and violent imagery. Later in his career he created a national scandal with his series called *Hitler=SS*, which was accused of racism and treating the Holocaust as a joke. Vullemin denied this, but the controversy seemed to sum up the air of danger that his work always carried.

As time went on, *L'Echo* increasingly became a pale shadow of its former self. Less comics were published in its pages, and more pictures of naked women appeared, which was a shame as the magazine had done more than any other to kickstart the adult comics phenomenon. Gotlib went on to found another anarchic comics magazine, *Fluide Glacial*, with the cartoonists Alexis and Jacques Diament. This magazine, dealing purely in humorous comics, featured cartoonists like Daniel Goossens (a very funny and talented cartoonist), Franquin (and his dark masterpiece *Idées Noires*), Masse, Solé, Édika (whose comics featuring the *Proko* family were surreal to say the least, and often veered into arguments between the author and his

Above: Claire Bretécher's cover to the first issue of *l'Écho des Savanes*. This novel magazine broke new ground for comics in France.
© *Claire Bretécher*

Right, opposite page: Detail from Moebius' (Jean Giraud) strip, *Arzach*. This was a strip that opened many doors for cartoonists to do personal work.
© *Jean Giraud, Les Humanoïdes Associés*

Schtroumpf

At the end of 1969, student Jacques Glénat-Guttin put together a simple, roneotyped (an early duplication process) fanzine, and in reference to both Peyo and the celebrated magazine about film, *Cahiers du Cinéma*, called it *Schtroumpf/Les Cahiers de la Bande Dessinée*. It was a humble beginning from which Glénat (he dropped the hyphenated surname) would never look back.

As time went on, the fanzine became a magazine, and Éditions Glénat, the company Glénat founded, went from

© Glénat

strength to strength, becoming one of the larger comics publishing houses. *Les Cahiers*, as the magazine became known, became famous for running in-depth features, studies and profiles on comics worldwide. Under editor Thierry Groensteen, who took over the editorial reins from issue 56 until issue 84, the magazine acquired a scholarly air that was like nothing before, and helped bring about a change in the general perception of comics.

creations) and Gotlib himself, who also provided the magazine's editorials.

SCREAMING METAL

In 1974, *L'Écho des Savanes* received a new member on its editorial team, Jean-Pierre Dionnet. Dionnet had first made his mark by writing for fanzines, and this led to him working as a comics writer on *Pilote*. Dionnet didn't reign long at *L'Echo*, as in 1975, he teamed up with friend Bernard Farkas, and artists Jean Giraud and Philippe Druillet to create a new, science-fiction based comic magazine for adults called *Métal Hurlant*, and a parent publishing company called Les Humanoïdes Associés. This magazine was a groundbreaker from the beginning, encouraging experimentation and non-linear storytelling.

From the first issue, *Métal Hurlant* contained many comic book milestones. Jean Giraud adopted his Moebius nom de plume and created one of the most iconic strips of all time, *Arzach*. This series of short strips, featuring a strange world filled with men riding pterodactyl-like creatures and giant monsters with unfeasibly large genitalia, was completely wordless, and often created 'on the fly', with Giraud literally making the story up as he drew the comic. Other artists like Druillet, Serge Clerc and Jacques Tardi weighed in with series and one-off strips that were massively

influential and shaped the perception of adult comics for years to come – which wasn't always a good thing. Unfortunately, there was an awful lot of dross as well as the great and the good, and *Métal* suffered more than most from a sense of being uneven. It inspired an English version of the magazine called *Heavy Metal*, which was more uneven than the original due to the editor's preference for stories that involved lots of naked flesh on display. The translations of the material left an awful lot to be desired too, often resulting in unintelligible messes.

Métal continued until 1987 when bad sales and general downturn in the BD market caused its closure. Les Humanoïdes Associés continued publishing however, and *Métal* was resurrected in 2002 with an English edition after the company changed hands.

TO BE CONTINUED...

In February 1978, Casterman, the Belgian publisher of the *Tintin* albums, dipped its toes into the waters of magazine publishing with the first issue of *À Suivre*. This excellently produced magazine promised to, "demand the masters of the new form [comic books] to express themselves in complete freedom... [*À Suivre*] will be the wild eruption of comics in literature." This aspiration was achieved by utilizing the work of two fantastic talents – the Italian Hugo Pratt (see the spotlight profile starting on page 204), and the Frenchman Jacques Tardi (see sidebar on page 159).

Throughout its run of 25 years, the magazine mostly lived up to its aim of presenting new chapters of great works every month, and it often featured new series from authors who were working for other publishers. Among the many artists involved were the Belgians François Schuiten and Benoît Peeters (Peeters is also a well-respected comics critic and author of books about the artform), Nicolas de Crécy (an amazing cartoonist whose work defies description), Francois Boucq, Comés and Jacques Loustal.

The magazine folded in 1987 during the downturn in the fortunes of comics in the late 1980s. More than most, À Suivre is missed as a venue for work that was challenging, amusing, occasionally infuriating, but always interesting.

FANDOM AND RESPECTABILITY

The 1960s brought about a change in the public perception of comic books whereby comics were no longer relegated to the realm of 'entertainment for children'. While the changing content of the comics themselves played a big part, it wasn't the only factor. It probably wasn't even the major factor. As early as 1963, the first organized fandom for comics emerged when a group of enthusiasts and amateurs (in the true French sense of the word) gathered to form Le Club des Bandes Dessinées. This club counted amongst its founders the film director Alain Resnais, the cartoonist Jean-Claude Forest (the creator of *Barbarella*), the critics Francis Lacassin and Pierre Couperie and the journalists Jacques Champreux and Jean-Claude Romer. These like-minded men came together to celebrate the comics of their youth with a sense of nostalgia, but also with an eye on the future. They published a magazine, named *Giff-Wiff*, that contained thoughtful studies on creators and strips from the 1930s and 1940s, and was the first of its kind in France. In 1964, the club changed its name (to CELEG – Centre d'Études des Littératures d'Expression Graphique) and its focus, to cover a broader survey of comics up to the contemporary scene.

CELEG lasted only until 1967, but was extraordinarily influential. The next major player in the nascent Franco-Belgian comics fan movement was born from a split in CELEG's leadership, when, in 1964, some CELEG members formed a rival group of comics amateurs called SOCERLID (la Société Civile d'Études et de Recherches des Littératures Dessinées).

Above: The cover of the 50th issue of *Métal Hurlant,* with a cover depicting the editor Jean-Pierre Dionnet.
© Etienne Robial, Les Humanoïdes Associés

Below: *Giff-Wiff,* the official publication of Le Club des Bandes Dessinées.
© Al Capp

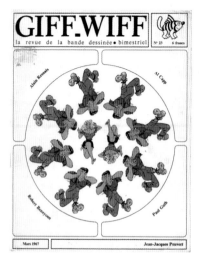

Below: A page from Philippe Druillet's outlandish, but groundbreaking adaptation of Gustave Flaubert's *Salammbô*, which originally ran in the pages of *Métal Hurlant*.
© *Philippe Druillet, Gustave Flaubert, Les Humanoïdes Associés*

Above: The cover of *Phénix* No. 46, one of the first comics fanzines in France. This issue features the Italian Franco Bonvicini's *Sturmtruppen*.
© *Franco Bonvicini, SOCERLID*

Left: *Bande Dessinée et Figuration Narrative* was a seminal exhibition that went a long way to convincing the French public that comics were, in fact, an artform. This is the cover to the French edition of the accompanying book.
© *SOCERLID*

Composed of critics and writers like Claude Moliterni, Pierre Couperie, Édouard François, Maurice Horn and Proto Destefanis, this new group went somewhat further than its parent organization and started to create a series of exhibitions to educate the general public and the art world on the value of comics. The first exhibition, called *Dix Millions d'Images* was presented at the Galerie de la Société Française de Photographie in September 1965. Relatively small, the show led to a much larger and prestigious event at the Louvre in Paris. The *Bande Dessinée et Figuration Narrative* exhibition opened on 2 April 1967 and ran for almost three months. After Paris, the exhibition travelled to London, Berlin, São Paulo and Helsinki, and spawned a book of the same name (later translated, rather boringly, as *The History of the Comic Strip*). The book was as ground-breaking as its parent exhibition, featuring chapters on the production of comics, narrative technique and the relationship of comics to other art forms, as well as a compact history lesson, subjects previously barely covered.

SOCERLID also produced a magazine called *Phénix* that carried reprints of old comics and in-depth studies of cartoonists past and present. *Phénix's* editorial team made a point of running articles on comics from the rest of the world, often showing work that had never been seen outside of its native country before, providing its readers with a window on the wider spectrum of comics, not just the French scene. The influence of *Phénix* on magazines about comics is still felt today, and without it comics scholarship would not exist – as we know it – today.

As the impact of a major comics exhibition at one of Europe's premier galleries sank in, it galvanized a grassroots movement of comics fandom. Soon, comics were attracting the attention of major cultural movers and shakers. Articles on and analysis of comics and their creators started to appear in the mainstream media, which in turn encouraged more artists to try their hand at comics production. Fanzines started to pop up everywhere, and small meetings were arranged where fans could meet creators, buy new albums and rare old ones, and generally celebrate comics.

Partway through *Phénix's* run, the publishing of the magazine was handed over to Dargaud. They took a hands-off approach and it continued much as it had done before, but it served to highlight an interesting, and increasing, phenomenon that was repeated the world over: the transformation of fanzines into professionally published magazines, and even, eventually, into full-scale publishing houses.

Phénix finally ground to a halt in 1977, 47 issues after its first edition – not the longest of runs for a magazine, but a very

Jacques Tardi

Born in 1946, Jacques Tardi is arguably one of the most important cartoonists in Francophone comics, certainly in the last quarter of the 20th Century.

Famed for his unique variation of la Ligne Claire style, Tardi began his comics career at the age of 24 drawing short stories written by Jean Giraud for *Pilote* magazine. He soon began writing his own work, and after several more shorter strips began to create a number of longer works: the *Adele Blanc-Sec* series, *Ici Même* (with Jean-Claude Forest), and *Griffu* (with Manchette). He also began a series of adaptions of the novels of Léo Malet, a series that has been very successful.

Tardi is perhaps best known for his series of albums about the First World War, a series that is best exemplified by the book, *C'Était La Guerre des Tranchées*, a haunting look at the horrors of war.

© Jacques Tardi, Casterman

Right: The cover of the first volume of Nicolas de Crécy's series *Monsieur Fruit*, the story of a rotund 'super' hero.
© *Nicolas de Crécy, Seuil*

Above: A page from Edmond Baudoin's strip *1 42 04 06 088 198*. Baudoin was one of the artists that *Futuropolis* effectively broke into the French comics scene, and his evocative brush style was an instant hit.
© *Edmond Baudoin, Autrement*

notable one nonetheless, not least for bringing an academic sensibility to fandom, and encouraging deeper analysis of comics.

FROM FANZINE TO PUBLISHER

When Les Humanoïdes Associés started to formulate what was to become *Métal Hurlant*, serious thought was given to the magazine's design. The designer they picked was Etienne Robial, a gifted and ardent comics fan who'd begun to make a name for himself as a small press publisher.

Robial started a fanzine in 1969 called Futuropolis (after the René Pellos strip from 1937) as part of the activities of the eponymous comic shop he co-owned in Paris. In 1972 – with the help of his then wife, the cartoonist Florence Cestac – Robial expanded the publishing side of Futuropolis while taking a back seat with the shop. Soon, Futuropolis had become a small, but fully-fledged publishing house with an impressive catalogue of books. At the same time, Robial and Cestac continued their respective careers as designer and cartoonist. Robial went on to design the comics magazine *À Suivre*, countless books for Futuropolis, the logo for the Paris St Germain Football Club and the identity for the Canal+ and M6 Television companies, the former of whom also employed him as Artistic Director. Meanwhile, Cestac created

a series of successful albums and gave us the iconic character *Harry Mickson*, who even had a football team (made up of cartoonists and comics editors) named after him. She eventually won the Grand Prix d'Angoulême, the highest achievement in European comics, in 2000.

Futuropolis published a who's who of cartoonists during its lifetime that included Jacques Tardi, Edmond Baudoin, Joost Swarte and Enki Bilal, as well as discovering new talent like Jean-Claude Götting and Jean-Christophe Menu. They reprinted the great and the good of the comics world, such as E.C. Segar (*Popeye/Thimble Theatre*), Alain Saint-Ogan (*Zig et Puce*), and Alex Raymond (*Flash Gordon*). All the books they produced were attractive, and set a standard for production that their rivals and even the large mainstream publishers had to work hard to meet. Robial's preference for black and white was apparent too, as they published an enormous amount of monochrome books. In publishing work without colour, Robial's desire for the purity and power of comics was well realized, and set a precedent in Francophone comics, as the publishing establishment believed – up until that point – that comics could only appear in colour. Futuropolis also instigated a series called 30/40 that published comics at the size they were originally drawn, rather than reducing them to fit a printed album page. This allowed the reader to experience the artwork as the cartoonist drew it, bringing the creator closer to the audience, and allowing them to better appreciate the work.

In 1986, the well-established French mainstream (not comics) publisher Gallimard, approached Robial and Cestac with a plan to invest in the company, and to co-create a series of reissues of classic novels, with design by Robial and illustrated by the top comics creators of the day. Robial and Cestac accepted the arrangement, and the investment, and set about creating the series of illustrated prose books. They paired up an interesting array of authors and illustrators, including Tardi with Celine, and Götting with Dostoyevsky, and the books were an immediate success.

Unfortunately, Robial fell out with Gallimard's management and decided to quit Futuropolis in 1994, 22 years after the launch of the company. The imprint fell into a state of lethargy, occasionally publishing, but mostly dormant. In 2005, however, news spread that Futuropolis was gearing up to publish new material after an infusion of new editorial and design talent in the shape of former Dupuis staffers Sebastien Gnaedig and Didier Gonord. The newcomers brought enthusiasm and a host of new talent along with a desire to publish fresh and interesting work. While they have a lot to live up to, and a reputation that is somewhat sacred to uphold, time will tell if their efforts are to be successful, and if they can reinstate the Futuropolis imprint to its former glory.

ANGOULÊME, ANGOULÊME, DEUX MINUTES D'ARRET

As the years rolled on, Francophone comics fandom became more professional. The small festivals that emerged at the beginning of the 1970s began to grow in size and stature, with the festival in the small French town of Angoulême becoming the great granddaddy of them all.

Initially started by local businessmen and comics enthusiasts Francis Groux, Pierre Pascal and Jean Mardikian, the small, sleepy Charente town, about an hour's drive north of Bordeaux, seemed an incongruous place to be the site of the world's most important comics festival. But strange though it may seem, that's just what has happened, although it took many years and political battles to reach the status it has today.

The first festival took place in January 1974, with guests including Burne Hogarth (the artist of *Tarzan* so beloved by a generation of French comics critics), Harvey Kurtzman, Maurice Tillieux and the winner of the first Grand Prix d'Angoulême – the annual prize given to comics' true greats – André Franquin. This first festival, while small, was successful

Above: An example of the 'bigfoot' style of Florence Cestac, the co-founder of Futuropolis. This book is notable because it is a 'survival guide' for would-be cartoonists entering the comics biz, and because it was written by the future director of the Angoulême Festival, Jean-Marc Thévenet.
© Florence Cestac, Jean-Marc Thévenet, Futuropolis

Above: The poster for the first Angoulême festival, drawn by Hugo Pratt.
© Hugo Pratt; FIBD, Angoulême

Below: The lavish catalogue for the 1989 Angoulême festival. This oversized softcover book had a cover by André Franquin.
© André Franquin; FIBD, Angoulême

and proved to the organizers that they were on the right track.

Between 1975 and 1990, the festival grew and grew, with ever-increasing attendances and a vast array of creators from all over the world as guests – Hergé, Eisner, Moebius, Tardi, Bilal... the list was endless. The festival soon cemented its reputation for vast retrospective exhibitions on various facets of comics and cartoonists, often with impressive sets and displays and accompanied by lavish catalogues.

In 1987, in line with the town's affirmation to be 'la ville de la Bande Dessinée', and backed by the French government, work began on a multi-million franc project to renovate the town's decrepit brewery into a special comics museum and resource centre. In 1990, the work was finished, and the Centre National de la Bande Dessinée et l'Image (CNBDI) opened its doors to the public. A vastly impressive building designed by the noted architect Roland Castro, himself a comics fan, it held an equally impressive range of exhibitions and a museum of comics that was quite astounding, especially to comics fans whose cultural impression of the medium wasn't as enlightened as the French. The CNBDI also led the way for the creation of other comics museums around the world, most notably the Centre Belge de la Bande Dessinée in Brussels – again, another wonderful museum and library housed in an

architecturally impressive building (a former Victor Horta designed department store), with a collection of original art to rival the CNBDI.

The festival, meanwhile, went through ups and downs over the years, unsurprisingly coinciding with the rises and falls in the BD market, but it managed to maintain its status in the comics world, helped not least by grants from the French government, and sponsorship from a bank and a large supermarket chain. Artistically, the festival isn't quite as impressive as it once was – certain exhibitions had to literally be seen to be believed, such as the Franquin retrospective and the *God Save the Comics* exhibition that focused on British creators – but it's still a vibrant place to soak up the world of comics, indulge in a few exhibitions featuring material you can see nowhere else, and to do a little business.

Many other festivals have sprung up around France and Belgium, and while none are as big or as internationally well-known as the Angoulême festival, many are thriving, both in terms of artistic merit and in size of attendance. The BD Boum festival in Blois is probably the next well-known festival after Angoulême, and is always worth a visit.

Left: The Centre National de la Bande Dessinée et l'Image, Angoulême, France. This magnificent converted brewery holds what is possibly the finest comics museum and library in the world. Trust us when we say the inside is as impressive as the outside. Photo: Jim Wheelock.
© Jim Wheelock

Below: An example of the scenography that often accompanies an exhibition at the Angoulême festival. This giant sculpture of Frank Margerin's *Lucien* character (and oversize panels from the comic series behind) were part of the show (put on the following year) dedicated to the cartoonist, when he won the Grand Prix d'Angoulême in 1992.
Photo: B. Brooks. © Frank Margerin; FIBD, Angoulême

Above: The front and back covers of *Labo,* the proto-Association book published by Futuropolis.
© *Futuropolis*

Below: Jean-Christophe Menu's auto-biographical book, *Livret de Phamille.*
© *JC Menu, l'Association*

THE ASSOCIATION

One of the last books published by Robial's Futuropolis was an anthology of new cartoonists' work called *Labo,* which was accompanied by an exhibition at the 1990 Angoulême festival. A black and white collection of exciting work by relative newcomers, *Labo* had contributions from a number of young artists (Jean-Christophe Menu, Stanislas and Mattt Konture) who had already formed a small collective called l'Association pour l'apologie du 9e Art Libre. These three men had a vision of what comics and comics publishing could be, and this coincided with the values of the *Labo* project. Unfortunately, only one edition of *Labo* was ever produced, but the experience was enough to convince these young cartoonists, plus some others from the project (David Beauchard, Lewis Trondheim, Killoffer and Mokéït), to expand the collective into an independent publishing house. In May of 1990, l'Association was officially formed, followed shortly by their first publication, *Logique de Guerre Comix,* in November.

From this small beginning, l'Asso (as it's fondly known) became incredibly influential on the world stage. Right from the start, the founders had a set of principles and a vision that they have stuck to. One of their principles was the belief in the power of black and white or two-colour work,

and the other was in a sense of high quality throughout, not just in their choice of creators, but also in production values and design.

l'Association publish a number of books each year, as well as a revue called *Lapin,* which they divide into collections sorted by size. There are the *Patte de Mouche,* small (10.5 x 15cm/4 x 6in) comics that are wonderfully made, the larger *Collection Ciboulette* (16.5 x 24cm/6 x 9in) books, and the normal album sized *Collection Éperluette* (22 x 26 or 29cm/8 x 10 or 11in). l'Asso are creating new collections all the time, the latest being the *Collection Eprouvette,* dedicated to critical works on comics themselves.

Many of the books l'Association have published have achieved success, not only critically, but also commercially. Menu and his colleagues have the knack for publishing books that help to keep the entire company afloat, while being lauded by the critics. Recently, the four-volume autobiographical *Persepolis* series by the Iranian-born Marjane Satrapi has been a huge international success for the publisher, allowing them to continue publishing other, less profitable works.

Three of the founders have made a name for themselves outside of the l'Association remit. Jean-Christophe Menu, the driving force behind the group, is known as a spiky, opinionated character, but his love of comics and his sense of fairness cannot be questioned. A superlative cartoonist, his book *Livret de Phamille*, is a wondrous autobiographical work, rich and poignant. As a publisher, he's not afraid to take a gamble, even if it affects him personally. A good example was the *Comix 2000* book that l'Association published to celebrate the new millennium. Featuring 324 authors from around the world, each one creating a wordless strip, and weighing in at 2048 pages, this monster of a book caused quite a stir when it was announced. It caused more of a stir when l'Association actually launched it, and even today, several years after publication, it is still causing a stir, but for the wrong reasons. Certain contractual differences (such as not being paid) have occurred between l'Asso and some of the cartoonists involved, particularly the foreign ones. Menu has stated publicly (on the *Comics Journal* Internet message boards) that due to a series of unfortunate and unforeseen circumstances, payments were late to a number of cartoonists, but l'Asso will endeavour to pay everyone eventually. Nevertheless, this has created some bad feeling towards the group and to Menu personally. While l'Asso handled the administration of the book badly (and have admitted as much publically), the fact that Menu is such an advocate for cartoonists' rights (and a man of integrity, if a little abrasive at times)

bodes well for the satisfactory outcome of this affair for everyone concerned. The only drawback to Menu the publisher, is the fact that Menu the cartoonist has had to take a bit of a back seat. Thankfully, though, he does still create comics, albeit not as prolifically as his partners.

Lewis Trondheim (real name Laurent Chabosy), the second of the three most notable l'Association partners, is something of a phenomenon in comics circles. Not the most polished of artists, he has nonetheless created a niche for himself. A wildly prolific cartoonist, publishing more than 35 titles in 10 years, Trondheim works with collaborators as well as alone. From the rollicking comedy-adventures of his *Lapinot* series (first published by l'Association and then by Dargaud), through his autobiographical comics (primarily *Approxitiviment*), to the heroic fantasy parody *Donjon* (with Joann Sfar, and numerous other collaborators), Trondheim's work cuts across many boundaries and appeals to many different people, not just comics fans. In recent years, Trondheim's own comics have tended towards the experimental; His *Mister O* album for Delcourt, for example, contained 29 one-page wordless strips featuring a little, round character trying (and failing) to get across a ravine.

While Trondheim himself admits he's not the greatest artist, he is a master cartoonist able to portray any number of

Above: The *Patte de Mouche* series of minicomics published by l'Association, seen here at about half the printed size. This example features a jam between two of the founders of the collective.
© *Lewis Trondheim, Mattt Konture, l'Association*

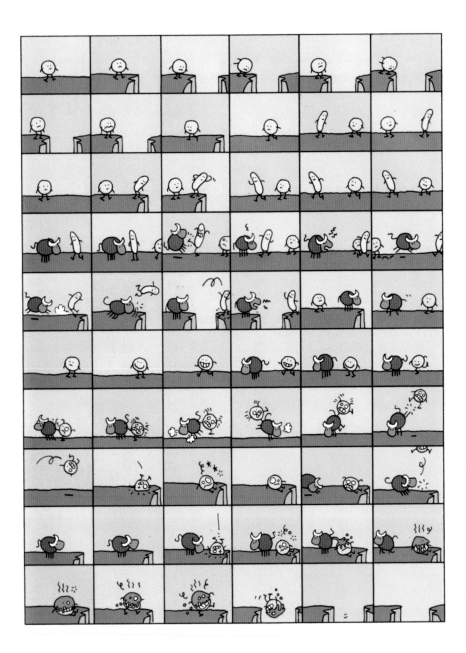

Left: A gem from the *Mister O* series of strips by the incredibly prolific Lewis Trondheim. *Mister O*, published by Delcourt, is the tale of a little man who's always trying to get to the other side of the ravine. And always fails. Hilariously.

Below: In 2005, Trondheim announced his retirement from comics. Still a relatively young man, he set out his reasons in a book called *Désoeuvré*, a comics essay about how he didn't want to end up like so many cartoonists, turning out crap for money as he got older. A brave move, but one that was tempered by the fact that he still continued to work on some of the many comics series he's been involved with.
Mister O © Lewis Trondheim, Delcourt
Désoeuvré © Lewis Trondheim, l'Association

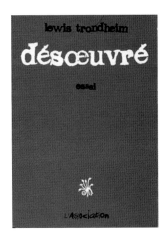

expressions and gestures in just a couple of lines.

The third and final of the most notable partners is David Beauchard. Specializing in comics that have the tenor of dreams, David B (as he is now known) is rightly acclaimed for his lush black and white imagery. After his first book, *Le Cheval Blême*, a collection of his (real) nightmares transposed into comics form, Beauchard concentrated on his autobiographical series about his brother's epilepsy and the effect it had on the whole family, l'*Ascension du Haut Mal*. Over three volumes, this series was to prove a critical and commercial hit, eventually winning the *Alph Art* award for best story at the 2000 Angoulême festival.

L'Association's ethos has always included the experimental as a large part of their raison d'être, and nowhere can this be seen more than in the project that they started in 1992: *OuBaPo*.

THE WORKSHOP FOR POTENTIAL COMICS

One of the most fascinating offshoots from French literary tradition is the OuLiPo, or Ouvroir de Littérature Potentielles – Workshop for Potential Literature. The 'potential' in the name refers to the creation of, "new structures and forms that can be used by [creators] in whatever manner they please." Formed by the poet Raymond Queneau and the mathematician François Le Lyonnais, the group explored the creation of prose and poetry under self-imposed and predetermined rules or constraints. These constraints, often mathematical in concept, determine the flow and dictate the principles the work must follow. Remarkably, this tends to increase the creativity of the writer by giving them something to 'push' against. Famous examples of Oulipian works are Georges Pérec's *La Vie: Mode d'Emploi* and Italo Calvino's *If on a Winter's Night a Traveller*.

After the formation of the parent group, many other new groups were formed with the idea of creation under constraint. Collectively, these groups are known as Ou-X-Po (where the X stands for the medium the group works in), and examples include OuPeinPo (Workshop for Potential Painting) and OuMuPo (Workshop for Potential Music). In 1992, the parent OuLiPo gave its blessing to the comics critic Thierry Groensteen and three members of l'Association (Jean-Christophe Menu, Lewis Trondheim and Killoffer) to form an Ou-X-Po devoted to the comics artform. OuBaPo, as it was called, started to work on creating an initial list of constraints that could be applied to the comics medium. First examples of these constraints started to filter out through work like Trondheim and Menu's book *Moins d'un quart de seconde pour vivre*. This book featured 100 strips

Above: The cover to the first *OuBaPo OuPus*.
© *Killoffer, OuBaPo, l'Association*

Below: A page from the masterful Daniel Goossens. From the book *Adieu Mélancolie* published by l'Association, this strip is a hilarous reworking of the old Princess and the Pea fairy tale.
© *Daniel Goossens, l'Association*

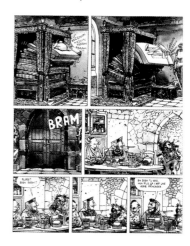

Above: David B.'s epic autobiographical series *l'Ascension du Haut Mal* was a breakout series for l'Association, mixing reality and dream-like sequences to relate his brother's battle with Epilepsy.
© *David B., l'Association*

made up from the repositioning of eight different panels to form the strip. It wasn't until 1997 and the publication of the first OuPus, that the initial constraints and the works derived from them were set out for all to see.

These initial constraints fell into two camps: Generative, or those the application of which led to the creation of completely new strips; and Transformative, or those that change already existing strips. In Groensteen's essay in the first OuPus, called *Un Premier Bocquet des Constraints*, he looked at the further subdivisions of these constraints, and while some of these further subdivisions were directly adapted from Oulipian constraints, like the N+7 constraint where the nouns in the text are changed with the seventh noun following in a specified dictionary (for example, "To Be or Not To Be: That is the quibble"), others were not. These constraints, like Scenic Restriction, where scenes in a strip are limited in how they are portrayed (for instance, every panel in a strip could be drawn from the same viewpoint) or Multireadability, where strips can be read in more than one direction, were referring to the comics medium and the comics medium alone.

By the time that *OuPus 1* was published, the number of members of OuBaPo had increased with the addition of the academic Anne Baraou, the critic Gilles

Ciment, and the cartoonists François Ayroles, Etienne Lécroart and Jochen Gerner. Like the parent group, OuBaPo does not solicit members; instead it votes people into membership and then approaches them in a sort of fait accompli). This influx of talent led to more oubapian works being produced, like the collaboration between Trondheim and the Spaniard Sergio García called *Les Trois Chemins*. This delightful book used the constraint of three separate but interlinking strips that ran directly across the page in the form of three roads that the characters walked and interacted along. Not only was it a fine experimental comic, but the story was excellent too, proving that OuBaPo was no mere intellectual exercise, but a valuable tool in the cartoonists' creative armoury.

In the early part of 2000, the French daily newspaper *Libération* approached OuBaPo with the request for a series of strips that would run that summer. The group complied, and every day from July to August, a new oubapian strip appeared. Six constraints were used by six cartoonists (Menu, Trondheim, Ayroles, Gerner, Killoffer and Lécroart) and these were then collected into the third *OuPus* (the second was still in the works, so it was bypassed).

The second *OuPus* came out in April 2003, and was a collection of comics based on the constraints first outlined in *OuPus 1*, with commentary by Jean-Christophe

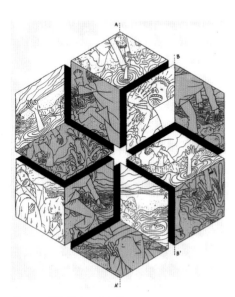

Above: Killoffer's OuBaPian homage to M.C. Escher which is also a pliage, or a strip that becomes another by folding the strip from point A to point B. This strip first appeared in the French newspaper *Libération*.
© *Killoffer, Libération*

Right: A page from the second book, *La Qu...*, in Marc-Antoine Mathieu's stunning four-volume *Julius Corentin Acquefacques* series. With OuBaPienne overtones, the series is a masterwork of kafkaesque machinations, metafiction and paper engineering.
© *Marc-Antoine Mathieu, Delcourt*

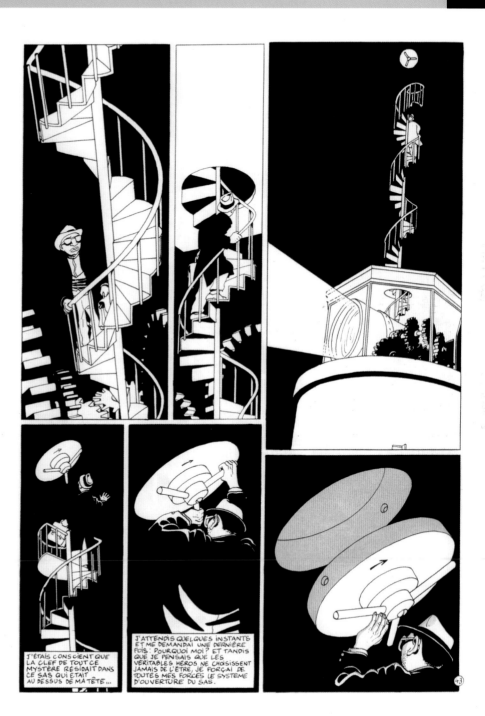

Above: Fabrice Neaud caused a stir when *Ego Comme X* brought out his series *Journal*, an intensely autobiographical and superbly realised set of albums.
© *Fabrice Neaud, Ego Comme X*

Menu. Additionally, the book featured a number of collaborative strips created at various comics festivals, and a number of guest cartoonists including Yves 'Tanitoc' Cotinat, Joann Sfar and Vincent Sardon. The last of these cartoonists also collaborated with Anne Baraou on *Coquetèle*, an oubapian game, made up of dice with comics panels on the faces, published by l'Association.

OuBaPo now has two foreign correspondents, Sergio García from Spain and Matt Madden from the USA, and Madden in particular, is proactive in sourcing new constraints via the website he set up (http://www.oubapo-america.com). All in all, OuBaPo shows no sign of slowing down, and indeed looks like becoming a world manifestation of comics experimentation.

THE RISE OF THE COLLECTIVE

The influence of the l'Association model was one that had an almost immediate impact. Cartoonists have always formed collectives, but now the collectives had a further goal in mind. Not content with just producing fanzines, these new collectives looked to producing revues and books with a more professional air. Foremost among these were the French Amok and the Belgian Freon, which were both established in the early 1990s and who shared a similar philosophy of comics as art. These two collectives published many important comics, including works by Vincent Fortemps, Thierry Van Hasselt, Denis and Oliver Deprez, Felipe Hernandez Cava and Raul, Stefano Ricci, Yvan Alagbé and Martin Tom Dieck, as well as two very important revues in *Cheval Sans Tête* and *Frigobox* respectively. Eventually they joined forces and recreated themselves as Fremok, and publish under this banner to this day.

Other collectives that emerged at this time included the brutal Le Dernier Cri (who pioneered la Ligne Brut, characterized by a ratty line and scatological and extreme sexual material), the classy Les Requins Marteaux, whose sense of humour is conveyed through the work of Winshluss and Cizo, Les Cartoonistes Dangereux – an international collective based in the UK, who published in both French and English, and included cartoonists like Charlie Adlard, Roger Langridge, Fareed Choudhury, Paul Peart-Smith, Jonathan Edwards and Dylan Horrocks – and Ego Comme X, the collective based in Angoulême, who specialized in comics that deal with real life, with Fabrice Neaud's *Journal* the pick of the bunch. *Journal*, currently up to its fourth volume, relates the story of the author's life as a gay man in and around the cartoonists' community in the Charente town. Neaud caused a minor scandal in Francophone comics with his frank depictions of fellow cartoonists,

Angoulême luminaries and his feelings towards them. Despite this, *Journal* has been critically acclaimed and is something of a tour de force of autobiographical story-telling.

The collective is as strong as ever in Franco-Belgian comics, and is still a force to be reckoned with.

THE MAINSTREAM ADOPTS MANGA AND BLACK AND WHITE

As the 20th Century gave way to the 21st Century, mainstream comics in France and Belgium changed. The genesis of this change had started much earlier, but as the 1990s progressed, the effects were felt more and more. Two things happened: the mainstream, larger publishers like Dargaud, Casterman and Glénat, started to take notice of what was happening in the world of the fanzine and the smaller publishers like l'Association, and at almost the same time, the Japanese metaphorically invaded.

Thanks to the sales of books by outfits such as l'Association and Cornelius, the big boys began to cast around for talent they had previously overlooked, if not outright ignored. Formats were experimented with, even to the extent of aping the style of books from the smaller publishers, and talent was headhunted. While this stuck in the craw of publishers like l'Association, and not without good reason, it meant that

for the first time in years, there was a freshness in the output of the mainstream, injected by authors such as David B, Lewis Trondheim and Marc-Antoine Mathieu (a graphic designer whose company created many impressive Angoulême exhibits). Mathieu's *Julius Corentin Acquefacques* series for Delcourt was a masterpiece of formal play mixed with a nightmarish Kafkaesque story, and stories like these could be seen at the larger publishers for the first time, a move that kept fans, if not smaller publishers, happy. Other important creators who broke through included Blutch, Dupuy and Barberian – whose *Monsieur Jean* series is a perfect comedy of social manners – and Pascal Rabaté and his delightful adaptation of Alexis Tolstoi's *Ibicus*.

The other major event to hit the mainstream comics scene was slower to emerge, but much, much larger. Thanks to the translation and broadcasting of Japanese cartoons on TV, young people in France and Belgium (and indeed, all over the world) began to be fascinated with the world of the Japanese manga. Publishers were not slow to pick up on this, and following others around the world, like the USA's Marvel, began to negotiate with Japanese publishers to buy the reprint rights to popular titles. Glénat was the first publisher to pick up on this coming trend when, in 1991, it released the French language translation of Katsuhiro Otomo's

Below: Philippe Dupuy and Charles Barberian work so closely together, that it's like they're two halves of the same person. Sharing the creative duties on all their comics equally, but with ever-changing roles, they have created some of the funniest and finest slice-of-life comedies ever, like the series *Monsieur Jean*, a page of which is shown below.
© Dupuy and Barberian, Les Humanoïdes Associés

Above: Some panels from a strip that Frédéric Boilet created for *BANG!* magazine, recalling events at the Angoulême festival, and showing his manga/BD hybrid style.
© *Frédéric Boilet*

breakthrough science-fiction epic *Akira* to immediate and quite startling success. This literally opened the floodgates to the Japanese invasion. Spearheaded by Glénat, the popularity of manga was soon picked up on by every major publishing house in France and Belgium, and they started negotiating with Japanese publishers like Kodansha, to buy properties for translation.

By 2003, translated manga made up 30% of the total sales of BD in France and Belgium. Teenagers, in particular, took to the manga format like ducks to water. Part of the attraction was the price: printed in black and white, on cheaper paper, the manga books are half the price of the traditional Francophone colour album. More than that however, the teenagers clutched them to their collective breasts due to their very difference from what their parents had grown up with; the manga gave them a window into a new, strange and fascinating world.

Creators too, were fascinated with these newcomers from the east. Soon, fanzines were full of young French and Belgian cartoonists emulating the manga style, and some were even picked up by publishers to create Francophone manga. Frédéric Boilet, a published cartoonist with a number of series for Glénat and Bayard to his name, was so infatuated with the new movement of Manga in Francophone comics that, after obtaining a grant from the French

government in 1990, he went to study in Japan.

In 1993, he received the first Morning Manga Fellowship, a grant for cartoonists from Japanese publisher Kodansha, allowing him to stay in Tokyo for a year. He now lives and works in Japan, creating comics for both Japanese and French publishers. He also created a manifesto about the interaction of the Francophone and Japanese comics scenes called *La Nouvelle Manga*, which he defined as, "[comics] that are neither completely BD nor completely Manga."

Not everyone took to the Japanese invasion with arms as open as Boilet. Many traditionalists were horrified at the thought of *Tetsuwan Atom* and *Dragonball* Z taking the place of *Tintin* and *Astérix* in the hearts of young people. Regardless, it seems that Manga are well and truly assimilated into the comics culture of the Francophones.

HOLDING THEIR OWN

Even though comics have come under pressure to maintain people's interest in the face of competing media, such as television, cinema, video games, DVD and the like (something that is true for every territory, but especially those in the First World), they have held their ground better than many would have thought. For the French and the Belgians at least, it seems that there's just something about the funny books with the mixture of words and pictures that keeps them coming back for more.

New and exciting publishers are cropping up all the time. For example, Thierry Groensteen, the comics critic and writer, is now the editor-in-chief of a new publishing house called Editions l'an 2, specializing in books about comics, a wide and wonderful range of albums and a critical magazine called *Neuvième Art* that was originally created as the annual journal of the CNBDI.

Other, more established publishers, are taking a leaf out of the independents' book, as we've seen, and are getting less conservative about the books they publish, whether in content, format or target audience. Even the once very depressed newsstand market has seen something of a revival, with a number of titles either about comics or containing comics, being launched and maintaining reasonable sales figures, certainly enough to keep them afloat. Newer titles like *BoDoi*, *Bédéka*, *Bandes Dessinées Magazine*, *BANG!* and *Ferraille Illustré* can all be found at the newsstand, while old favourites like *Spirou*, *Fluide Glacial* and *Vecu* are still going strong.

Even though the market for comics has gone up and down over the years, it does remain a readily accepted truth that comic books' spiritual home (at least in the West) is in the hearts and minds of the French and the Belgians. The number of books published continues to go up year on year, and the increasing number of festivals, exhibitions and coverage from other media continues to point to the good health of the scene in France and Belgium, both artistically and commercially.

Above: The first four panels from *La Fille du Professeur* by Joann Sfar and Emmanuel Guibert. The witty script and superlative artwork sent this album into the critical stratosphere, and with good reason.
© Joann Sfar, Emmanuel Guibert, Dupuis

Left: *Neuvième Art*, Thierry Groensteen's critical and analytical journal on comics that is the true heir to *Phénix* and *Les Cahiers de la Bande Dessinée*.
© Editions l'An 2, CNBDI

Above: Some panels from the brush of Pascal Rabaté, showing his wonderful sense of lighting, as well as his use of subtle caricature.
© Pascal Rabaté

HERGÉ

HERGÉ

Young Belgian, Georges Remi, had two main interests: the Boy Scouts, and drawing. Both of these were to have an enormous impact on his life, and help to make him the most influential European comics artist to have lived.

Born on 22 May 1907, in a small suburb of Brussels called Etterbeek, the young Georges spent his time in school doodling, and thinking about the Scouts, of which he was an enthusiastic member. An above average student, especially in art, he enjoyed school, but inbetween his dreams of becoming a newspaper reporter, he started to draw strips for *The Belgian Boy Scout* magazine featuring a character called *Totor*, a scout who was strangely reminiscent of a character he would create in the future. It was here that he adopted his pen-name of Hergé (which is the French pronunciation of his reversed initials).

Soon after creating *Totor*, Hergé was approached by the editor-in-chief of the right-wing newspaper, *Le Vingtième Siècle*, the priest Abbé Wallez. Wallez wanted Hergé to create comics for the youth supplement of the newspaper, *Le Petit Vingtième*.

One of Hergé's many cartoons illustrating the scouting lifestyle.
© Hergé, Moulinsart

Hergé agreed and started working on a new strip featuring a dashing boy reporter. The first episode of the new strip, *Tintin au Pays des Soviets,* appeared in the newspaper on 10 January 1929, and it wasn't long before Hergé's latest creation had a massive following, even culminating in staged homecomings for the character that were attended by hundreds of members of the public.

In 1932, the Brussels publishing house Casterman started issuing the collected *Petit Vingtième* stories in album format, an arrangement that has lasted to this day. It was also the year that Hergé married his girlfriend Germaine, and met a man who was to have a profound effect on his life and work: Chang Chong-Jen from China. A student at the Academy of Fine Arts in Brussels, Chang's initial impact was to insist that Hergé research the places where he was to send his character in order to create a sense of verisimultude.

As the Second World War ravaged Europe, *le Vingtième Siècle* stopped publishing, and Hergé went to work for the newspaper *Le Soir,* as the editor-in-chief of the youth supplement *Soir Jeunesse*, where he continued the adventures of *Tintin*. This was a move that would later dog Hergé, as *Le Soir* was completely under Nazi control, a fact that led to charges of collaboration after the war ended.

During this time, Hergé began using (and relying on) assistants. After the war, when he and Raymond Leblanc had started the magazine *Tintin*, he formed the Studio Hergé to help him redraw and recolour the early work to be republished. This crossed over to the new stories he created, and to help with the workload he assembled a fine team of cartoonists including Bob de Moor, Edgar P. Jacobs, Jacques Martin and Roger Leloup, all of whom went on to create their own successful series.

One of the colourists he employed at Studio Hergé was a young woman named Fanny Vlamynch, and in 1956, Hergé and Fanny began a relationship which was to end his marriage to Germaine. Despite finding a new love, he started to suffer with depression, and the time between new albums became longer and longer. Nevertheless, the public demand for more *Tintin* stories kept Hergé coming back to a character that, over time, he had become to resent.

Resentment aside, the period between 1950 and 1962 saw Hergé create what are commonly thought to be his two finest works – *Tintin au Tibet* and *Le Bijoux de la Castafiore*. Both are notable for entirely different reasons; the former is a wonderful adventure romp about *Tintin* searching for his lost friend, and the latter is a funny farce that is entirely character driven.

The last full *Tintin* book, *Tintin et les Picaros,* was published in 1974 to a mixed reaction. The public loved it, but the critics didn't. It would be four years before Hergé started another book. In the meantime, he married Fanny and received many awards including the Grand Prix d'Angoulême, the Grand Prix St-Michel and the Belgian Order of the Crown.

In 1979, the 50th anniversary of *Tintin* took place, and was marked by many events and celebrations, including the issue of a stamp by the Belgian Post Office. The year after, the first signs of the illness that would kill Hergé started to appear. He became tired easily and he was later diagnosed with Leukemia.

For all the awards and money that he made, Hergé's greatest thrill came when, in 1981, he was finally reunited with Chang, with whom he had lost touch just before the war.

Hergé died on the 3 March 1983, after a week in a coma. His last *Tintin* book, *Tintin et l'Alph-Art*, was published posthumously and in an unfinished state.

A self-portrait of Hergé 'created' by *Tintin*.
© *Hergé, Moulinsart*

A coloured drawing Hergé created for Raymond Leblanc on the occasion of *Tintin* magazine's seventh anniversary.
© *Hergé, Moulinsart*

Above: A scene from Spanish cartoonist Miguelanxo Prado's adaptation of the classic fairy tale, *Peter and the Wolf*. Prado's wonderful artwork and writing style have made books like *Trazo de Tiza* appear in many critics '"Ideal Library of Comics'.
© *Miguelanxo Prado*

6

CONTINENTAL
COMICS

There's more to comics in Europe than the output of France and Belgium. In this chapter, we look at the greater European comics scene and check out how countries as diverse as Portugal, Holland and Germany 'do' comics.

Above: A semi-finished page from Lo Hartog van Banda and Dick Matena's series *De Argonautjes*. © *Dick Matena, Lo Hartog van Banda*

Right: The Chris Ware minicomic 'business card' for the Lambiek comic shop in Amsterdam. © *Chris Ware, Lambiek*

From Portugal in the south, to Holland and Germany in the north, comics stretch across the language barriers, influence creators across borders, and unify Europe like no other art form.

The fact that the majority of European countries produce comic books, and the sheer number of states involved (43 and growing), means that this chapter is inevitably a whistle-stop tour of eurocomics. The main comics-producing nations in Europe – aside from France and Belgium – are Spain, Holland, Italy and Germany, but the others have their contribution to make too.

THE NETHERLANDS

Holland has a fine tradition of comics and cartoonists. From the earliest works of sequential art dating from the Middle Ages, right up to the work of young cartoonists like Maaike Hartjes and Erik Kriek, Holland has been at the vanguard of comics creation. Even though comics, in the form of sequences of pictures and occasional word balloons, had been around since the late 1400s, comics as we know them today only started appearing in Holland after the First World War, mainly in newspapers and magazines. Many Dutch companies started using comics in advertizing in the late 1930s, with some organizations commissioning artists to create new, intricate campaigns, while others used artists to rip off popular characters like Segar's *Popeye*.

In 1936, the first issue of *Sjors* was published, the first truly Dutch comics magazine.

During WWII, many artists, like Alfred Mazure, either stopped drawing or made bland comics to avoid their art being used by the German invaders, but some collaborated and put their art in the thrall of Nazi propaganda. Most cartoonists could continue their work however, and due to the prohibition on the importation on US material, original Dutch comics were promoted. Marten Toonder's studio, started to cash in on this gap in the market, would eventually produce some of the most famed Dutch comics ever, including *Tom Poes*, *Kappy* and *Panda*. Drawn in a wonderful Disneyesque style, Toonder's comics worked on many levels and were as popular with adults as they were with children.

Members of Toonder's studio included such wonderful cartoonists as Dick Matena, Fred Julsing Jr, Piet Wijn and Carol Voges, many of whom went on to have long and successful careers of their own.

After the war, things started to return to normal and by the 1950s the number of newspapers published increased, and therefore so did the number of cartoon strips. Some of the more popular – apart from those produced by Toonder's stable – were by artists like Ben van den Born (whose wordless strip *Professor Pi* was world renowned), Schmidt and Westendorp (*Tante Patient*) and Carol Voges (*Jimmy Brown*). Imported strips increased as well, especially those from the USA, and in 1952 the first issue of *Donald Duck Weekblad* was launched to great success. Still published today, many Dutch cartoonists have contributed stories and art to the magazine, including Dick Matena, Marten Toonder and Eddie De Jong. In the 1960s, a Dutch version of *MAD* magazine appeared, and like the other international editions, was a mix of reprint from the parent US magazine and new, original material from Dutch artists like Willy Lohmann. Just as the American *MAD* was an inspiration and impetus to the US underground cartoonists, so the Dutch version seemed to usher in a new age of comics in Holland. Comics from other European countries, like *Astérix* and *Lucky Luke*, were translated into Dutch for the first

time, giving rise to the idea that comics were an art form worthy of study, in the minds of the general public.

In 1962, a new comics magazine, *Pep*, was launched, and towards the end of the decade it featured material from a new generation of Dutch cartoonists. Important works like *Agent 327* by Martin Lodewijk, *De Argonautjes* by Dick Matena and *De Generaal* by Peter de Smet made their first appearance in *Pep*. *Pep* later transmogrified into *Eppo* magazine and later still into *Sjors and Sjimmie stripblad*, but managed to maintain its status as the most important comics magazine for children published in Holland. *Tina*, a comics magazine for girls, was launched in 1967 and – unlike most other Dutch comics of the period – is still being published today. It had a fine roster of talent contributing stories, including Dick Vlottes, Patty Klein, Jan Steeman, Andries Brandt, Peter de Smet (again) and Piet Wijn.

Fandom started to take off with the establishment of the Het Stripschap comic society and its magazine *Stripschrift*. Het Stripschap organized the first Dutch comic convention, called The Day of The Strip, in 1968. That same year, the first comic shop in Holland, *Lambiek*, opened in Amsterdam. As the 1960s came to an end, fandom became more active in creating comics as well as writing about them. The influence of the US underground scene was particularly strong in Holland, with Martin

Above: A page of *Tuimel & Professor Ich*, by the wonderful Fred Julsing Jr. The son of a cartoonist, Julsing Jr died in January 2005. © *Fred Julsing Jr.*

Below: The cover to the 30th anniversary issue of *Stripschrift*, one of the longest running fanzines in the world. Illustration by Gerard Leever. © *Gerard Leever, Het Stripschap*

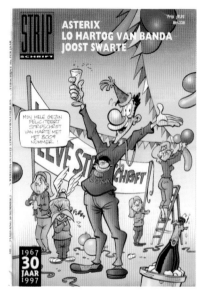

Above: *Tante Leny* was an incredibly important magazine in Dutch comics history, created by Evert Geradts and his wife Leny Zwalve.
© *Evert Geradts*

Right: A panel by Hein De Kort, showing his signature style of artwork.
© *Hein De Kort*

Beumer and Olaf Stoop forming the Real Free Press, specializing in reprints of US underground and classic comics, as well as importing magazines from other parts of Europe, such as France's *Métal Hurlant* and *El Vibora* from Spain.

By 1972, the first issue of *Tante Leny Presenteert*, the first real Dutch underground comic, had been released. *Tante Leny* was a landmark magazine for Dutch comics in many ways, not least due to its somewhat stellar line-up of young Dutch talent. Artists like Peter Pontiac, Evert Geradts, Marc Smeets and Joost Swarte made their debuts in its pages. Swarte also published a small press comic called *Modern Papier*, which merged with *Tante Leny* on its 11th issue. *Tante Leny Presenteert* continued until 1978, its 25th issue marking the end of an era for Dutch comics.

In 1975, Jan Van Haasteren and the comics writer-turned-cartoonist Patty Klein launched a new magazine, *De Vrije Balloen*. Not strictly an underground comic, *De Vrije Balloen* nevertheless had an underground vibe as a place where new and established artists could create strips with few boundaries. Cartoonists working for the mainstream, like Robert Van Der Kroft and Andries Brandt, found themselves sharing pages with a new generation of Dutch creators like Wim Stevenhagen and Gerrit de Jager. *De Vrije Balloen* had an impressively long life for an underground comic, lasting

for 62 issues and nine years, and was enormously influential.

Another facet of comics in the Netherlands, especially through the 1970s and beyond, was the political content. The comics of artists such as Willem, Jaap Vegter and Joost Swarte carried comment on social issues that was, at times, quite profound and had a real impact on their audience. The increasing political focus and social mores of the era meant the time was ripe for a new wave of comics in the 1980s. Increasingly, strips about families and their foibles started to appear, including the offbeat *Familie Doorzon* by Gerrit De Jager. Running in the magazine *Nieuwe Revu*, De Jager's series portrayed a family filled with stereotypical characters found in an atypical Dutch household. Unsurprisingly, the series became a huge hit as the Dutch instantly recognized themselves in the strip. De Jager's wonderfully expressive artwork didn't hurt either.

At the same time, artists like Hein de Kort and Eric Schreurs started to appear in magazines like *Nieuwe Revu* and *De Waarheid*, and their approach to comics – irreverent, vulgar and manic – was a shock to the system after the clear line stylings of Swarte, Theo van den Boogaard and Robert van der Kroft. Shock aside, they were just as influential to the newer generation of Dutch cartoonists as were the adherents of La Ligne Claire.

Dutch comics today are in a state of flux. The mainstream comics world is a disaster area, with comics mainstays like *Sjors* and *Sjimmie Maanblad* suddenly disappearing. At the same time, established cartoonists like Hanco Kolk, Peter de Wit and Eddie de Jong found new outlets in newspaper strips. A new small-press movement was established and is still going strong today. Artist Robert van der Kroft started a new comics and culture magazine called *Zone 5300* in 1994. Other small-press magazines like *De Stripper* appeared, providing showcases for cartoonists who would have struggled to be seen and had little chance of making a living from their comics. Many of these cartoonists worked as graphic designers and used this expertise in their self-publishing efforts. Hand in hand with the rise in self-publishing was the emergence of autobiographical comics, reflecting the worldwide phenomenon. Spearheading this new wave of cartoonists were artists like Barbara Stok and Maaike Hartjes, who created engaging comics with a simplicity that belies their depth. Another recent movement in the Netherlands was the emergence of experimental comics like those created by Erik Kriek, Stefan van Dinther and Tobias Schalken (the latter two created *Eiland* magazine). Kriek's comics are, on the surface, more traditional than the *Eiland* cartoonists, but all three share a desire to get behind the mechanics of the medium, thereby creating better and more insightful comics.

Fandom continues to act as the support mechanism to all of this activity, with news magazines like *Stripschrift* and *Zozolala*, and conventions like the annual Haarlem festival providing means for fans to discover the new movements in Dutch comics.

The other area that Dutch cartoonists in their droves have been exploring is the possible format of the future, the webcomic. Many sites carry the latest work by both new and more established creators. Seemingly making up for the relative lack of publications in which to present their work, the Dutch comics community has jumped upon the Internet as a means of communication with each other and the outside world.

Above: A page of Maaike Hartjes *Dagboek,* a diary comic.
© *Maaike Hartjes*

Below: The superb artwork of Marten Toonder, the Walt Disney of Dutch comics.
© *Marten Toonder*

Above: *Corriere dei Piccoli,* the first magazine to carry comics in Italy.
© *Corriere della Sera*

Above: Giovan Battista Carpi's interpretation of *Donald Duck* for *Topolino* magazine. The Italian Disney artists are among the best in the world.
© *Disney*

ITALY

After France and Belgium, Italy has the richest European comics heritage. Called fumetti, after the puff of smoke-like thought balloon, comics in Italy were introduced by the children's magazine *Corriere dei Piccoli* – a supplement of the newspaper *Corriere della Sera* – in 1908. At first, the comics published were reprints of US newspaper strips like *Happy Hooligan* and *Little Nemo in Slumberland*. They were 'adapted' for Italian audiences, however, by removing the balloons – thought to be 'miseducating' – and substituted with rhyming captions underneath the pictures in a kind of libretto. Soon, strips created by Italian cartoonists, with the same type of formatting, started to appear in *Corriere dei Piccoli*. These Italian strips included *Signor Bonaventura* by Sergio Tofano, *Bil Bol Bul* by Attilio Mussino and *Quadratino* by Antonio Rubino, all of which were enormously popular and were drawn in styles that mimicked popular fine art movements like Cubism, Dadaism and Modernism. The irony of these early comics was that although they were very popular, the rejection of typical comics techniques (like word balloons) by the editorial staff of *Corriere dei Piccoli* only reinforced the negative impression of comics as a juvenile medium, fit only for children and idiots in the minds of the populace. This misconception would take

decades to be broken down in the minds of the general public in Italy.

The first cracks in this attitude began to appear around the beginning of the 1930s, when the first magazines for young adults were launched. Called giornali, these magazines were very much like early children's comics in the UK in format and content, including titles such as *l'Avventuroso*. One of the most famous was *Topolino* (the Italian for *Mickey Mouse*), which was created in 1932 and is still published today, the Italians being another nation that loves Disney comics. These titles, and the others that sprouted up, reprinted American newspaper strips and Disney series, but unlike before, they kept the original formatting, word balloons and all. In addition to the reprints, the publications also featured Italian cartoonists' original work. One comic in particular, *Il Vittorioso*, featured no reprints at all, but instead filled its pages with homegrown material. One cartoonist who came to national attention at this time was Benito Jacovitti, who for many years was the most beloved comics creator in Italy and was hugely influential. His many series and characters became the benchmark for humour comics in Italy for years.

Like French and Belgian comics, the Italian strips serialized in the giornali were collected into books called albi. Unlike most of their Francophone counterparts however, albi were published in many different formats, the most popular being the landscape formato all'italiana, which measured 13 x 9.6cm (5 x 4in).

During the Second World War, the fascist government of Mussolini banned the importation of American comics and movies, afraid that the Italian public would be 'seduced' by the American lifestyle. Mussolini also made the publishers revert to the old Italian stylization of running a libretto under the pictures with no word balloons. To get around this ban, as the US series were very popular, the publishers changed the names and appearances of the characters and farmed them out to Italian creators. Thus *Tarzan* became *Sigfried* (complete with a shirt to cover his naked chest) and *The Phantom* became *The Mystery Man*. The last US character to be banned was *Mickey Mouse*, as, ironically, Mussolini's children were big fans of the Disney characters. When he was banned, *Mickey* magically became *Tuffolino*, and was pretty much traced from Floyd Gottfredson's original, by Pierlorenzo De Vita.

When the war was over, and Mussolini dead, the importation of American comics started up again. New giornali began to pop up, replacing those produced before and during the war. Titles like l'*Avventura* reprinted all the old US newspaper strips that the Italian public had missed during the war, and brought in newer strips like *Dick Tracy* and *Rip Kirby*. The public's tastes

had moved on from the old formula however, so a different approach was taken – smaller magazines that were the size of US comic books, but with more pages, were created. These carried complete stories and were a big hit. Fewer and fewer US newspaper strips were imported and reprinted, and even those that were still popular, like *The Phantom*, *Mandrake* and *Flash Gordon*, started to have Italian cartoonists take over the creative chores (*Flash Gordon*, in fact, was written for a time by film director Federico Fellini). An attempt at a purely Italian superhero was undertaken just after the end of the war when the legendary cartoonist Hugo Pratt (see spotlight on page 204), Mario Faustinelli and Dino Battaglia teamed up to create l'*Asso di Picche*. But in spite of the talent on show, the magazine wasn't a success. In fact, superheroes never really took off in Italy until the late 1960s.

As the 1950s came around, changes were afoot. *Topolino*, the best-selling magazine, dropped all non-Disney strips and adopted a pocket-sized format. The magazine became even more successful, and today Italy is the primary producer of Disney comics, with artists like Luciano Bottaro, Giovan Battista Carpi, Romano Scarpi, Giorgio Cavazzanò and Massimo De Vita creating fine stories using the American characters, much in the same vein as Carl Barks and Floyd Gottfredson.

Benito Jacovitti

Born in 1923 in Termoli, Italy, Jacovitti's first cartoons were published in the satirical magazine *Il Brivido* in 1939, when he was still a student at high school. He followed up this early work with the adventures of his most famous creation, *Pippo*, in the catholic weekly *Il Vittorioso* in 1940. *Pippo* was soon joined by two friends, *Pertica* and *Palla* to form the *Three P's*, a strip that ran until 1967.

Jacovitti was a prolific cartoonist and he went on to produce many famous strips for a variety of magazines, including *Il Barbiere della Prateria*, *Chicchirichi* and *Raimondo il Vagabondo* for *Vittorioso*, *Cocco Bill* for *Il Giorno* and *Zorry Kid* for *Corriere dei Piccoli*. He also adapted *Pinocchio* and the *Kama Sutra* into comics, and worked as a publisher and teacher. Jacovitti remained as Italy's best-loved cartoonist until his death in 1997.

Cocco Bill © Benito Jacovitti

Left: The cover from an issue of the first fumetti neri, *Diabolik*.
© Astorina Srl

Below: A page from the hugely successful *Dylan Dog* created by the comics writer Tiziano Sclavi. This page, from issue 26, is drawn by Giampiero Castertano.
© *Sergio Bonelli Editore*

The success of *Topolino* led to many other publishers creating similar formats and styles, often featuring funny animals and humour.

Many new publishers started to appear at this time, but the most important was the Milanese Bonelli company. Formed in 1948 with the first of their many titles, the western series *Tex*, the Bonelli company carved a niche for themselves that stands to this day. In so doing, they also created a new format for their comics that would become an industry standard – a 96+ page, 16 x 21cm (6 x 8in), black and white book with around six panels on a page. Bonelli is still the powerhouse in the Italian comics industry today, with a large market share (along with Disney) and an amazing 25 million books sold every year. They publish several titles ranging from *Tex* and the groundbreaking horror series *Dylan Dog* (created by Tiziano Sclavi), to the detective series *Napoleone* (created by Carlo Ambrosini), and they have been very successful at selling the rights to their properties abroad. In 1999, US publisher Dark Horse translated three Bonelli series; *Dylan Dog*, *Martin Mystery* and *Nathan Never*.

The Italian comics scene ticked along until the 1960s, when, like most other comics-producing countries, things underwent an uprising. In 1962, the first issue of a new series, *Diabolik*, created by sisters Angela and Luciana Giussani, was

published. Utilizing another new format, a complete 128-page story with two panels a page, *Diabolik* featured – for the first time in Italian comics – a villain as the main character. The move inspired several imitations, and these fumetti neri, or black comics, became a thriving sub-genre with *Kriminal*, by Luciano Secchi and Roberto 'Magnus' Raviola, being *Diabolik's* biggest rival in the sales stakes.

The fumetti neri had another offshoot – the erotic comic. This trend, taking the format of comics like *Diabolik*, was started by Giorgio Cavedon's *Isabella*, and became an inordinately prosperous and ubiquitous one. Mainly softcore to begin with, the comics had become decidedly hardcore by the 1980s, a fact that led to a number of calls from the Catholic church and government bodies for them to be banned. What the critics couldn't stop however, was the rise of distinguished cartoonists like Guido Crepax, Milo Manara and Vittorio Giardino, and the widespread use of the comics medium as a vehicle for erotica.

In 1965, the first of the 'prestige' magazines devoted to comics appeared, *Linus*. Named after the Charles Schulz *Peanuts* character, *Linus* had a touch of the fanzine about it, even though it was a professional newsstand magazine. Several of its patrons were from the world of 'high' culture, like author Umberto Eco and Oreste Del Buono, and it made the media and the public sit up and take notice of comics with a more respectful attitude. Its appearance led to the publication of several fanzines (the first, *Comic Club 104*, was co-founded by the future comics writer Alfredo Castelli), and the same year the first Salone Internazionale dei Comics was held in Bordighera. The Salone was moved to Lucca in 1966 and, until the rise of the French Angoulême festival, was the most important comics event in Europe.

As well as featuring comics, *Linus* contained scholarly articles on comics and reprints of important old material from the USA and other places, as well as introducing the work of famous Italian authors such as Milo Manara, Paolo Eleuteri Serpieri, Attilio Micheluzzi, Bonvi and Tanino Liberatore, amongst others. It also led to a number of competitors like *Eureka* and *Comic Art*, and its importance to the growth of European comics as an art form, particularly in Italy, cannot be stated earnestly enough.

During the 1970s, several movements within Italian comics started to draw lines of demarcation: the family weeklies like *Topolino*, *il Giornalino* – sold exclusively through churches – and *Corriere dei Ragazzi* (the former *Corriere dei Piccoli*, now reprinting many Franco-Belgian strips, as well as producing original series by top Italian cartoonists like Sergio Toppi, Dino Battaglia and Milo Manara); the fumetti neri and

erotic comics; the adventure weeklies like *Skorpio* and *Lancio Story*; the Bonelli comics and suddenly, a number of new, independent and innovative comics (the so-called new wave), started by *Cannibale* in 1977.

Created by a group of cartoonists, including Lorenzo Mattotti, Tanino Liberatore, Stefano Tamburini and Andrea Pazienza – many of whom had made their name in other artistic fields like graphic design, fine art and fashion – *Cannibale* was like nothing seen before in Italy. Featuring stories that were very raw in intent (but not in technique), Tamburini stated that *Cannibale* was created, "with the smell of Tear Gas in our nostrils." *Cannibale* lasted only two years, but its influence was far-reaching. As the 1980s got underway, the spiritual heir to *Cannibale* was launched. Named *Frigidaire*, this magazine differed from its predecessor by toning down the emotional impact while losing none of the verve. It contained work by creators such as the Valvoline group, a collective including Igort, Marcello Jori, Giorgio Carpinteri, and Massimo Mattoli (famous for his bizarre mixture of Saturday morning cartoons, extreme violence and pornography, as embodied in his *Squeak the Mouse* and *Superwest* series). Other members included Nicola Corona and Liberatore, the latter teaming up with old compatriot Tamburini to create the hyper-realistic and violent series *Ranxerox*. As with most countries, the

Above: The first issue of *Linus*, one of the most important comics magazines in the world. The cover features the magazine's namesake, *Linus Van Pelt*, from the *Peanuts* strip.
© *Charles Schulz, UFS, Milano Libri Srl*

Below: One of the less-offensive panels in Massimo Mattoli's hilarious *Superwest* album. Mattoli, a gifted cartoonist, often caused offense with his violent, gory and sometimes pornographic comics.
© *Massimo Mattoli*

Above: Francesca Ghermandi has used her silent strip *Pastil* to reach a wider world audience for her work.
© *Francesca Ghermandi, Ed. Phoenix*

Below: Lorenzo Mattotti has become one of Italy's most respected illustrators as well as one of its top comics authors.
© *Lorenzo Mattotti, Jerry Kramsky, Ed. Hazard*

comics industry in Italy was hit by competition from a number of other media, primarily television. Until 1976, the Italian government had a complete monopoly on the country's TV output, with the state effectively controlling what the public could watch. When a loophole in the legislation was found, a multitude of private TV stations suddenly erupted, flinging the comics market into turmoil. Where people had been coming to comics for their daily entertainment, TV could now provide a free alternative 24 hours a day. Many comics disappeared overnight, and the only survivors were those who could offer something different. The Bonelli comics — with their long stories that would take over an hour to read — began to flourish and centre themselves in the marketplace. Manga started to make inroads in the Italian market, as elsewhere in Europe, in the 1990s. Although sales are good, the influence of the Japanese style was a little less all-pervading than in other countries.

A small-press movement began to pick up momentum in the early 1990s, as artists who found it difficult to break into the major companies started to publish themselves. They found a place to sell their comics through the growing number of comic shops that were springing up, even though the majority of titles were still sold via newsstands and kiosks. The small-press led to smaller, independent publishers, like Kappa Edizioni and Lizard, which were set up along the same lines as France's l'Association. These publishers work with the intent of producing comics of real quality and artistic merit, and with collectives like the Mano group, founded by the fabulous Stefano Ricci, the grassroots level of comics in Italy is thriving. Newer cartoonists like Francesca Ghermandi, Stefano Piccoli and Vanna Vinci took to these new outlets for their work enthusiastically, and produced work that was on a par with the best that other European nations could offer. Still today, fanzines like *Fumo di China* and *Schizzo* are supplementing *Linus* with news and articles on comics, and there are new and exciting projects coming out of the smaller houses. A new magazine called *Orme* looks set to continue this trend of ground-breaking work with a mix of established and young creators. The increasing cross-pollination of influences from abroad with the Italian classics means that the comics industry in Italy is as vibrant and thrilling as ever.

Right, opposite page: A page from the strip *Identikit* by the fantastic Stefano Ricci. Due to the methods Ricci uses to create his comics, his original pages are almost three dimensional, and have real texture, which is hard to reproduce on the printed page.
© Stefano Ricci

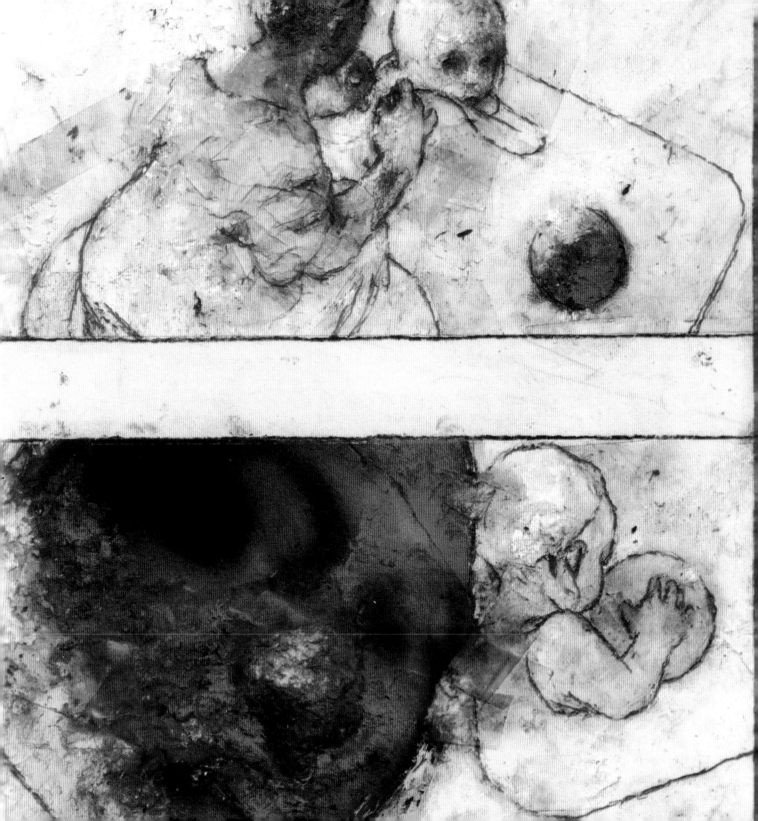

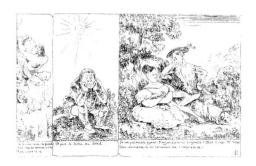

Above: Rodolphe Töpffer, the father of modern comics, from *M. Vieux-Bois.*

Below: A page from Zep's *Titeuf* series, one of the most successful strips in Francophone comics in recent times.
© *Zep, Glénat*

SWITZERLAND

It's ironic that the country that gave us the father of modern comics, Rodolphe Töpffer, has never really set the world on fire with its comics output – that is, until recently. While not shouting about it from the rooftops, in typical Swiss fashion, there has been something of a quiet comics revolution happening in this small central European country. Switzerland put itself on the comics world map in the early days of the medium. A schoolteacher and writer from Geneva, Töpffer created his histoires en images and gained instant notoriety, as well as a whole plethora of imitators and bootleggers. Unfortunately, after Töpffer, the Swiss never really followed up on this early promise and lagged behind their neighbours in France, Germany and Italy in terms of their reputation for comics.

That is not to say that the Swiss haven't produced their fair share of cartoonists; throughout the years the Swiss, partly due to their geographical location, have yielded a number of well-regarded creators who have worked in most of Europe's comics industries. Certainly, names like Ceppi, Cosey, Ab'Aigre and Rosinski spring to mind as Swiss cartoonists who have found fame elsewhere. Even so, the Swiss never really had an indigenous comics industry as such, forcing cartoonists to seek outlets for their work elsewhere. In fact, the

nearest thing that Switzerland has had to a truly international comics character is the parrot *Globi*. Created as an advertising mascot for the Globus chain of department stores, *Globi* was conceived in 1932 by Globus' advertising chief Ignazius Schiele and caricaturist Robert Lips, and was incredibly successful, with some 60-odd albums to its name. There have been other attempts at a homegrown industry, but none of them had any longevity.

Recently however, this has started to change. In both the French and German-speaking sections of Switzerland, fans and amateur cartoonists started to create their own magazines and comics. As early as the 1970s, fanzines like *Le Phylactère* and *Guete Morge Comix* started to appear, and an organized fandom began to emerge. As the 1980s came around, a number of festivals had begun, including the respected Sierre and Lazern events. Newer fanzines such as *SWOF* and *INK!* helped to create a fan network in the country that allowed young cartoonists to present their work to other fans, and get the necessary feedback for artistic growth. Additionally, schemes like the immense collection of comics in the Municipal Library in Lausanne, organized by the comics historian Cuno Affolter, furthered the infiltration of comics into the general Swiss culture. Today, the Swiss have a comics scene, which, while small, is something to be proud of. There are many cartoonists creating fine work abroad, as they have always done, but who are now also creating for small independent publishing houses like Edition Moderne, Drozophile, B.ü.L.B. and Atrabile. The general culture in Switzerland is now very favourable to the creation of high-quality comics, and many cartoonists supplement their income by drawing for public and private organizations.

Of all the fanzines that are published in Switzerland, the most important is the German-language *Strapazin*, from Edition Moderne based in Zurich. Not only did *Strapazin*, edited by David Basler, publish comics by some of the world's finest cartoonists (like Jacques Tardi, José Muñoz, Alberto Breccia and Edmond Baudoin), but it also made a virtue out of promoting homegrown artists, especially those who found breaking into commercial comics either tough, or undesirable. *Strapazin* also pushes the envelope of comics magazine design, and one particular feature is that cartoonists produce all the advertisements. The advertisers don't know which cartoonist will create their ad, and the ads themselves, which measure a couple of inches square, are printed in grids. This most-effective and visually striking method of working sums up the *Strapazin* experience. The magazine also has a neat line in articles about comics, and presents features on comics and creators from all over the

world, making it a fine all-round magazine for anyone passionate about comics, especially those of a more alternative nature.

The artists working in Switzerland today are a mixed bunch, producing material in a variety of genres, media and styles, but are all high quality. From the best-selling, knockabout comics of Zep, the creator of the stratospheric *Titeuf* for Glénat, to the dark, scratchboard nightmares of Thomas Ott, via the weird and wonderful cut-out comics of Anna Sommer, the Swiss comics scene is a vibrant and powerful arena. Some other artists of note include the Genevois cartoonists Frederik Peeters, whose *Pilules Bleues* is an immensely powerful autobiographical book deserving its many accolades; Pierre Wazem, the creator of the award-winning *Bretagne* and an artist of rare and exceptional talent; and Nicolas Robel who, aside from being a prodigiously able cartoonist with an impressionistic style and unusual colour sense, is also the brains behind the design/comics house, B.ü.L.B. B.ü.L.B. are famed for their packaging which redefines the term 'minicomic'. Other great cartoonists like Tom Tirabosco, Alex Balardi, Mike van Audenhove and Karoline Schreiber also promote Swiss comics at the highest level. Indeed, the country where comics were arguably born is making great strides in the medium's future development as an artform.

Above: *Strapazin*, the most important comics magazine in Switzerland.
© *Strapazin*, Pierre Thomé

Below: The excellent Frederik Peeters from his book, Pilules Bleues.
© *Frederik Peeters*, Atrabile

Above: *Comixene,* the
original German comics
fanzine.
© *Edition B & K*

Below: Walter Moers' strip,
Kleines Arschloch.
© *Walter Moers*

GERMANY

In stark contrast to most of its European neighbours, comics in Germany have traditionally fared very badly. If comics are thought of at all, it is mostly as a medium for children, or the lowest trash created simply for morons. This low status was mostly the result of many campaigns against literature of 'questionable' values and 'offensive' material, campaigns that have dogged comics in Germany for many years. Ironically, Germany was the birthplace of one of modern comics pioneers, Wilhelm Busch, who created the strip *Max und Moritz* in 1865. Unfortunately though, the potential of the medium went largely over the heads of the German public.

While it is fair to say that comics aren't held in the highest regard in Germany, there is still a history of comics publishing. For the most part, it consisted of reprints of foreign material, and while that's still true today, original material isn't unknown. After WWII, like their European counterparts, German publishers like Ehapa Verlag started to import American comics and reprint them after translation. While none of these were successful, it didn't stop Ehapa from trying its hand at importing other comics, particularly Disney comics, and eventually strips from other European countries like France and Belgium. The Disney comics, appearing in *Micky Maus*

magazine, fared much better than other US imports, and created the basis for Ehapa to continue its comics line.

Few homegrown comics appeared in the early days. Rolf Kauka created his legendary series *Fix und Foxi* in 1953, and for many years this was the only really successful German comics series. In East Germany before the fall of the Berlin wall, the situation was even worse. Practically all comic strips were banned as, "vehicles of imperialist propaganda", with the result that most children's magazines resembled comics from before the 1930s. Only one magazine from East Germany, *Mosaik*, really made an impression, and after the fall of the wall, it consolidated itself and now publishes traditional comics. Between the end of the war and the late 1970s, the situation for comics in Germany was somewhat bleak, but companies like Ehapa, Carlsen and Alpha continued to reprint comics from abroad and a fanbase slowly began to build. As the 1980s came into full swing, the situation started to change, albeit on a small scale. Fanzines, often the catalyst for homegrown cartoonists, started to appear, with titles like *Comixene* creating the biggest effect. *Comixene*, edited by a host of notable German fans (including Andreas Knigge, Klaus Strzyz and Hartmut Becker), created a mood in which comics were talked about as something more than trash, and its influence led to other fanzines like

RRAAHH!, *ICOM Info* and *Comic Reddition* being published.

In the late 1980s, German cartoonists started to make inroads into the world comics scene. Walter Moers became famous for his strip *Kleines Arschloch*, about a small boy who really is a pain in the backside. Ralf König created satirical strips about gay life included *Das Killer Kondom* (later made into a movie). Matthais Schultheiss became famous in France and the USA with his science-fiction themed works, and Anke Feuchtenberger's strange dream-like strips spawned countless imitators. Small independent publishing houses began to appear, the most influential being Jochen Enterprises. Jochen bucked the trend of the larger houses, guided by foreign examples like l'Association and Cornelius. They published homegrown talent like Tom, OI, Reinhard Kleist, Lillian Mousli and Fil, cartoonists who previously would have had little chance to be published. When Jochen called it a day and folded in 2000, it left a large hole in the German comics scene that has been hard to fill, although newer publishers like Reprodukt and Zwerchfell Verlag have attempted to plug the gap.

The comics industry in Germany remains in a state of flux today as the larger publishers maintain their position of mainly reprinting work from abroad. Nonetheless, the smaller publisher is here to stay, and many cartoonists are self-

publishing as well. Creators like the marvellous Ulf K, Isabel Kreitz, Martin Tom Dieck and Kat Menschik are becoming as fêted at home as they are abroad, and with good reason. Meanwhile, fandom continues to press on with the good fight. The festivals at Erlangen has become a real Mecca for comics enthusiasts, not only from Germany, but from around the world. New fanzines are alive and well too, with titles such as *Panel*, *Plop* and *Epidermophytie* publishing the work of even newer cartoonists. The Web too, is a breeding ground for the new generation of German cartoonists, whilst historians like Andy Konkykru (who is a fine cartoonist and small-press publisher in his own right) use the Net as a means of disseminating information on comics. While the scene in Germany isn't as large as most others in Europe, it is one that refuses to die in the face of apathy from the general public, and gets a little more vital with each passing day.

Above: A rare colour strip by the wonderful Ulf K, an amazingly versatile cartoonist.
© *Ulf K, Bries*

Left: *Fix und Foxi* by Rolf Kauka, one of the most popular German comics ever, allowing Kauka to create a studio along the same lines as Marten Toonder and Hergé.
© *Kauka Promedia Inc.*

Left: A proto-comic by early Spanish comics artist Apel les Mestres.

Right: *Anita Diminuta* by Jésus Blasco, one of Spanish comics most revered creators.
© *Jésus Blasco*

Below: *TBO,* the longest running children's comic in Spain.
© *Ediciones B*

Below: *Mortadelo y Filemón* by Francesco Ibáñez.
© *Ibáñez, Ediciones B*

SPAIN

Spanish comics have undergone a roller-coaster ride ever since they started to appear in the late 1800s. Even so, Iberia's love for the Ninth Art remains something of a given.

The first real comics started to appear towards the end of the 19th Century, but before that, the Spanish painter Tomás Padró had started to work with the page as a narrative space, culminating in his strip *Las Delicias de la Torre* which appeared in 1866. Padró's student, Apel les Mestres, carried on where his mentor left off and in 1880, he created a series of strips for a variety of magazines. At about the time, Wilhelm Busch started to be published in Spain, and inspired more artists to draw pictures in sequence.

In 1904, the first attempt at a magazine with comics as a significant component of its content was published. Called *Monos*, the majority of its pages were given over to proto-comics, satirical or otherwise.

In 1915, another milestone in Spanish comics was reached – the first modern comic. *Dominguín* was an attractive large-format magazine, in much the same vein as the American Sunday supplements that included the cream of the cartoonists then working in Spain. Artists like Ricard Opisso and Joan Llaverías created high-quality work matched by the production of the

magazine. Sadly, *Dominguín* lasted only 20 issues, but in that time it set a standard for future Spanish comics.

Two years later, the first issue of *TBO* hit the streets. This comic was so successful that one of the names by which comics are known in Spain is 'Tebeos'. *TBO* spawned masses of imitators after its launch, but the most popular was *Pulgarcito* launched in 1921, which was published by Bruguera, who became the biggest name in Spanish comics publishing. Both *TBO* and *Pulgarcito* became household names and both would survive the Spanish Civil War and go on to be published for over 2,000 issues each. The success of *TBO* led to the creation of B.B., the first in a long line of comics for girls, in 1922.

By the 1930s, magazines and newspapers in Spain started to reprint comics from America, including Disney comics, much like the rest of Europe. These reprints became very influential to the new generation of cartoonists coming through at that time. By 1938 however, the reprinting stopped due to the effects of the Spanish Civil War, particularly the paper shortages. That year also saw the publication of *Chicos*, a magazine that many comics historians say is arguably the finest Spanish comic ever. *Chicos* featured work by some of the most celebrated Spanish cartoonists ever: Angel Puigmiquel, Emilio Freixas and Arturo Moreno and Jésus Blasco (who would later work for the UK publisher Fleetway on such series as *The Steel Claw*, and later still for Belgian comic *Spirou*).

After the Civil War ended in 1939, many titles were relaunched to an eager public. Cartoonists, buoyed by the resumption of these magazines, started to create work that would become iconic. Strips like *La Familia Ulises* by Benejam in *TBO*, and *Carpanta & Zipi Zape* by Escobar, *Doña Urraca* by Jorge (later taken over by Jorge's son, Jordi Bernet, who would later become famous in his own right for his work on the strip *Tornado*) and, the most celebrated, *Mortadelo y Filemón* in *Pulgarcito* by Francesco Ibáñez (a former accountant who became one of Spain's most famous cartoonists). Ibáñez later created the strip *El Botones Sacarino*, a direct panel-for-panel copy of André Franquin's *Gaston Lagaffe* series. This further astounds when you realize that this was not the first or last time that Ibáñez had paid 'homage' to the Belgian.

The 1950s saw the Spanish comics industry further consolidate its success with ever-increasing print runs, dozens of new titles, and massive sales. The Bruguera publishing house came to real prominence at this time, and slowly assumed dominance in the marketplace. It issued new titles, like the adventure comic *El Capitán Trueno* by Victor Mora, which first appeared in 1956. By the end of the 1960s, Bruguera had a virtual monopoly on

publishing comics in Spain. While great for Bruguera, this was bad for Spanish comics. The monopoly led to poor remuneration for artists and plunged their status downwards in an ever-decreasing spiral. The worsening conditions led artists to form agencies that would look outside the relatively small Spanish market to the wider world of comics production. The most important of these agencies was Selecciones Illustradas, set up by former cartoonist Josep Toutain. SI (as it was commonly called), and its main rival Bardon Art, created a whole new market for cartoonists in places like the USA, the UK and Europe. Great names in Spanish comics like Carlos Giménez, who later parodied his time at SI in his marvellous series, *Los Profesionales*, Josep M Beá, Luis García, Luis Bermejo and Alfonso Font all joined the agencies and became published outside their homeland. Some, like Carlos Ezquerra who worked for UK comics and co-created the famous *Judge Dredd* character, became more well known abroad than at home.

Bruguera's monopoly also created another, more long-term problem. As the company's magazines were so successful, they refused to move with the times and change any of the formulae that had made them so profitable through the 1950s and 1960s. The net result was that the general comics-buying public started losing interest in something that they had seen

Carlos Giménez

One of Spain's finest cartoonists, Carlos Giménez was born in 1941, and spent much of his early life in an orphanage, an experience that he would draw on in his future work. His first steps on his career as a comics author were taken as an assistant to the Spanish cartoonist Manuel López Blanco, along with fellow cartoonist Esteban Maroto. From there, he stepped out on his own and created the *Buck John* series for Ed. Maga.

He began working for the Selecciones Illustradas agency where he drew strips like *Gringo* and *Delta 99*, and series like *Roy Tiger* for the German comics market. Giménez also collaborated with Victor Mora on the series *Dani Futuro* for a number of magazines, including *Tintin*, but by 1977 had started creating *Paracuellos,* the first of a number of autobiographical series. This was soon followed by the series *Los Profesionales* and *Barrio*. Giménez is still in demand today as a versatile cartoonist who can turn his hand to many styles, but is also loved for his series detailing his own life and the life of the country he hails from.

© *Carlos Giménez*

Above: The wonderful, surreal *Bardín el Superrealista* by the inimitable Max.
© Max

Below: Albert Monteys' *Tato*, the hilarous stories of a Pizza delivery man.
© Albert Monteys, Ed. El Jueves

countless times before. The drop in sales coincided with an increase in reprinting of foreign material from the USA, Europe and increasingly, Japan. Persisting to this day, some would argue it has strangled the indigenous Spanish comics market.

As the rise of the comics agencies continued, so the artists involved began to work on material that was outside of the normal genre comics they were employed to create, and was instead more personal. These comics were the first in what were later termed 'Art comics' and they, along with the changing political climate in the 1970s, the rise of fandom and magazines about comics like *Cuto*, *Sunday*, and Antonio Martin's *BANG*, combined with less official censorship, opened the way for a new kind of comics aimed at an adult audience. Titles like *1984*, *Comix Internacional* (the last two published by Josep Toutain) and, most importantly, *El Vibora*, were launched and artists started leaving the agencies (or at least putting them on hold) to work for this new generation of comics magazine. As these magazines started to catch the public's imagination, more titles were launched. Comics like *CIMOC*, *Ramblas* and *Cairo* all started to bring comics for adults into the marketplace, with a mixture of foreign reprints and new homegrown material. Cartoonists whose creativity would captivate comics readers worldwide, began their careers in these titles. *El Vibora*,

especially, brought us artists like Max, Pere Joan, Gallardo, Cifré, Daniel Torres (who, like Max, draws in a beautiful clear line style), Miguelanxo Prado, Sento and Mique Beltran.

Sadly, it didn't last. The mainstream continued shrinking, taking the majority of these magazines with them. As the 1980s reached their end, only a handful of titles were being published. Humour magazines like *El Jueves*, children's comics like *TBO* and sex comics like *Kiss* and, in its later years, *El Vibora* (both of which resemble hardcore pornography more than cutting-edge comics) fared slightly better, but were always in danger of cancellation. Yet, as in so many other countries, the cloud did have a silver lining in the shape of fandom. More and more specialist comic shops were popping up, and with them the number of fanzines grew. Magazines like Joan Navarro's *Krazy Comics* gave a way for like-minded amateurs to contact each other. Comics festivals started to appear, like the excellent Saló Internacional del Comic in Barcelona, and soon small publishing houses grew out of the fanzine scene. These houses, like Norma, Cameleón Ediciones, Dude, La Factoría de Ideas, Sinsentido and Zinco all started publishing the work of new Spanish cartoonists. These included Albert Monteys, Pablo Velarde (whose strip *Quentin Lerroux* is a splendidly funny tale of a man, a chicken and his cleaning lady),

David Ramírez (who transcended his manga influences to great effect), German García, Carlos Portela, Raúl and Sanjulián. They paid the bills by reprinting US comics and, more frequently (and more successfully), manga. These small publishers often produced magazines about comics too, like *Viñetas, Neuróptica, U, El Pequeño Nemo* and *Dentro de La Viñeta*, helping to influence more young cartoonists.

One small publisher in particular deserves to be singled out. In 1993, the cartoonists Max and Pere Joan decided to publish an anthology comic, inspired by l'Association's *Lapin* and the war in Bosnia. The result, *Nosotros Somos Los Muertos*, raised the bar on what an anthology comic should be. Featuring top drawer cartoonists from all over the world, *Nosotros* was an unqualified critical (if not commercial) success. Max and Pere Joan also started to publish some small series of comics in a US-style format, but with far higher design and production values. Max's character, *Bardín el Superrealista* – a small everyman-type cartoon character in a very strange world – was packaged this way, as was the *Raspa Kids Club*, a book that has to be seen to be believed – it's that good – by a young cartoonist called Alex Fito who quickly outgrew his influences to gain his own strange voice. *Nosotros* is still published, albeit very infrequently, and has a new publisher in Inrevés Edicions. Fans of great comics

everywhere always await a new issue with baited breath.

Although the Spanish mainstream, what there is of it, is saturated with reprints of manga and American comics, there is cause for good cheer. Every year, new and excellent cartoonists like Javier Olivares, Miguel B. Núñez and Gabi Beltran appear. Fanzines and comics are published, and the silver lining, although slightly tarnished, is still there. The Web too, is playing its part, with blogs like *La Cárcel de Papel* providing information to those who need it, and webzines featuring new cartoonists keeping the industry alive.

Above: A page from Alex Fito's *Raspa Kids Club*, a wonderfully sick and funny series that's impeccably drawn.
© Alex Fito

Below: Pablo Velarde's superb *Quentin Lerroux*, a very funny strip by a very talented cartoonist.
© Pablo Velarde

Right: *U*, one of the best magazines about comics in Spain, here with an excellent cover by José Luis Ágreda, whose book *Cosecha Rosa* won best book prizes at the Salo del Comic, Barcelona.
© José Luis Ágreda, La Factoría de Ideas

PORTUGAL

Banda Desenhada, as the Portuguese call comics (they also call them Quadrinhos), entered the public's consciousness in the late 1880s when Rafael Bordalo Pinheiro, influenced by the German, Wilhelm Busch, began to publish his sequences of picture narratives in such magazines as *O Binoculo*, *A Berlinda* (both of which he started), *El Mundo Comico* and *El Bazar*. Several albums collecting his work were published, and in addition to his comics, Pinheiro also founded a ceramics factory that still operates today. He wasn't the first artist in Portugal to create comics, as artists like Manuel de Macedo, Nogueira da Silva and Flora had come before him, but Pinheiro's work cemented the comics form into Portuguese popular culture.

Illustrated magazines and children's papers continued to publish comics right into the early 20th Century, and the man who is considered to be one of the fathers of the Portuguese children's comic is Jose Stuart Carvalhais. His long career started in 1915 when he created the series *Quim e Manecas* in *O Século Cómico* magazine. He continued this strip for 38 years, stopping just eight years before he died. He was also one of the first European cartoonists to use word balloons. In 1920, Carvalhais and another cartoonist, Jose Ângelo Cottinelli Telmo, co-founded *ABC-Zinho*, a very

Above: A repugnant panel from a strip by Raphael Bordallo Pinheiro depicting a man who has squashed a chicken on his travels. As you do.

successful children's magazine that contained many comics. Cottinelli Telmo drew a popular series called *Pirilau* for the magazine, and *ABC-Zinho* contained work by the best Portuguese artists of the era, including the prolific Carlos Botelho who started his career colouring Telmo's *Pirilau* series.

In the 1930s and 1940s, many great comics were published in Portugal. These ranged from *ABC-Zinho's* successor, *O Senhor Doutor*, along with *Tic-Tac* and *O Papagaio*, to *O Mosquito*. Unlike in other countries during this time, the standard of Portuguese comics was high, and the importation of foreign work relatively low. There was a comic called *Mickey* that reprinted Disney material, but the war stopped the importation of most comics to Portugal. There were many fine cartoonists working in Portugal during these years, but among the most influential were Fernando Bento, who specialized in adaptations of literary works, Eduardo Texeira Coelho, who later worked for *Vaillant* in France, Vítor Péon, who also worked in France and in the UK, José Garcês, who found success later in his career with the four-volume *Historia de Portugal em BD*, and Jayme Cortez, who began his career as Coelho's assistant.

Censorship reared its ugly head in the 1950s, as in the rest of the world, unleashed partly due to the swamping of the Portuguese comics market with reprints of foreign comics. A censorship bureau

(Direcção dos Serviços de Censura) was created and legislation was passed to stop the influx of foreign comics. In effect, the Bill said that 75% of all comics published must be Portuguese, which was good news indeed to native cartoonists, even if it was a blow to some readers. Comics like *Mundo de Aventuras* more than filled the gap, and introduced more
talented cartoonists to the audience. Of these, Carlos Roque, a superb humorous cartoonist who later worked for *Spirou*, José Antunes and Victor Mesquita, who made his debut at 17 and later went on to be the founder of the influential comics magazine *Visão*, really stand out.

After the heady years of the past three decades, the 1960s were like a bucket of cold water for comics in Portugal. Originality went out of the window, and foreign reprints began to glut the market again. Some cartoonists like Eugénio Silva managed to rise above the general mire, but for the most part it was a forgettable decade for comics in Portugal. The 1970s brought with it a little of the old originality, with anthologies like Mesquita's *Visão*, which came out in 1975 and was a breath of fresh air. Filled with new Portuguese talent like Ze Paulo, José Maria André, Manuel Pedro, Carlos Barradas and Zepe, *Visão* represented a leap forward like the one that happened in France with *L'Echo des Savanes*. *Visão* only lasted for 12 issues, but

changed Portugal's perception of comics forever. It was about this time that fanzines started to make their mark with the formation of the Clube Português de Banda Desenhada in 1976, which brought with it an attempt to rehabilitate Portuguese comics. It also inspired others to publish fanzines, and titles like *Evaristo*, *O Estripador* and the C.P.B.D's own *Boletin* appeared.

The first comics festival in Lisbon took place in 1980 and was followed five years later by the Porto version.

In 1988, the publisher Meriberica-Liber published 44 issues of its large-format colour revue, *Selecções BD*, which, although about 70% reprint, did open its doors to new Portuguese talent. Soon after, in 1990, the first Amadora festival was staged to great acclaim.

In 1993, the magazine *Quadrado* was launched. It had a changeable format, was exceptionally well designed and had a mixture of comics, scholarly articles and interviews (by comics historians and critics like João Paulo Cotrim, Domingos Isabelinho, Leonardo de Sá and Pedro Cleto). It managed to focus on new homegrown cartoonists as well as provide a platform for presenting the best of the rest of the world. Three years later, the Bedeteca de Lisboa opened. This fantastic resource is a library, a national repository, an information hub and a centre where Portuguese comics are celebrated and studied. The Bedeteca also

Above: A page by Victor Mesquita, the founder of *Visão* magazine, and one of the most important cartoonists from Portugal.
© *Victor Mesquita*

Above: *Quadrado,* arguably the most important comics magazine in Portugal.
© *Bedeteca de Lisboa*

Left: A professional graphic designer, André Carrilho is also a superb cartoonist with a lovely sense of colour and pacing.
© *André Carrilho*

Above: José Carlos Fernandes is one of the most stylish cartoonists to come out of Portugal in recent years.
© *José Carlos Fernandes*

started publishing an anthology called *LX Comics,* and then took over the publishing of *Quadrado,* bringing together two of the best things to happen to Portuguese comics in years.

The time since the turn of the century has been one of consolidation for the comics industry in Portugal. Most comics published today contain reprints of foreign material, mostly from the USA, France and Japan. There are increasing signs however, that the native cartoonists are producing fine work that is being published by home-grown publishers. Artists like André Carrilho, Ana Cortesão, Victor Borges, Daniel Lima, Jorge Mateus, and José Carlos Fernandes, Pedro Borges and Vasco Colombo are creating work that deserves to be read by a larger audience, especially in their home country. Smaller independent publishers and collectives like Chili com Carne are creating interesting revues and books that are getting noticed abroad, while the Internet has provided a boon for cartoonists in the quest to get their work seen by the general public and other fans.

EASTERN EUROPE

"Comics in Eastern Europe? What comics in Eastern Europe?" is a question that could understandably be on the lips of anyone other than local comic fans. In fact, the comics scene throughout the various countries of Eastern Europe is fractured, but very much alive.

In order to fit everything in, this look at the work and cartoonists in these countries will likewise be fractured, but we hope to at least convey a sense of the comics culture there.

SERBIA AND, BOSNIA-HERZEGOVINA

Even before the war that tore apart the countries of the former Yugoslavia, comics were never treated seriously, though Yugoslavia did have a history of comics publishing and produced a number of important cartoonists including Jules Radilovic, the Neugebauer brothers and Andrija Maurovic. Bosnia had an ambassador for comics in the form of Ervin Rustemagic who, aside from being a well-known comics enthusiast and historian, formed Strip Art Features, an agency representing cartoonists to comics publishers (much in the same vein as Josep Toutain's Selecciones Illustradas), in the 1980s. He was also the founder of Strip Art magazine, which won 1984's Yellow Kid award for best comics magazine at the Italian Lucca festival. Rustemagic became disenchanted early on in his career with the dearth of opportunities for cartoonists in his homeland and started looking to work with the Western comics scene. After the war broke out, and the siege of Sarajevo started, Rustemagic's offices and their repository of priceless and irreplaceable original artwork was destroyed by tanks, forcing him and his family to flee to Slovenia where they remain and work today. Another casualty of the siege was the Serbian comics journalist Karim Zaimovic, who was mortally wounded by a grenade. Zaimovic was one of those rare people who, like Thierry Groensteen in France or Paul Gravett in the UK, worked tirelessly to elevate the public's opinion of the comics art form. Even though he and Rustemagic weren't cartoonists, their loss was particularly hard for the Serbian comics scene.

Nevertheless, comics production continues in Serbia, albeit on a small scale, and often with little or no reward. Cartoonists like Zoran Janjetov, Darko Perovic, Rajko Milosevic Gera, Sasa Rakezic, Branislav Kerac, Bojan Redzic, Nenad Vukmirovic, Dejan Nenadov and many others are all either abroad or working for foreign publications, while at home fanzines like Patagonia, Tron and Niznaf have introduced the new generation of

Jules Radilovic

Born in 1928 in Maribor, Slovenia, this incredibly important cartoonist was one of the first former Yugoslavian comics artists to have their work syndicated around the world. Equally good at realistic and humorous comics, Radilovic began working in the comics industry in 1952 after working at the Studio for Animated Films in Zagreb. In 1956, he started collaborating with the scriptwriter Zvonimir Furtiner with whom Radilovic created the series *Izumi i Otkrica* for the German Rolf Kauka studio, and the historical epic *Kroz Minula Stoljeca* in the Yugoslavian magazine *Plavi Vjesnik*.

Radilovic's most famous series was the detective parody *Herlock Shomes* that ran until 1972, but he also worked on a variety of other series, including the WWII series *De Partizanen* for the Dutch magazine *Eppo*, and series like *Baca Izvidjac* and *Jamie McPheters* for Ervin Rustemagic's Strip Art Features syndicate.

Herlock Shomes © Jules Radilovic/Zvonimir Furtiner

Above: The dynamic artwork of Edvin Biukovic, who sadly died of cancer at the tender age of 30 in 1999. This is from the US series *Grendel Tales*, written by Darko Macan.
© Edvin Biukovic, Matt Wagner

Below: The stunning black and white art of Mirko Ilic, one of the founders of the influential *Novi Kvadrat*.
© Mirko Ilic

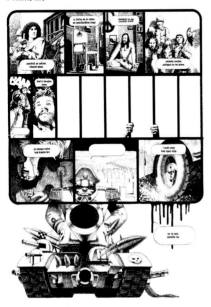

cartoonists like Dragan Rokvic, Wostok, Enisa Bravo and Berlin Tuzlic.

CROATIA

The early history of Croatia's comics industry is tied up in the history of Yugoslavia's. In 1954, a new magazine called *Plavi Vjesnik* was created. This magazine, which lasted 19 years, carried an array of comics by the finest cartoonists in Yugoslavia at the time, including Jules Radilovic, Andrija Maurovic, the Neugebauers, Zarko Beker, and Oto Reisinger. Many of these cartoonists were based in Croatia, and more than a few of them were influenced by American and other foreign comics that they had seen.

At its height, *Plavac* (as the magazine was colloquially known) had a circulation of 170,000 and was known as the magazine for children and adults who wanted to follow comics. Unfortunately, a series of editorial faux pas led to the magazine practically dropping all comics from its pages, and the corresponding drop in sales led to its eventual demise. At about the same time, Croatian publishers also discovered cheap imports of foreign comics, mainly from the UK, US, France and Italy, and this forced almost all cartoonists to look for work in other media like animation and advertising. For the next few years, the Croatian comics market slumped into a

state of despair with almost no home-grown cartoonists published.

In 1976, a group of young cartoonists formed a collective called Novi Kvadrat, and turned Croatian comics on their head during the three years they worked together. Influenced by adult comics from France that they couldn't read, the group – which included Mirko Ilic, Ninoslav Kunc, Radovan Devlic, Kresimir Zimonic, Emir Mesic, Igor Kordej and Josko Marusic – remade comics in their own image, dealing with subjects like philosophy, satire and social criticism. After Novi Kvadrat disbanded, some members vanished from sight, while others moved into other artistic fields. Ilic went to America and became a renowned illustrator and graphic designer. Others went on to create longer-format comics, like Devlic and Kordej, while Kresimir Zimonic decided to try to elevate comics to the level of art all by himself. He formed the Croatian Union of Comics Creators, started the biennial comics festival in Vinkovci and edited the comics fanzine/magazine *Patak* for over 10 years. *Patak* introduced a great many excellent creators like Darko Macan, Daniel Zezelj, Edvin Biukovic, Zeljko Pahek and Magda Dulcic, but went into a slump and finally hiatus when the war broke out.

Croatian comics nowadays are divided into reprints of foreign material (mostly Disney, Bonelli comics and some manga), children's magazines like *Modra Lasta* or *Smib* (which are distributed through schools, and where Croatian cartoonists can earn a living) and fanzines like *Endem*, *Stripoholic* and *Variete Radikale*, which do their best to promote young cartoonists. There is also *Kvadrat*, a magazine about comics, which has detailed criticism, a little like a Croatian *Les Cahiers de la Bande Dessinée*.

SLOVENIA

The biggest thing in Slovenian comics in the past decade or so has been *Stripburger*, a magazine devoted to alternative comics. This magazine was born out of the hard-core music and graffiti scenes, and took some time to come to be the influential and international magazine it is now. With the authors willing to take risks, both in format and in content (issues have been oversized, pocket-sized and silk-screened), *Stripburger* is a wonderful insight into the world of young cartoonists, especially in Slovenia, today. An editorial committee, which can sometimes produce some unusual decisions, pilots the editorial direction of the magazine, but people as passionate about comics as Igor Prassel and Jakob Klemencic never go far wrong. A healthy scene has grown up around *Stripburger*, and there are some fine cartoonists working out of Slovenia, including the aforementioned Jakob Klemencic, Gregor

Mastnak, Damijan Sovec, Milos Radosavljevic and Zoran Smiljanic.

CZECH REPUBLIC

Comics have been a rare commodity in the Czech Republic over the years. Due to the communist regime, any comics that appeared before the 1989 'velvet revolution' were scrupulously analyzed for any hints of subversive imperialist influence. As a result, comics were thought to be capitalist rubbish for people who couldn't read real books.

There were exceptions, like the *Rychlé šípy* stories created by Jaroslav Fogler and Jan Fischer (and later a whole host of cartoonists including Bohumil Konecny, Václav Junek and Marko Cermak), and subsequently the work of Karel Saudek who had seen Western comics and applied the form to his own. Unfortunately, his work was often left unfinished due to censorship, even though it was published in magazines like *Mlady Svet*. In the 1980s, the *Ctyrlistek* series of comic books was issued for children, created by Ljuba Stiplova and Jaroslav Nemecek. After the 1989 revolution, the Czech people got their first taste of comics with foreign works, but it didn't really click. It was a difficult start. Nonetheless, a few enthusiasts got together and started to form small publishers to reprint foreign comics and publish new

Above: The Croatian comics fanzine, *Kvadrat*. Cover by Jules Radilovic.
© *Jules Radilovic*

Right: The work of Daniel Zezelj has rightly won him many fans in Western comics publishing houses.
© *Daniel Zezelj*

Above: The evocative brushwork of Slovenian cartoonist Jakob Klemencic.
© *Jakob Klemencic*

Below: Sasa Rakezic (AKA Aleksandar Zograf) and his strange, dream-like comics.
© *Sasa Rakezic*

Czech artists. Two magazines stand out: *Crew2*, dedicated to introducing the Czech public to the wider world of comics, and *Argh!*, which does the same job for home-grown cartoonists.

POLAND

Of all the countries in the former Eastern Bloc, Poland has perhaps the largest comics scene – you could almost call it an industry. As in most countries, comics in Poland have been looked down upon as trash for subnormal people and slow children. Much of this attitude was created by the communist regime, which on one hand dismissed comics as imperialist garbage, and on the other used them for propaganda amongst children and adolescents. During these years, such morally edifying comics like *Kapitan Kloss*, *Kapitan Zbik* and the still-published *Tytus Romek I A'Tomek* had their salad days.

After the fall of communism, it was a fallow time for Polish comics, as the free market discovered that publishing comic books was a quick way to the poorhouse. Fortunately, an independent comics scene began to fill the gap left by the sudden lack of interest by the established publishers. These independents mainly reprinted comics from abroad (like *Thorgal*, incidentally co-created by the most famous Polish cartoonist, Grzegorz Rosinski), and so

fanzines began cropping up to publish Poland's ever-increasing pool of local talent. The most important magazines are *AQQ*, *Arena Komiks* and *KKK* (nothing to do with the American organization with the same initials) – all of which are a mix of articles and news about comics, and strips by young Polish cartoonists. Among the artists featured are cartoonists like Jacek Celadin, Ola Czubek, Krzysztof Ostrowski, Tomek Tomaszewski, Tomek Piorunowski and Michel Sledzinski. The latter was also the creator of one of the most successful recent anthologies in Poland, *Produkt*.

The pan-European publisher Egmont also set up a division in Poland in the mid-1990s, and began to publish a new magazine called *Swiat Komiksu*. The success of the magazine has also led Egmont to publishing albums, some reprints and others of Polish cartoonists' work, such as *Breakoff* by Robert Adler and Tobiasz Piatowski. A local publisher, Siedmiorog, followed Egmont's lead, and started to publish Polish comics in album format, the first being the surreal *Mikropolis* by Krzysztof Gawronkiewicz and Dennis Wodja. Festivals are also a big part of the Polish comics scene with the two main ones being the Lodz and Warsaw festivals, which have a mix of foreign visitors and panels featuring local comics. Like most other European events, the festivals in Poland also have exhibitions, awards and lectures on different aspects of comics.

Attendances have been growing for these festivals, with 2,000 to 3,000 people going through the doors over three days.

Although there are scenes in other Eastern European countries, those described above are the most active in terms of comic book output. Others, like Russia and Hungary, have a comics industry that is small but slowly growing. Whether comics have a place in the general culture of the former Eastern Bloc countries, or if they are to stay as an underground, almost cult-like medium, remains to be seen.

Left: The wonderful Darko Macan, here making a comment on receiving an award...
© Darko Macan

Left: A special issue of the Slovenian comics magazine, Stripburger, featuring a cover by Polish cartoonist Wostok.
© Strip Core, Wostok

Right: Dennis Wodja's surreal cartooning for his series Mikropolis.
© Dennis Wodja, Krzysztof Gawronkiewicz

HUGO PRATT

Above: Early work from Pratt's Argentinean days: *Sgt. Kirk*, written by Hector Oesterheld.
© *Hugo Pratt, Hector Oesterheld*

Below: One of the *Occident* series of watercolours painted in 1982, this beautiful picture shows a quiet moment for *Corto*.
© *Hugo Pratt*

Hugo Pratt was a true man of the world, and as a cartoonist he more than lived up to this image, having worked in several countries around the world by the time of his death in 1995.

Born in Italy in 1927, Pratt's early life was one of a seasoned traveller, a pattern he would follow for the rest of his life, as he moved along with his parents to Venice, then Ethiopia (back then an Italian colony) and then back to Venice after Italy's defeat in Africa.

He attended the Venice Academy of Fine Arts where, in 1945, he met Mario Faustinelli. With Faustinelli, and the writer Alberto Ongaro and artist Dino Battaglia, he created his first comics work called *Asso Di Picche* about a Batman-like superhero. While the opportunities for cartoonists in post-war Italy weren't good, he did become part of the Venice group, a loose association of comics writers and artists along with Faustinelli, Battaglia, Ongaro and Paolo Campani, who worked together on projects for comics publishers. Even so, the situation in Italy was so bad that Pratt and Faustinelli accepted an offer by Cesare Civita to work for his Abril publishing house in Buenos Aires, Argentina.

After working with Abril for a while, he met up with Argentine comics writing legend Hector Oesterheld, and started supplying artwork for Oesterheld's comics company Ed. Frontera. With Oesterheld, Pratt created some of his most famous early comics – *Sgt.Kirk*, *Ernie Pike*, *Anna Della Jungla*, *Wheeling* and others. These comics were rightly acclaimed, and Pratt's evocative artwork perfectly comple-mented Oesterheld's humanist stories.

For a while, Pratt moved to São Paulo, Brazil, to teach on the comics drawing class started by Enrique Lipzyc at the Escula Panamericana de Arte, but he tired of the teaching life and moved back to Argentina. It wasn't long before he got itchy feet again, and in 1959 Pratt moved to London to start working for Fleetway Publications, drawing for their pocket-sized War Picture Library comics. He also got some occasional work draw-ing for the *Daily Mirror* and *Sunday Pictorial*, but it wasn't enough to keep him in London, and with assistant Gisela Dester quitting comics, he briefly went back to Argentina to become the editor of the *Misterix* comics magazine.

In 1962, Pratt moved back to Italy, where he met up with his old friend Battaglia, who was drawing adaptations of popular fiction and historical stories for the *Corriere dei Piccoli*, a children's comic based in Milan. By the end of that year, Pratt had started drawing similar material to Battaglia for *Corriere dei Piccoli*. This work bored and frustrated Pratt, but he needed the money, especially since he had married for the second time.

By 1967, Pratt had been kicked off *Corriere dei Piccoli* due to his characteristic boat-rocking. By lucky chance, at around the same time, he was approached with the idea of publishing translations of some of his Argentinean work. Thus *Sgt. Kirk* magazine was born. In addition to the translated reprints, Pratt also worked on a new strip called *Una Ballata del Mare Salato*, set in the South Seas. One of the characters within the strip, originally a supporting actor, began to take over. This character was to become *Corto Maltese*, Pratt's most famous creation. In the meantime though, *Una Ballata* became a critical and public success. It also allowed Pratt to again experiment with his artistic style and was something of a revelation, both to the reader and to Pratt himself.

While at the Lucca comics festival, Pratt was introduced to the editor-in-chief of Editions Vaillant in Paris, Georges Rieu. Rieu was impressed by *Una Ballata*, and asked Pratt to

contrubute to *Pif*. When *Sgt. Kirk* folded in late 1969, Pratt found himself working on a strip featuring *Corto Maltese*, and in the 4 April 1970 issue of *Pif*, the first *Corto* story, *Le Secret de Tristam Bantam* appeared. In 1973, he transferred the strip to the Belgian magazine *Tintin* and an older audience saw *Corto*. Soon Casterman were collecting *Corto Maltese* into albums, and the Italian magazine *Linus* featured the first episode of a new *Corto* story, *Corto Sconte della Arcana*.

Even though Pratt now had fame and was comfortably well off, he continued working and travelling. In addition to the *Corto Maltese* strips, he also found time to create a number of independent comic series, including a couple with fellow Italian cartoonist Milo Manara.

Pratt died of cancer in 1995 at his home in Switzerland. Comics had lost one of its heroes, a man not content to stay within one style or mode of storytelling, but who wanted his comics to reflect the wider world of experience. His comics not only showed his graphic versatility, but also his use of fantasy elements in his stories. Pratt wasn't afraid to use dream imagery or adventure to tell his stories, and while this may have been confusing or off-putting in a lesser artist, Pratt's pure mastery of the comics form always ensured his readers were with him every step of the way.

Above: *Corto Maltese* talks tough. From *Una Ballata del Mare Salato*.
© Hugo Pratt, Casterman, Harvill Press

Below: Pratt's rough layouts were better than many cartoonists' finished work.
© Hugo Pratt

Above: A marvellous sequence from Argentine cartoonist Eduardo Risso's breakout US series, *100 Bullets*.
© *Eduardo Risso, DC Comics*

7

SOUTH OF THE BORDER

South American comics have a rich and varied history. They also have been the stage on which some incredible things have occurred. From 'disappearances' of a major creator and many members of his family, to incredible sales figures...

Above: *Sarrasqueta,* arguably the first major Argentine comics character, here drawn by Manuel Redondo.
© *Estate of Manuel Redondo*

The four main comic-producing nations of South American consist of Argentina, Brazil, Mexico and Cuba, and while other countries 'south of the border' do have comics scenes, they are not quite as big as this quartet.

ARGENTINA

Argentina's love affair with the comics medium started in the early 20th Century. Like most other prosperous countries in the world at the time, satirical magazines and broadsheets were in vogue, featuring caricatures and narrative sequences of pictures. Often called 'proto-comics', these early attempts at graphic narrative emerged in Argentina in the latter part of the 19th Century. In 1912, one of these magazines, *Caras y Caretas,* featured the first true comic strip to be seen in South America. Created by Manuel Redondo, the strip was called *Viruta y Chicharrón* and was later discovered by comics historians to have been a copy of an obscure comic strip called *Spareribs and Gravy* by the North American cartoonist George McManus, the creator of the famed strip *Bringing Up Baby.* Regardless of its

dishonest origins, *Viruta y Chicharrón* became a massive hit and this convinced the editors of *Caras y Caretas* to open the doors to more comics. Redondo followed up his first success when he took over the creative duties on another strip in *Caras y Caretas* – called *Sarrasqueta* – from its creator, Alonso. Widely thought to be the father of modern Argentine comics, Redondo continued working on *Sarrasqueta* until his death in 1928.

The success of Redondo's strips meant that nearly every publication in the country jumped on the bandwagon and comics appeared in every newspaper and magazine. Many were uniformly awful, but a number of wonderful cartoonists got the chance to show off their talents, the pick of the bunch being Arturo Lanteri, Dante Quinterno and Arístides Rechaín.

The first magazine dedicated solely to comics, *El Tony,* was published in 1928 by Editorial Páginas de Columba, a company formed by the cartoonist Ramón Columba and his brother. *El Tony* was originally a tabloid format, much like early comics in the UK, and was mainly filled with translated foreign comics from the USA and UK.

Little by little though, Argentine cartoonists started to find a home in El Tony, with the first being Raúl Roux, a talented artist who also created the first non-humour strip in Argentina, an adaptation of the Brothers Grimm fairy tale, Hansel and Gretel.

1928 was a banner year for the nascent Argentine comics industry, as it also saw the creation of Patoruzú by Dante Quinterno. Originally a supporting character in the strip Don Gil Contento, Patoruzú – the chieftain of a long-lost Patagonian Indian tribe – soon became so popular that the strip was renamed and the Indian became the main character, eventually getting his own magazine in 1936. Incredibly successful, Patoruzú the comic book was edited by Quinterno and was a mix of humour and adventure serials. Among the artists Quinterno employed, was the fantastically talented José Luis Salinas, who went on to draw the US strip The Cisco Kid. Like El Tony, Patoruzú spawned a multitude of imitators. Most of these featured cheap reprints of foreign strips, but one or two excellent cartoonists like Carlos Clemen and the young Alberto Breccia worked for these magazines, where they stood out like a sore thumb.

In 1940, Patoruzú had a stable of talented cartoonists working on the magazine with the most beloved being Guillermo Davito, the creator of the strip Oscar Dientes de Leche. Four years later, Davito left to form his own comic Rico Tipo, a phenomenal success

and the major competitor to Patoruzú and El Tony. Every major cartoonist in Argentina queued up to work for Davito's magazine, due to the fact that it was aimed at a different audience to its competitors – adults. At around the same time, a magazine strictly for children called Billiken was using a superb and very influential cartoonist named Lino Palacio to illustrate their covers. Palacio was also the creator of many much loved strips like Don Fulgencio and Ramona. These series were still being published when members of his own family murdered Palacio in 1984, a case that shocked Argentina.

A year later, in 1941, Patoruzú fathered a spin-off magazine, featuring the Indian chieftan as a child, called Patoruzito, and which along with its parent magazine, gave Quinterno the major share of the Argentine market for several years. Unlike its competitors, Patoruzito consisted purely of adventure strips, even though some were drawn in a semi-comedic style. Writers Mirco Repetto and Leonardo Wadel, and artists Tulio Lovato, José Luis Salinas, Raúl Roux, Alberto Breccia, the Italian Bruno Premiani, the marvellous Eduardo Ferro and Roberto Battaglia (who created the revered sitcom Don Pascual) all shared cramped space with reprints of US strips by masters like Alex Raymond and Frank Godwin, to create a magazine that fired the public's thirst for thrills.

Dante Quinterno

Born in 1909 in San Vicente, Quinterno began his career as a cartoonist when the magazine El Suplemento published his strip Pan y Truco. He then had some moderate success with other strips, but his luck changed when the newspaper Crítica started publishing his series Don Gil Contento in 1928. Soon, a supporting character became incredibly popular, and the strip changed both its name and focus: Patoruzú was born.

By the middle of the 1930s Patoruzú had his own comic book series, and Quinterno had started his successful comics publishing house after first travelling to the US and working with Disney in 1933.

The great Dutch cartoonist Marten Toonder met Quinterno when he was 19, and cited the Argentinean as the spur to his own cartooning career, while it is feasible that René Goscinny, the creator of Astérix, was influenced by Quinterno and his creation when he was a boy in Argentina.

Quinterno died in 2003, leaving a legacy of fine comics behind him.

Patoruzito © Dante Quinterno

Above: An issue of *Salgari,* with a cover featuring the Hugo Pratt series *As de Espadas.*
© *Hugo Pratt, Dino Battaglia, Ed. Abril*

Below: A panel from the Hector Oesterheld and Francisco Solano Lopez smash series, *El Eternauta.*
© *Hector Oesterheld, Francisco Solano Lopez*

That desire for adventure comics was further fed when, in 1947, the Italian publisher Cesare Civita created a new comics publishing company in Argentina called Editoria Abril. Civita's first publication, the comic *Salgari,* was an immediate hit, and mainly had strips written and drawn by a team of cartoonists that he had brought with him from Italy. With strips like *Misterix, As de Espadas* (the Argentine translation of the Italian series) and others created by mercurial talents like Dino Battaglia, Hugo Pratt and others, *Salgari* was very influential as well as successful. Many other publishers tried to wrestle market share from Civita, Quinterno, Davito and Columba's titles, but few came close. Indeed, from the late 1940s to the late 1950s, these four men tied up the entire comics industry in Argentina.

Competition was not long in coming though, as in 1957, a new publishing company set up shop. Called Editoria Frontera, it would change the face of Argentine comics by doing two things: first, it aimed its publications at a new, mature audience; and second, the founder of the company was a young writer who cut his teeth writing for Ed. Abril's magazines, and was to become the most important comics writer in Argentine comics history, if not in the world: Hector Germán Oesterheld.

Frontera launched two magazines, *Hora Cera* and the eponymous *Frontera,* both mostly written by Oesterheld himself. Right from the beginning, these two magazines stood out in a crowded marketplace thanks to Oesterheld's writing – a supreme blend of humanity and poetry – and excellent artwork by the cream of Argentine (and Italian) artists, talents like Alberto Breccia, Francisco Solano Lopez, Carlos Roume, Arturo Del Castillo and Hugo Pratt. Of the many stories Oesterheld wrote for these magazines, two stand out as classics. *El Eternauta,* with artwork by Francisco Solano Lopez, was the story of an eternal time traveller who meets Oesterheld himself, and tells him the saga of his 100-plus lives. The other was *Ernie Pike,* with artwork by Hugo Pratt. It was the story of a war reporter, and it showed war for what it is – an evil business where there are no good guys or bad guys, just death.

Unfortunately by 1959, Ed. Frontera started to fail as Oesterheld's best artists started to leave for pastures new. Pratt returned to his native Italy, and Breccia, Solano Lopez and others started accepting work from foreign publishers. Oesterheld tried to steady the ship by bringing in talented newcomers like Leo Durañona, Juan Gimenez, and José Muñoz (a former student of Breccia's), but nothing seemed to work and Frontera closed its doors in 1962. Meanwhile, Civita sold his company to a new outfit called Yago. The new company's first act was to launch a revamp of one of Civita's old comics, *Misterix*, and employed Oesterheld to oversee it.

Oesterheld threw himself enthusiastically into the work for Yago, and with his long-term collaborator, Alberto Breccia, he created what was unquestionably one of the finest series ever created: *Mort Cinder*. Using a device from *El Eternauta*, *Mort Cinder* related the stories told by the immortal title character – who had seen every major and minor period in the Earth's history – to his confidant, the English antiquarian *Ezra Winston*. Unable to die, the eponymous character is stricken with grief and anguish over the things he has seen, but is doomed to live on. These harrowing stories were ably illustrated by Breccia who was then coming to fruition as an artist. Using a range of techniques to fit the mood of the story, the artwork was like nothing seen before, but amazingly only hinted at what was to come from this astounding cartoonist. The stories and the artwork complemented each other so well, it's hard to believe that two people, rather than one single visionary cartoonist, created the strip.

Misterix, under Oesterheld's supervision, was something of a tour de force, and was arguably the only interesting adventure comics magazine being published in Argentina at the time. Most of the cartoonists who had worked with Oesterheld at Ed. Frontera came over to *Misterix* and so he

had a host of talent such as Del Castillo, Muñoz, Durañona and others to choose from. A number of new talents were given their chance on the magazine too, including writer Ray Collins and artist Ernesto Garcia Seijas. Sadly, *Misterix* was cancelled in 1967, but only after introducing the Argentine public to some wonderful comics.

Back when Oesterheld was setting up Frontera with his brother Jorge, in 1957, another new magazine came onto the scene. Founded by the humour cartoonist Jose Carlos Colombres (who went by the pen name Landrú, in homage to the French assassin who was guillotined the same day that Colombres was born), *Tia Vicenta* did for humour comics what Frontera's magazines did for adventure. Specializing in a satirical, politically motivated humour, it poked fun at every element of Argentine life, with a staff of very talented cartoonists like Oski, Caloi, Ceo, Jorge Limura and the rising star, Joaquín Salvador Lavado, better known as Quino.

After leaving *Tia Vicenta* in 1964, Quino continued to work for advertising agencies, something he'd always done while simultaneously working on comics. He decided to re-work an idea he had pitched for a campaign to sell a line of home appliances, and send it to the papers as a daily strip. The newspaper *El Mundo* took him up on his offer and *Mafalda* was born. From this

Above: *Ernie Pike* drawn by Hugo Pratt. Pratt based the character's looks on the writer Hector Oesterheld's features.
© *Hugo Pratt/ Hector Oesterheld*

Below: The stunning *Mort Cinder* by Hector Oesterheld and Alberto Breccia.
© *Hector Oesterheld, Alberto Breccia*

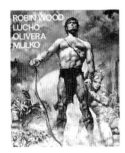

Left: One of the colla-borations between the writer Robin Wood and the artist Lucho Olivera.
© Robin Wood, Lucho Olivera

Above: A panel from Hector Oesterheld and Alberto & Enrique Breccia's *La Vida del Ché*.
© Hector Oesterheld, Alberto & Enrique Breccia

Right, opposite page: Another fabulous scene from Oesterheld and Breccia's *Mort Cinder*, showing the fantastic and innovative technique of Alberto Breccia.
© Hector Oesterheld, Alberto Breccia

innocuous introduction, one of the most successful strips of all time was created. Reminiscent of Charles Schulz's *Peanuts*, both in artistic style and in depth of character, *Mafalda*, the eponymous six year old lead character, became the mouth-piece for Quino to express his, and the Argentine people's, social and political concerns. Not only was it an intelligent, erudite comic strip, it was damned funny too. For 10 years, Quino created a high-light of not just Argentinian, but world comics, but in 1973, complaining of burnout, he ended the strip. Considering its enormous popularity, this was a courageous decision.

Towards the end of the 1960s, the only publisher still producing adventure comics was the Editoria Columba group. While these comics were still doing relatively okay in the marketplace, creatively they were uninteresting to say the least. About this time however, a new young writer named Robin Wood was brought in to revitalize the line. His well-crafted and engaging stories gave Columba's tired line a much-needed kick up the backside. Thanks to his breadth of stories – he was equally skilled at writing comics about mobsters in the 1930s as he was crafting a comedy about a young couple – and some well chosen artists like Lito Fernandez, Carlos Castilla, Carlos Vogt, Lucho Olivera, Ricardo Villagrán and Cacho Mandrafina,

titles like *El Tony* started to get sales figures they hadn't seen in years. Buoyed by this upturn in their fortunes, Columba added more titles, and most of these lasted until the middle of 2000.

Oesterheld again teamed up with Alberto Breccia for two series at the end of the 1960s. The first, *Vida del Ché*, was a biography of the Argentine revolutionary Ché Guevara, who helped overthrow the Cuban dictator Fulgencio Batista. Oesterheld, always a humanitarian, had started to lean further towards the left by this point in his life, and *Ché* was a state-ment that would later lead to tragedy for Oesterheld and his family.

Nevertheless, it was a high-water mark in Argentine comics at that point, and the artwork by Breccia and his son Enrique was stunning. The second series that the two men worked on was a revamping of Oesterheld's earlier series *El Eternauta*. The re-working wasn't a success however – probably due to the fact that Oesterheld played up the political angle of the story, and Breccia's artwork was maybe a little too experimental – and it was abruptly dropped from the pages of *Gente* magazine.

As the 1970s began, Argentina started to change. The military government imposed greater censorship on the media, including comics. The political *Tia Vicenta* found itself on the wrong end of the censorship and began to lose its way, while

Quino

The creator of one of the world's most popular comic strips, Quino, was born Joaquín Salvador Lavado in Mendoza, Argentina in July 1932. Taking after his uncle, the painter Joaquín Tejón, Quino discovered an aptitude for art from an early age. After entering the School of Fine Arts in Mendoza, he discovered the magazine *Rico Tipo*, and the world of comics opened up to him. He proceeded to try to sell cartoons everywhere he could, and in due course found some measure of success. But it wasn't until 1964, when he created his great strip *Mafalda*, that he really moved into the upper-tier of world cartoonists.

Mafalda was successful from the start, and something about the strip's way of reflecting the life, times and preoccupations of the Argentinean people struck a chord with the general public.

Even though *Mafalda* was incredibly popular, and spawned a vast merchandising effort, Quino decided to retire the strip in 1973. Since then, he has concentrated on creating one-off strips and panels.

Mafalda © Quino

Rico Tipo was cancelled. Even *Patoruzú* found its sales diminishing. It was time for a change, and in 1972, Argentine comics got it with the foundation of two new magazines: *Hortensia* and *Satiricon*. These magazines put the cartoonists from *Tia Vicenta* to good use, despite their different bent – *Satiricon* was, as its name suggests, far more caustic than its country cousin *Hortensia*. Nonetheless, *Hortensia* discovered a cartoonist who was not only very significant, but who was also a master of satiric parody – Roberto Fontanarrosa. In the wake of these magazines, many imitators were published, and while many of the cartoonists who worked for *Hortensia* and *Satiricon* also worked for these competitors (Fontanarrosa included), only one, *Humor*, surpassed the originals. Despite threats, heavy censorship and one or two cancellations, for 20 years *Humor* battled against the military regime led by dictator Jorge Videla, using the only weapons it had – a fine blend of great comics and satirical articles lampooning the government. When *Humor* finally folded in 1999, having survived the despotic regime that it so railed against, it left a massive gap in the Argentine comics scene that has yet to be filled.

The 1970s also brought about a large downturn in the fortunes of the adventure comics, that affected all publishers. *Patoruzito* was cancelled, and artists scrabbled around looking for work. Some like Oswal found the children's magazines to be a perfect fit, but others weren't so suited. A magazine, *Top*, was launched, featuring many great artists and writers, like Oesterheld, Fernandez, Horatio Altuna and others, but it didn't last. Oesterheld also found work on Columba's titles, which were the only comics to do okay during this time, and some outstanding artists like Altuna and the young José Luis Garcia Lopez – who was later to leave Argentina and make an impact on North American comics – joined him. The political and economic problems however, combined with comics' global scourge, TV, meant that the 1970s were dark days indeed for the Argentine comics industry.

In 1974 came the one ray of light for the times – Ediciones Record launched a new magazine called *Skorpio*. It was notable in that it contained the work of pretty much all the major cartoonists in Argentina, and it gave them a creative freedom that was unheralded. Artists like Solano Lopez, Altuna and Alberto Breccia were joined by newer talents like Juan Zanotto, Juan Gimenez, Leo Durañona, Alberto Salinas (the son of José Luis Salinas) and Enrique Breccia. Hugo Pratt also returned to Argentine comics with the debut of his masterwork *Corto Maltese* in *Skorpio*. The magazine also collected the best writers too. Oesterheld was joined by

Robin Wood, Ray Collins and several gifted newcomers like Carlos Trillo and Ricardo Barreiro. *Skorpio* was not only an artistic success, but it went down very well with the public too, leading to Record creating more titles. Unfortunately, none were anywhere near the quality of *Skorpio*, although some talented new artists like Quinque Alcatena were developed in their pages.

When the military took power in 1976, a black cloud descended over Argentine comics. Many cartoonists who didn't share the fascist ideas of the dictatorship were forced out of the country, or worse. One who decided not to go into exile was Oesterheld. Instead, he started working on a sequel to *El Eternauta* with Solano Lopez that was tantamount to a political tract against the ruling regime. It wasn't long before it was noticed, and he and his family became targeted as enemies of the state. In 1977, Oesterheld was arrested and taken from his home, along with four of his daughters, who belonged to a Peronist movement and two of whom were pregnant. None returned. It is assumed that Oesterheld was tortured and killed by the brutal regime despite pleas from Oesterheld's wife Elsa Sanchez and a petition circulated by Amnesty International. Two years later, the Italian journalist and comics writer Alberto Ongaro enquired about Oesterheld and was chillingly told, "We did away with him

because he wrote the most beautiful story about Ché [Guevara] ever done."

As the 1980s dawned, the publisher of *Humor* decided to create a sister magazine, and imaginatively called it *SuperHumor*. The uninspiring title aside, *SuperHumor* was a magazine to rank alongside *Skorpio*, attracting exceptional talent to create both humorous and realistic strips, including Alberto and Enrique Breccia, Ceo, Tabaré, Fontanarrosa, Trillo, Solano Lopez and others from *Skorpio*. One exceptional talent that *SuperHumor* found was Breccia's daughter (and Enriqué's sister) Patricia, who used the magazine to break into comics – the family business, as it were. During this time, Columba's comics also started taking talent and readers away from *Skorpio*, with many readers attracted by the team of Robin Wood and Ricardo Villagrán. Columba also started to promote some very gifted neophytes, such as the marvellous Eduardo Risso and Jorge Zaffino.

At the end of the military dictatorship in 1983, cartoonists and publishers celebrated democracy with a newfound freedom of expression. Editorial La Urraca, the publisher of *Humor* and *SuperHumor*, decided to cancel the latter title and replace it with a magazine that was to become a landmark in South American comics – *Fierro*. Based on European comics magazines like *Circus*, *Comic Art* and *Linus*, *Fierro* collected a creative team with some of the best Argentine

Left: After the military Junta were deposed in Argentina, this poster, featuring characters he had created, appeared to ask what had happened to Oesterheld in the years previously.
© Elsa Sanchez Oesterheld

Below: *Skorpio*, one of the most renowned comics anthologies to come out of Argentina. Cover by Francisco Solano Lopez.
© Francisco Solano Lopez, Ed. Record

cartoonists available. Some artists came back from exile after the fall of the military, but others stayed away after becoming top cartoonists in the US and Europe where they could make far more money. Nevertheless, *Fierro* featured comics by local talents like Muñoz and Sampayo (reprinting their classic *Joe's Bar* and *Aleck Sinner* strips from European magazines), Carlos Trillo, Solano Lopez, Gimenez, Altuna, Tati, Juan Sasturain, Carlos Nine, Durañona, Risso, Sanyu, Fontanarrosa and the Breccias (including Breccia's other daughter, Cristina). It also began reprinting the best in foreign comics including work by Pratt, Manara, Tardi, Prado, Crumb and others, and promoting the work of newcomers who had been working for fanzines, particularly the minicomics that were popular with Argentine comics fans at that time. Of the talents that *Fierro* picked up from these fan efforts, El Tomi, Pablo Fayo, Esteban Podetti and Pablo Pez were conspicuous in their capacity as cartoonists. Even with the stellar line-up however, *Fierro* never did as well as its competitors, and after cutting costs several times (meaning that its more well-known talents were replaced with newcomers) to cope with the crippling economy in Argentina in the 1980s, it finally folded in 1992 with its 100th issue.

The comics industry in the late 1980s and early 1990s in Argentina was a place where experimentation was at a peak, but sales were low. Carlos Trillo started his own publishing house in 1989 and began to publish a comics magazine called *Puertitas*. Originally containing humour strips as well as adventure ones, it eventually became an adventure-only title that specialized in stories that weren't quite as dark as those in *Fierro*, with artists like Altuna, Risso, Mandrafina and Zaffino producing luscious artwork. It also featured foreign comics, including work by Bernet, Manara, Joe Kubert and the Hernandez Brothers. Again, though the quality was high, the market couldn't support it, and *Puertitas* disappeared after 48 issues. As for other publishers like Columba, Record and La Urracha, they began flinging magazines at the market to see what would stick. In quick succession, readers were treated to a revamp of *Skorpio*, several new titles like *Pais Canibal*, *Coctel* and *El Tajo*, and the return of old favourites like *Hora Cera* and *Tid-Bits*. Even though these magazines were filled with talent, both from home and abroad, nothing seemed to work and many had runs of less than eight issues.

Argentine comics next phase was spearheaded by the growing legion of comics fans. In 1992, a fanzine called *Cazador* was picked up by La Urracha and turned into a professional magazine. Created by Lucas (Jorge Luis Pereira) and Ariel Olivetti, *Cazador* was clearly inspired by North American comics, especially DC's *Lobo*

Above left: *Puertitas,* Carlos Trillo's comic magazine.
© *Carlos Trillo*

Above right: A page by Roberto Fontanarrosa from *Humor.*
© *Roberto Fontanarrosa*

Below: The cover to the first issue of *Fierro,* a very influential anthology.
© *Ed. La Urraca*

Left, opposite page: A panel from *Joe's Bar* by José Muñoz.
© *José Muñoz, Carlos Sampayo*

Above: *Cazador* by Lucas and Ariel Olivetti.
© Lucas, Ariel Olivetti

Right: *Comiqueando*, the premier magazine about comics in Argentina.

Below: Toni Torres and Mariano Navarro's *Caballero Rojo*.
© Toni Torres, Mariano Navarro

series (with art by the UK's Simon Bisley). This hit the Argentine market like a bombshell, and along with Sanyu's superhero comic *Tres Historias*, led the Argentine publishers to start reprinting US comics by the bucket load. They were popular, and more importantly, they were cheaper to produce than using local talent.

Around this time, the first comic shops were starting to open, and although the old publishers practically ignored them as a sales outlet, the new generation of fans did not. Soon, the minicomics of the late 1980s led to small publishers setting up and producing comics for the direct market (comic shops). In 1993, cartoonist Sergio Langer produced the first issue of his annual *Lapiz Japonés*, modelled on the American anthology *RAW*, filled with work by the most progressive cartoonists and graphic designers around, including many from the minicomics scene. Langer produced five issues of *Lapiz Japonés*, and it remained a hotbed of experimentation until it folded.

In 1996, the first issue of *Comiqueando* emerged, a magazine about comics containing news and criticism ably edited by Andrés Accorsi, which also featured a comics section that showcased the best new cartoonists in Argentina, including Fernando Calvi, Lucas Varela (also one of Argentina's top graphic designers), Juan Bobillo, Mariano Navarro and Gustavo Sala. The comics section of *Comiqueando* also featured works by more established cartoonists who were finding it hard to get their work seen in Argentina, especially after the cancellation of *Skorpio* at the end of 1995. *Comiqueando* is still thriving today, and is an important resource for anyone passionate about comics, particularly of the Argentine variety. Other news and criticism fanzines popped up in the wake of *Comiqueando*, with most having a Web presence too. One of the better ones is *Sonaste Maneco*, which is available as a free PDF from the web site of the publisher, La Bañadera del Comic.

By now, the mainstream publishers were convinced that the old-style Argentine comics were a fast way to bankruptcy, and that the new US-style comic books were the way forward after the success of *Cazador*. More titles were spun-off from series that began in fanzines, with *Comiqueando* providing particularly rich pickings for the larger publishers, and cartoonists like Calvi, Navarro and Toni Torres were given their own books. The latter duo created the superhero comic *Caballero Rojo* that also included contributions from Risso (who was also making quite an impact in foreign comics along with fellow Argentineans Carlos Trillo and Carlos Nine), Olivetti and Quinque Alcatena. Navarro and Torres eventually took over the publishing of *Caballero Rojo* themselves, and relaunched the book in 2000. Most of the other books

Above: A page from José Muñoz and Carlos Sampayo's gritty drama, *Sinner*.
© José Muñoz, Carlos Sampayo

Below: The exciting storytelling and stunning artwork of Eduardo Risso, here from a story written by Carlos Trillo.
© Eduardo Risso, Carlos Trillo

launched around this time, however, weren't as successful and many folded after a few issues.

Even though the major publishers were shying away from the anthology format, smaller publishers attempted to revitalize it. This led to a number of anthologies being released from 1996 onwards, with *Suelteme!* and *Hacha* being two of note.

As the 1990s ended, the collapsing Argentine economy caused many comic shops to close, despite a boom in mini-comics, fanzines and magazines reprinting manga. The Buenos Aires Fantabaires comic festival also appeared, along the same lines as the festival in Barcelona, Spain.

Two projects grabbed the headlines at the end of the 20th Century. The first, a new *El Eternauta* story created by Solano Lopez and Pablo Maiztegui, was published weekly in a supplement to several Sunday newspapers called *Nueva*. Although nowhere near as good as the original, the whole story was later collected into a full-colour book published by Club del Comic – a chain of comic shops – and the creators are working on more *El Eternauta* stories. The second project was called *4 Segundos*, created by Alejo Garcia Valdearena and Feliciano Garcia Zecchin, and was an excellent attempt to get away from superheroes and fantasy, and create a sitcom in comics format. The strip also appeared in a manga-influenced anthology called *Ultra*, along with *Convergencia* by Leandro Oberto and Pier Brito, and other examples of new Argentine comics.

The latest great hope for the old-style Argentinean anthology came in 2004, when the small publishing house Ediciones Gargola launched *Bastión Comix*, a mix of homegrown talent, with cartoonists like Ricardo Villagrán, and imported reprints, with the hope of capturing the public's attention as *El Tony* and *Skorpio* once did.

The beginning of the 21st Century still saw the Argentine economy in the toilet, and comics publishers cancelling titles left, right and centre. It seemed that comics in Argentina were, if not doomed, then mortally wounded. The situation is not quite as bad as it could be, artistically at least, as Argentinean cartoonists are becoming more and more popular abroad, with many of them earning a living in US, French or Italian comics. At home, fanzines like *Comiqueando*, *El Historietista*, the online *Portalcomic.com* and *Rebrote.com* and others are giving a home to the new voices in comics, and although the mainstream is all but gone – with manga and other reprints being the majority of material published, there is always hope that the Argentinean blic will rekindle their long love affair with the Ninth Art.

Right: *4 Segundos,* a popular independent comic book.
© *Valderena, Zecchin*

Below: *Superhumor,* an important anthology.
© *Ed. La Urraca*

Left, opposite page: The cover from Alan Moore's graphic novel *A Small Killing,* illustrated by the Argentinean cartoonist Oscar Zarate. Zarate has also illustrated graphic novels by Alexei Sayle (the UK comedian) and a number of "…*for beginners*" books.
© *Oscar Zarate, Alan Moore, Victor Gollancz*

Left: *Gibi*, the most famous name in Brazilian Comics.
© *Lee Falk, KFS*

Right: An *O Tico-Tico* Annual cover.
© *Respective Copyright Holders*

Above: The influential and funny Laerte, one of Brazil's finest cartoonists.
© *Laerte*

Right, opposite page: A striking image from Brazilian cartoonist Samuel Casal, one of the new breed of Brazilian talents.
© *Samuel Casal*

BRAZIL

Brazil's comics industry doesn't have quite the breadth of history as the Argentine scene, but that's not to say that there haven't been fine Brazilian comics or cartoonists. On the contrary – the Brazilians have produced more than their fair share of stand-out creators and strips.

Comics first arrived on Brazil's shores thanks to an Italian immigrant, Angelo Agostini, who, in 1869, started to create strips for the magazines *Vida Fluminense*, *Revista Illustrada* and *O Mahlo*. In 1905, Agostini was asked to help create a new children's magazine, called *O Tico-Tico*, which went on to be the mainstay children's magazine in Brazil for 50 years. Many of the comics in *O Tico-Tico* were adapted from US comics after the advent of World War I, but even so, its pages were home to a host of good early cartoonists like Nino Borges, Luis Sá, and J. Carlos (the creator of the popular series *Lamparina*).

Although *O Tico-Tico* didn't fold until the 1950s, its (and all its imitators) days were effectively numbered when a newspaper from São Paulo called *A Gazeta* started a children's pullout called *A Gazetinha*. A little later, Adolfo Aizen's *Suplemento Juvenil* – a tabloid weekly originally started in 1935 in the daily newspaper *A Nação* that transformed into a standalone, three times a week magazine – started to import comics from the USA. *A Gazetinha* also used local artists to produce strips, among them, a certain Messias de Mello, possibly the most prolific comics creator in the history of Brazilian comics. Immediately popular, these two publications inspired a host of imitations, the best known being *O Globo Juvenil*, whose president Roberto Mahinho signed a deal with the US King Features Syndicate to reprint their stable of strips in his magazine. Later, *O Globo* started to publish the adventures of *Gibi*, a small black boy, as a comic book. This was so successful that even today, the name *Gibi* is a slang term for comics in Brazil.

In 1945, Adolfo Aizen closed down the *Suplemento Juvenil* and instead started a publishing house called Brasil-America, or EBAL, that began to publish comic books similar to his main competitor *O Globo*. Most of the material that EBAL published was reprints of US comics, but he was also careful to use Brazilian cartoonists to improve the quality of his comics and thereby deflect any criticisms parents or teachers would have against them. To this end, he created a series called *Edições Maravilhosas*, which contained classics of Brazilian literature and tales of Brazilian history adapted by Brazilian cartoonists.

Another Italian immigrant, Victor Civita, set the next stage of the evolution of comics in Brazil in motion, at the beginning of the 1950s. Victor's brother

Mauricio De Souza

Often called the 'Walt Disney of Brazil', De Souza is an example of a local cartoonist taking on the big boys (in this case, Disney themselves) and winning.

Born in 1936 in a small town outside São Paulo, De Souza grew up loving the comics, especially the work of Will Eisner who he discovered in the pages of *Gibi*. At 17, he become a crime reporter for the *Folha de São Paulo* newspaper, but by 1949 he had quit this job and dedicated himself to creating comics. After creating a number of characters, he based a strip on his daughter and *A Turma de Mônica* was born.

Mônica © Mauricio De Souza

This series, about a small girl and her strange coterie of friends, soon caught on and was turned into a full-colour monthly magazine published by Ed. Abril. De Souza formed a studio, much in the same vein as Marten Toonder, and soon other titles based on his characters appeared. A large scale merchandising operation grew up around the characters, and they now account for around 79% of the children's comics market in Brazil.

Cesare had already created the publishing house Abril in Argentina in 1947, and he offered his brother the chance to do the same in Brazil. Like Cesare, Victor started the Brazilian arm of Abril (which, ironically was to become far bigger than the parent company) by publishing comics. The first, *O Pato Donald*, was a reprint of Disney's *Donald Duck* comics (with translated strips by Carl Barks among others) which was, predictably, a massive success. Abril followed this title up with the magazines *Mickey*, *Zé Carioca* and *Tito Patinhas*, again reprinting Disney comics, but with original stories by Brazilian cartoonists as well.

Despite the difficulties faced by other publishers when trying to launch titles, due to the monopolistic effect of the Disney and US reprints, the 1950s saw the appearance of other types of comics in the market. Jayme Cortez, a Portuguese cartoonist who emigrated to Brazil, launched his series *Sérgio do Amazonas* to initial success, but it and others like *Anjo* by Flávio Colin didn't last very long due to the oppressive market conditions. Nevertheless, Cortez created and curated, not only Brazil's, but the world's first exposition devoted to comics, appropriately called the First International Comics Exhibition, in June 1951. Held in São Paulo, it was the first event of its kind anywhere in the world, and not only displayed original artwork, but also set up a series of panels analyzing

how comics worked and their relationship to other media like film and prose.

In 1960, a new comic for children was released (for the first time a Brazilian created the whole comic on his own) and it was successful from the start. Called *A Turma o Pererê*, it was created by one of Brazil's most famous cartoonists, Ziraldo Alves Pinto, and only the military coup d'etat stopped its production.

In the late 1950s and early 1960s, a form of comics other than the foreign reprints began to gain popularity. Vanguarded by the small printer turned publisher Editoria La Selva, the horror comics movement in Brazil started creating series in the vein of EC's comics in the United States – the same comics that caused the famous witchhunt against the medium in North America. Unlike the US though, the Brazilian public loved these comics, and publishers did all they could to encourage local artists to create more. In fact, it was the publishing of horror comics that kept many Brazilian cartoonists and publishers afloat.

The massive popularity of the horror comics helped pave the way for pornographic comics, and several of these were created by the same man – the mysterious Carlos Zéfiro, who was finally unmasked in 1991 as Alcides Caminha, a middle-class civil servant, and a most unlikely candidate for a porn cartoonist.

In 1970, Abril approached newspaper strip cartoonist Mauricio De Souza (who had already created a comic book – Bidu – in the 1950s for Ed. Continental) with a view to turning his popular strip Mônica's Gang into a comic book. De Souza readily agreed, and together they turned the resulting full-colour monthly magazine Mônica into a million-plus selling title, eventually outselling the Disney titles by a wide margin. This, along with the estimated annual merchandizing revenue of US$350 million (£184 million) turned De Souza into the most successful cartoonist in Brazilian comics history.

Until the 1980s, children's comics like Mônica and Pererê, and the horror comics dominated the Brazilian market. There were underground comics like Pau Brasil, Grimoire, Dejá Vu and Panacéia, but these troublemakers were short lived. O Balão was a fanzine that came out around this time, created by architecture students and heavily influenced by US underground cartoonists like Crumb. It became the most important contemporary publication because of the artists it introduced – like Luiz Gé, Henfil, Fortuna, Paulo Caruso and Laerte – and because of the inspiration it gave to the next generation of Brazilian cartoonists. One thus inspired was Arnaldo Angeli Filho Cirne, who started the magazine Chiclete com Banana with his friend Toninho Mendes at the end of 1985. At the same

Two images from the very talented Mozart Couto, a well-respected and famed Brazilian cartoonist, who had worked both at home and abroad in Belgium and the USA.

Left: A page from O Sonho de Ran, written and drawn by Couto.
© Mozart Couto

Right: The poster for the third Belo Horizonte comics festival painted by Mozart Couto.
© Mozart Couto, FIQ

Above: A page from the extremely talented José Aguiar.
© José Aguiar

Below: From *Front*, a page by Quinho, a marvellous cartoonist.
© Quinho

Right, opposite page: Cover illustration from *Front* by Osvaldo Pavanelli, a superb comics author and stylish illustrator.
© Osvaldo Pavanelli

time, Luiz Gé and Laerte started *Circo* in São Paulo. Both of these magazines had a huge impact on Brazilian comics. They used the normal means of distribution, but their contents – satirical, politicized and sceptical – were like nothing seen before. The success of these magazines ensured that others followed. In next to no time, *Piratas do Tielê* (a spin-off from *Chiclete com Banana*, featuring Laerte's masterwork), *O Pasquim* (by Glauco), *Geraldão* (another spin-off from *Chiclete com Banana*), *Udigrudi*, *Porrada!*, *Animal* (edited by Fabio Zimbres, a tireless worker for the cause of small-press comics in Brazil, and a fine cartoonist in his own right), *Níquel Náusea* (featuring the work of Fernando Gonzales), *Front* (with the cartoonists Osvaldo Pavanelli, Kipper, Marcelo D'Salete, Quinho, José Aguiar and Samuel Casal) and others had appeared. The larger publishers like O Globo and Abril fought back by launching titles that were adult comics containing mostly imported comics from the USA, and the market again became saturated with foreign material, mainly superheroes. While most Brazilian cartoonists prefer to create comic books or strips, some have now started to create entire books, or graphic novels, if you will. Of these, the most renowned is Lourenço Mutarelli, who started out drawing for Mauricio de Souza's studios, moved on to creating strips for the magazines *Chiclete com Banana*, *Animal* and *Front*, and then went on

to win acclaim for his books *Transubstanciação* and *O Dobro de Cinco*.

While the comics scene in Brazil has had something of a chaotic time, it cannot be denied that the Brazilians love comics, even if at times it's been very hard to get hold of them. As well as the first International Exhibition of Comics, Brazil was the first country to have a regular newspaper column dedicated to the art form, and the first to offer a university course on the world of comics. Even now, the Brazilian comics community have grasped new technology, and sites like *CyberComix* (the Web version of the fanzine) and *Nona Arte* (which carries lots of downloadable comics in PDF format, many of them by the talented creators of the comics theory magazine *Mondo Quadrado*, André Diniz and Antonio Eder) regularly carry comics by young Brazilian authors. It would seem that while there are people like Fabio Zimbres and Waldomiro Verguerio (the current coordinator of the University of São Paulo's Centre for Research on Comics at the School of Communication and Arts) continually boosting the homegrown creators to the rest of the world, then the comics scene in Brazil will continue to survive and thrive.

Above: Andrés C. Audiffred's *El Señor Pestaña*.
© *Andrés C. Audiffred*

Right, opposite page: The wonderful Juan Arthenack, one of the pioneers of Mexican comics.
© *Juan Arthenack*

MEXICO

It has often been said that the biggest market for comics in the world is Japan. While this is undoubtedly true, it isn't quite the full answer. Another country has, at times, been just as voracious a consumer and producer of comics as the Japanese, and that country is Mexico.

Comics as we know them today, began in Mexico at the end of the 19th Century, much like everywhere else in the world. In 1880, the tobacco company El Buen Tono contracted the Catalan artist Planas to create illustrated stories that were included in cigar boxes. Twenty three years later, a similar campaign by the same company introduced the character *Ranilla* by the artist Juan Bautista Urrutia. Making its debut in 1897 was the weekly humour magazine *Cómico*, publishing silent comics with some signed by artists like J.P.H., Alcade and Olvera. Other weekly magazines followed suit, and five years later the anthology *Caras y Caretas* started featuring a silent strip called *Filippo*. Artists like Medina, Vargas, Alvaro Pruneda, Mr. Torres and Ernesto García Cabral contributed strips to the ever-increasing array of satirical magazines published in Mexico at the time.

In 1910, the first strip appeared in the Sunday newspaper *El Imparcial*. Called *Caldera el Argüendero*, it opened the doors for other newspapers to follow suit and run comics, mostly imported from the United States. Unfortunately for the newspapers and their readers, it seems that the US suppliers weren't too worried about punctuality when sending the material to their Mexican clientele. Strips often arrived past deadline or not at all. This situation led the director of the *Heraldo de México* newspaper, Gonzalo de la Parra, to contact Alvaro Pruneda's son, Salvador, to create a new strip for them, one that wouldn't have the problems the US strips had, because it would be created by Mexicans. Along with the writer Carlos Fernandez Benedicto, Pruenda Jr. created the strip *Don Catalino*, which eventually ran in *El Democrata* and *El Nacional* as well. The shortage of American strips also led the newspaper *El Universal* to run a competition to find a new strip in 1925. The contest was won by Hugh Tilghman with his strip *Mamerto y Sus Conocencias*, a parody of the US strip *Bringing Up Father* by George McManus (whose work was incredibly influential in South America). The competition also uncovered numerous other cartoonists and their strips, all of which gained publishing deals, including the quite wonderful Juan Arthenack's *Prudencio y Su Familia* and *Adelaido El Conquistador*, and Jesús Acosta's *Chupamirto*. Other homegrown strips published at this time included Carlos Neve's *Segundo 1º Rey de Moscovia* and *Rocambole*, and Andrés C. Audiffred's *Señor Pestaña*.

Above: The frankly bizarre *Kalimán*, the Asian-garbed Mexican superhero.
© *Editora del Bajio*

Below: Sixto Valencia's iconic character, *Memín Pinguín*.
© *Sixto Valencia Burgos*

Left: German Butze's *Los SuperSabios*, a seminal Mexican series that proved to be very popular.
© *German Butze*

Other pioneers of the comics form in Mexico were cartoonists like Alfonso Ontiveros, Bismark Mier, Miguel Patiño and Alfredo Valdez, all of whom created comics that would help fix the medium in the minds of the Mexican public as a homegrown tradition, and not just something imported from the States. Many young cartoonists, attracted by the new form of expression, moved from the provinces to Mexico City to try to get strips published. Publishers also caught the 'comics fever', and soon the newsstands were filled with magazines – like *Macaco*, *Pinocho* and *Pin Pon* – carrying comics. Most were short-lived, but this didn't deter publishers at the beginning of the 1930s.

In 1932, the first comic book devoted to one character was published. Based upon the *El Universal* strip *Adelaido El Conquistador* by Juan Arthenack, the eponymous comic was a precursor of what was to come. The first title really to find a wide audience was the weekly (like most comics in Mexico) *Paquín* in 1934, with *Paquito* (1935), *Pepin*, *Paquita* (a comic for women), *Ti-To* (the first US comic book reprint), and *Chamaco* (1936) all following in quick succession. 1936 also saw the formation of Artistas Unidos, the first studio cum syndicate of Mexican cartoonists, set up by Ramon Valdiosera, Antonio Gutiérrez, Juan Reyes Baiker, Daniel Lopez and Jesús Quintero. Valdiosera's vision for this

association was to eventually sell works to foreign publishers, and he was on the verge of signing a contract with the American King Features Syndicate to supply strips by Mexican artists – working under assumed English-sounding pen names – when Pearl Harbor was attacked.

The period from the 1930s to the early 1960s are often referred to as Mexico's 'Golden Age of Comics', parallelling the experience of their northern neighbours. At their most popular, around 1943, comics would often be published daily and around 500,000 would be sold each day. *Pepin*, the most popular of the bunch, appeared eight times a week (twice on Sundays), and its influence was so prevalent that even today some Mexicans call comic books 'Pepines'. Not everybody loved comics though; in 1943, the Catholic Legion of Decency mounted an anti-comics campaign that led to the formation of La Comisión Calificadora de Publicaciones y Revistas Illustradas, a body that had no real support of the law, but had enormous power. It remains operational today, but is largely ineffectual.

The two most popular comics, *Pepin* and *Chamaco*, also published the most important strips. Many talented artists were coming to the fore in the 1940s and 1950s, such as German Butze (*Los Supersabios*) and Guillermo Marin (who created the first romantic comics series in Mexico, *Cumbres*

Above: A cover from an issue of *Paquín* from 1937.

Right: A cover of *Chamaco* by German Butze.
© *German Butze*

Left: Gabriel Vargas' exceptionally popular series, *La Familia Burrón*.
© Gabriel Vargas

Right: Ángel Mora's ecological fable *Chanoc*.
© Ángel Mora

Left: *Lagrimas, Risas y Amor*, the most popular Romance titles in Mexico.
© Ed. Argumentos

Right, opposite page: Detail from *Anibal 5* by Alejandro Jodorowsky and Manuel Moro Cid, a very influential Mexican comic that has been reprinted in France, among other places.
© Alejandro Jodorowsky, Manuel Moro Cid

De Ensueño, and would also draw readers into his strips if they sent in photographs), José G. Cruz (who pioneered the use of the photo-montage technique where photographed characters were stuck on top of painted backgrounds), and Gabriel Vargas (who began his career with a competitor to Butze's *SuperSabios*, called *Los SuperLocos*, and later created the massively popular strip *La Familia Burrón* in 1948). Other names included Arturo Castillas, Sixto Valencia (who created the popular series *Memín Pinguín*), Antonio Gutiérrez, Leopoldo Zea Salas (an extremely prolific cartoonist, he worked on 12 different series at once) and Adolfo Mariño (the first cartoonist to create comics for adults with *Yolanda and Picante*, and who would be later jailed for several days for, "perverting the children"). Constantino Rabago and Jorge Pérez Valdés created a professional organization for cartoonists, Sociedad Mexicana de Dibujantes, in 1957, with over 200 members, showing the breadth of professional talent in Mexico at this time.

After the war, there was a growth of publishers producing comics. Several genres sprung up, including sport (with soccer and boxing being the two most popular), adventure, science-fiction and superheroes. Romance comics were also popular, with Editorial Herrerias forming a group of women writers to create the stories. Guillermo de la Parra and Yolanda

Vargas Dulché also formed a publishing company called Argumentos to publish romance comics, such as *Doctor Corazon*, *Amor y Fuego* and, in 1962, *Lagrimas-Risas y Amor*, which today sells over a million copies a week. Another enormously popular title was *Kalimán* by Modesto Vázquez Gonzalez and Rafael Cutberto Navarro, the tale of a turban-wearing psychic superhero.

As time went on and the 1970s approached, more titles flooded onto the market. Some featured reprints of US comics (including the ubiquitous Disney comics), but many homegrown comics were featured too. In the children's market, established cartoonists like German Butze, Alfonso Tirado and Gabriel Vargas continued to create new characters and comics, while in the adult market, more and more artists were being attracted to the freedom. These included the famed film director and comics writer Alejandro Jodorowsky, who created the book *Anibal 5* with artist Manuel Moro Cid, Ruben Lara (*Fantomas*) Ángel Mora (*Chanoc*), Sealtiel Alatriste (*Johnny Galaxy*) and Ignacio Sierra (*El Amor de los Volcanes*). Sergio Aragones and Sergio Macedo, both of whom would find fame in international comics, also started creating comics around this time.

Possibly the most important cartoonist working in Mexico at this time, and possibly to this day, is the revolutionary Ríus (the pen-name of Eduardo Del Rio).

DIBUJADA A TODO COLOR

Left: Taller del Perro co-founder Frik.
© *Frik*

Right: A page by Ricardo Peláez
from *Sensacional de Chilangos*.
© *Ricardo Peláez*

Left: Another co-founder of the Taller
del Perro collective, Edgar Clément.
© *Edgar Clément*

Right: The stylish comics
of José Quintero.
© *José Quintero*

Ríus specializes in highly critical political comics targeting the Mexican government (though not exclusively), dressed in straight-ahead humour, like his series *Los Supermachos* and *Los Agachados*. In 1969, he so got up the nose of the Institutional Ruling Party, that the military kidnapped him and staged a mock execution by firing squad. After inflicting this psychological torture, they ordered Ríus to stop creating satirical comics, particularly those aimed at the IRP. To his credit, he completely ignored them and continues to annoy governments everywhere to this day.

In the 1970s, four publishers were responsible for around half of the total comics output in Mexico: Argumentos, Novaro, Herrerías and Promotora K. By the 1990s, the largest publishers were Vid (formerly Novaro), EJEA and Novedades. This complete turnover was due to the massive economic downturn of the 1980s. Publishers scaled back the production of comics and further changed the format to a standard 96-page digest size book. Regardless of this recession, it was estimated that as recently as 1999, the total sales of all comics in Mexico was around 20 million a month; not bad for an industry in 'crisis'. EJEA and Novedades specialize in new types of comics, often with lurid content, which remain unique to modern Mexican comics. There truly is nothing like *Almas Perversas* and *La Ley de la Calle* anywhere

else in the world. Sick, twisted and very funny (in all the wrong ways), these comics follow a long Mexican tradition of giving the public what the publisher thinks it wants, which is normally the lowest common denominator. Artists on these books, all of whom are very gifted, include Zenaido Velázquez, Mario Guevara, Oscar Bazaldúa Nava (who was an assistant to Sixto Valencia) and the king of the basura (as these trashy comics are colloqually known), Garmaléon. This last artist is thought to actually be Ángel Mora, creator of *Chanoc*, working under an assumed name.

In spite of the comics that totally dominate the Mexican market, or maybe because of them, there are still comics that aspire to show comics as an art form and not just as a diversion for the poor. For a time, the magazine *Gallito Comics* was the main venue for independent comics in Mexico, but now artists like Rafael Gallur, Ekó, Humburto Ramos (who works for US comics in the main) and the cartoonists who make up the collective Taller del Perro – Ricardo Peláez, José Quintero, Edgar Clément and Erik Proaño Frik – and who self-publish the anthology of independent cartoonists called *Sensacional de Chilangos*, carry the flag for new Mexican comics that promote the art form.

Above: A poignant cartoon by Ríus, one of the most important cartoonists from Mexico.
© *Ríus*

Below: The anthology *Sensacional de Chilangos*, put together by the Mexican comics collective Taller del Perro.
© *Taller del Perro*

Above: Juan Padrón Blanco's famed *Elpido Valdés*.
© Juan Padrón Blanco

Below: The superb *Supertiñosa* by Virgilio Martinez Gainza.
© Virgilio Martinez Gainza

CUBA

Cuban comics didn't really get going until the time of the revolution in the late 1950s when Fidel Castro and Ché Guevara overthrew dictator Fulgencio Batista. Until that point, most comics took the form of newspaper strips and pages in magazines like *El Pais Gráfic* and *Hoy Infintil*. Before the revolution, certain cartoonists who were sympathetic to Castro's rebels would fill their comics with hidden messages of support, such as those in *Pucho y Sus Perrerias* by Marcos Behemaras and Virgilio Martinez Gainza, that appeared in the clandestine satirical magazine *Mella*. Virgilio – who signed his comics 'Laura' before the revolution – was a cartoonist of admirable skill, especially in mimicry of other cartoonists, much like a Cuban Wally Wood or Bill Elder. This skill was especially to the fore in the parody of *Superman* he did in the pages of *Mella's* comics supplement called *Supertiñosa*. One of the most famous Cuban cartoonists however, wasn't so fond of the revolution, and fled to America in May 1960. His name was Antonio Prohías, and until his retirement in 1990, he was the creator of the strip *Spy Vs. Spy* (originally started as an anti-Castro cartoon) for *MAD* magazine.

After the revolution, comics really started to spread in Cuba. They began to appear in all sorts of publications, from the aforementioned *Mella* to the official magazines of the Cuban police force, navy and other branches of the armed services. Daily newspapers continued their tradition of publishing comics supplements too, but instead of the now-banned US importations that were a staple before the uprising, local cartoonists had the space. In supplements like *Muñequitos de Revolutión*, Cuban creators like Hérnan Henríquez, Heriberto Maza and Tulio Raggi were creating their stories for a captivated audience.

In 1961, a magazine was created that was to become Cuba's most important comics magazine, *El Pionero*. Originally, the magazine was a supplement of the daily newspaper *Hoy*, and was aimed at very small children, but in 1964 the magazine dropped the 'El' from its name, changed the logo and targeted an older audience. It became a standalone magazine in 1972, and was published weekly until 1990 when it hit a hiatus until 1999, after which it reappeared as a monthly. Many of the classic characters and creators of Cuban comics, such as Gaínza, Lorenzo Sosa, Manuel Lemar Cuervo and Roberto Alfonso Cruz appeared in *Pionero*, with one of the most popular strips being Juan Padrón Blanco's *Elpido Valdés*.

In 1965, the publishing house Ediciones en Colores was created by the government department Comisión de

Orientacion Revolucionaria to further expand the use of the comics medium. They launched four monthly revues, *Aventuras*, *Muñequitos*, *Din Don* and *Fantásticos*, which originally contained US strips, but these were soon phased out to make way for Cuban cartoonists and their work. Many great names of Cuban comics worked for these magazines, including Fabio Alonso, Newton Estapé, Karla Barro, Felipe García Rodriguez, Juan José, and Juan Padrón Blanco. These magazines were very successful, and only paper shortages stopped their publication in 1968.

A new magazine, ©*Línea*, was launched in 1973 at the behest of the Grupo P-Ele, otherwise known as the comics department of the information agency Prensa Latina. ©*Línea* was a different type of magazine from anything published in Cuba before. For a start, it was primarily a magazine about comics, and it gave information about comics in other countries along with analyses of strips and essays about creators and the ideology of different comics. It also promoted many creators and strips, with the works of Estapé, Morales Vega, Delgado and Raggi among them. Another of the magazine's initiatives before it folded in 1977, was the creation of a weekly magazine called *Anticomics*, which was completely created in Cuba but was printed and distributed solely in Mexico. Unsurprisingly, neither the local publishing mafia nor the

CIA appreciated this, and stopped the magazine's distribution by either buying or destroying all the issues.

As *Pionero* slowly targeted teenagers instead of children, it was supplemented in 1980 with a new magazine called *Zunzún*, which aimed to pick up with young children where *Pionero* left off. Its success was ensured when popular comics like *Elpido Valdés* by Padrón Blanco, *Cucho* by Gaínza and *Matojo* by Cuervo moved across to it from *Pionero*.

The middle of the 1980s saw the first Cuban magazines aimed at adults. Published by Editorial Pablo de la Torriente, three magazines were launched: the weekly tabloid format *El Mune*, which featured comics and articles about comics history and criticism; the monthly comic book *Cómicos* and the twice-a-year *Pablo*, which also featured comics by and features on such international cartoonists as Alberto Breccia, Carlos Giménez, Quino and José Muñoz, and was converted to the official publication of the Asociación Latinoamericana de Historietistas in 1990. Another publication of Ed. Pablo de la Torriente was the series *Historietas*, a magazine that was actually a monograph on a particular cartoonist. The public (and the Cuban cartoonist community) took these publications to their hearts, and the magazines sold rapidly, often between 50,000 and 80,000 copies an issue. Even today,

Above: A quite lovely page by the Cuban comics legend Tulio Raggi.
© *Tulio Raggi*

Below: A classic page from Roberto Alfonso Cruz's strip *Guabay*.
© *Roberto Alfonso Cruz*

Above: The work of Luis Lorenzo Sosa.
© *Luis Lorenzo Sosa*

Below: A page by José Delgado Vélez,
otherwise known as Delga.
© *José Delgado Vélez*

Right, opposite page: A beautiful colour page (from
Dracula, Dracul, Vlad?, Bah...) by possibly the finest
South American comics creator, Alberto Breccia.
© *Alberto Breccia*

Ed. Pablo de la Torriente still publish a magazine devoted to Latin American comics called *Revista Latinoamericana de Estudios Sobre la Historieta*, packed full of scholarly articles on the South American comics scene. This enthusiasm for comics by the public caught on with the comics community, and many cartoonists ramped up production. Artists and poets too, like Félix Guerra, René Medros Félix and Eduardo Muñoz Bachs, who had never before touched the comics, began to get involved.

Sadly the trend didn't continue indefinitely. Changes in world politics, namely the move away from communism towards democracy, meant that Cuba's economic position became extremely difficult. One of the first activities to feel the pinch was publishing, and particularly comics publishing. While some comics like *Zunzún* continued, albeit in very reduced circumstances, most found it hard to carry on and stopped. The magazines of Ed. Pablo de la Torriente did continue, though they suffered badly by coming out irregularly, with very poor quality and even enforced changes of format.

Even though these shortages hit the comics industry hard, there was a new magazine launched during this time. Called *Mi Barrio*, and published irregularly, it dealt with the problems faced by Cubans in their everyday lives during this period of tough economic conditions. Even though today things are a little better for Cuban comics, every day is still a struggle. Nevertheless, the tenacity of the Cuban people shines through, and this includes the cartoonists. Nobody knows what the future may bring for Cuba's comics industry, but while dedicated cartoonists and fans are still enjoying comics, hope is always there.

Above: A later page by Virgilio Martinez Gainza, from his series *Cucho*.
© *Virgilio Martinez Gainza*

WORLD-CLASS CREATORS: breccia

ALBERTO BRECCIA

Above: A page from Juan Sasturain and Alberto Breccia's classic series *Perramus*, a vicious satire of Argentina under military rule.
© *Juan Sasturain, Alberto Breccia*

Below: The ultimate panel from Carlos Trillo and Breccia's short story *La Gallina Degollada* from 1978.
© *Carlos Trillo, Alberto Breccia*

The most famous Argentinean comics artist wasn't actually from Argentina. Alberto Breccia was born in Montevideo, Uruguay in 1919, but moved with his family to Buenos Aires in Argentina when he was three. He became a cartoonist at the age of 17 as a way out of working in a meat packing house, and started getting paid work drawing cartoons and comics for a number of Argentine humour magazines, including the famous *Tid-Bits*.

In 1945, he joined the staff of Argentina's most popular comic at the time, *Patoruzito*, to draw a series called *Jean de la Martinica*. Soon after, he took over a comic called *Vito Nervio* which showed the influence of Milton Caniff in his work.

During the Fifties, he worked on a number of features, but in 1956 he met the man that would change his life and career, as well as the entire Argentine comics scene forever: Hector Oesterheld. With Oesterheld, Breccia started to create the comics for which he would become so famous, including such series as *Sherlock Time*, *Doctor Morgue*, and the most famous of all, *Mort Cinder*.

With this last series, Breccia started on the first of his long line of experiments with technique in order to create the moody and chilling visuals that the script required. Not content with using brush and ink, he used collage, sponges, photographs and even a bicycle sprocket in one episode.

Around this time, Breccia started teaching at the newly formed Escula Panamerican de Arte, lecturing on the comics course. Some of his students were to become the new generation of Argentine cartoonists including José Muñoz, Walter Fahrer, Ruben Sosa, Mandrafina and others.

In 1960, Breccia began to be noticed by publishers outside of Argentina, and he began to work for Britain's Fleetway. He considered moving to England, but the illness of his first wife kept him in Argentina, where he started on *Mort Cinder*. Breccia later said in an interview that, "For me [*Mort Cinder*] holds significance since my wife was dying while I was working on it. In 1961 I made 4,500 pesos a week while my wife needed 5,000 pesos a day just for prescriptions". He later told an interviewer that he had worked out all his frustrations with his and his wife's situation on the pages of *Mort Cinder*, making it ever more poignant to read.

A short story he worked on in 1966, *Richard Long*, saw the start of Breccia's acclaimed and unique collage method, something he would put to excellent use in the future.

In the late '60s, Oesterheld and Breccia created the book *La Vida del Ché*, a biography in comics form of Ché Guevara, which also marked the debut in comics of Breccia's son Enrique. Unfortunately, this book was to cause an inordinate amount of trouble for all concerned. The originals were lost, Oesterheld and the publisher were 'disappeared' (a euphemism for being kidnapped, tortured and usually murdered by the Argentine govenrnment at the time), and Breccia could only save copies of the work by burying it in his garden.

By the '70s, Breccia was indulging his passion for adapting classic horror stories to comics, including works by Poe and H.P. Lovecraft. His adaptation of Lovecraft's *Cthulhu Mythos* was something of a masterpiece, and Breccia later said of his choice of subject matter, "A cartoonist's work is in the public eye. To be suspect equalled a death sentence".

In 1974, Breccia had started collaborating with the writer Carlos Trillo on a series of gritty stories, set in the Buenos Aires he depicted so well, called *Un Tal Daneri*. He continued this and his horror adaptations while the military were still in power, to deflect any suspicion they may have had of him.

When the military gave up power in 1983 after the Falklands conflict, Breccia and the rest of the Argentine comics community went into high gear. He started to produce fully painted, darkly humorous stories, and later started working on what would be his masterwork, the political allegory *Perramus,* with writer Juan Sasturain. Scathing in its veiled look at the recent history of Argentina, *Perramus* brought Breccia's experimental nature to the fore. His work on this book is rightly acclaimed as a tour de force of different techniques while fully supporting the narrative.

Breccia had been discovered by the European comics community some years before when his and Oesterheld's work was reprinted in the Italian magazine *Linus*, and he won a number of international comics awards including Lucca's Yellow Kid.

In addition to his son Enrique becoming a cartoonist, Breccia's daughters Patricia and Cristina also followed in their father's footsteps and became comics artists, a fact that made Breccia the elder very proud.

Breccia died on 10 November 1993, aged 74. He left behind a legacy of work that has to be savoured in its entirety to be really appreciated. Breccia was not only a master of the comics artform, he elevated it to another level completely.

Above: A page from *Ano 1870*.
© *Alberto Breccia*

Below: A wonderful page from *Dracula, Dracul, Vlad?, bah...*
© *Alberto Breccia*

Above: Sweden's *Fantomen* reprinted Lee Falk's classic *The Phantom* newspaper strip and helped influence a whole generation of Scandinavian comic creators. This issue is from 1969. © *King Features Syndicate*.

8

SNOW, DUCKS AND PHANTOMS

Above: *Donald Duck's* Swedish debut on the cover of the first issue of his eponymous *Kalle Anka & Co* in September 1948. The anthology featured other Disney characters including *Mickey Mouse, Pluto* and *Goofy* .
© *Walt Disney Enterprises*

It seems slightly odd that in the part of Europe that gave us bloodthirsty, village-burning Vikings, a cartoon duck should be one of the best-loved characters in comics. Yet in Scandinavia wherever you go – Norway, Denmark, Sweden or Finland – the ubiquitous Donald is there.

The reason that *Donald Duck* – or *Kalle Anka* as he's known in Sweden – is so popular in the Nordic countries can be put down to the tenacity of one man, a German called Robert S. Hartman. As a representative of Walt Disney Productions, Hartman was sent to Sweden in the mid-1930s to supervise merchandise produced in Scandinavia, distributed at the time by a company called Sagokonst (AKA The Art of Fables).

During his trip, he noticed a small studio called L'Ataljé Dekoratör had produced some illustrated cards published by Sagokonst. The Disney characters were perfectly 'on-model', so Hartman contracted the studio to create the Swedish equivalent of the English *Mickey Mouse Weekly*. In 1937, a new magazine called *Musse Pigg Tidningen* (*Mickey Mouse Magazine*) was published by L'Ataljé Dekoratör. Despite *Musse Pigg Tidningen's* high production values, the monthly comic lasted only 23 issues, closing in 1938. Its influence however, on Scandinavian comics is undeniable. While

some material was reprinted from *Mickey Mouse Weekly*, most of the stories were locally created by writer Roland Romell and artists Birger Allernäs, Lars Bylund and Åke Skjöld. Hartman left Disney in 1941 to become a respected doctor of philosophy, but not before helping set up Disney offices in every single Scandinavian country, ensuring that 'Uncle Walt's' creations became indelibly ingrained in the Nordic psyche.

Although it was *Mickey* who forged the path to the frozen north, it was *Donald* who appealed more to the Scandinavian sensibilities, and in 1948, *Kalle Anka & Co* was launched in Sweden. The anthology featuring the avian anti-hero has remained in print ever since. Today, some 434,000 Swedes read *Donald Duck* every week and it continues to be the most popular comic on the market. *Aku Ankka* is a clear favourite in Finland, selling 270,000 copies an issue, and in 2001, the Finnish Post Office even issued a five-stamp miniature sheet dedicated to *Donald Duck* to celebrate his 50th anniversary in Finland. Yet it's in Norway where the duck reigns supreme. It is

Left: Norway's most popular comic strip *Nemi*, written and drawn by Lise Myhre. This image comes from the pirate special of her own magazine, published monthly by Egmont.
© *Lise Myhre*

Above: American reprints dominated Scandinavian comics for the first half of the 20th Century. Titles like the Swedish *Serie Nytt* (*New Comics*) reprinted National Comics' (DC Comics) characters such as *Hopalong Cassidy* and *Blackhawk* in 1961.
© DC Comics

Opposite page, bottom: *The Phantom* as high art in the Kemi Museum of Contemporary Art, Helsinki. The painting was created by 1972 by pop artists Leo Niemi and Matti Helenius.
Photo: T. Pilcher
© *Leo Niemi and Matti Helenius*

estimated that one in four Norwegians read the title every week – that's a staggering 1.3 million readers, figures US publishers dream about these days. *Donald Duck* has become the Scandinavian equivalent of the UK's *Beano* or *Dandy*, a comic that generations have grown up with, from grandparents to grandchildren.

Another successful US import that has flourished in the north is Lee Falk's 1936 creation, *The Phantom*. This gun-toting, spandex-wearing jungle hero has had a deep cultural impact on Scandinavians – something they bizarrely share with Australia and India – where Falk's character has entertained children for generations. In Sweden the title is known as *Fantomen*, in Norway it's *Fantomet* and in Finland the title's called *Musta Naamio*.

Swedish publisher Lukas Bonnier (of the powerful Bonnier publishing family) recalled the creation of *Fantomen*. "During a visit to New York in the early '50s, I summoned my courage and went to King Features Syndicate and asked if I could buy the comic book rights for a character called *Dragos* that I had seen in the newspaper *Svenska Dagbladet*... I was told the character's name was *The Phantom* in English, and that it should be his name all over the world. I was also informed that the King Features' licensee was Bull's Press Service, and that they had the newspaper strip rights for the Scandinavian market. When I returned

home, I went to 'uncle' [Bjarne] Steinsvik, owner and manager of Bull's... Before the *Fantomen* there had been only one real comic in Sweden, namely *Kalle Anka*, published by Gutenberghus of Denmark [later Egmont]." Steinsvik had not considered putting a collection of the strips into a comic book, but, "Comic magazine rights were swiftly created, and with a contract in my hand, I walked out from Bull's," remembered an astute Bonnier.

FANTOMEN TAKES OFF

Despite his father's initial doubts about Bonnier junior's publishing venture, the first issue of the full-colour fortnightly *Fantomen* was launched on 5 October 1950 and was an instant hit. During its first year, it was selling 72,000 copies per issue. As an anthology, the 36-page comic initially comprised of *The Phantom*, *Louie* by Harry Hanan, *Nancy* by Ernie Bushmiller, *Curly Kayoe* by Sam Leff and *Hopalong Cassidy*. *Fantomen* took its lead from other great European comic anthologies such as *Spirou*, *Pilote* and *Tintin*, which featured a multitude of comic characters. But the main reason for the anthology format was because of the Swedish Post Office who distributed the comic via mail to subscribers. According to bizarre Post Office regulations, one feature was not allowed to take up more than half of the interior pages. This limited the actual *Phantom* stories to a maximum of 12 pages. These regulations remained in effect right up until the 1980s, which explains the ongoing popularity of the anthology in Sweden and Scandinavia as a whole.

Things started looking bleak in the mid-1950s however, when television stole a major chunk of sales, and *Fantomen* switched to black and white with issue 22 (1955). The publishers then decided to switch *Fantomen* to a weekly in 1958. This move proved to be nearly fatal for sales, and the title quickly switched back to a fortnightly schedule by the following year and the magazine increased from 36 to 68 pages. Sales were still a little unstable, and with the magazine needing more material than was available, it dropped to a monthly publishing schedule in 1960.

In order to save the comic, editor Ebbe Zetterstad secured the rights to produce brand-new *Phantom* stories for the Swedish market. The first Swedish-created *Phantom* story was drawn by Bertil Wilhelmsson and appeared in issue 8 in 1963. Wilhelmsson wrote some of the stories and the rest were written by Zetterstad, but only 19 stories were created in this way between 1963 and 1967, and Bonnier Press still relied heavily on reprints. In 1964, the comics department of Bonnier Press was renamed Semic – a combination of the word 'comic' and its Swedish equivalent,

'serier'. From then on, they increased the number of *Fantomen* issues each year until it was back on a fortnightly schedule by 1968. A Scandinavian 'Team Fantomen' was put together to produce new adventures, and included Wilhelmsson, Anders Thorell, Germano Ferri and Turkish-born artist Özcan Eralp. Team Fantomen expanded to include *Fantomen's* legendary cover artist Rolf Gohs, who started in 1957 and still contributes to this day.

GOLDEN AGE OF TEAM FANTOMEN

Led by the new writer/editor Ulf Granberg in 1973, the team focused on producing completely new stories. The addition of Spanish-born artist Jaime Vallvé (who lived in Denmark) marked the Swedish renaissance of *The Phantom*. Vallvé's first story in #1 (1972) became the style guide for future artists as the 1970s marked *Fantomen's* high-point. Average sales were over 160,000 copies per issue and the two best-selling issues in the history of the magazine, #6 (1978) and #20 (1979), sold well over 200,000 copies each, thanks to a wedding and birth of twins.

A decade later saw several new Scandinavians join Team Fantomen: Eirik Ildahl, Knut Westad, Diane Alfredsson and Claes Reimerthi, among others. As the magazine developed its 'Swedishness', readers took a greater interest in the

Above: Norway's *Fantomet's Kronike* reprints classic American and Swedish strips. © *King Features Syndicate Inc*

Above: *Pyton* and its sister title *MegaPyton* were short lived but important *MAD*-style humour anthologies with an underground comix edge. The cult '90s titles not only featured top Scandinavian creators like Frode Øverli and Tommy, but reprinted strips from France's *Fluide Glacial* and one of the UK's greatest cartoonists, Hunt Emerson.

© *The Respective Copyright holders*

homegrown creative teams, which was reflected in the growing sales figures. Research showed that in 1980, *Fantomen* was more popular than TV among Swedish teenagers, although that might just be an indictment of Swedish TV at the time. By the mid-1980s, overwhelmed by the amount of work involved editorially, Ulf Granberg left to become editor-in-chief/publisher in charge of Team Fantomen's efforts. Without Granberg's guiding hand however, sales began to drop at the end of the 1980s, and the title reverted to colour with #1(1991). Disastrously, this had the opposite effect and many older readers dropped the comic. The decision to print in colour didn't stop the decline in sales; it simply lowered the average age of the readers.

In 1997, the Bonnier family sold off Semic to Danish publishers Egmont, best known for producing Scandinavia's Disney comics. Months later, Egmont bought the only remaining competitor in Swedish comics publishing, Atlantic. Atlantic were responsible for many of the big American licenses from Marvel and DC Comics and so for a brief period, Egmont had a complete monopoly on the Swedish comics market.

Egmont changed *Fantomen's* focus to a younger age group and managed to stabilize sales around 35,000 to 40,000 copies per issue, still a respectable figure

for comics in Sweden. While much of the magazine still contains reprints of Falk's original newspaper strips, a large portion of new material is now created by local talent. Perhaps then, it is appropriate, given *The Phantom's* antipodean connection, that New Zealander (and former editor of the UK's *2000 AD*) David Bishop is writing new adventures for "The Ghost Who Walks" in Sweden, and that these stories are subsequently reprinted by FREW Publications in Australia.

NORWAY'S NEWSPAPER STRIPS

The influence of American newspaper strips, such as *The Phantom*, is palpable in Scandinavian comics, from the best-selling *Larson* (reprinting Gary Larson's *The Far Side*, among others) to Bill Watterson's *Calvin and Hobbes* (or *Tommy og Tigern*, as it's known in Norway). And it's not just in reprints. Nordic artists have been heavily influenced creatively as well, with Lars Lauvik's *Eon* owing a huge stylistic debt to Berke Breathed's *Bloom County* and *Outland*. Not only that, but many of the comics are laid out in the classic four panel 'gag' formation of newspaper strips. As Norwegian new-wave cartoonist Jason points out, "For some reason, newspaper strips are probably the most popular form of comics in Norway." However, to say that Nordic comics consist solely of US newspaper reprints would do the industry a great disservice. There are hundreds of very talented home-grown creators producing a wide variety of material. The comics industry as a whole is thriving in Norway, and in fact it is the world's second biggest comics-reading country, per capita, after Japan (although Mexico has a much larger population and consequently sells a greater volume of comics a month). The strong sales are partly explained because everybody reads comics in Norway and there is no stigma attached to adults reading comics on the train on the way to work, and partly because the comics community is expanding rapidly due to a new breed of young artists and scriptwriters. Jippi Publishing is a central force in this 'new wave', a company founded and run by comic creators.

FORRESTEN

Jippi's main publication, the anthology *Forresten*, is published twice a year. Its 68 pages showcase all of the artists in the collective and boasts on the cover, "Norway's Premier Underground Comix".

In 1999, with their eye focused on the international community, Jippi announced on their web site, "We believe that our material should be interesting for more readers than just Norwegians so […] we will present a monthly translated comic

here on the Net." Since then, they have showcased talents such as Ronny Haugeland and his controversial strip *Downs Duck*, about a bird with Downs Syndrome.

Jippi also publishes various artists' solo project, and one whom they helped along the way is Jason. "Jippi is a small publishing company, consisting for the most part of two people. They publish young cartoonists that have trouble seeing their work printed at larger publishers," recounted the Norwegian creator. "Recently, I have been published by such a larger publisher, but I still keep in contact with Jippi..."

Jason, AKA John Arne Saeteröy, was born in Molde, Norway in 1965 and started his comics career at the tender age of 15, drawing cartoons for the magazine KonK. As Jason himself says, he, "went to art school in Oslo from the late '80s to early '90s, and worked as an illustrator and cartoonist since then. My first album was published in 1995, drawn in a realistic style." It was this style – heavily influenced by the Franco-Belgian comics scene – that Jason was soon to drop. "Two years later [1997], I got my own comic book, *Mjau Mjau*, where I started working more in the direction of animal characters."

He has recently broken through into the English-language market with cutting-edge US publisher Fantagraphics Books translating his *Hey, Wait...* and *The Iron Wagon* graphic novels. In 2001, he was listed in

Above: Not-so funny animal stories by Norwegian cartoonist Jason in his latest graphic novel, *Why Are You Doing This?* Originally from Oslo, Jason now lives in Portland, Oregon in the USA. © *Jason.*

Below: Jason's earlier work from his surreal strip, *Invasion of the Giant Snails*. © *Jason.*

Above: *Bild & Bubbla*, Sweden's comics journal. Cover by Don Rosa. © *Walt Disney Enterprises*

Below: The Serieteket library in Stockholm, Sweden. Photo: T. Pilcher.

Time magazine's 'Best of' comic creators. Jason however, remains modest about his new-found international fame, "It's nice, but it's one man's opinion."

Another man with opinions, most of them humorous, is Frode Øverli, whose hugely popular *Pondus* anthology contains work by fellow Norwegians such as Mads Eriksen and Lars Lauvik.

CONVENTIONS AND COLLECTIONS

With rare exceptions, such as *The Phantom*, Scandinavia is dominated by humorous titles and anthologies, and these markets have thrived in recent years, so much so that Norway also has its own regular convention, Raptus, which was founded in 1995 in Bergen, Norway's second largest city. The festival stretches across a whole weekend with exhibitions, panels, auctions, children's programmes, educational courses and signings. The crowds have steadily grown over the years and now usually number a very respectable 3,500 – 4,000. Raptus also regularly attracts overseas guests such as America's Sergio Aragones and Britain's Warren Ellis and Lew Stringer, among others.

Norway also has its own Museum of Cartoon Art (Tegneseriemuseet). The original building served as a museum, a comics and fanzines shop, a second-hand bookshop and a venue for comics-related

events with guests like US *Donald Duck* artist Don Rosa being invited over. The original location in Langes gate, Oslo, ran into difficulties so the manager, Jan Petter Krogh, moved it one hour north to Brandbu. The privately funded and run comics museum was officially re-opened on 1 October 2001 by Tove Bakke (Norwegian Council for Cultural Affairs, with a special responsibility for comics affairs – a nonexistent role in the UK or USA), Morten Harper (president of the Norwegian Comics Association) and Hege Høiby (chief editor of *Fantomet*). Set in the former headquarters of the region's main newspaper, the museum is devoted to the collection, preservation, exhibition and study of cartoon art, and displays master-pieces from its permanent collection alongside rotating exhibitions. Education is a cornerstone of the museum's mission and it seems to be inspiring new Norwegian talent all the time.

One of the great Norwegian success stories of recent years has been Lise Myhre and her humorous strip Nemi. First appearing in 1997 in *Larson* magazine #7, *Nemi Montoya* exploded onto an unsuspecting readership. The series about an acerbic Goth girl has become a phenomenon and has spawned its own anthology magazine. Despite her gothic appearance, Myhre is tired of being confused with her creation, "Honestly, I'm sick of people thinking that the series is so damned autobiographical," she wrote on her web site. "I mean sure, we have certain common characteristics. It would be almost impossible to develop a truthful person based on an entirely fictional basis of reference... I see *Nemi* as an imaginary friend rather than a reflection of my life or myself. *Nemi* acts, speaks and thinks things that I wouldn't have." But what Myhre has thought and acted upon is that rare editorial control over her anthology's back-up strips. Her choices are a mixed bag of American reprints, such as Frank Cho's *Liberty Meadows*, and Norwegian strips such as *Rex Rudi*. *Nemi*'s success has led to the strip running in London's free daily newspaper, *Metro*, exposing the Norwegian Goth to a whole new audience. Myhre's roots however, are still very Scandinavian, "My greatest inspiration has been Charlie Christensen, a Swedish comic book artist, who is still, to this day, the best artist I know of."

WHEN DUCKS COLLIDE

Arne Anka, written and drawn by Charlie Christensen, first appeared in November 1983 in the magazine *399*. This anthropomorphic comic strip about a failed alcoholic, womanizing poet duck in Stockholm, struck a cord with Swedes and was popular from the outset. Two years later, however, *399* folded and *Arne* moved

to three new homes. The uniqueness of *Arne Anka* had attracted the attention of *Metallarbetaren* (The Metalworker), the weekly newspaper of the metalworker's union. Bizarrely, they began running Christensen's strip in 1987, perhaps seeing an affinity with this working-class hero duck. Other diverse publications that ran *Arne* were the free entertainment guide *Träffpunkt Stockholm* (Meeting Place Stockholm), and the comic anthology *Galago*. One of Sweden's longest-running alternative anthologies, *Galago* was founded in 1985. Currently it is published quarterly by a collective of cartoonists, but its future has recently looked bleak.

The winter of 1988 was also bleak for Christensen, when The Walt Disney Company finally focused its attention on the hapless *Arne*. It's well documented that the behemoth from the United States has little tolerance when it believes its copyright has been infringed, and *Arne Anka* was no exception. He bore a striking resemblance, physically and mentally, to a *Donald Duck*, with adult sensibilities (in other words sex, drugs and alcohol. And sex). Christensen even worked under the pseudonym Alexander Barks, as an in-joke referring to Carl Barks, the writer/artist godfather of Disney's duck comics, and considered one of the biggest influences on Scandinavian comics ever.

Träffpunkt Stockholm, *Galago* and *Metallarbetaren*, all received legal threats from

Above: Frode Øverli's very popular humour comic *Pondus*. © *Frode Øverli*

Below: The *Pondus* anthology also features Mads Eriksen's excellent semi-autobiographical strip *M*. © *Mads Eriksen*

Fahrenheit

Fahrenheit started life as an international comics anthology in 1991. In a similar vein to *RAW*, it contained a huge variety of styles, from cartoony to photo-realistic. Regulars included Mårdøn Smet's *Stig & Martha* and Lars Horneman's *Frieda*. Edited by Paw Mathiasen, the funky Danish anthology has featured an impressive array of international talent including Craig Au Yeung (Hong Kong), Robert Crumb (USA), Jean-Christophe Menu (France), Thomas Ott (Switzerland), Dave Sim (Canada) and Mark Stafford (England), among others.

© Lars Horneman

The company began publishing books like *Bord* (1996) and *Stol* (1999), (*Table* and *Chair*) both by Søren Behncke. These companion books contained a series of mostly silent one page gags, with either piece of furniture in a starring role. Fahrenheit also started translating and publishing foreign titles by the likes of Jason from Norway and *The League of Extraordinary Gentlemen*. In 1998, *Fahrenheit* launched a comic news magazine, *Strip!*

Disney to cease publication of Christensen's strip. In the Winter 1989 issue of *Metallarbetaren*, the magazine scathingly declared that, "Walt Disney consider themselves the holder of all the copyright in the world on comics with the presence of ducks as main characters." *Träffpunkt* saw it as censorship but chose to retouch the duck and rename him *Arnes Ande* (The Spirit of Arne). *Galago* dropped the cartoon altogether, while *Metallarbetaren* first had their legal advisers evaluate the copyright situation and then eliminated any similarities with the Disney product, just as US publisher Marvel did with Steve Gerber's *Howard the Duck*.

DISNEY DUCK DEATH

However, Christensen got his revenge on the giant animation conglomerate in an inspired twist. In March 1989, the strip had *Arne* apparently crushed and killed by a one ton weight, labelled Walt Disney & Co. Yet his death is faked and he undergoes plastic surgery to remove his beak (thus any duck-like similarities). In January 1990, Christensen brought in his masterstroke, a false bill for his duck. Thus if Disney ever started any legal murmurings again, he could simply whip off the bill. Now *Arne* could look like the American prototype without being accused of epigonism. Eventually, the visible string around

Arne's head, securing the false bill, disappeared and Disney gave up hunting other people's ducks. Christensen himself gave up on his own duck, and in 1995 moved to Pamplona, Spain. Since then, he has worked on the comic adaptation of the classic Viking story *Röde Orm* (Red Snake) and has drawn *Bar Nero* for the sports magazine *Offside*. *Arne Anka* remains the only strip that has been awarded an Urhunden – Sweden's highest comics award – not twice, but three times in 1990, 1992 and 1994. Awards don't pay bills however, but sales do, and Arne has sold a very respectable 350,000 per album.

Another respected Swedish publication is Scandinavia's highly regarded comics review magazine, *Bild & Bubbla* (Pictures and Balloons). Originally called *Thud* in 1968, the magazine changed its name in the 1970s. Almost 40 years on, it is still going strong and is currently edited by comics scholar and author Fredrik Strömberg. The magazine discusses comics from all over the world, not just Scandinavia, and its closest relative in the English language is the equally respected *Comics Journal* in America.

Stockholm is host to one of those rare gems, a comic book library. The Serieteket (founded in 1996) is run by Kristiina Kolehmeinen and is part of the city's huge Kulturhaus arts complex. It boasts over 10,000 titles from all over the world, 70%

of which covers 15 languages. Anyone can walk in, sit down and start reading. Members can borrow a staggering 40 books at any one time for up to a month. It's a panelologist's wet dream. Kolehmeinen is rightly passionate about comics and the Serieteket's role, "We are here to educate," she stated simply. In 2004, it managed to illuminate over 130,000 visitors and had over 45,000 loans. Despite this, the Serieteket remains a constant source of bemusement to Kolehmeinen's more traditional librarian colleagues. Originally from Finland, Kolehmeinen feels that her homeland is possibly the most ignored of Scandinavian comic countries, and unjustly so. While the population is small, comics there are highly regarded and many graphic novels from all over the world can be found in regular bookshops. Finland even boasts the most northern comic convention in the world, in the logging town of Kemi, near the Arctic Circle.

FINLAND'S FUNNIES

Finland's most famous cartoon export is undeniably *The Moomins*, created by Tove Jansson in 1939. Jansson was from the 8% minority of Swedish-speaking Finns and came from a creative family. Her father was a respected sculptor, she studied art in Helsinki, Stockholm and Paris, and she was an accomplished painter, cartoonist, illustrator and writer. Her first comic collection, *Kometjakten*, featured the *Moomins*, little troll-like creatures. Their inoffensive little adventures grabbed the hearts of young and old across the world, and in 1954 they became a running feature in the UK's *Evening News*. By 1958, Tove had roped in her younger brother Lars, first on the script, then on the artwork. In 1961, Lars took over the entire strip, while Tove concentrated on books and painting. Lars continued drawing the strip until 1974, and when Telecable's animated *Moomin* series started in 1989, he joined on as a creative consultant and co-writer. Up until his death in 2000, Lars supervised all the artistic quality of *Moomins* productions from merchandise, comic books and albums, through theatre, opera and film, to radio, television and multimedia.

Tove Jansson and her lifelong girlfriend – graphic artist Tuukikki Peitila – spent 25 summers on the island of Klovharu, before she returned to Helsinki, to die a year after Lars at the age of 86. Her contribution to Finnish culture is incalculable. *Moomin* novels have been translated into 34 languages and *Moomin* cartoons have been read by millions of people. There is a *Moomin* museum in Tampere, Finland, which houses many original illustrations, seasonal exhibitions and a five-storey replica of the *Moominhouse*. There's even a

Above: The Serieteket, part of Stockholm's Kulturhaus, is a vast repository of the world's comics. Warning: days can be lost here browsing the shelves!
Photo: T Pilcher.
© Tim Pilcher

Below: Finland's Matti Harlberg drew this surreal strip *God's Night Off.*
© Matti Harlberg

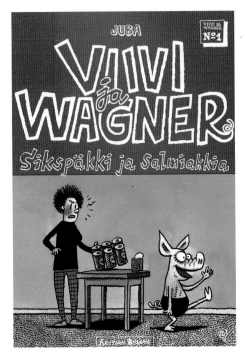

Above: *Viivi ja Wagner* has made Finnish cartoonist Juba a very rich man. Limited edition prints of the characters are sold in fine art galleries in Helsinki and there is an endless stream of merchandise.
© *Juba*

Right: Charlie Christensen's *Arne Anka* is a women-chasing duck who is in touch with his 'inner pig'.
© *Charlie Christensen*

Moominworld theme park in Naantali – Finland's equivalent to Disney World or France's *Parc Astérix*. Even today, Tove Jansson influences new generations of Finnish comic creators and illustrators. Things however, have changed somewhat.

ARCTIC ARTISTIC ARGUMENTS

In a recent article in the Finnish student magazine, *Ylioppilaslehti*, Kari Puikkonen of Like Publishing – one of the two largest comics publishers in Finland – bleakly remarked, "There is no sense publishing Finnish comics. Finns don't buy domestic comic series. The comics we choose to publish are more or less just a matter of improving our profile." Such is a rather strange point of view for someone publishing comics, but Merja Heikkinen of the Central Committee for the Arts disagreed. "There is a marginal market for Finnish prose as well, but that doesn't stop its publication… Finland accepted the comic strip as an art form in the '90s. Now comic artists receive their share of support and financial aid."

Generally, the quality of Finnish comic creators is of a higher standard than Sweden's, due to the fact that so many have had formal art school training, as opposed to being fans creating small-press comics at home. One of these art-school graduates, Hans Nissen, also remained sceptical about Finnish comics, despite creating them for the past 13 years, "I can count on one hand the number of comic artists in Finland that I am interested in. Although the Finnish comic is high quality internationally, it is immature compared to other art forms. Comics are the bastards of the art world." A sad, but true fact, in much of the world.

Kivi Larmola, former editor of Finland's Comic Strip Society's magazine *Sarjainfo*, admitted that no one can make a living in Finland as a comic artist. "A Finnish comic strip album sells about as much as a collection of poetry: few sell more than 2,000 copies." Larmola still feels that comics are managing just fine in Finland, regardless. There's always an exception to the rule however, and Finland's is *Viivi ja Wagner* by Juba.

Viivi is an eco-friendly, politically correct, right-on woman who unfortunately shares her life with a beer-swilling male chauvinist (literal) pig called *Wagner*. The strip has made Juba, real name Jussi Tuomola, a millionaire, with each of the collected books (seven so far) selling over 400,000 copies.

Tuomola started drawing comics for titles like *Alpha*, *Myrkky* and the Finnish *MAD* in 1991, but it wasn't until 1997 that he created his unlikely couple in the newspaper *Helsingin Sanomat*. Since then, *Viivi ja Wagner* strips have been translated all over

Scandinavia and across Europe and have even been turned into a set of Finnish postage stamps in 2003, and a stage play the previous year.

DENMARK'S DELIGHTFUL DRAWINGS

Denmark's comic industry has more similarities with the rest of Europe than Scandinavia, both stylistically and in terms of publishing programmes. While many other Scandinavian album collections are made up of newspaper strips, Denmark's read more as complete stories than as a series of gags every four panels. The story-telling is slightly more sophisticated and there is a tendency to cover more diverse genres than humour.

Having said that, one of the best cartoonists working today is satirist Mårdøn Smet. Smet originally trained to be a stonecutter, but gravitated to the Danish underground comic scene. His work is obviously inspired by Franco-Belgian comics, US cartoons and the work of the American 1960s underground cartoonists, most notably Robert Williams. Considering his funny, but highly brutal and offensive strips, it is a surprise that he also worked on the children's *Mumitroldene* (The Moomin Trolls) comic, based on Tove Jansson's creations, in 1991. His *Mumitroldene* album *Den Lange Vej Hjem* (The Long Way Home) was chosen as best album of the year in 1995. He was

asked to leave shortly after however, as it was possible that his artistic style differed from what the publishers were looking for. Either that or they saw his other work and got scared. Yet for a while, this Jekyll and Hyde of Nordic comics had settled nicely into his dual role of providing sequential story telling for adults and kids, particularly, with his sex and violence pastiche, *Stig & Martha*, also started in 1991.

BELGIAN INFLUENCE

Another creator with all-ages appeal is Sussi Bech. Bech's epic *Nofret* tells the story of a young girl growing up in ancient Egypt. Started in 1986, the series has reached over 11 volumes and looks set to keep expanding. Bech's artistic style, in the clear line tradition made famous by Hergé and the other Belgian cartoonists, is markedly different from the majority of Scandinavian artwork. This has meant that her work is regularly published in France, Holland and Indonesia.

Like Jason from Norway, and the rest of the Scandinavian 'new wave', Danish artists are emerging from the tundra onto the world stage, most notably Teddy Kristiansen and Peter Snejbjerg. The former made a name for himself early on with his first album, *Superman og Fredsbomben* (*Superman and the Tale of Five Cities*) in 1990. It was written by Niels Søndergaard – who had been

Above: Mårdøn Smet's savagely funny, and continually excellent strip, *Stig & Martha*. Smet (AKA Morten Schmidt) also drew the superb occult detective parody, *Hieronymus Borsch*.
© *Mårdøn Smet*

Below: Finnish cartoonist Kati Kovacs now lives 'la dolce vita' in Italy, where her work is also published.
© *Kati Kovacs/Like Publishing.*

Below: A detail from Peter Snejbjerg's 1998 graphic novel, *Mareridt*.
© *Peter Snejbjerg*

Above: Teddy Kristiansen's 1994 painting for the DC Comics/Vertigo trading card, *The Falconer*, from *The Books of Magic*.
© *DC Comics*

Denmark's main *Superman* translator for years – and it was the first Superman story drawn outside of the USA with DC Comics' permission. The story is a true Scandinavian special; starting in Amsterdam it travels to Helsinki and Copenhagen, then Oslo, and culminates in Stockholm. However, rumour has it that DC was a little unnerved by certain adult elements of the story, which included prostitution, a subject that wouldn't be alluded to in a US version of *Superman*.

Peter Snejbjerg began his comics career producing short stories for various anthologies, including *Kulørte Sider* (*Pulp Pages*). His magnum opus *Hypernauten* began here, but stopped midway when the magazine folded. However, the lavish sci-fi fantasy strip was collected into a 200-page album in 1990. The following year, he contributed to the horror anthology *Slim* (*Slime*) and he drew the fast-paced mystical Egyptian adventure *Den Skjulte Protokol* (*The Hidden Protocol*), written by Morten Hesseldahl.

VIKINGS INVADE AMERICA

Like many creators around the world, forced to search abroad for regular comics work, both Kristiansen and Snejbjerg looked to American shores.

In 1992, the two artists collaborated on Henning Kure's short-lived *Tarzan* project

for US publisher Malibu, and a year later Kristiansen was nominated for the US Eisner Award. From then on, both artists have contributed regularly to numerous American publishers, most notably DC Comics' Vertigo imprint, with titles such as Neil Gaiman's *The Sandman* and *House of Secrets* (with Steve Seagle), *The Books of Magic*, *The Dreaming*, DC's *Starman* and *The Light Brigade*. Despite finding international success, both artists remain true to their roots and continue to live and work in Copenhagen.

While being European, Scandinavian comics have a unique identity. Although humour is all-pervasive, there is an historical fondness for American newspaper strips in general that's almost unique for Europe. There is also a huge amount of cross-pollination across the countries, from creative influences and cultural ideas, partly for historical and geographical reasons and partly because of language similarities. There is a great deal of talent making names for themselves in their own territories, yet it is almost certain that more and more Nordic creators are going to step into the global spotlight and join the international pantheon of lauded comic creators.

Above: *Excreta: Stories of Bodily Fluids* was inspired by Ole Comoll Christensen's training in medicine. He then worked for toy manufacturer Lego before becoming a full time comic artist in 1991. Christensen works at the Gimle Studios in Copenhagen, alongside Peter Snejbjerg and others.
© *Ole Comoll Christensen*

PETER MADSEN

PETER MADSEN

Above: The cover to *Thor's Wedding*, the second book in the *Valhalla* series.
© Peter Madsen, Henning Krue, Hans Rancke, Per Vadmand, Søren Håkansson and Carlsen Comics

One of Denmark's most famous comic creators, Peter Madsen, was born in 1958.

In the autumn of 1973, at the tender age of 16, he showed up at the Copenhagen Comics Festival with a stack of drawings, like so many other hopefuls. Unlike the others however, he impressed Danish publishers Interpresse, and their comics editor, Uno Krüger, gave him work. For the next two years, Madsen's work was published in the anthology *Seriemagasinet*, and in 1976 he published the fanzine *Knulp* with Rune Kidde and others.

When Henning Kure, Interpresse's album editor, was looking for an artist for a new series of books, Peter Madsen was top of the list. Madsen started work on the humorous series *Valhalla* in 1977. It was a comedic romp through the old Nordic myths in the style of Goscinny and Uderzo's *Asterix*. Hans Rancke Madsen, Henning Kure, Peter Madsen and Per Vadmand, (who joined the team in 1979) all co-wrote the series with Søren Håkansson colouring Peter Madsen's artwork. The first album appeared in 1979 and two more followed in 1980 and 1982, after which Madsen became connected with the production of the animated film *Valhalla*, first as writer then director when Jeffrey James Varab, the original director, left over artistic differences. The film was plagued by production problems and was the most expensive animated project in Denmark at the time, costing over 22 million kroner ($5.7 million/£3 million), but it helped establish a stable cartoon industry, including Scandinavia's largest animation studio, A. Film. Released in 1986, *Valhalla* received mixed critical reviews, but it was a box-office smash in Scandinavia.

After the film, Madsen continued working on the *Valhalla* series, producing 12 books to date. The series was a hit all across Scandinavia and was even translated into Dutch, German and French, but has never made it into English. Several of Madsen's drawings and comics from 1975–82 appeared in the collection *Hen ad Vejen* (*Along the Road*), and in 1988 he produced two contributions to Bogfabrikken publisher's erotic comics anthology, *Danske Fristelser* (*Danish Delights*). Like so many other cartoonists, Peter Madsen also studied medicine alongside his drawing. He collected his experiences as a young medical student in *Grønlandsk Dagbog* (*Greenland Diary*), published in 1990. It went on to win that year's Best Drawn Series Award at the Danish Comic Artists Convention.

In 1995, Madsen interpreted the New Testament for the Danish Bible Society. After three years work and 136 pages of watercolour paintings the Dane produced *Menneskesønnen* (*The Son of Man*), relating the life of Jesus. The graphic novel went on to win The Danish Award for Best Colour Comic in 1995, and the Angoulême Christian Comics Prize the following year.

In 2005, to celebrate the bicentenary of Hans Christian Andersen, the Belgian Comic Strip Centre in Brussels held an exhibition of Madsen's paintings from his graphic novel adaptation of *Historien om en Mor* (*The Story of a Mother*). Originally written in 1847, Andersen's story is of a mother forced to give up her sick child to Death, but who then battles It to bring her kid back to life. Madsen's masterful adaptation is just as moving as Andersen's tale and proves what a powerful storyteller the artist continues to be.

Right: *Thor* gets his hammer back!
© *Peter Madsen*

Above: A sequence from *The Mouse*, a moving tale about the loss of innocence.
© *Peter Madsen*

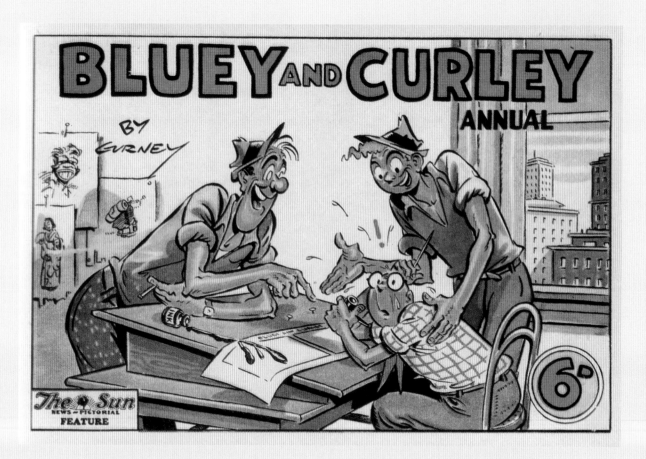

Above: The *Bluey and Curley* annual, reprinting the famous Australian newspaper strip by Alex Gurney, featuring the two Aussie soldiers and their lives both in and out of the Army. This strip became immensely popular with the Australian public, who could relate to the characters' slang, attitudes and sense of irreverence towards all levels of authority.
© *Alex Gurney*

9

DOWN UNDER WONDERS

Australasia. The world 'down under'. Not the first place that many would consider to be a hotbed of comics activity, but, as we'll see, appearances can be very deceptive...

Above: Panels from an early *You and Me* strip by Stan Cross.
©*Estate of Stan Cross*

Above: Syd Nicholls' *Fatty Finn,* the major competitor to James Bancks' *Ginger Meggs.*
© *Estate of Syd Nicholls*

Of course, Australasia has never really had much of what you would call a comics 'industry'. Nevertheless, the part played in the world comics scene by both Australia and New Zealand is not inconsiderable, due to the sheer number of cartoonists they have produced, many of whom now work for foreign publishers.

IMPORTATION AND EXPLOITATION

Both New Zealand and Australia have benefited and lost out, in terms of their comics business, through being members of the British Commonwealth. While comics from the UK were imported and widely distributed, this had the damaging effect of suppressing the indigenous output. Attempts were made to create local versions of the imported 'papers' from the UK and the USA as early as the late 1880s, but for the most part, the native scene was dominated by imported comics, sometimes reprinted with new covers and a local price.

During the 1920s and 1930s, some efforts were made to introduce locally

produced comics, and it was around this time that the first continuing Australian comic strip was published, in a magazine called *Smiths Weekly*. Called *You and Me*, and later *The Potts*, the strip was created by Stan Cross, and it became one of Australia's longest-running strips, characterized by its typically Aussie, hard-edged humour.

Local newspapers in Australia started to copy their US contemporaries and produce supplements containing comics, normally in a Sunday edition. Foremost among these were the *Sydney Sunday-Sun*, with its supplement called *Sunbeams*, and the *Sunday Times* with *Pranks*. *Sunbeams* was especially notable for introducing a strip in 1921 called *Us Fellers*, by the artist James Bancks. This strip featured a character that was to become a national icon: *Ginger Meggs*. Bancks' character owed much to the kid strips that were the vogue in the USA, but with a uniquely Aussie twist. *Ginger Meggs*, and a later strip, *Fatty Finn* by Syd Nicholls, were remarkably Australian, being full of native vernacular as opposed to the idioms of the UK and the US.

In New Zealand in 1924, Noel Cook, an Auckland-based cartoonist, drew one of the earliest science-fiction strips, *Peter and All the Roving Folk*, for the Australian *Sunday Times* supplement, *Pranks*. Tim Bollinger, a New Zealand cartoonist and comics historian, noted in his essay "A Low Art in A Low Place", that Cook was offered a contract with the US syndicate Bell to continue the strip in America. Inexplicably, Cook turned down the offer and instead watched *Buck Rogers* become the first US Sci-fi strip. Nonetheless, it was a foretaste of the transportable nature of New Zealand cartoonists and their work.

Australian newspapers and their supplements like *Pranks* and *Sunbeams*, featured mostly homegrown talent, with only the occasional imported strip. As the Great Depression set in however, many newspapers (including the *Sunday Times*) folded, and those that were left looked to cut their costs by running imported strips. Luckily though, Australian publishers started to experiment with the idea of comic books.

The first true Australian comic was *The Kookaburra*, launched in 1931, with a similar format and look to many of the comics from the UK at that time. Although it didn't outlast the year, it did provide something of a glimpse into the Australian psyche at the time, with strips like *Bloodthirsty Ben & Callous Claude* and *Lucy Lubra the Artful Abo*. Full of racist imagery, they simply reflected the times in a country where prejudice against the native

Australian people was a state-sanctioned public pastime.

Syd Nicholls, the creator of *Fatty Finn*, moved into publishing and brought out *Fatty Finn's Weekly* in May 1934. Taking a cue from the UK children's comics around at the time, it was the result of simple necessity on Nicholls' part – he had been fired from his job on the *Sunday Star* due to cutbacks. Like *The Kookaburra*, it was a valiant attempt, but it too folded within a year of launch, despite involvement from Frank Packer, the founder of the Packer Media empire.

The newspapers in New Zealand followed their Australian counterparts by launching colour supplements, "for the kiddies" in the 1930s. Mostly filled with American strips like *Mutt and Jeff* and *Bringing Up Father*, there was the occasional glimpse of a homegrown strip, but far less than their Australian equivalents. Even so, more and more imported comics began flooding into both New Zealand and Australia, leading to a deluge of magazines reprinting US and UK comics in much the same manner as *Famous Funnies* and other early comic books in the USA.

The tide was turned against this invasion of foreign material in the late 1930s in both Australia and New Zealand, although the way it was done differed between the two countries. In New Zealand, the government became

James Bancks

Bancks, the son of an Irish railway worker, was born in 1889 in New South Wales, Australia. Shortly after leaving school he decided to become a cartoonist, and after selling some cartoons to *The Arrow* magazine, he accepted a job on *The Bulletin* newspaper where he remained until 1922. While at *The Bulletin*, he submitted strips to the *Sydney Sunday-Sun*, and in 1921, they started to run Bancks' strip *Us Fellers*. One of the minor characters in the strip, a small boy named *Ginger Meggs*, would soon become the main draw of the series, and would catapult Bancks to stardom.

Ginger Meggs © The James Bancks Estate

It wasn't long before *Ginger* had imitators, the main one being Syd Nicholls' *Fatty Finn*. Bancks wasn't overly bothered by this until he got into a dispute with Nicholls over the usage of the term 'Beaut' in both strips. The two men fell out over who was first to use the term and didn't really speak again.

Bancks died in 1952 from a heart attack, but his creation goes on still, now drawn by James Kemsley.

Above: A truly Australian comic if ever there was one! The aptly-named *Wocko the Beaut* by Emile Mercier, Frank Johnson Publications' star cartoonist.
© *Emile Mercier, Frank Johnson Publications*

Below: Emile Mercier again, with another one of his uniquely Australian takes on comics. *Supa Dupa Man*, the Aussie conterpart to the more well known American hero, is famed for his cry, "You Beaut!"
© *Emile Mercier, Frank Johnson Publications*

concerned about the levels of American adventure strips being imported and reprinted, and were alarmed at their so-called 'dangers'. To combat this 'threat' to the children, they implemented new import controls that, while tough on the US reprints and imports, were soft on the more palatable UK imports. Because the UK strips had fewer word balloons and additional librettos running under the pictures, they were deemed more beneficial to the education and morals of minors. Conversely, in Australia the impetus to stop the influx of foreign material came from the artists rather than the authorities, and protests were arranged to show displeasure with the continued importation of foreign material at the cost of homegrown work.

These measures apart, the importation of strips from the US and the UK almost totally stopped when World War II broke out. A total ban on US comics and/or syndicated proofs of strips was implemented in Australia. To pick up the slack, a number of publishers with an opportunistic eye started producing comics. Unfortunately, the war had imposed another limitation upon them, namely the ban on new continuing titles due to the restriction on newsprint for non-essential services. The publishers however, got around this by releasing many one-shot publications that just happened to have continuing stories in them. While a novel solution, this must

have been a complete nightmare for anyone actually wanting to follow a story through to its completion!

Of the many publishers who were printing comics during this time, the foremost was probably Frank Johnson Publications (FJP). This company took full advantage of the new prohibitions on the importation of foreign material and employed local artists to create its four new one-shot comics a month. FJP's speciality was adapting Australia's tradition of irreverent humour to the US comic book. Embodying this tradition was the work of perhaps FJP's best known cartoonist, Emile Mercier. Born in 1901, Mercier had worked for a number of Australian newspapers as an artist after emigrating there in 1919. His forté was to take US-type heroes and adapt them to a peculiarly Australian context, complete with Aussie slang. His most famous characters included *Supa Dupa Man*, *Tripalong Hoppity* and *Wocko The Beaut*.

Other artists working for FJP included New Zealanders such as the aforementioned Noel Cook and the strangely named Unk White. The latter was responsible for FJP's first adventure strip, *Blue Hardy and the Diamond-eyed Pygmies*. Despite objections from church leaders and other establishment figures over the importation of Australian comics into New Zealand (for much the same reasons as the objections against US comics), FJP and other publishers' titles

Above: The short-lived *Fatty Finn's Weekly*, a brave attempt by Syd Nicholls to create a UK-style weekly comic featuring his popular character.
© *Estate of Syd Nicholls*

Above: Eric Resetar, the 'boy wonder' of early New Zealand comics.
© *Eric Resetar*

Above: A title panel from a strip by Harry Bennet, the loveable rogue of New Zealand comics history.
© *Harry Bennet*

were readily available to an expectant public.

As the war drew to a close, publishers started to ignore the rules about continuing comics. Syd Miller, who was also a cartoonist, published the first of the new continuing comics, *Monster Comics*; a tabloid containing strips and prose, it set the stage for the wholesale transformation of the one-shots into continuing series.

The other effect of the end of the war was the lifting of the embargo against foreign comics. Reprints of US comics like *Superman*, the Disney characters and *Captain Marvel* flooded onto the market, a situation that would eventually spell doom for the locally produced comics.

The immediate post-war period also saw the emergence of two artists/publishers in New Zealand who kept the home-grown ethos alive. The first was Harry Bennet, a likeable entrepreneur with a penchant for ducking and diving. From 1945 until the early part of the next decade, Bennet drew and published *Supreme Comics* for 30 issues almost single-handedly, as well as producing several one-shot titles. The other cartoonist was Eric Resetar, who often worked under the pseudonym of 'Hec Rose'. In 1941, when he was just a 12 year old schoolboy, Resetar approached a local printing firm with an eye to getting them to publish the stories he'd produced for schoolmates. The printer, who liked the

boy's confidence, advised him to contact the NZ Minister of Internal Affairs to ask for an allocation of paper for the job. Resetar did this, and to the surprise of all concerned, the ministry granted him twice the requested amount of paper. If the ministry had expected the comics produced by a 12 year old boy to be slightly higher in tone than what was being produced elsewhere, they were in for a bit of a shock. Resetar's comics were full of blood and guts, and got ever more violent. Resetar continued working into the 1950s, when he tried to tone down his act for reasons that soon became apparent.

THE GHOST WHO WALKS

Also in New Zealand, native publishers had started producing collections of syndicated newspaper strips, mainly from the States, but also some from Australia. These collections, often featuring new covers by local artists, were immensely popular from the outset, but the out and out winner in the popularity stakes was the reprints of Lee Falk's strip *The Phantom*. For some reason that is almost completely unfathomable, *The Phantom* proved to be something of a phenomenon. In September 1948, FREW, an Australian publishing house founded by four men who each put in £500 (Australian), and used the initial letter of their surnames to create the company

Right: A page of *Ginger Meggs* from *Sunbeams*, the *Sydney Sunday-Star's* comics supplement. James Bancks, the creator of *Ginger Meggs*, saw his character become a national icon on the back of his tight scripts and attractive artwork that summed up the spirit of Australia.
© *The James Bancks Estate*

Above: The cover of the 50th Anniversary issue of the Australian *Phantom* comic, published by four-man publishing outfit, Frew.
© *Frew Publications, KFS*

Below: Australia's answer to Milton Caniff, John Dixon and his *Air Hawk and the Flying Doctors* series.
© *John Dixon*

name, started publishing the regular *Phantom* comic, a title that is still running today. New Zealand followed suit in 1950, and a company called Feature Productions based in Wellington, in the South Island, started publishing a regular comic of the *Phantom* that ran for 550 issues. To quote Tim Bollinger again, "Stories of little old ladies with cupboards full of *Phantom* comics in this pre-television age were not uncommon." FREW took up the slack and started distributing the Australian version in New Zealand and Papua New Guinea, which it does to this day. It should be noted, that although the *Phantom* is very popular in Scandinavian and India, the character's phenomenal success is not replicated on the same scale anywhere else in the world, including the strip's native America.

THE FIFTIES, A TIME OF RECESSION

As the 1950s got going, comics in Australasia entered a recession brought about by the unfortunate combination of four ongoing global patterns that threatened local comics across the planet: the rise in the cost of production, the resumption of foreign importation, the effect of a new medium – television, and the advent of a worldwide censorship movement.

The publication of Frederick Wertham's 1953 treatise on comics and their

'harmful' effect on children, *Seduction of the Innocent*, had an impact not only on comics in the USA where the book first appeared, but also in the UK and its colonies, including New Zealand and Australia. It didn't matter that very few of the comics featured in Wertham's book had ever been seen in either New Zealand or Australia, the censors jumped on all comics as the cause of society's ills, and little things like facts weren't going to stand in their way. By the end of the decade, both countries had set up committees that looked into the comics being published and had issued banning orders and legislation prohibiting certain types of comics.

As a reaction to the legislation, the publishers followed the example of their American counterparts and neutered themselves; they toned down the material and began issuing more 'wholesome' comics. In New Zealand, the only US comics allowed into the country were the bland *Classic Comics*, with their dull adaptations of classic novels, which passed the censors' criteria for being literary and morally uplifting (they're based on real books, don't you know…), while in Australia, very few homegrown comics survived the backlash, with only series like Paul Wheelahan's *Davy Crockett*, John Dixon's *Catman* and *Air Hawk and the Flying Doctors*, and Maurice Bramley's *Phantom Commando* (the Aussies having a thing for series with the word *Phantom* in the title) surviving into the 1960s.

COMICS GO UNDERGROUND. AGAIN.

As in the US, and to a lesser extent the UK, comics went somewhat underground in New Zealand. Many kids who were reading comics in the 1950s were now being educated at universities and were becoming cartoonists themselves, determined to bring back a bit of the spunk that they remembered comics having. All kinds of student magazines – especially those published around the time of the annual graduation event known as 'capping' – and newspapers cropped up, each one giving opportunities to young cartoonists who had something to say, but nowhere to say it. One magazine in particular stands out – *Cock*. Editor Chris Wheeler put together a publication that was the epitome of the 1960s' underground magazine: satirical, political and subversive. Featuring cartoonists like Bob Brockie (now a famed political cartoonist), *Cock* ran for 17 issues from 1967 to 1973.

The same situation did not exist in Australia. Instead, comics went into a state of further decline. The few homegrown titles that were still being published at the end of the 1950s had disappeared by the middle of the next decade, while reprints such as *The Phantom* and the Disney titles took up the slack and increased their sales. Comics from the US publisher Marvel had started to be imported into Australia too, and like everywhere else at that time, captured the imagination of comics readers new and old.

THE SEVENTIES' RESURGENCE

The new decade would see a fresh impetus in comics publishing in both New Zealand and Australia. This newfound upswing in comic books wasn't generated by the traditional comics publishing houses however, as they had all but disappeared or had transformed into reprint houses. The new surge in comics was generated by the cartoonists themselves, who in the best tradition of comics fandom, had started to self-publish.

The influence from the American undergrounds was palpable, and in Australia, the emergence of radical magazines meant that local cartoonists had places to publish their work. Of the many cartoonists working at the time however, only a few created actual comic books. Gerald Carr was one of these exceptions, and he created his nationally distributed horror comic *Vampire!* in 1975, after working for different publishers in the late 1960s and early 1970s. *Vampire!* was very much along the same lines as the horror comics published by Warren in America,

Above: Gerald Carr's *Vampire!* magazine, an attempt to bring adult comics to the Australian public. Carr still creates comics, and distributes them under his *Vixen* imprint.
© *Gerald Carr*

Below: Jason Paulos has won many admirers with his series *Hairbutt the Hippo*, which features his accomplished artwork.
© *Jason Paulos*

like *Creepy* and *Eerie*, but nowhere near as successful.

In New Zealand, a hippy named Barry Linton had his comics published in the Auckland student newspaper *Craccum* and the underground magazine *The Ponsonby Rag*, and thereby inadvertently became one of the most influential cartoonists to come out of the country. His style was a lush, erotic one that could only have come from an island in the Pacific. He travelled around New Zealand in the late 1960s and early 1970s, meeting up with like-minded people and, especially, other cartoonists, like Laurence Clark, Joe Wylie and Colin Wilson, who eventually would become the founding artists behind the inspirational anthology *Strips*.

Strips was the creation of Colin Wilson, who was (and still is) an incredibly talented comics artist who went on to draw for comics in the UK (where he worked on *2000 AD*), USA and mainland Europe, even taking over the art duties on the *Young Blueberry* series from his artistic hero Jean Giraud. He also created the first full-colour comic book published in New Zealand, *Captain Sunshine*, an advertising vehicle for a frankly rubbish plastic sundial watch, featuring an 'ecological' superhero. Unsurprisingly, both the watch and the comic book were an unmitigated disaster.

In creating *Strips*, Wilson gathered a group of cartoonists who were producing eclectic and innovative work, especially in terms of what had been seen in New Zealand until then. As well as the commercial stylings of Wilson, and the 'Pacific R. Crumb' like Linton, *Strips* also featured the work of Wylie, Laurence Clark (whose epic story *The Frame* was an experimental work of metafiction) and Terence Hogan (later to go on to be a notable art director and designer).

Over its 10 year run *Strips* printed the first work of many New Zealand cartoonists, including Chris Knox, a musician in the bands Toy Love and Tall Dwarfs who later went on to produce his own fanzine *Jesus on a Stick*, Peter Rees, who was later published by American alternative publisher Fantagraphics Books and Dylan Horrocks (see Creator Spotlight on page 278).

INTO THE EIGHTIES

One of the side effects of the mass reprinting and importation of foreign comics, especially those from the USA, was the wholesale influencing of the newer generation of cartoonists. This was especially true in Australia, where young comics fans had been fed on a diet of almost exclusively foreign comics. As the 1980s began, more and more fanzines began to crop up. Some, like *Star Heroes* (which went under different names at different times in its history), were clearly influenced by American

Above: The luscious artwork of a truly original cartoonist, the New Zealander Barry Linton.
© Barry Linton

Below: The ultimate panel in the ultimate episode of Laurence Clark's comics within comics series *The Frame*.
© Laurence Clark

Left, opposite page: A page from the second album, *Mantell*, of the three-volume series *Dans l'Ombre du Soleil* by Colin Wilson. The series also featured colouring by Wilson's wife Janet Gale.
© Colin Wilson, Glénat

Above: *Strips* was one of the most important comics anthologies to come out of New Zealand. Cover by Kevin Jenkinson & Laurence Clark.
© *Kevin Jenkinson & Laurence Clark*

Above: *Fox Comics*, an important multi-national anthology created out of Australia by cartoonist David Vodicka, and later published by US comics publisher Fantagraphics.
© *David Vodicka, Fantagraphics Books*

superheroes, even to the extent of featuring art by American artist Tom Sutton, while others like *Outcast* and *Inkspots* took their cue from less mainstream sources like the growing alternative scene in the USA and magazines like *Métal Hurlant* in Europe.

In 1983, *Oz Comics* was launched and, though short-lived, seemed to help spread the word of alternative homegrown comics further. Of the cartoonists featured in *Oz*, David de Vries (a New Zealander), Glen Lumsden and Gary Chaloner stand out. All of these artists went on to work for a number of American publishers as well as self-publishing their own work at home. Lumsden and De Vries even created a new series of *Phantom* comics in 1994, continuing a beloved tradition.

This new-found hive of activity intensified when, in Melbourne, cartoonist David Vodicka started a new fanzine, *Fox Comics*, which became a focus for the growing Melbourne scene. Twenty seven issues of *Fox Comics* were released between 1984 and 1990, the last four published by US-based comics publisher Fantagraphics, along with a number of specials after the main magazine had folded. In those 27 issues, *Fox Comics* introduced a number of important Australian cartoonists, such as Philip Bentley, Gerard Ashcroft, Chloë Brookes-Kenworthy and Vodicka himself, as well as showcasing cartoonists from abroad like Dylan Horrocks from New Zealand and Glenn Dakin and Eddie Campbell from the UK.

De Vries and Lumsden branched out into publishing their own comic called *Cyclone* in 1985, and this was the starting point for a number of other independent titles like Gary Chaloner's *Jackaroo*. Another anthology launched at around the same time was *Phantastique*, edited by Steve Carter, an anthology of horror comics that fell foul of the moral watchdogs and only lasted four issues.

RAZOR

Unfortunately, *Strips* came to an end after 22 issues. While a sad day for the New Zealand comics scene, a natural successor was waiting in the wings: *Razor*. Created by Dylan Horrocks and Cornelius Stone (who is something of a local legend in Auckland), *Razor* grew out of the friendship between the two cartoonists, both of whom were rabid comic fans. Under the guidance of Stone and Horrocks, *Razor* became the *Strips* for the 1990s, and featured an eclectic mix of cartoonists, including Roger Langridge, Warwick Gray (who moved to England and started working in comics publishing) and Richard Bird (who also moved to the UK and helped set up the international collective Les Cartoonistes Dangereux, before moving into film and TV). There was also Tony Renouf, Graeme

Left: Richard Bird, a superb comics stylist, went to the UK to try to find work in the comics industry but instead started working in film and TV as a director. Film and TV's gain is comics loss.
© Richard Bird

Right: Warwick Gray, another fabulous cartoonist from New Zealand who moved to the UK to work in comics. He did find work in comics as an editor and writer, but unfortunately doesn't draw anymore, a real shame.
© Warwick Gray

Left: *Razor*, another important magazine to come from New Zealand. Cover by Cornelius Stone, the magazine's co-creator. Stone often used many techniques to create his comics, including photography that he either retouched or traced over.
© *Cornelius Stone*

Below: A whimsical page by Tony Renouf, a contributor to *Razor* and one of New Zealand's most tireless supporters of small-press homegrown comics.
© *Tony Renouf*

Below: The delightfully ribald Karl Wills and his minicomic creation *Backdoor Gran*. There's more than a touch of E.C. Segar about this cartoonist.
© *Karl Wills*

Romanes (whose wonderful letters in comics form had to be seen to be believed) and Paul Rogers, who worked with the journalist/comics writer Stephen Jewell, and who now teaches cartooning. This mix of raw and polished talent made the magazine an exciting melting pot of traditional storytelling and experimentation. Although *Razor* didn't last long (1985 to1992), it did seem to signal a change in how cartoonists in New Zealand saw themselves and their place in the world comics scene. Several of the creators involved went off to work in the UK or the USA, and this led *Razor* to be as influential to the next generation as *Strips* was to the previous.

FROM THEN 'TIL NOW

After the influence of *Fox Comics* in Australia and *Razor* in New Zealand, antipodean cartoonists began to spread their wings and started to look at getting their names known abroad. Eddie Campbell, the Scottish cartoonist who was such a force in the small-press scene in the UK, and later, the artist on the Alan Moore-written series *From Hell*, moved to Australia. His arrival led to a small enclave of comics fans in Brisbane starting an small comics publishing venture called *DeeVee*. Edited by Marcus Moore, *DeeVee* was a minor success internationally and featured comics by cartoonists like Gary Chaloner, Pete Mullins and Eddie

Campbell, as well as others from all over Australia and abroad.

The scene in Australia is as unpredictable now as it has always been, but there are always new cartoonists, like Trudy Cooper (*Platinum Grit*) and Dillon Naylor (*Batrisha*) coming through, and established names like Jason Paulos (*Hairbutt the Hippo*) doing interesting work. Fandom also has an active role, with conventions like OzCon happening every so often, and excellent fanzines like *Eat Comics*, edited by Tonia Walden, being published. The recent announcement of the creation of the Ledger Awards for outstanding achievement in Australian comics (named after the late Australian cartoonist, colourist and airbrush artist Peter Ledger) by the fanzine *Oz Comics* and the cartoonist Gary Chaloner, also bodes well for the future of Australian comics.

In New Zealand, the industry is just as active, with an ever-increasing list of fine cartoonists who work on their comics both at home and abroad. Of the cartoonists who have left and gone overseas, the most prominent is Roger Langridge. After moving to London, Langridge worked for a number of publishers all over the world, including Fantagraphics, DC and Dark Horse in the USA, Fleetway/Rebellion (2000 *AD* and *The Megazine*), Deadline and Eaglemoss in the UK, and Kôdansha (Japan), as well as working on his own

Cornelius Stone

Possibly one of the most important figures in the development of the New Zealand comics scene in recent times, Cornelius Stone is best summed up as the locus of the creative energy of more than one generation of cartoonists from New Zealand.

As well as *Razor*, Stone has also published the revues *Family of Sex, UFO* and *Roundabout*, and is the co-creator of the classic series *Knuckles the Malevolent Nun* with Roger Langridge, a strip that is surreal, funny and somewhat offensive.

Stone is also a playwright (several of his plays have links to his comics), and a cartoonist with a penchant for experimentation.

While a fine writer, Stone's true gift is for creating a scene that allowed many cartoonists to flourish and find their own voice.

Knuckles © Cornelius Stone, Roger Langridge

Above: The lush brushwork of Adam Jamieson, one of the best young creators to come out of New Zealand.
© Adam Jamieson

Right: The incomparable Chris Knox, a multi-talented cartoonist and musician. This strip illustrates one of his own song lyrics.
© Chris Knox

series *Fred The Clown* and doing illustration work to pay the rent. Langridge is a veritable workaholic, and possibly the most organized cartoonist in the world. His artwork is distinctive, even when he has to draw in someone else's style – something at which he excels. He could be summed up as his generation's E.C. Segar (the creator of *Popeye*), and if there was any justice in the world, he would be one of the most famous cartoonists on the planet.

Cartoonists like Langridge and Horrocks have had an enormous influence on the newer comics creators coming up in New Zealand. There are people like Karl Wills, whose *Comicbook Factory* turns out beautifully drawn and uproariously funny, dirty minicomics, Anthony Ellison – a political cartoonist whose work has a lovely line and a wicked sense of humour, Ant Sang – famed for his minicomic, *Filth* and Chris Slaine, whose graphic novel *Maui*, is an accomplished reworking of old Maori legends with a distinctive and attractive visual style. All have broken through and are themselves influencing a new generation of cartoonists.

Courses in comics – like those taught by Paul Rogers – are becoming more prevalent, and the fruits of these initiatives are there for all to see. Students whom Rogers has mentored, such as Kelvin Soh, Alex Beart and Simon Rattaray, have all gone on to do their own minicomics or

contributed to each other's, thus keeping the scene alive. Newer collectives like SeeSaw, formed by husband and wife Timothy Kidd and Sophie McMillan, with friend Adam Jamieson, are also doing their bit to keep the sheer diversity of the types of comics available in New Zealand alive. Other collectives of note are Oats, formed by Stefan Neville, and Funtime, formed by Darren Schroeder. What can be seen from all of this activity is that there is no one unique New Zealand style. The country displays a mix of US, UK, European and Japanese stylings, and the scope of subject matter is breathtaking. From Jared Lane and Jason Brice's comic *Avatar* – about the effect that rape has on a group of students – to Saret Em's genre-stretching minicomics, there is anything and everything in NZ comics. For the true comics connoisseur, the Australasian scene, and particularly the community in New Zealand, is one well worth investigating.

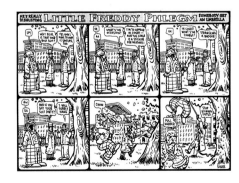

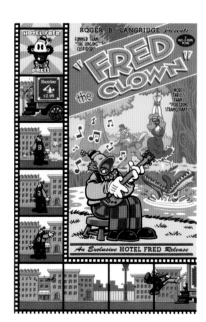

Above: A striking cover, making exceptional use of colour for Langridge's self-published series *Fred the Clown*.
© *Roger Langridge*

Right: Langridge plays with the comics form in this page of *Fred the Clown*, a technique he uses almost effortlessly.
© *Roger Langridge*

Left, previous page: Roger Langridge shows his uncanny ability to mimic the styles of other cartoonists. In this strip, he pays homage to Winsor McCay's *Little Sammy Sneeze*.
© *Roger Langridge*

DYLAN HORROCKS

~dylan horrocks~

Above: The cover from New Zealand cartoonist Dylan Horrocks' magnum opus, *Hicksville*. The story of a journalist trying to track down the truth about the world's most successful comic book artist, *Hicksville* is a tour de force of storytelling and a passionate love poem to an artform.
© *Dylan Horrocks*

Right: *Atlas* is something of a sequel to *Hicksville*, and shares some of the same characters. The same obsessive love of comics is there, but this time it's tempered by a sense of real tension.
© *Dylan Horrocks*

Dylan Horrocks is a man who has something of a love-hate relationship with his chosen medium of expression: comics. While his love for the artform cannot be denied, and indeed it has led him right around the world and back, it does seem to affect him in the strangest of ways.

Born in Auckland, New Zealand in 1966, Horrocks was born into a family that was no stranger to popular culture. His father, Roger, is the head of department of Film, Television and Media studies at the University of Auckland, and his uncle Nigel is a celebrated DJ on New Zealand radio. The favoured bedtime reading in the Horrocks household was Hergé's *Tintin*, Carl Barks' *Donald Duck* comics and Tove Janssen's *Moomin* stories.

No wonder then, that the young Dylan had a natural affinity for comics, and that by the age of 15 was contributing a strip called *Zap Zoney of the Space Patrol* to local children's magazines like *Jabberwocky*.

While reading English at university, he met Cornelius Stone, a local legend, and together they launched *Razor* magazine, a venue for cartoonists to do esoteric, experimental and

personal work. Until its demise in the early Nineties, *Razor* was a hub for local cartoonists and a benchmark in the New Zealand comics scene. In addition to his work for *Razor*, he contributed strips to many student magazines and anthology comics, including the Australian *Fox Comics*, and started to build up a reputation as a cartoonist of real worth. He also took on a pseudonym, Kupe – the name of the mythical first settler of Aotearoa, the Maori name for New Zealand – but this was rather short-lived.

In 1989, he decided to go to England to look for work as a cartoonist, starting a minicomic called *Pickle* (after Dill pickles - dill, Dylan - get it?), but unfortunately soon after he arrived, he started to suffer from a comics phobia, which reared its ugly head as a panic attack whenever he tried to enter a comic shop or read anything but the briefest of strips. He eventually weaned himself back onto comics by writing and drawing them, and desensitising himself with foreign language comics like bandes dessinées and Manga – anything he couldn't read, basically. He documented this period in his life in an issue of *Pickle* called *The Last Fox Story*, and still suffers from this affliction, although not quite as badly.

Resigning himself to a cartoonist's life, he co-founded the cartoonist collective Les Cartoonistes Dangereux, before reinventing *Pickle* as an American comic book for Michel Vrana's Tragedy Strikes Press (later Black Eye Books) in 1992. Ten issues of *Pickle* appeared over the next five years, garnering good reviews and a couple of Ignatz awards. In 1998 *Pickle's* main serial, *Hicksville,* was collected as a graphic novel by Black Eye.

Hicksville is Horrocks' masterpiece. The story of Leonard Batts, a journalist who works for the American *Comics World* magazine, and his voyage to a small town called Hicksville (which just happens to be a Heaven on Earth for the comics enthusiast) in New Zealand. There, he goes in search of the secret behind Dick Burger, the world's most famous cartoonist.

What follows is a tour de force of comics storytelling with some amazingly inventive plot lines and a series of characters that are well-drawn (in both senses of the phrase). *Hicksville* went on to be reprinted by Canadian publisher Drawn & Quarterly, and has appeared in French (published by l'Association), Spanish and Italian editions. It has also been nominated for several awards, including the Prix d'Alph-Art for Best Album, the Critic's Prize at Angoulême, a Harvey award

and two Ignatz awards, and was named as one of the books of the year by *The Comics Journal*.

After the success of *Hicksville*, Horrocks started writing for DC Comics, where he worked on the series *Batgirl*, and *Hunter: the Age of Magic*. He also created a weekly strip for the *NZ Listener* magazine, health promotional comics for the government and contributed comics and illustrations for many outlets.

In 2001 he created the first issue of a new series called *Atlas* for Drawn & Quarterly. Something of a follow-up to *Hicksville*, *Atlas* again features Leonard Batts, who travels to the Eastern European country of Cornicopia in search of celebrated cartoonist Emil Kopen. Sadly, only the first issue was published, due to Horrocks' workload, but it is hoped by his many fans that he will soon pick up where he left off.

In addition to being a cartoonist, Horrocks is also a comics historian who has written about comics for a number of magazines, given lectures and talks, and in 1998, put together an exhibition called *Nga Pakiwaituhi o Aotearoa* about New Zealand comics, along with a 100-page accompanying catalogue.

Horrocks, who lives on a beach with his wife and two children, is a pivotal figure in NZ comics, spanning the *Strips-Razor* eras and beyond. His influence can be seen throughout the last 20 or so years of New Zealand comics, and it's not over yet.

Above: A page from Horrocks' unfinished series *Café Underground,* a tale of unrequited love set in Auckland.
© *Dylan Horrocks*

Below: A scene from *Atlas* depicting the author being interrogated by a foreign government.
© *Dylan Horrocks*

Vol. 505 Rs.25

The Gita

Amar Chitra Katha: the Glorious Heritage of India

Above: Amar Chitra Katha's 1977 version of the classic Hindi text, *The Bhagavad-Gita*, adapted by writer/editor Anant Pai and artist Pratap Mulick.
© *India Book House Ltd*

10

ASHRAMS, APARTHEID & ARABIAN TALES

While not renowned for its great comic book industries, the developing world has produced some first-class comic creators and masterpieces of sequential storytelling. From India to Africa and the Middle East, the comic is no less important in these regions than in any other part of the globe.

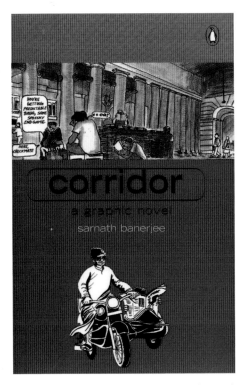

Above: Sarnath Banerjee's best-selling 2004 graphic novel, *Corridor*, set in Delhi.
© Sarnath Banerjee

Indigenous comics in India have been around for over 40 years and have secured an important place in the country's popular culture. Heavily influenced by British comics until independence in 1947, India didn't get its first homegrown comic characters until as late as 1960.

When cartoonist Pran Kumar Sharma – one of the founding fathers of Indian comics – created the teenager *Dabu* and his mentor, *Professor Adhikari*, for Delhi newspaper *Milap*, he broke the monopoly of syndicated foreign comics strips. He followed it up with *Shrimatiji*, a strip about the misadventures of an atypical Indian housewife, and in 1969, Pran created *Chacha Chaudhary* and *Sabu*, a duo who combine brain and brawn to fight crime. *Chaudhary* is a frail, elderly, but remarkably intelligent man, who always wears his trademark red turban and is accompanied by his trusty dog. His partner, *Sabu*, is a giant of a man who just happens to come from Jupiter. Published by Diamond Comics, the series captured the market and the pair went on to become the most popular comic

personalities in India. Pran created other popular titles like *Raman and Bhagat Ji* and *Billoo, Pinki & Uncle Sulemani*, but none grabbed the public's imagination quite like *Chacha Chaudhary*.

INDRAJAL COMICS

The 1960s were the boom time for Indian comics. A young Anant Pai was working at the *Times of India* (*TOI*) when his boss decided to move into comics to generate extra revenue when the printing presses were quiet. Foregoing *Superman*, *TOI* licensed the American *Phantom* newspaper strips by Lee Falk and reprinted them in the monthly *Indrajal Comics*, launched in March 1964. The first 16 to 24 pages were made up of *The Phantom*, and the rest consisted of other King Features characters like *Flash Gordon*, *Mandrake the Magician* and *Buzz Sawyer*. India succumbed to the charm of Lee Falk's character like so many before it, including Australia and Scandinavia, and on 1 January 1967 *Indrajal*'s popularity meant it switched to a fortnightly schedule with issue 35. Anant Pai's editorial skills were honed on

Right: An interior page from
the excellent *Corridor*.
© *Sarnath Banerjee*

Left: Amar Chitra Katha comics are printed in numerous languages. This painting is by the exceptional cover artist, C. M. Vitankar.
© *India Book House Ltd*

Below: Heavy philosophy from *The Gita*, adapted by Anant Pai and Pratap Mulick.
© *India Book House Ltd*

the title and he soon became the driving force in Indian comics. Many of *The Phantom*'s adventures took place in or nearby India and because of American faux pas, Pai and the other editors needed to make several 'politically correct' changes. The dwarf Bengali tribe became the Denkali, as there are no pygmy people in Bengal, an uninformed characterization which would probably have infuriated Indian readers. The Singh Brotherhood was renamed the 'Singa' pirates so as not to offend the Sikh population, and the deadly nemesis of the 20th Phantom, Rama (an Indian deity), was changed to the common Ramalu (the Indian equivalent of Smith or Jones). The covers for the first 50-something issues of *Indrajal Comics* were painted by B. Govind, whose artwork is still highly revered amongst fans, and is on par with those of artist George Wilson's work for the US Gold Key's comicbook series.

TELEVISUAL REVELATION

Pai was happy working on *Indrajal*, but in 1967 he had a revelation, "Television had just begun in India on an experimental basis. One fine evening in Delhi, I happened to pass by a shop that had a television on display. I stopped to watch out of curiosity. A quiz was on; the question asked was 'Who is the mother of Ram?' [seventh incarnation of the Indian god Vishnu]

None of the participants knew the answer. The next question on Greek gods was answered by all. I realized that there was a need for informing the youth of India of our own culture… Then, like a flash of lightning, it stuck me that here was a way… I was also aware of the [comic book] craze thanks to my job at *Times*' *Indrajal Comics*. I took my idea to many publishers but in vain," Pai recalled.

AMAR CHITRA KATHA

Pai eventually found a home at the publishing company of India Book House (IBH), and probably the most influential Indian comics imprint ever was born, the mythological *Amar Chitra Katha* (ACK). ACK proved extremely popular, with over 86 million copies sold in the last 25 years.

The self-contained comic books told over 384 stories based on tales from Indian culture and history. Artists such as Ram Waeerkar, Dilip Kadam, Souren Roy and Pratap Mulick helped breath life into tales of Vishnu, Ganesha and the whole Indian pantheon. Waeerkar and Mulick were renowned for their detailed research and Kadam had his own studio team, Trishul Comico Art. Based in Pune, Kadam and his son Omkar supervised a team of around 10 artists creating comics and animation work. Another key artist on the ACK titles was C. M. Vitankar, who drew *Ganesha* (1975), *Tales*

Above: Amar Chitra Katha's *Prahlad,* adapted by Kamala Chandrakant and drawn by Souren Roy. The story is based on the traditional Bhagawat and Vishnu Puranas.
© *India Book House Ltd*

of *Shiva* (1978), *Arjuna, the Monkey and the Boy* (1979) and *Karttikeya* (1981). ACK went on to produce titles based on famous historical Indian people such as Gandhi, Nehru and Buddha and eventually diversified to world personalities.

"I must say that the *Amar Chitra Katha* that I did on Krishna is one of the most satisfying ones in my career. I also got a lot of satisfaction from doing *The Gita*," Pai fondly remembered. The comics have been translated into an incredible 38 languages. "The largest order for any title was for 50,000 copies of *Jesus Christ*, in a local

language called Ibaan by an organization in Africa."

However, 'Uncle' Pai wasn't happy resting on his laurels, and in 1980 he created another comics sensation, *Tinkle*. This comic magazine contained strips, puzzles and features in the style of the *Beano* from the UK, and became India's best-loved comic. *Tinkle* is still published today, and for one of its characters, *Suppandi*, all of the stories are suggested by readers, and then drawn by professional artists. This interactive element generates a staggering 6,000 letters a week.

In the 1970s and 1980s, comics were the premier children's mass medium. For many, comics became an affordable and parentally approved mode of entertainment. However, cable television soon began to steal readers away. The remedy for many publishers in the late 1980s and early 1990s lay in the introduction of more blood and gore, as comics were geared towards an older teenage audience. "I feel that there is a lot of violence in animation today," bemoaned Pai. "Today the IQ in children is quite high but the EQ [emotional quota] is low."

Despite the trend to more extreme comics and animation, or rather because of it, Diamond Comics, who emphasized simple all-ages stories, continued to be the leader of the pack. "We are still at the top because we are clean," said Gulshan Rai,

Below: Krishna visits Mirabai in her eponymous comic, beautifully drawn by Yusuf Lien.
© India Book House Ltd

editor and director of Diamond Comics. "Characters like *Chacha Chaudhary*, *Billu* and *Pinki* are very popular because they are taken from the family environment."

CHACHA CHAUDHARY

In a population of nearly one billion, one of the hardest problems for Indian publishers is the huge diversity of languages spoken across the country, "*Chacha Chaudhary* still comes out in 10 languages, including Hindi and English, and sells almost 10 million copies [an issue]," Pran said. The creator believes his character's continued appeal lies in the fact that he solves problems using his intelligence, unlike western heroes such as Superman who primarily perform physical feats. "*Chacha Chaudhary* is a typically Indian middle class character, whose brain works faster than a computer," said Pran.

Despite television – the global scourge of comics – stealing readers, the Indian comic industry embraced the small screen. In 2002, 32 years after the character first appeared, *Chacha Chaudhary* was finally brought to television in a massive 200-part series of all-new adventures, aired three times a week. "The comic series is still quite strong," said Pran. "But we have to keep pace with the changing times. TV has come up as a strong medium for family entertainment and this production is aimed

at catering to that demand." The show was unafraid to tackle complex contemporary events such as 9/11, and creator Pran was not overly concerned about the sensitivity of the subjects for a family show, "Don't the children see all this happening in the TV news everyday? I am not creating anything totally unheard of. Today children are far more sensible."

An optimistic Pai concurred, "I think given today's markets and global culture, we ought to teach the child the right values of life when he is young and ready to imbibe. There are so many simple values that make life better, these values when conveyed through animation or comics are such that whether the child is in India or Russia or France or US, the values are universal. Making content with such universal messages makes the entire world an audience." Yet according to Ram Mohan, one of the founders of Indian animation, "To convert the vast treasury of stories and design heritage into animated content we require a good deal of money, just as the Japanese developed anime we need to have our Indian ethos." Ram Mohan's company has been creating comics for the John Hopkins University aimed at adolescents in Bangladesh and related to health issues. "Comics always have an appeal. Even food and agriculture related organizations come out with comics to educate the rural population Recently,

Rogan Gosh

Peter Milligan and Brendan McCarthy's wonderfully frivolous series (named after a curry) first appeared in 1990 in the UK's ill-fated *Revolver*. Originally a six-part serial, it was collected into a single volume by Vertigo in 1994. Set partly in an Indian restaurant in Stoke Newington, London, the comic wore its influences spilled all down its front.

In the foreword, McCarthy related his own love of Indian comics and in particular *Amar Chitra Katha*, "...The English-language comic scene has rapidly become more international... So *Chitra Katha* may well find a market outside the sub-continent, and if this first look at Indian comics helps the process along, then I'm all for it!"

It has obviously sparked an interest as, in 2005, fellow Vertigo creators Grant Morrison and Philip Bond launched *Vimanarama* about British-Asians, arranged marriages and ancient gods.

Above: Another fantastic Amar Chitra Katha cover by the prolific C. M. Vitankar.
© India Book House Ltd

India's rising literacy rates and buying power have meant changing spending habits. The population of nearly one billion is the youngest in the world, and by 2015, India will have 550 million people under the age of 20. "These kids are liberalization's children," said Arvind K. Singhal of New Delhi-based retail consultancy KSA Technopak. "They are exposed to global trends through TV and the Internet and are not spending-averse." While hundreds of millions of Indians still live in poverty, there are also malls, millionaires and middle class children looking for comics. They've long had *Spider-Man*, *Batman*, and the rest, but now it is time for their own. Until recently, despite a thriving culture of myths that lends itself to sequential storytelling, Indian comic books have generally low production values, compared to many other countries.

After 26 years and 803 issues, Indrajal Comics finally closed its doors on The Phantom in April 1990. "The Ghost Who Walks" then strolled over to Diamond Comics, followed by a quick saunter to Rani Comics and eventually came to rest in June 2000 at Egmont Publications and Indian Express Group (who later became Egmont Imagination). Egmont relaunched the masked hero as an English-language series, reprinting stories created by the Scandinavian Team Fantomen.

In 2004, film director Shekhar Kapur and self-help guru Deepak Chopra set up the ultimate Indian outsource comics company. Previously, their Gotham Entertainment Group (GEG), named after and run by Chopra's son, had licensed America's Marvel and DC Comics' titles in the vast sub-continent. Gotham Chopra was the story editor of Image Comics' *Bulletproof Monk* and he produced the movie version.

HOT 'N' SPICY SPIDER-MAN

Then GEG set up Gotham Studios to create its own localized version of *Spider-Man*. Gone was mild photographer Peter Parker and in came Pavitr Prabhaka, who wears a dhoti, a loose rural Indian garment. Now Mumbai-based, the web-slinger gained his powers from a mysterious sadhu, or holy man, not from a radioactive spider, and his enemy, the Green Goblin, is the reincarnation of an ancient Indian demon called Rakshasa. Other echoes of the US version include Pavitr courting Mira Jain, not Mary Jane; Uncle Ben is Uncle Bhim; Aunt May becomes Aunt Maya. "The superheroes of tomorrow will be cross-cultural and will transcend nationalistic boundaries," said Chopra senior. "Unlike traditional translations of American comics, *Spider-Man India* will become the first-ever 'transcreation', where we reinvent the origin of a Western property." Gotham studios is intent on using its Indian talent pool to create

Above: An early character design for *Spider-Man: India's* alter ego, *Pavitr Prabhaka, by* Jeevan J Kang.
© *Marvel Comics*

Right: *Spider-Man: India* was co-written by Suresh Seetharaman, Sharad Devarajan and Jeevan J Kang, who also supplied the artwork. The first four issues were collected and published in America in 2005.
© *Marvel Comics*

comics for US publishers, to help reduce their costs. "A legion of Indians became software programmers, but we hope the new generation of Indians returns to what India was renowned for – its creativity," said Sharad Devarajan, CEO of Gotham Studios. The Indian version of *Spider-Man* was also sold outside India, to an American audience.

Despite these events, Rohit Gupta, a Bombay-based writer whose weekly newspaper column reaches over six million readers, remains sceptical about the Asian version of the wall-crawler. "It may have been fun to read a hundred years ago during the British Raj. Today, it's laughable in a country where computers and cell phones are everywhere, and to a people whose Gods can kick the ass of any superhero."

Of course, this viewpoint could be sour grapes, as Gupta also runs Apollo Bunder Comics, an independent comics studio, founded in December 2003. "The very first comic we produced as a studio – *The Doppler Effect*, adapted into a graphic novel by Gabriel Greenberg – examined and protested the violence that happened in Gujarat a couple of years ago," said the writer/ publisher, referring to 2002's bloody riots when over 1,000 people were killed. "We are also making a graphic novel to conduct propaganda for child relief in India." Meanwhile, Gupta's newspaper strip *SOS* (*Special Officer Savant*) is published in *Mid-Day*,

Mumbai's biggest daily newspaper. Gupta's peer, Sharad Sharma, also runs an adult education venture called World Comics – associated with a Finnish organization of the same name – that uses sequential art to change lives in rural India by involving people in making comics about their issues.

Meanwhile, comics are also taking off in India in new and unexpected places. Sarnath Banerjee's *Corridor* has become the first of the new wave of Indian graphic novels to be internationally recognized, and was a bestselling and critical hit, reprinting three times.

It relates the interconnecting stories of a second-hand bookseller in Delhi and his customers. Banerjee's commissioning editor at Penguin Books, India, V. K. Karthika, believed there was interest in further graphic novels, but finding the talent is hard.

AFRICA: THE DRAWN CONTINENT

Africa is a notoriously difficult continent for any type of publisher, but especially so for comic publishers. Faced with poor distribution infrastructures, lack of financing, the general public's disdain for comics and the growth of non-reading, television-focused consumers, it's a wonder there's a comic industry at all. But there is in many countries, and it's growing, albeit slowly.

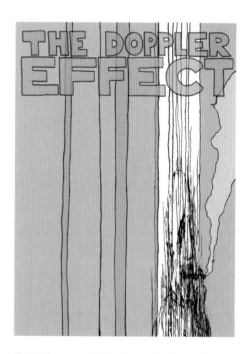

Above: Indian writer Rohit Gupta's novel, *The Doppler Effect,* was adapted into a comic by Gabriel Greenberg.
© *Rohit Gupta and Gabriel Greenberg*

Left, opposite page: *Chacha Chaudhary* and the giant, *Sabu* by Indian cartoonist Pran Kumar Sharma.
© *Pran Features*

Above: Africa's Posh and Becks get married in the wedding special of *Supa Strikas*. But not even his bride could keep goalkeeper, Bongane 'Big Bo' Bonani, from playing on his wedding day! The strip is written by Bruce Legg and drawn by a huge team including, Bonisa Bonani, Peter Woodbridge, Mfundo Ndevu, Michael Crafford, Janine Corneilse, John-Evans Wagenaar and Henri Roberts.

© Strika Entertainment / Supa Strikas Football Club

No country proves that comics are an extension and expression of a nation's psyche more than South Africa. Historically, local comics have never been able to move out of the shadow of national events and the cultural stresses that form the country. Politics, sport and societal concerns dominate society and this is reflected in the comics South Africans create and with which they identify. However, many comics and creators have often been criticized for being too 'worthy' and unsurprisingly, nearly all South African comics have evolved to become art with a message, and find it hard to just be simple light entertainment.

South African readers still shoehorn comics into two categories: kiddie comics and intellectual cartoons. Highbrow political strips are socially acceptable because of their commentary and specific viewpoint, while superheroes, manga and European imports are perceived as childish. Local retailers put comics out of the reach of the youth market in terms of pricing and by putting them on the top shelf. Comics have become a luxury item the average person can't afford. Coupled with literacy problems and competition from movies, television and computer games, the going is tough, but not really that different from the problems other countries face.

Cartoonist Rico Schacherl was born in Vienna, Austria, and emigrated with his

family to Johannesburg, South Africa, when he was young. After studying architecture and graphic design, he eventually met up with South African Harry Dugmore, a former academic and trade unionist, and they founded the country's first satirical magazine *Laughing Stock*, SA's version of *MAD*. Unfortunately, it folded after a year. Meanwhile, American writer Stephen Francis moved to SA when he married his Afrikaans wife. Francis was a big fan of *Laughing Stock* and joined the team just as the magazine was in its death throes. In 1992, the trio of Schacherl, Dugmore and Francis created the comic strip *Madam & Eve*, about the relational dynamics between a white woman and her black housekeeper (inspired by Francis' mother-in-law and her help). The comic was picked up by the SA newspaper, *The Weekly Mail* (now *Mail & Guardian*), in June 1992. As soon as readers entered the home of Gwen Anderson (Madam) and Eve Sisulu (Eve) the series took off, becoming South Africa's best-known and longest-running newspaper strip. Its success results from the writers' ability to tap into, and put a twist on, local concerns and views. It has gone on to spawn several collections, a successful TV series, and has been syndicated around the world.

While US writer Francis has reaped success in SA, his home country's comics haven't fared that well. South Africans tend

Above: Africa's biggest football comic, *Supa Strikas* successfully gets sponsorship for everything from the ball (Nike) to the team's kit (South African petroleum company CalTex).
© *Strika Entertainment / Supa Strikas Football Club*

Above and Below: Harry Dugmore, Stephen Francis and Rico Schacherl's *Madam & Eve*. The hugely popular strip satirizes life in post-apartheid South Africa.
© *Rapid Phrase Entertainment*

Above: Afrikaans artist Johan de Lange's *Vis Stories* from the *Africa Comics* anthology.
© *Johan de Lange*

Left: Joe Dog's disturbing dream sequence in the European clear line style, from his strip *1974*. Dog set up *Bitterkomix* with fellow South African creator Conrad Botes.
© *Anton Kannemeyer*

to respond better to European comics because, more often than not, the writing is superior to the formulaic approach taken by American publishers. Who needs *Superman* or *Batman* when you can tell the story of Nelson Mandela's *Long Walk to Freedom* in a comic format?

SUPA STRIKAS

Some in-roads have been made in reaching the masses by pan-African projects such as the *Supa Strikas* comic supplement, currently running in several countries' national newspapers. This African version of Britain's football comic, *Roy of the Rovers*, has been partly funded by South African businesses. The companies that sponsor it get their advertising on almost every panel and the newspaper attracts the youth market while the artists and writers get the exposure and experience they need. A similar system is run in the UK's *Striker 3D* comic.

BITTERKOMIX

In an evolving South African society, comic books have taken on a role in literacy training, AIDS awareness and environmental activism, and in promoting democratic political processes. Inspired by First World graphic novels and Third World literacy programmes, artists and writers regularly produce original comic books for the state

health department, the Department of Environmental Affairs, the African National Congress, the state education departments and the Red Cross. One of the more successful creators to achieve international recognition is Conrad Botes. Born in Ladysmith, Cape Province, South Africa, in 1969, he studied graphic design and illustration at the University of Stellenbosch, where he met Anton Kannemeyer (aka Joe Dog) on the same course. The two founded the ground-breaking magazine *Bitterkomix* in 1992, which was the only independent comicbook magazine in South Africa at the time. It had socio-political, satirical content, offering South African creators a chance to show their work. Together with Ryk Hattingh, Botes later created *Die Foster Bende*, which was published in June 2000. Botes and Joe Dog's work has also appeared in European comics such as *Formaline*, *Zone 5300*, *Lapin* and the *Comix 2000* anthology. They continue to publish their work in *Bitterkomix*, and have regular exhibitions in South Africa and Europe. In 1998, Joe Dog created the graphic novel *Zeke and the Mine Snake*, a tale about mining labourers in South Africa, with writer Vuka Shift. Currently, Joe Dog lectures on illustration and silk-screening at Wits Technikon college, Johannesburg.

For South African comics producers, general funding is still hard to come by and more support is being shown by

Above: A painting by Conrad Botes, *Bitterkomix* co-founder.
© Conrad Botes

Below: Henri Roberts' self-published *Venge*. Roberts also contributes to *Supa Strikas*.
© Henri Roberts

Above: Ruth Wairimu Karani and Kham's *Macho Ya Mji* (*City Eyes*) is the story of a blind beggar and two street boys who help the police prevent crimes in Nairobi, Kenya.
© *Sasa Sema Publications Ltd*

foreign governments for art projects, most notably the Swiss Pro Helvetia Office and the French government who organized the 2003 Comics Galore nationwide festival. They flew international artists to South Africa as well as organizing lectures and a convention in Johannesburg with *Bitterkomix*. The Festival of International Comic Art is a six-month programme of events including exhibitions, an international conference, workshops, lectures and book launches dedicated to Comic Art in South Africa. The Comics Galore festival is intended to become an annual event.

SOUTH AFRICAN ANTI-HERO

In March 2004, Cape Town's Henri Roberts released his self-produced six-issue miniseries, *Venge*. It tells the story of a confused, deformed man awakening in New York in 2020, on the run from the powers that be as he tries to discover what has happened to him. Roberts owes more than a nod to the early 1990s' wave of American superhero artists such as Todd McFarlane and Rob Liefield, and *Venge* himself comes across as a monosyllabic mix of *Spawn* and *Batman*. Yet *Venge* is a rarity in SA comics for several reasons. Not only did Roberts write and letter the title, he also fully painted it and published it in a glossy, oversized format. It is also simple superhero fare, unencumbered by the social responsibilities of many

South African titles. Roberts believes, "Most locally produced comics lack strong stories and characters. I find local content very boring. Quality is key. Do work that can compete internationally, dammit."

Elsewhere, comics are being used by UNICEF in Somalia to enhance child survival and development. During the 1994 cholera epidemic in Somalia, over 500,000 anti-cholera cartoon leaflets and 20,000 posters were distributed, and 20,000 copies of the 74-page Somali version of UNICEF's popular *Facts For Life* have rolled off the press, redrawn as a graphic novel by one of Somalia's top cartoonists. This educational graphic novel features a day-to-day account of a perplexed Somali mother and father who learn what to do in case of the four disastrous 'Ds': diarrhoea, dysentery, diphtheria and dyslexia.

AFRICAN NATIONAL COMICS

Considering Nigeria has the largest population in the continent (one in six Africans is Nigerian), it's unsurprising that comics influence is strongest there, but it wasn't until September 2004 that Nigeria's capital hosted the first ever Lagos Comics Carnival. The free event gave a voice to the growing wealth of local creators who grew up on Marvel and DC. Regarding Nigerian artists breaking through onto the international stage, comics creator Baba Aminu thought,

Left: Conrad Botes' darkly humorous strip for *Comix 2000*.
© *Conrad Botes*

Right: Tanzanian cartoonist Gado's Swahili graphic novel, *Abunuwasi*. The strip adapts three East Africa coast folk stories of a trickster called Abunuwasi who outwits rich and greedy men and brings justice to the poor.
© *Godfrey Mwampembwa*

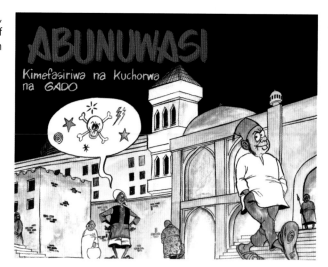

Left: A self-portrait of Godfrey Mwampembwa, better known as Gado. He was was named Kenyan Cartoonist of the Year in 1999.
© *Godfrey Mwampembwa*

Right: The poster for Lagos' first comic carnival in 2004, which was part of the 6th Lagos Book and Art festival.

Left: Nigerian superhero *Powerman* was forced to change his name to *Powerbolt* when reprinted in the UK. The panels were numbered to help readers follow the story. Art by Brian Bolland.
© *Brian Bolland*

Right: The cover to *Powerman* #6 by Brian Bolland.
© *Brian Bolland*

"It's all an issue of timing. It'll happen really soon, judging by the level of talent available here at the convention. Nigeria has great comic book history... Dave Gibbons and Brian Bolland first began their careers here, in Nigeria… If that's not good karma, I don't know what is."

NUBIAN SUPERHEROES

Both British artists, Gibbons and Bolland had already done a lot of work for UK fanzines when, in 1975, they got their big break. As Gibbons recalled, "My agent, Bardon Press Features, who specialized in comics, had been approached by an executive of a Nigerian advertising agency. He and his wife had seen a gap in the market in Nigeria, in that the only comics that were available were imports featuring exclusively white heroes. They set up a company over here [in the UK] called Pikin Press to publish comics with black characters. There was *Powerman* and another, which was aimed at girls."

Gibbons designed *Powerman* and his logo, while he and Brian Bolland alternated on the art chores, "We both did a 14-page episode a month and it was published every fortnight." The anthology also featured the black sheriff, *Jango*. Other British artists involved included Eric Bradbury, Ron Smith and Ron Tiner and Spaniard Carlos Ezquerra. The stories were written by UK-based IPC scripter stalwarts Donne Avenell and Norman Worker. "I wasn't aware of African comics," admitted Gibbons, "although I remember asking why they didn't get African creators to work on the strips. I was told that they would probably emerge once the comics business got established. We had some difficulty adjusting to local customs and conventions," recalled the UK-based creator. "For example, a fat stomach was a sign of success and power, not gluttony or greed. And it wasn't considered sexist for macho *Powerman* to always get off with the girls, who found him universally irresistible. That's what we were told anyway!"

"*Powerman* was later reprinted, beyond our control, in South Africa and *The Comics Journal* had a field day, accusing us of supporting apartheid, since we only had black characters in our stories!" Gibbons remembered. "In fact, there was one white character, a dishonest blond Aryan property developer, called Boss Blitzer, whom *Powerman* brought to justice."

The Gibbons/Bolland *Powerman* stories were reprinted in the UK by Acme Press in 1988, but had the named changed to *Powerbolt* for legal reasons, as Marvel Comics already had a black superhero called *Powerman*. Both artists went on to make a name for themselves in 1977 working on Britain's most celebrated action comic, *2000 AD*, drawing *Judge Dredd* and *Dan Dare*.

Above: *Komerera: The Runaway Bride* by Tuf Mulokwa is set in the Mau Mau era during Kenya's war of independence in the 1950s.
© *Sasa Sema Publications Ltd*

Right: Tayo Fatunla's self-portrait.
© *Tayo Fatunla*

They then went on to be some of the biggest stars in American comics, with Gibbons drawing the seminal graphic novel *Watchmen*, written by fellow ex-2000 *AD* scribe, Alan Moore.

NIGERIAN CARTOONIST

Tayo Fatunla was born in London in 1961 but, at a young age, was taken back to Nigeria where he grew up initially reading British comics like 2000 *AD*. "While in my primary school, I came across *Mighty Thor* comic book. And I fell in love with American comic superheroes from then on," Fatunla recalled. "When I was a young teenager in Nigeria," the artist reminisced, "[Marvel Comics'] *Black Panther* and *Luke Cage* were characters I enjoyed reading. They were the first black superheroes I came across. At that time, we had a constant flow of comics into Nigeria..."

Fatunla studied at the Joe Kubert School, alongside Kubert's sons Adam and Andy, before returning to Nigeria to draw editorial cartoons for *West Africa*, a pan-African weekly magazine, for 12 years. He also went on to draw for the *Nigerian Punch*, *Daily Times*, *National Concord*, *The Guardian* and *Nigerian Herald* newspapers and a news magazine called *This Week*. He created the popular character *Omoba* (Prince) who, despite being at the bottom of the social scale, made satirical jibes at Nigerian

political, economic and social issues. These are classic subject matters in Nigeria, and Fatunla wears his roots on his sleeve, "I have been influenced by Nigerian cartoonists such as Kenny Adamson, Dr. Dele Jegede, Toyin Akingbule." Fatunla's book on black history, *Our Roots*, was based on the strip that he has drawn for London's black newspaper *The Voice* since 1989. In 1995, it was syndicated in the USA thanks to Jerry Robinson (the former *Batman* artist).

Unsurprisingly, due to comics 'Ninth Art' status in Francophone countries, the French-speaking African nations such as Algeria and Morocco also create many comics relating to social and economic issues. In the forefront of such comics are the European publishing companies Africa E Mediteraneo (Africa and Mediterranean), based in Italy, and Marisa Paolucci's Africartoon. Both often run competitions, encouraging published and unpublished African comics artists in both continents, and so the cross-fertilization of ideas continues.

ARABIAN TALES

In the remaining Arabic states, comic strips are generally regarded as child fodder. There are exceptions however, and many titles have enormous readerships and a political and ideological range extending from secular modernist to Islamic religious

Below: Tayo Fatunla's first collection of black history, *Our Roots* which was originally serialized in the UK newspaper, *The Voice*.
© *Tayo Fatunla*

Above: Samuel Mulokwa's (AKA Tuf) first published comic book was the 1998 *Manywele*, created while Tuf was still at school. It's the story of an innocent Rasta who is jailed, but ultimately saves everyone from a terrible disease which causes people to grow hair all over their body and to literally die laughing. The Swahili graphic novel dealt with religious hypocrisy, tribalism and honour.

© *Sasa Sema Publications, Kenya*

Right: Politics are never very far away in Arabic comics. This biography of Egypt's first president, Nasser, took its title from his Arabic name, *Jamal Abd Al-Nasir* and was drawn by Muhammad Al-Dhakiri.

© *Muhammad Al-Dhakiri*

Above: Cairo's biggest comic publisher, Nahdet Misr, not only publishes DC Comics and Disney's magazines, but also releases local fables and classic stories in sequential form.
© *Nahdet Misr*

perspectives. In Abu Dhabi, United Arab Emirates, the most successful and most pan-Arab comic-strip magazine, *Mâjid*, is produced. With a weekly circulation of 175,000, *Mâjid* is probably the most widely read children's magazine in the region, delighting readers in every Arab state, with the exception of Syria. In Cairo, copies at the newsstands are snatched up the day they are put on sale. One of *Mâjid's* popular strips is the global adventures of *Kaslân Jiddan. Kaslân* is a naughty boy who gets into comic scrapes by trying to play the adult.

THE LEBANESE EXPERIENCE

Illustrated Publications (IP), a Beirut firm, built a profitable comic book business based on the Arabs' fierce pride in their own language. Until 1964, the majority of comic books in the Middle East were in either English or French, a hangover from the colonial days. Then, a forward-looking editor realized that it might be possible to make a few Dirhams by encouraging children to read about their culture in their own language, just like Anant Pai in India. IP built up sales of around 2.6 million copies a year and distributed them in 17 countries to an estimated 270,000 avid kids. "Kids from Saudi Arabia to Morocco were so enthusiastic that we had to stop answering their letters," said Leila Shaheen da Cruz, editor-in-chief of Illustrated

Publications. "It was taking too much time." IP's first Arabic comic was *Superman*, launched on 4 February 1964 – a month before *Indrajal Comics* launched in India. But Clark Kent switched his identity, becoming mild mannered reporter Nabil Fawzi, working on Al-Kawkab Al Yawmi. The following year, the dynamic duo, *Sobhi and Zakkour, AKA Batman and Robin* appeared, pursued by *The Lone Ranger, Bonanza, Little Lulu, Tarzan*, and most recently, *The Flash*.

Arabic comics, like Japanese manga, read from right to left. That meant that the filmed reproductions of the original artwork had to be reversed before printing plates could be made, a process that immediately produced a sack of letters demanding why the S on Superman's costume was backwards. IP also had to soothe tradition-minded parents who were not entirely convinced that their children's Arabic was going to be improved by superhero slugfests, so they added eight pages of educational games, stories and contests.

When nationalistic readers objected to the amount of Western material, IP agreed that Arab culture had enough ideas for at least one locally created comic. Unfortunately, it proved impractical. "That kind of artwork, story continuity and long-range planning," said da Cruz, "is still unfamiliar to most local artists or is too expensive. The adventures of *Sinbad the Sailor*, for example, would be a natural out here,

Above: Marjane Satrapi's *Persepolis 2: The Story of a Return* is the 2004 sequel to her international bestseller, *Persepolis*. Both graphic novels deal with the author's fraught childhood growing up during the Iranian Islamic revolution.
© *Marjane Satrapi*

Right: The popular pan-Arabic children's comic, *Mâjid*.
© *Mâjid*

Below: Cheeky *Kaslân Jiddan* gets up to his usual tricks from the pages of *Mâjid* magazine.
© *Mâjid*

Left: Turkey's *GirGir* magazine was founded by cartoonist brothers Oguz and Tekin Aral in 1972. The satirical anthology soon became a national institute and helped launch the careers of many young Turkish comics artists.
© *GirGir*

Right, opposite page: Mete Erden's strip *Polis Abuziddin* from *GirGir* shows that Turkey's police haven't improved much since *Midnight Express*.
© *Mete Erden*

and we know that there would be a rich market for an adventure strip based on the exploits of Arab commandos. But so far we haven't found a local cartoonist who is not either inexperienced or overpriced." Elsewhere in the Middle East, Egypt's first locally published children's magazine, funnily enough called *Sinbad*, was launched in 1952, but in 1956, rival publishers Dar Al-Hilal's Egyptian comic book series *Samir* was launched and the battle for the nation's reading habits began. By 1959, *Sinbad* was in troubled waters, when Nadia Nashaa — the then editor-in-chief of *Samir* — dealt the killer blow to *Sinbad* by acquiring the Arabic rights to translate *Mickey Mouse* comics. "Dar

Al-Hilal was a reputable company at that time," says Dr. Shahira Khalil, the current editor-in-chief of *Samir*. "The magazines published by Dar Al-Hilal were very successful, so there was no problem at all to have the copyright for *Mickey* here." *Mickey* took off as readers identified with the American characters, whose names were Arabized to *Batoot* (*Donald Duck*), *Bondock* (*Goofy*) and *Amm Dahab* (*Uncle Scrooge*). For years, Dar Al-Hilal had the monopoly in Egypt, with *Samir* and *Mickey* — which soon over took its sister title with sales of 56,000 — the only two children's magazines on the market. Then, at the end of 2004, Disney slapped Dar Al-Hilal in the

Above: Algerian Cartoonist Abd Al Karim Qudiri's hero *SuperDabza*.
© Abd Al Karim Qudiri

Right: Arabic superhero, *Jalila*, by Faye Perozych, Rafael Albuquerque and Rafael Kras.
© *AK Comics Inc*

Below: Fantasy adventure comic *Rakan* by Todd Vicino, Rafael Albuquerque and Rafael Kras.
© *AK Comics Inc*

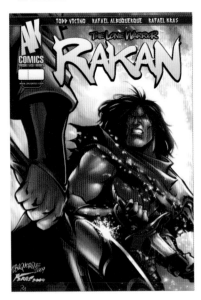

face after 44 years of cooperation, and handed the licence to rivals Nahdet Misr.

The new *Mickey* title was relaunched in 2005 with Egypt's First Lady Suzanne Mubarak – the Arab world's leading advocate of literacy and children's programs – writing the introduction to Nahdet Misr's first issue. The title now sells 60,000 copies a week and it makes $1.4 million (£750,000) a year. Despite this success, "Comics are not yet a big part of Egyptian culture," says Farrah, the current *Mickey* editor. "We don't have a significant role in the world of comics."

TRUTH, JUSTICE & THE ARAB WAY

All that changed however, at beginning of 2005, when Cairo-based publisher AK Comics launched the first Arabic superhero line. AK attempted it in the USA the previous year, but found the market too crowded for unknown superheroes. AK's founder, Dr. Ayman Kandeel, then decided to launch them in Egypt. The series features *Amgad Darweesh*, a mild-mannered philosophy professor who is secretly *Zein*, the Last Pharaoh, a 14,000 year old crime fighter. Endowed with supernatural strength and a mission to "fight evil until the end of time", he lives in Origin City, which, with its pyramids, traffic and random chaos, looks suspiciously like Cairo. Other characters include *Rakan*, a hairy medieval warrior

in Mesopotamia, *Jalila*, a brainy Levantine scientist and fighter for justice, and *Aya*, a North African described as, "a vixen who roams the region on her supercharged motorbike confronting crime wherever it rears its ugly head."

AK Comics distribute 7,000 copies in Arabic and 5,000 in English to Egypt, Saudi Arabia, the Persian Gulf states, Lebanon, Syria and North Africa. They even print 10,000 issues on black and white newsprint for poorer Egyptians. The glossies cost 80 US cents (42 pence); the black and white versions about 20 US cents (10 pence). The titles have really taken off, with Egypt Air stocking the books for in-flight reading. AK Comics is on a mission, "To fill the cultural gap created over the years by providing essentially Arab role models – in our case, Arab superheroes – to become a source of pride to our young generations. I grew up reading Spider-Man and loved him," said Marwan El-Nashar, managing director and editor, "but I couldn't get into Peter Parker. I mean, he lived in New York. I always wondered why there weren't any Arabs leaping off buildings." Nashar finally reached the obvious question, "Why can't the Middle East have its own heroes?"

AK Comics is a real product of globalization. Because Egypt had no homegrown tradition of comic strips (unless you count hieroglyphics), AK Comics outsourced the

artwork to Studio G in California. This cultural cross-fertilization led to some problems with the attributes of the two female do-gooders, *Jalila* and *Aya*, creating decency jitters. "We've had issues where censors go through page by page and blacken out the breasts with a marker," said Nashar. It seems some things simply just don't travel well, pneumatic breasts being two of them.

Right: Sid Ali Melouah is Algeria's foremost cartoonist. Unfortunately, due to death threats from Muslim fundamentalists, he had to flee to France. This strip, *The Touareg*, was produced for the Algerian government.
© *Algerian Department of the Environment*

ANANT PAI

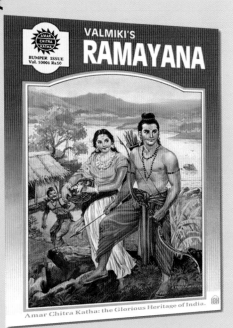

Above: Amar Chitra Katha's *The Ramayana* adaptation.
© India Book House Ltd

Left: The Phantom appeared in the Anant Pai-edited Indrajarl Comics.
© King Features Syndicate Inc

Without a doubt, the pioneer of Indian comics is Anant 'Uncle' Pai. In fact, Pai is Indian comics.

The writer/editor/publisher was born in Karkala, Karnataka, India, in 1931 and he initially studied science. However, his true passion lay in publishing, and in 1954 he started an editorial career, eventually becoming a junior executive in the *Times of India*'s (*TOI*) book division. He was at the cradle of Indian comics with the creation of *Indrajal Comics* in 1964. "P K Roy, my boss, told me, 'Anant, our printing machines are busy during season, but they are not in use during off-season. Let's take some licenses to comics and use our printing equipment.' He then asked me if *Superman* would be a good license to buy and I conducted a small survey and I found out that kids preferred *The Phantom* to *Superman*." Pai soon became frustrated at *TOI*, and in 1967, "I left a very good job at the TOI to pursue my interest in Indian comics. Finally, I met G L Mirchandani and H G Mirchandani who showed some interest in 1970." The Mirchandanis ran the publishing company India Book House, and shared Pai's dream of educational comics. "They

were however, cautious to begin with, and asked me to work on some fairy tales that they had rights to, for the Indian region," recalled Uncle Pai. "The first 10 issues of the *Amar Chitra Katha* [*Immortal Picture Stories*] were therefore not Indian culture or mythology, but tales like *Red Riding Hood* and *Jack and the Beanstalk*."

However, that situation soon changed and each of the comics in the series was dedicated to a person or event in Indian history, religion or mythology. Pai – being a true renaissance man, speaking eight languages – conceptualized all of these, and wrote most of them.

But as the *Far Eastern Economic Review* (February 1984) astutely pointed out, "Pai's avowed objective was not a business, but a vehicle to educate." He was concerned that too many Indian children knew plenty about Western history but practically nothing of their own culture and heritage. This rich vein was tapped into by a total of 436 comics titles, published every fortnight, covering classic tales from the epic *Mahabharata* and featuring gods such as Ganesha, the elephant god, and Hanuman, the

trickster monkey from the Hindu pantheon. By the mid-1990s, global sales
had topped an incredible 79 million
copies of the English-language versions alone.

Two years after launching *Amar
Chitra Katha*, Anant Pai founded Rang
Rekha Features, India's first comic and
cartoon syndicate, and in 1980 he
launched the children's magazine
Tinkle. Each issue was packed with 96
full-colour pages with comics and features such as *It Happened to Me* and
Tinkle Tricks and Treats. Over 25 years
later, the magazine is still going strong,
receiving a staggering 60,000 letters a
week from children, and the publisher
is affectionately called 'Uncle' Pai.

Despite being in his late seventies,
Pai continues to look for new ways to
educate and entertain, "I am releasing
an animated VCD. It is full of universal
values for kids told in simple yet
engaging story format." It even features a singing animated Uncle Pai.
"Even today I am amazed and overwhelmed by the kind of love and
warmth I receive wherever I go in the
world," said the modest Pai. "The kind
of fascination that children the world
over have for *Tinkle* and *Amar Chitra
Katha* is amazing."

Amar Chitra Katha: the Glorious Heritage of India

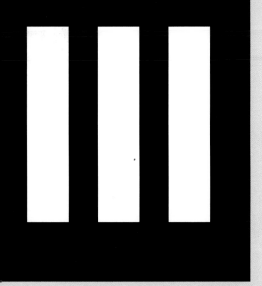

INDEX

BIBLIOGRAPHY

Marvel: Five Fabulous Decades of the World's Greatest Comics
Les Daniels
Harry N. Abrahams Inc, Publishers, 1993
0810925664

Comicbook Encyclopedia
Ron Goulart
Harper Collins, 2004
0060538163

Hong Kong Comics: A History of Manhua
Wendy Siuyi Wong
Princeton Architectural Press, 2002
1568982690

A History of Komiks of the Philippines and Other Countries
Cynthia Roxas, Joaquin Arevalo, JR. et al.
Islas Filipinas Publishing Co. Inc, 1984

Adult Comics: An Introduction
Roger Sabin
Routledge, 1993
0415044197

Comix: The Underground Revolution
Dez Skinn
Collins & Brown, 2004
184340186X

500 Comicbook Action Heroes
Mike Conroy
Chrysalis Books, 2002
1844110044

Gare du Nord
Edited by Rolf Classon
Tago Forlag, 1997
9186540912

Manga: Sixty Years of Japanese Comics
Paul Gravett
Laurence King Publishing, 2004
1856693910

Manga! Manga!: The World of Japanese Comics
Frederik L. Schodt
Kodansha America, 1998
0870117521

Dreamland Japan: Writings on Modern Manga
Frederik L. Schodt
Stone Bridge Press, 1996
188065623X

500 Comicbook Villains
Mike Conroy
Collins & Brown, 2004
184340205X

The World Encyclopaedia of Comics
ed. Maurice Horn
Chelsea House, 1998
079104856X

Larousse de la BD
Patrick Gaumer
Larousse, 2005
2035054168

BD Guide 2005
ed. Claude Moliterni, Philippe Mellot, Laurent Turpin, Michel Denni, Nathalie Michel-Szelechowska
Presses de la Cité, 2004
2258065232

Histoire Mondiale de la BD
Ed. Claude Moliterni
Pierre Horay, 1989
2705801650

Système de la Bande Dessinée
Thierry Groensteen
Presses Universitaires de France, 1999
2130501834

Les Maîtres de la Bande Dessinée Européenne
Ed. Thierry Groensteen
Seuil/Bibliothèque Nationale de France
2020436574

Comics The Art of the Comic Strip
Ed. Walter Herdeg & David Pascal
The Graphis Press

Comics, Comix & Graphic Novels
Roger Sabin
Phaidon Press
0714839930

Understanding Comics
Scott McCloud
HarperCollins Publishers
006097625X

Reinventing Comics
Scott McCloud
HarperCollins Publishers
0060953500

MAGAZINES

The Comics Journal
Comic Art
9e Art
International Journal of Comic Art
The Imp
Bild & Bubbla
Rackham
Bang!
U
Hop!
PLG
Phénix
Les Cahiers de la Bande Dessinée
Quadrado
Escape
The Panelhouse

WEBSITES

http://www.lambiek.com
http://www.comicsresearch.org
http://www.rpi.edu/~bulloj/comxbib.html
http://bugpowder.com/
http://www.comicsreporter.com/
http://www.ninthart.com/
http://www.scottmccloud.com/
http://www.graphicnovelreview.com/current.php
http://www.du9.org/
http://plg.ifrance.com/
http://www.indyworld.com/indy/
http://www.labanacomic.com.ar/home.htm
http://www.afnews.info/news.asp
http://www.tcj.com/
http://www.terra.com.br/cybercomix/
http://www.bedeteca.com/index.php
http://www.bdangouleme.com

ACKNOWLEGMENTS

TIM WOULD LIKE TO THANK:

Many, many people were helpful in making this book happen. Roger Langridge for the fantastic cover and for always being the consummate pro. Dave Gibbons for his excellent introduction and for being an inspiration, not only as a creator, but as a human being as well. Steve Holland for sharing his knowledge of British comics and writing skills with a keyboard. Kristiina Kolehmeinen at the Stockholm Serieteket, and Peter Snejbjerg for their Scandinavian hospitality and knowledge. To Paul Hudson at Comic Showcase, Art Young (ex-Vertigo), Dez Skinn and Mike Conroy at Comics International and everyone else who has given me a job over the years that has meant I could work in my greatest passion, comics. Garth Ennis and Joe 'Cheeky' Melchior simply for being top mates who understand the sad addiction that is comics. Craig Charles for your funky radio show that kept me going in the long dark nights. Of course a major nod to Chris Stone at Chrysalis Books who keeps hiring me regardless! Adele, Megan and Oskar, your patience and understanding never cease to amaze me, thank you. Thanks to Dad for getting me into comics in the first place, and Mum for not throwing them away! A big shout out to anyone I've ever met or spoken to on the phone and especially to _____(fill your name in here). A massive "Hurrah!" to Robert Harding Computers in Brighton for helping us through our darkest hours when all others failed. Liz and Sophie for allowing me to disrupt your house and steal your husband and dad. And finally to Brad Brooks, I couldn't have done it with out ya, mate! Now, I've got this idea for another book…

BRAD WOULD LIKE TO THANK:

First and foremost, Liz and Sophie for being the loveliest people in the world and putting up with me. Mum, who I never tell how much I love and appreciate her. All the guys on Thimble Theatre/LCD, especially Faz, Paul P., Scott, David, Dave, Charlie, Dylan, Roger, Cheeky, Pete, Gene Gene (and Kate), Yves, Jim, Paul G., Billy, and the rest of the gang. The Prayer Boyz: Greg, Richard, Adam, Fadi, Hennie, Tom & Ryan. The Design Collective: James, Wendy and Matthew. All the gang at Gosh, especially Barry and Tony. The Mongolfiers, especially Roger, Ian and Steve. Everyone on the Comics Scholars e-list. Mark Nevins, Bart Beaty, Rui Cartaxo and the old gang from Comix@. Thierry Groensteen, Jean-Pierre Mercier, Jean-Paul Jennequin, and Philippe Morin. Everyone at Lambiek. Chris Stone, for being the consummate editor (i.e. he didn't get angry). Chris McNab and Andy Nicolson for their help. Roger Langridge for the amazing cover. Len and Margaret for their wonderful support. For all our friends and family everywhere. Apple, for their wonderful computers. Arsenal Football Club, for many long years of joy. For anyone I've forgotten, and finally Tim, Adele, Megan and Oskar, without whom this book would have never been started.

ABOUT THE AUTHORS

Tim Pilcher has spent 16 years as a writer and editor in the comic industry. He was an assistant editor at DC Comics' *Vertigo* imprint and the associate editor on *Comics International*, the UK's tradepaper. He has written and contributed to numerous books on pop culture including: *Spliffs 2*, *Comix: The Underground Revolution*, *500 Great Comicbook Action Heroes*, *The Slings & Arrows Comic Guide* and *The Complete Cartooning Course* with Brad Brooks.

Brad Brooks has been involved with comics for most of his professional life as an editor, cartoonist, writer and journalist/historian. Co-founder of the collective *Les Cartoonistes Dangereux*, he is a partner in design consultancy *Sequential Design*. Married with a daughter, Brad is obsessed with Apple Macs, Design, Arsenal Football Club and, of course, comics. He also sits on the international editorial board of the *International Journal of Comic Art*.